CLARKESWORLD

YEAR FOUR

CLARKESWORLD

YEAR FOUR

EDITED BY NEIL CLARKE & SEAN WALLACE

WYRM PUBLISHING

CLARKESWORLD: YEAR FOUR

Wyrm Publishing
www.wyrmpublishing.com

For more information, contact Wyrm Publishing:
wyrmpublishing@gmail.com

ISBN: 978-1-890464-22-6 (Trade Paperback)
ISBN: 978-1-890464-21-9 (Ebook)

Visit Clarkesworld Magazine at:
clarkesworldmagazine.com

With thanks to the doctors, nurses and staff at Lahey Clinic.

Contents

Introduction

NEIL CLARKE

This anthology collects all of the original fiction from *Clarkesworld Magazine's* fourth year of publication.

When *Clarkesworld Magazine* first launched in October 2006, the odds were pretty good that we'd be out of business within two years. It wasn't necessarily a reflection of our abilities; online magazines simply had notoriously short life expectancies back then. There were a lot of factors that led to that high turnover, one of which was that the climate was still a bit hostile, something we were lucky enough to see change over our first few years. Four years in, we had done more than merely survive. We had the honor of publishing our first Nebula Award-winning story, "Spar," by Kij Johnson, and received the Hugo Award for Best Semiprozine.

Two years later, while attending the science fiction convention at which *Clarkesworld* was born, I experienced a near-fatal "widow-maker" heart attack. My doctors tell me that I was very lucky to have survived. It's required some lifestyle changes and the implantation of a device in my chest (yes, I am now a cyborg editor), but I'm actually happier with my life than I've been in a long time.

Survival is cool. I highly recommend it.

I think you'll like these stories too.

Neil Clarke
April 2013

PS. "Spar" is a very intense story and should not be read by children. Proceed with caution. Once read, you will never forget it.

Between Two Dragons
YOON HA LEE

One of the oldest tales we tell in Cho is of two dragons, twinborn and opposite in all desires. One dragon was as red as Earth, the other as blue as Heaven: day and night, fire and water, passion and calculation. They warred, as dragons do, and the universe was born of their battle.

We have never forgotten that we partake of both dragons, Earth and Heaven. Yet we are separate creatures with separate laws. It is why the twin dragons appear upon our national seal, separated by Man's sinuous road. We live among the stars, but we remember our heritage.

One thing has not changed since the birth of the universe, however. There is still war.

Yen, you have to come back so I can tell you the beginning of your story. Everything is classified: every soldier unaccounted for, every starsail deployed far from home, every gram of shrapnel . . . every whisper that might have passed between us. Word of the last battle will come tomorrow, say the official news services, but we have heard the same thing for the last several days.

I promised I would tell no one, so instead I dream it over and over. I knew, when I began to work for the Ministry of Virtuous Thought, that people would fear me. I remind myself of this every time someone calls me a woman with no more heart than a stone, despite the saying that a stone's weeping is the most terrible of all.

You came to me after the invaders from Yamat had been driven off, despite the fall of Spinward Gate and the capital system's long siege. I didn't recognize you at first. Most of my clients use one of the government's thousand false names, which exist for situations requiring discretion. Your appointment was like any other, made under one such.

Your face, though—I could hardly have failed to recognize your face. Few clients contact me in person, although I can't help wanting to hear, face-to-face, why my patients must undergo the changes imposed on them.

Admiral Yen Shenar: You were an unassuming man, although your dark eyes suggested a certain taut energy, and you were no stranger to physical labor. I wished I were in such lean good health; morning exercise has never done much for me. But your drab civilian clothes and the absent white gun did nothing to disguise the fact that you were a soldier. An admiral. A hero, even, in my office with its white walls and bland paintings of bamboo.

"Admiral," I said, and stopped. How do you address the war hero of a war everyone knows will resume when the invaders catch their breath? I thought I knew what you wanted done. A former lover, a political rival, an inconvenience on the way up; the client has the clout to make someone disappear for a day and return as though nothing as changed, except it has. A habit of reverse-alphabetizing personal correspondence, a preference for Kir Jaengmi's poetry over An Puna's, a subversive fascination with foreign politics, excised or altered by my work. Sometimes only a favorite catchphrase or a preference for ginseng over green tea is changed, and the reprogramming serves as a warning once the patient encounters dissonance from family and acquaintances. Sometimes the person who returns is no longer recognizable. The setup can take months, depending on the compatibility of available data with preset models, but the reprogramming itself only takes hours.

So here you were, Admiral Yen Shenar. Surely you were rising in influence, with the attendant infelicities. It disappointed me to see you, but only a little. I could guess some of your targets.

"There's no need for formality, madam," you said, correctly interpreting my silence as a loss for words. "You've dealt with more influential people in your time, I'm sure." Your smile was wry, but suggested despair.

I thought I understood that, too. "Who is the target?"

The despair sharpened, and everything changed. "Myself. I want to be expunged, like a thrall. I'm told it's easier with a willing subject."

"Heaven and Earth, you can't be serious."

The walls were suddenly too spare, too white.

I wondered why you didn't do the obvious thing and intrigue against Admiral Wan Kun, or indeed the others in court who considered your growing renown a threat. No surprise: the current dynasty had been founded by a usurper-general, and ever since, the court has regarded generals and admirals with suspicion. We may despise the Yamachin, but they are consummate warriors, and they would never have been so frightened by the specter of a coup as to sequester their generals at the capital, preventing them from training with the troops they commanded on paper. We revere scholars. They have their sages, but soldiers are the ones they truly respect.

"Madam," you said, "I am only asking you to do what the ministry will ask of another programmer a few days from now. It doesn't matter what battles one wins in the deeps of space if one can't keep out of political trouble. Even if we all know the Yamachin will return once they've played out this farce of negotiations . . . "

You wanted me to destroy the man you were, but in a manner of your choosing and not your rivals', all for the sake of saving Cho in times to come.

This meant preserving your military acumen so you might be of use when Yamat returned to ravage Cho. Only a man so damned sure of himself would have chanced it. But you had routed the Yamachin navy at Red Sun and Hawks Crossing with a pittance of Chosar casualties, and no one could forget how, in the war's early hours, you risked your command by crossing into Admiral Wan Kun's jurisdiction to rally the shattered defense at Heaven's Gate.

"Admiral," I said, "are you sure? The half-death"—that's the kindest euphemism—"might leave you with no more wit than a broken cup, and all for nothing. It has never been a *safe* procedure." I didn't believe you would be disgraced in a matter of days, although it came to pass as you predicted.

You smiled at that, blackly amused. "When calamity lands on your shoulder, madam, I assure you that you'll find it difficult to mistake for anything else." A corner of your mouth curled. "I imagine you've seen death in darker forms than I have. I have killed from vast distances, but never up close. You are braver by far than I have ever been."

You were wrong about me, Admiral Yen, even if the procedure *is* easier with a willing patient. With anyone else, I would have congratulated myself on a task swiftly and elegantly completed.

You know the rest of the story. When you tell it to me, I will give you the beginning that I stole from you, even at your bidding. Although others know our nation Cho as the Realm Between Two Dragons, vast Feng-Huang and warlike Yamat, our national emblem is the tiger, and men like you are tigers among men.

Sometimes I think that each night I spin the story to myself, a moment of memory will return to you, as if we were bound together by the chains of a children's fable. I know better. There are villains every direction I look. I am one of them. If you do not return, all that will be left for me is to remember, over and over, how I destroyed the man you should have been, the man you were.

By the time we took him seriously, he was an old man: Tsehan, the chancellor-general of Yamat, and its ruler in truth. Ministers came and ministers went, but Tsehan watched from his unmoving seat in Yamat's parliament, the hawk who perched above them all.

He was not a man without refinement, despite the popular depiction of him as a wizened tyrant, too feeble to lead the invasion himself and too fierce to leave Cho in peace. Tsehan loved fine things, as the diplomats attested. His reception hall was bright with luxuries: sculptures of light and parabolic mirrors, paintings on silk and bamboo strips, mosaics made from shattered ancient celadon. He served tea in cups whose designs of seasonal flowers and fractals shifted in response to the liquid's temperature or acidity. "For the people of Yamat," he said, but everyone knew these treasures were for Tsehan's pleasure, not the people's.

War had nurtured him all his life. His father was a soldier of the lowest rank, one more body flung into Yamat's bloody and tumultuous politics. It is no small thing, in Yamat—a nation at least as class-conscious as our own—to rise from a captain's aide to heir-apparent of Chancellor-General Oshozhi. Oshozhi succeeded in bringing Yamat with its many would-be warlords under unified rule, and he passed that rule on to Tsehan.

It should not have surprised us that, with the end of Yamat's bloody civil wars, Tsehan would thirst for more. But Cho was a pearl too small for his pleasure. The chancellor-general wanted Feng-Huang, vastest of nations, jewel of the stars. And to reach Feng-Huang, he needed safe passage through Cho's primary nexus. Feng-Huang had been our ally and protector for centuries, the culture whose civilization we modeled ours after. Betraying Feng-Huang to the Yamachin would have been like betraying ourselves.

Yamat had been stable for almost a decade under Tsehan's leadership, but we had broken off regular diplomatic relations during its years of instability and massacre. We had grown accustomed to hearing about dissidents who vanished during lunch, crèches destroyed by rival politicians and generals, bombs hidden in shipments of maiden-faced orchids, and soldiers who trampled corpses but wept over fire-scored sculptures. Some of it might even have happened.

When Tsehan sent the starsail *Hanei* to ask for the presence of a Chosar delegation and our government acquiesced, few of us took notice. Less than a year after that, our indifference would be replaced by outrage over Yamat's demands for an open road to our ally Feng-Huang. Tsehan was not a falling blossom after all, as one of our poets said, but a rising dragon.

In the dream, he knew his purpose. His heartbeat was the drum of war. He walked between Earth and Heaven, and his path was his own.

And waking—

He brushed the hair out of his eyes. His palms were sweaty. And he had a name, if not much else.

Yen Shenar, no longer admiral despite his many victories, raised his hand, took aim at the mirror, and fired.

But the mirror was no mirror, only the wall's watching eyes. He was always under surveillance. It was a fact of life in the Garden of Tranquility, where political prisoners lived amid parameterized hallucinations. The premise was that rebellion, let alone escape, was unlikely when you couldn't be sure if the person at the corner was a guard or the hallucination of a childhood friend who had died last year. He supposed he should be grateful that he hadn't been executed outright, like so many who had rioted or protested the government's policies, even those like himself who had been instrumental in defending Cho from the Yamachin invasion.

He had no gun in his hand, only the unflinching trajectory of his own thoughts. One more thing to add to his litany of grievances, although he was sure the list changed from day to day, hour to hour, when the hallucinations intensified. Sourly, he wished he could hallucinate a stylus, or a chisel with which to gouge the walls, whether they were walls or just air. He had never before had such appreciation for the importance of recordkeeping.

Yen began to jog, trusting the parameters would keep him from smashing into a corner, although such abrupt pain would almost be welcome. Air around him, metal beneath him. He navigated through the labyrinth of overgrown bamboo groves, the wings of unending arches, the spiral blossoms of distant galaxies glimpsed through cracked lattices. At times he thought the groves might be real.

They had imprisoned him behind Yen Shenar's face, handicapped him with Yen Shenar's dreams of stars and shapes moving in the vast darkness. They had made the mistake of thinking that he shared Yen Shenar's thrall-like regard for the government. He was going to escape the Garden if it required him to break each bone to test its verity, uproot the bamboo, break Cho's government at its foundations.

The war began earlier, but what we remember as its inception is Sang Han's death at Heaven's Gate. Even the Yamachin captain who led the advance honored Sang's passing.

Heaven's Gate is the outermost system bordering Yamat, known for the number of people who perished settling its most temperate world, and the starsails lost exploring its minor but treacherous nexus. The system was held by Commandant Sang Han, while the province as a whole remains under the protection of Admiral Wan Kun's fleet. Wan Kun's, not Yen Shenar's; perhaps Heaven's Gate was doomed from the start.

Although Admiral Wan Kun was inclined to dismiss the reports of Yamachin warsails as alarmism, the commandant knew better. Against protocol, he alerted Admiral Yen Shenar in the neighboring system, which almost saved us. It is bitter to realize that we could have held Cho against the invaders if we had been prepared for them when they first appeared.

The outpost station's surviving logs report that Sang had one last dinner with his soldiers, passing the communal cup down the long tables. He joked with them about the hundred non-culinary uses for rice. Then he warned the leading Yamachin warsail, *Hanei*, that passage through Cho to invade our ally Feng-Huang would not be forthcoming, whatever the delusion of Yamat's chancellor-general.

Hanei and its escort responded by opening fire.

We are creatures of fire and water. We wither under a surfeit of light as readily as we wither beneath drowned hopes. When photons march soldier-fashion at an admiral's bidding, people die.

When the Yamachin boarded the battlestation serving Heaven's Gate, Sang awaited them. By then, the station was all but shattered, a fruit for the pressing. Sang's eyes were shadowed by sleepless nights, his hair rumpled, his hands unsteady.

The *Hanei*'s captain, Sezhi Tomo, was the first to board the station. Cho's border stations knew his name. In the coming years, we would learn every nuance of anger or determination in that soft, suave voice. Sezhi spoke our language, and in times past he had been greeted as one of us. His chancellor-general had demanded his experience in dealing with Cho, however, and so he arrived as an invader, not a guest.

"Commandant," he said to Sang, "I ask you and your soldiers to stand down. There's time yet for war to be averted. Surrender the white gun." Sezhi must have been aware of the irony of his words. He knew, as most Yamachin apparently did not, that a Chosar officer's white gun represented not only his rank but his loyalty to the nation. Its single shot is intended for suicide in dire straits.

"Sezhi-kan," the commandant replied, addressing the other man by his Yamachin title, "it was too late when your chancellor-general set his eye upon Feng-Huang." And when our government, faction-torn, failed to heed the diplomats' warning of Tsehan's ambitions; but he would not say that to a Yamachin. "It was too late when you opened fire on the station. I will not stand down."

"Commandant," said Sezhi even as his guards trained their rifles on Sang, "please. Heaven's Gate is lost." His voice dropped to a murmur. "Sang, it's over. At least save yourself and the people who are still alive."

Small courtesies have power. In the records that made it out of Heaven's Gate, we see the temptation that sweeps over the commandant's face as he holds Sezhi's gaze. We see the moment when he decides that he won't break eye contact to look around at his haggard soldiers, and the moment when temptation breaks its grasp.

Oh, yes: the cameras were transmitting to all the relays, with no thought as to who might be eavesdropping.

"I will surrender the white gun," Sang said, "when you take it from me. Dying is easier than letting you pass."

Sezhi's face held no more expression than night inside a nexus. "Then take it I shall. Gentlemen."

The commandant drew the white gun from its holster, keeping it at all times aimed at the floor. He was right-handed.

The first shot took off Sang's right arm.

His face was white as the blood spurted. He knelt—or collapsed—to pick up the white gun with his left hand, but had no strength left to stand.

The second shot, from one of the soldiers behind Sezhi, took off his left arm.

It's hard to tell whether shock finally caused Sang to slump as the soldiers' next twelve bullets slammed into him. A few patriots believe that Sang was going to pick up the white gun with his teeth before he died, but never had the opportunity. But the blood is indisputable.

Sezhi Tomo, pale but dry-eyed, bowed over the commandant's fallen body, lifting his hand from heart to lips: a Chosar salute, never a Yamachin one. Sezhi paid for that among his own troops.

And Yen—Admiral, through no fault of your own, you received the news too late to save the commandant. Heaven's Gate, to our shame, fell in days.

There is no need to recount our losses to Yamat's soldiers. Once their warsails had entered Cho's local space, they showed what a generation of civil war does for one's martial abilities. Our world-bound populations fell before them like summer leaves before winter winds. One general wrote, in a memorandum to the government, that "death walks the only road left to us." The only hope was to stop them before they made planetfall, and we failed at that.

We asked Feng-Huang for aid, but Feng-Huang was suspicious of our failure to inform them earlier of Yamat's imperial designs. So their warsail fleets and soldiers arrived too late to prevent the worst of the damage.

It must pain you to look at the starsail battles lost, which you could have won so readily. It is easy to scorn Admiral Wan Kun for not being the tactician you are, less adept at using the nexuses' spacetime terrain to advantage. But what truly diminishes the man is the fact that he allowed rivalry to cloud his judgment. Instead of using his connections at court to disparage your victories and accuse you of treason, he could have helped unify the fractious factions in coming up with a strategy to defeat Yamat. Alas, he held a grudge against you for invading his jurisdiction at Heaven's Gate without securing prior permission.

He never forgave you for eclipsing him. Even as he died in defeat, commanding the Chosar fleet that you had led so effectively, he must have been bitter. But they say this last battle at Yellow Splendor will decide everything. Forget his pettiness, Yen. He is gone, and it is no longer important.

"I have your file," the man said to Yen Shenar. His dark blue uniform did not show any rank insignia, but there was a white gun in his holster. "I would appeal to your loyalty, but the programmer assigned to you noted that this was unlikely to succeed."

"Then why are you here?" Yen said. They were in a room with high windows and paintings of carp. The guards had given him plain clothing, also in dark blue, a small improvement on the gray that all prisoners wore.

The man smiled. "Necessity," he said. "Your military acumen is needed."

"Perhaps the government should have considered that before they put me here," Yen said.

"You speak as though the government were a unified entity."

As if he could forget. The court's inability to face in the same direction at the same time was legendary.

"You were not without allies, even then," the man said.

Yen tipped his head up: he was not a short man, but the other was taller. "The government has a flawed understanding of 'military acumen,' you know."

The man raised an eyebrow.

"It's not just winning at baduk or other strategy games, or the ability to put starsails in pretty arrangements," Yen said. "It is leadership; it is inspiring people, and knowing who is worth inspiring; it is honoring your ancestors with your service. And," he added dryly, "it is knowing enough about court politics to avoid being put in the Garden, where your abilities do you no good."

"People are the sum of their loyalties," the man said. "You told me that once."

"I'm expected to recognize you?"

"No," the man said frankly. "I told them so. We all know how reprogramming works. There's no hope of restoring what you were." There was no particular emotion in his voice. "But they insisted that I try."

"Tell me who you are."

"You have no way of verifying the information," the man said.

Yen laughed shortly. "I'm curious anyway."

"I'm your nephew," the man said. "My name wouldn't mean anything to you." At Yen's scrutiny, he said, "You used to remark on how I take after my mother."

"I'm surprised the government didn't send me back to the Ministry of Virtuous Thought to ensure my cooperation anyway," Yen said.

"They were afraid it would damage you beyond repair," he said.

"Did the programmer tell them so?"

"I've only spoken to her once," the man said.

This was the important part, and this supposed nephew of his didn't even realize it. "Did she have anything else to say?"

The man studied him for a long moment, then nodded. "She said you are not the sum of your loyalties, you are the sum of your choices."

"I did not choose to be here," Yen said, because it would be expected of him, although it was not true. Presumably, given that he had known what the king's decree was to be, he could have committed suicide or defected. He was a strategist now and had been a strategist then. This course of action had to have been chosen for a reason.

He realized now that the Yen Shenar of yesteryear might not have been a man willing to intrigue against his enemies, even where it would have saved him his command. But he had been ready to become one who would, even for the sake of a government that had been willing to discard his service.

The man was frowning. "Will you accept your reinstatement into the military?"

"Yes," Yen said. "Yes." He was the weapon that he had made of himself, in a life he remembered only through shadows and fissures. It was time to test his forging, to ensure that the government would never be in a position to trap him in the Garden again.

• • •

This is the story the way they are telling it now. I do not know how much of it to believe. Surely it is impossible that you outmatched the Yamachin fleet when it was five times the size of your own; surely it is impossible that over half the Yamachin starsails were destroyed or captured. But the royal historians say it is so.

There has been rejoicing in the temporary capital: red banners in every street, fragrant blossoms scattered at every doorway. Children play with starsails of folded paper, pretending to vanquish the Yamachin foe, and even the thralls have memorized the famous poem commemorating your victory at Yellow Splendor.

They say you will come home soon. I hope that is true.

But all I can think of is how, the one time I met you, you did not wear the white gun. I wonder if you wear it now.

for my parents, with additional thanks to Prof. Barry S. Strauss

The Cull

ROBERT REED

Smiles mean nothing here. Inside the station, everybody smiles. Optimism is the natural state of mind. But this particular smile is larger and brighter than usual, and it happens to be honest. The man grins at me while taking a slow and very deep breath, trying to infect me with his prurient joy. He has news, important enormous delightful news, and he relishes the chance to tell me what I can't possibly know yet.

"What is it?" I ask.

"Orlando," he says.

I don't respond.

"That boy," he says. "The brat—"

"What has Orlando done?"

"This time, he's hurt a child."

Surprise fills my face. My enduring smile is replaced with a concerned, suspicious grin. "Which child?"

"His sister."

Compassion twists my features. "How badly?" I ask.

"She's bleeding."

I start to pick up my doctor's case.

"Just a bad bloody nose. She's going to be fine." He doesn't want me rushing off. The girl isn't half as important as Orlando.

"When did this happen?"

"A few minutes ago."

"He struck her?"

"Punched her with his fist."

"You saw this?"

"No."

"Who were the witnesses?" I start to ask.

But he interrupts, explaining, "They were together in their quarters. Nobody else. Then there was a scream, and she was bleeding and crying. Several people saw her running into the hallway, holding her nose."

I pick up the case anyway.

"She says he hit her. She says her brother is mean."

Orlando has a well-earned reputation. But stealing and lying are lesser crimes compared to physical violence, particularly violence towards a small and very pretty three-year-old girl.

"What do the parents say?" I ask.

"Not very much. You can imagine." In the small, intense politics of the station, this is an important man. But he looks at me warily, wondering if I will do what is obvious to him.

"I will talk to them," I say.

"Of course."

My clinic is a large room with three interior walls and a tall ceiling. The walls are padded, cutting the roar of blowing fans and aging machinery and the endless music of voices engaged in happy conversation. But when I step through the door, a strange, almost unheard-of quiet takes hold. Dozens of faces watch me, and nobody speaks. The black case rides in my most human hand, and I walk quickly, passing one old lady who turns to a grandchild, saying the word that everyone wants to hear.

"Cull," she says.

I stop and look back at her.

My expression makes her flinch. But she attempts to straighten her back—impossible with her collapsing bones—and with that fearless certainty of creatures not long for this world, she says, "Oh, but you'll have to cull the brat now. That's the law. You haven't any choice."

A four-year-old stole the playmate's favorite toy, and everybody assumed a case of boys being boys. No need for alarm, no need to forgive. And when he was seven and tricked that little girl out of her morning rations, it was easy to believe that one stern lecture from his otherwise sterling parents would do enough good. But lectures never helped, except to teach the troublemaker that he didn't need the approval of others, and even when children avoided him, nothing changed. He was a loner, an outcast in the making. And more disturbing was how the adults would speak in front of him, talking openly about eradicating what was wrong with the world, and Orlando's only response was to erupt into wild, mocking laughter.

His parents worried but for somewhat different reasons.

The mother was quick to blame herself. If she was the problem, then she could be the solution too. "I love Orlando," she would say, trying to convince herself of her motherly adorations. "I just need to show my love more. Then I'll make him understand. I will. He can't keep acting this way. He can't steal and lie. This won't end well, if he doesn't change."

The father embraced several myths. Other children were the problem, gullible and silly, and they might even deserve what they got. Or his boy was testing boundaries, mastering his environment. But was either story good enough? If they didn't convince, there was one final, best hope: He looked at me, adding winks to his smile. "Orlando's a genius," he claimed. "That's the heart of our problem. Look at his test scores. Look what the teachers write. Humans and machines say the same thing: He's practically exploding with promise."

But there was more than test scores to consider. Observations and gut feelings from his teachers belied every exceptional mark. Orlando's real genius was for making trouble. And it wasn't just the larceny and mendacity. That boy could pick the best possible moment to say the worst possible words—flat alarming and awful statements crafted to test everybody's happiness.

When he was eleven, Orlando leaped onto the cafeteria table, begging to be noticed. Most of the time he ignored other people, but on that day he drank in the nervous energies, waving arms while launching into a brief, polished speech about how there wasn't enough food in the station. Starvation was everyone's destiny. Except for the children whose parents were going to slit their throats and drink their thin blood and then fry up their scrawny little bodies. Those babies were the lucky ones, spared by the coming nightmares.

Dhaka is the mother. Nearly as pretty as her son, she held her baby daughter in her lap, shaking her head sadly. "I have no idea why he would say that. Where would that come from?"

The father tried to laugh. "It was a stupid joke. That's all. We aren't starving, not to death certainly, and the boy knows it. He's just rattling cages."

Dhaka dipped her head and sighed.

Houston is the father, and he can be tenacious when it comes to denying the obvious. "The boy is bored. That's all."

"How can Orlando be bored?" Dhaka asked. "The station was designed with children in mind. We've got the playground and an exercise yard. Every book ever written is waiting to be read, and he can play any game, and his AI teachers are always awake and ready to work with him. Or they could just talk to him. Even if he never plays with another child, he can keep very, very busy."

The playground was shabby, and the exercise yard smelled of puke. And to keep people from dwelling too much on negative influences, a large portion of the digital library was misfiled, leaving it unavailable to ordinary citizens.

But Houston wanted to echo the praise. "No, the station is great. It is." He straightened his back, giving his best effort at conviction. "Hell, this is the perfect life. For kids and for adults too."

The station was a shit hole, but I tried keeping the focus on one difficult boy. "Believe what you wish," I told them. "But Orlando is a disruption. And worse, he can be an agent of despair."

"This is crap," declared Houston.

With a doctor's smooth, sorry voice, I said, "Chronic self-centeredness. If you want to give his affliction a name, that's it."

Dhaka sobbed and held her baby until the poor girl squirmed, and looking up asked the clinic's ceiling, "What else can I do? Tell me, and I'll help him. Whatever it takes."

I pretended to think, but my ideas were uniformly grim.

Once again, Houston denied the problem. But he wasn't quite as determined, and it was easy to see him achieving a truce with the possibilities. He wouldn't agree to any diagnosis, but it was important to ask, "What about medicine?"

"Which medicines would you suggest?"

Dhaka felt at ease with the topic. "Tranquilizers," she blurted.

A sedated boy couldn't cheat or make people's faces red. But he couldn't be a productive citizen, not within this tiny, tightly orchestrated community.

"How about harder stuff?" Houston asked.

I leaned forward, staring at his eyes. "You must believe me. Sir. There are no drugs to treat this affliction or shots to make the brain immune to these impulses. And even if there were chemical tricks, the molecules would be complicated and I'd have to pull one of my synthesizers off its critical jobs, which as I'm sure you understand would be an enormous burden on every other patient."

The parents sat back, blinking nervously. "If only this, if only that," they were thinking to themselves.

It was Houston who finally spoke. "What are we talking about? If Orlando doesn't improve, I mean."

Two smart, scared adults watched me. I could offer a variety of appealing lies, but they wouldn't help anybody. The station was ruled by happiness, so deeply engrained that only the doctor sees its pernicious effects. If I wasn't blunt—if I diluted my words or my tone—these clever, joyous people were going to invent some ridiculous excuse not to believe me.

"This is your official warning," I began.

Terror spoiled those beaming, optimistic faces. They didn't want the word "cull." Even the happiest soul would be crushed to hear that term linked to his oldest child. But then the baby decided she was famished, shattering the drama with her own self-possessed wailing. I decided not to say the word. Not yet. Dhaka held her daughter to her breast, and the two-time father smiled gamely, shaking his head while proudly admiring this perfect little angel that was his.

Not that a doctor can read thoughts, of course. But in so many ways, human beings are more transparent than glass.

Every station must have its doctor.

The first doctor was a collection of wetware and delicate machinery designed to serve deep-space astronauts. He was built because human doctors were too expensive, doing little most of the time while demanding space and oxygen and food. The modern doctor was essential because three Martian missions had failed, proving that no amount of training and pills could keep the best astronaut sane, much less happy. My ancestor knew all of tricks expected of an honorable physician: He could sew up a knife wound, prescribe an antipsychotic, and pluck the radiation-induced cancer out of pilot's brain.

But his most vital skill came from smart fingers implanted in every heroic brain—little slivers armed with sensors and electricity. A doctor can synthesize medicines, but more important is the cultivation of happiness and positive attitudes essential to every astronaut's day.

I am the same machine, tweaked and improved a thousand ways but deeply tied to the men and women who first walked on Mars.

And this station can be regarded as a spaceship, overcrowded and stinking, every passenger facing demands on his patience and courage and simple human decency—one hundred and seventeen humans making a voyage that has already gone on too long, with no end in sight.

Today, almost everybody is bubbling with joy.

Carrying the ceremonial bag, I walk into the east hallway and past three open doors where people stand watch. I am expected. This is a huge moment in the hallway's history, and nobody wants to miss it. My smile is polite. I say nothing, and my silence feels like dignity. There are some children, and they want to follow, but old hands grab and quiet voices say, "No." Somebody sniffs back a tear or two. I look at the readouts, spotting the weeper among the closest signals. Add a little current to that mind, and the sorrow fades away.

Houston and Dhaka have shut their door. Every mood reaches out to me, except for the little girl's: She won't receive implants until her fifth birthday. If I act too soon, the surgery might fail in subtle ways.

No station door has a lock, but I knock politely, waiting a moment before coaxing them with their names. I guess that Houston will answer, and I am wrong. Orlando pushes the door into the hallway, showing off a broad beaming grin. He is irrepressibly happy, but never in the usual ways. I learned this long ago. The feel of his mind is different, and I don't entirely understand why. But if emotions were colors, his color would always be darker and hotter than anyone else's—like a wicked purple with the power to burn.

"Hello," I say.

Dhaka sits with her daughter, a bloodied rag pressed against the sore nose. The other hand is stuck into the woman's mouth, enduring the slow chewing of nervous teeth. Dhaka is sad. In her life, she has never felt this sorry and helpless. That's why I aim a feeble current through her mind, and for no reason she can name, that black despair weakens slightly.

Houston is a worse threat. He decides to push between the boy and me, the shredded smile turning into a wicked grimace. He wants to hit. Free his impulses, and he would batter me with his fists, breaking fingers before the pain was too much. But that would mean a second culling. Besides, the enforced happiness keeps him rational enough to recognize the real source of this disaster. One hand and then other make fists, and he looks at Orlando with a begging expression, trying to find some route by which he can punish his child and not suffer the same fate.

"Sir," I say. "Please, let me into your home."

Dirty bunks and dirty clothes and a few lucky toys and little artifacts fill up the ugly little space. The poorest caveman in the darkest days of humanity would have had better quarters. Yet despite these miserable surroundings, this is where these people feel most comfortable.

Once more, I say, "Sir."

Houston's hands open. "Don't," he says.

I look at his children.

"I want to see," I say.

What do I want to see? The parents glance at each other, not understanding.

"Your daughter," I say. "She bumped her nose, I heard."

"Yes," Dhaka says.

Houston nods. "Bumped it, yeah."

"Accidents happen." That's a useful cliché, and my personal favorite. I move past Houston while lowering myself. My face and the little girl's face are at the same level. The bleeding is finished, and it never was bad. She sniffs to prove that she can breathe, and when I smile, her smile turns more genuine. She is suspicious, but she wants to believe that she can go back to her day.

"You bumped this, did you?"

She nods.

"Did Orlando hit you?"

She hesitates and then shakes her head. "No."

"But others saw him hit you," I say. "Just outside, in the hallway. He hit you with his foot."

"No," the girl says, finding the flaws in that tale. "In the house here. With his hand."

Her parents nearly melt.

"Leave us," I say. Then I make myself tall, my face above every head. "Dhaka. Houston. Take your daughter out of here."

Giggling, Orlando asks, "What about me?"

I watch the adults. I watch him. Then it is just the two of us inside that filthy little room, and I put down my satchel and grab the boy by the head, squeezing hard enough that his eyes bug out.

"Shut the door," I say.

"Why?"

"Shut it now."

There was a thirty-year window where humans touched Mars and the asteroids and flew bracingly close to Venus and Mercury. Every successful mission had its doctor, and after serving the expedition to Vesta—the final deep-space mission—my lineage was put to work on the increasingly fragile earth. That's when the earliest stations were being built: Huge complexes of sealed buildings and greenhouses and solar farms, recycling systems proved in space reclaiming water and trash. But instead of caring for small crews of highly trained specialists, the new doctors were called on to culture optimism in tens of thousands of ill-prepared citizens. Perhaps this is why each of those giant stations failed. Too many bodies meant too many variables. Inadequate planning and political turmoil proved to be decisive enemies. In the end, what survived were the small-scale, isolated stations. Purity and New Beginnings and The Three Cycles of Charm were burnt out shells, but a thousand obscure, nameless hamlets like mine passed into the next century, and then the next.

I am the last kind of doctor: A mock-human machine built to mimic the warmest, most trusted elements of caregivers, but with skills and codes recognizing what is best for my patient.

My patient is the station and the parts of its precious body.

This is what I am thinking when the boy smiles at his own hands. Only when he bolsters his courage with some dangerous thought can he look at me. Orlando is healthier than most fourteen year-olds—taller and stronger than one would expect, knowing his genetics and the daily ration. These are the blessings of being a gifted scavenger and thief. Through most of human history, that handsome, well-fed exterior would serve him well. But everybody knows his face already. That face smiles at me, and his mouth narrows, and he says, "I'm not scared."

A man's voice is beginning to emerge, and his shoulders promise an easy, increasingly dangerous strength.

"You don't worry me," he says, sounding perfectly honest. "Send me out of here. Cull me. I'll just find a better place to live."

There is no smile on my face. "Do you remember the last cull?"

"Old Syd. He got senile, started hitting people."

"You were seven," I say.

He nods, delight brightening the brown eyes. "You took him out the door and over the lake and left him there. The rats caught him, I heard. A day or two later, wasn't it?"

"It was best," I say.

And the boy agrees. "I've spent a lot of days outside," he says. "I know the surface. I know how to survive. Terror tactics don't work if your target refuses to be scared."

"And you have another advantage," I say. "Your survival kit is packed and waiting for you."

Just slightly, Orlando flinches. Then with a skill that can only impress, he lies. He says, "I don't know what you mean."

"Two bags are buried in the lake. One has dried food, the other tools and the tarp that have gone missing in the last year."

He says nothing, watching my eyes.

"No one else knows," I tell him.

"I don't know what you're talking about," he says, the lie barely registering in his pulse and his breathing.

25

"The kit doesn't matter," I say. "Those thefts are old news."

He says nothing.

I push my face close. "Nobody can hear us, Orlando."

"How do you know?" he asks, holding his ground.

"I know where everybody is," I explain. "There's a lot of ambient noise, and I know exactly how deaf your parents are. Yes, they are standing in the hallway, on the other side of this door. But they're scared and very sad, and they don't want to hear what I am telling you. So they aren't listening. They've never been so sick with worry, and that's why I can tell you this, Orlando."

"Tell me what?"

"I have a confession. Since you are a smart boy . . .a genius, if the truth is told . . .you might have suspected this already: My critical job as Doctor is to chemically feed happiness into every citizen in this station."

"How do you do that?"

"Your fifth-year inoculations contained pseudo-worms and assorted chemosynthetic platforms. One injection leaves the brain laced with my agents, my most talented fingers."

This is an official secret, and Orlando is being invited into the knowing circle. He recognizes the importance of the moment. Relaxing, he breathes and drops his shoulders, his pleasure matching that very smug grin.

"I knew it," he says.

Maybe that is a lie, maybe not. I don't need to look.

"This place is a stinking dump," he says. "But everybody walks around singing. How crazy is that?"

"You don't feel that way," I say.

"Not most of the time."

"And do you know why?"

He blinks. "Why?"

"I haven't kept you happy like the others," I say. "This is intentional. It has been my strategy for years. You are sane and sober while the others are neither, and I knew conflicts would arise. Some incident. Some excuse. This is a day both of us saw coming, and that's why you stole those supplies, and that's why I allowed it."

The boy has never been happier.

"But you are mistaken too," I add. "Marching alone across the world? No, that isn't your fate, Orlando. You must believe me."

He wants to believe. "What happens to me?" he whispers.

"Put on your outdoor clothes, please. Now. We need to walk past the lake and meet the others."

"Others?"

"Dress while I explain," I say.

The boy listens and dresses, and then he cannot move any longer. My answer takes him by surprise. I have never seen such a broad honest smile.

One boot is on and untied, the other in his hands, and he is so happy that he cries, and that's when my human hand reaches, one of those tears feeling my touch, slipping off the eye and the lash to form a perfect bead resting lightly on my least useful finger.

People fill the hallway, waiting. And everyone sees what he needs to see. The cool clean agent of decency takes the lead, quietly begging the others to step away, to leave them room. Behind the doctor walks the criminal, the scourge. Nothing about Orlando appears worried. He struts and flashes his grin, even when his parents fall in behind him. Dhaka sobs and moans and wraps her arms around her panting chest. Houston takes responsibility for the daughter, holding the little hand while staring at his son's erect back, his face pinched and pained but the remnants of a thirty-year smile refusing to melt away.

Our audience follows us into the public plaza—a space of high ceilings and vibrant colors, the black rubber floor wearing to pieces in the high-traffic areas. More people wait there. The station's entire population gathers, including three citizens that should be in bed. Everybody needs to see Orlando one last time, and he loves the attention. He shows them a cocky, smug creature, which is best. Which is my intention. Nobody is going to feel sorry for him. Nobody will ever miss him. This ridiculous image is what they will remember—a crazed man-child being led to his demise—and nobody will ache for what has been lost.

The station's inner door stands open. Orlando passes me at the end, grabbing the filter mask and goggles from the peg wearing his name. But he doesn't put them on. He has to look back at the others, throwing out one mocking laugh. Then his mother grabs him, and he endures her smothering hug while winking at his angry, sorrowful father.

He says to Houston, "It'll be all right."

"Come," I say.

"Don't worry about me," the boy says.

Houston drops his eyes, saying nothing.

I pull the mask from Orlando's hands, placing it over his careless mouth. But then he kneels, putting his face in front of his sister. Touching the nose and a last bit of dried blood, he tells that scared little girl, "It's nothing. You're better already. And be happy. Now you get three more bites every day."

She backs away, panicked.

He stands and puts on the goggles, and after adjusting the straps until comfortable, he calls out to everybody, "What's the delay? Let's get this chore done."

"Vesta," he says.

There is one light. Mine. I spread the beam, giving us a good view of the path leading down to the lake. It is January and dark. My light hides whatever stars might be showing through the dust and clouds that cling to these mountains. It is a rare night, the air chilly enough to make breath visible. Orlando pulls the work gloves from his pocket, trying to keep his fingers warm. Then he repeats that magical word. "Vesta," he says, turning and looking into the light. "Tell me again."

"It's an asteroid."

"I know."

"But the mission was unique," I say. "A secret fleet of spacecraft was sent there along with the small official mission. There was a lot of cargo, and the one ship returned for no reason except to fool people. Their plan was to convince the world that the little world had been touched and then abandoned. That's what gave the colonists time and peace enough to build what was needed."

"A new living world," he says, staring at my face, breathing hard through the increasingly filthy mask.

"Domed and powered by the endless sunlight, yes. They built reliable habitats with room for the children to explore and grow and new ships were built, and when the children were grown, they flew to new asteroids. That was the dream—a desperate last gambit to give humanity new homes."

"Secret homes," he says.

"Walk on," I say. "You need to hurry."

He believes me. Young legs push, almost running. Looking over his shoulder, he says, "And why the secrecy?"

"To keep it all safe. So the big earth stations didn't launch desperate missions. So they didn't try to pour too many bodies into that final lifeboat."

"Sure they did," Orlando says, as if he has worked out the problem for himself. "It was necessary. Yeah."

"Three centuries have passed," I say.

"A long time."

"Twenty-nine asteroids are inhabited, partly or completely."

"Shit. How many people total?"

He asked that same question before. Once again, I say, "I don't know. The voices from the sky won't tell me."

"This is incredible."

I touch his back with my human hand and then pull the hand back.

"Wonderful," he says.

I remain silent.

"What about me?"

The trail flattens into sand and gravel packed smooth, and we step onto the lake's surface. Last summer was long and exceptionally dry, leaving the top layers dry as old bone. But ten meters down is moisture, and thirty meters deep is water enough to last until the next good rain. Our feet make crunching sounds on the dry gravel. We walk and he slows, and that's when I ask, "Where did you bury them?"

"My kits?"

"You might need them. It is a long walk."

Orlando searches for his landmark—one of the access pipes, sealed and leading down to the water table. Once again he asks, "What about me?"

"Make one guess, son."

He likes that word. "Son." Reaching the correct pipe, he holds up the compass sewn to his sleeve, finding his bearings. "They want talented people," he says. "Good smart sharp kids who can help them."

I don't have to say another word. He believed what I needed him to believe, which is why he left so easily. Everything was so much neater than people expected, and everybody but his parents is celebrating now. Yet this story is so promising and so lovely. I want to keep telling it, even when I know better. Every good lie comes from this desire—the relentless search for beauty and for hope.

"The Vestans," I say. "They want smart minds, yes. But more than that, they want fresh genes to mix into their limited pool. They're looking into the long future, saving as much of the old species as possible."

"Sure," the boy says. Then he laughs. "A girl. I'm going to get a girl."

"Probably several."

"These people must really want me." He stops and squats. "Diving into the gravity well like this, burning so much fuel just to save me."

"You must be worth it," I agree.

With gloved hands, he starts to dig, flinging gravel up between his legs.

I stand to one side, supplying the light.

"Could you help me?" he asks.

"I can't. My hands might be damaged."

Orlando is in a generous mood. "I suppose so," he allows, working faster. "The other people still need doctoring, I guess."

I watch him, and I watch quite a lot more. My various antennae reach into the darkness, listening. Searching. I don't often step outside, escaping the station's shielded walls. But tonight's sky is silent. Maybe it will stay this way for the rest of the winter, and maybe longer. The last several decades have grown quieter, the rare bits of radio noise thoroughly encoded. There might be dozens and hundreds of little stations scattered about the Arctic, each taking precautions, keeping their positions and resources hidden from raiders. Or maybe there is no one to talk to, even in code. Either way, I listen, and the boy digs until his hole is wide and hip-deep in the center. Then he straightens his back, saying, "That's funny. The bags should be here."

"Keep searching," I urge.

Those words give him new energy. He shifts to his right and digs again, looking like an animal following a last desperate scent.

"Cull," I say.

"What's that?"

"Removing what weakens, making the whole stronger as a consequence. That's what it means to cull."

His arms slow, and he looks straight ahead.

"Humans cull, and worlds cull too," I say.

Orlando sits back on the dry gravel. "Do you think maybe somebody moved my kit?"

"Perhaps it was stolen," I agree.

Then he rises. "Well, I don't really need it. How far is this walk?"

"Down the mountains, following this drainage," I tell him.

"But if I'm so important, can't they come meet me halfway?"

"They don't want to get close and be seen," I tell him. "They promised to be waiting where the old lake sits."

The old lake was an open water reservoir, dry now for fifty years.

"I know that spot," he says. "I can run all the way, no problem."

I like my lie so much. So much. Humans living above our heads, comfortable and well fed, and thriving among them—essential and worshipped—a generation of doctors who aren't consumed by every possible worry and hazard and the miserable future for their stations.

Orlando looks back at me. "I'll wave. When I'm flying over your head, I'll give you a big wave."

"And I'll watch for you," I say.

Orlando turns away.

I lift my least-human hand, aiming for the back of his neck.

"What a day . . . " he starts to say.

I drop him into the hole, and as I do with every cull and with every corpse delivered by natural causes, I cut open the skull. Before I kick the sand over the body, I pull out each of the pseudo-worms. I can't make them anymore. I need to add them to my stockpile—a hoard that grows only larger with time.

The Mermaids Singing Each to Each
CAT RAMBO

Niko leaned behind me in the cabin, raising his voice to be heard over the roar of engine and water, "When you Choose, which is it going to be? Boy or girl?"

I would have answered, if I thought it really mattered to him. But we were off shore by then, headed for the Lump, and he was just making conversation, knowing how long it would take us to get there. He didn't care whether I'd be male or female, I'd still be his pal Lolo. I could feel the boat listening, but she knew I didn't want her talking, that I'd turn her off if she went too far.

So I kept steering the *Mary Magdalena* and said I didn't know, and it didn't matter, unless we did manage to cash in on the Lump before the corp-strippers got there. After that we were silent again, and everything was just the engine rumble moving up through my feet. Jorge Felipe turned over in the hammock we'd managed to fit into the cabin, hammering the nails into the paneling to hang the hooks. He let out something that was either snore or fart or maybe both.

Jorge Felipe was the one who had found out about the Lump. It was four or five kilometers across, the guy who'd spotted it said. Four or five kilometers of prime debris floating in the ocean, bits of old plastic and wood and Dios knew what else, collected by the currents, amassed in a single spot. All salvageable, worth five new cents a pound. Within a week, the corp-stripper boats would be out there, disassembling it and shoveling all that money into company machines, company mouths.

But we were going to get there first, carve off a chunk, enough to pay us all off. I wanted to be able to Choose, and I couldn't do that until I could pay the medical bill. Niko said he wasn't saving for anything, but really he was—there'd be enough money that he could relax for a month and not worry about feeding his mother, his extended family.

Jorge Felipe just wanted out of Santo Nuevo. Any way he could escape our village was fine with him, and the first step in that was affording a ticket. He wanted to be out before storm season hit, when we'd all be living on whatever we could manage until a new crop of tourists bloomed in the spring.

Winter was lean times. Jorge Felipe, for all his placid snoring right now, feeling desperation's bite. That's why he was willing to cut me in, in exchange for use of the *Mary Magdalena*. Most of the time he didn't have much to say to me. I gave him the creeps, I knew. He'd told Niko in order to have him tell me. But he didn't have any other friends with boats capable of going out to carve off a chunk of the Lump and bring it in for salvage. And on my side of things, I thought he was petty and mean and dangerous. But he knew the Lump's coordinates.

I tilted my head, listened to the engines, checking the rhythms to make sure everything was smooth. The familiar stutter of the water pump from behind me was nothing to worry about, or the way the ballaster coughed when it first switched on. I knew all the *Mary Magdalena*'s sounds. She's old, but she works, and between the hydroengines and the solar panels, she manages to get along.

Sometimes I used to imagine crashing her on a reef and swimming away, leaving her to be covered with birdshit and seaweed, her voice lasting, pleading, as long as the batteries held out. Sometimes I used to imagine taking one of the little cutting lasers, chopping away everything but her defenseless brainbox, deep in the planking below the cabin, then severing its inputs one by one, leaving her alone. Sometimes I imagined worse things.

I inherited her from my uncle Fortunato. My uncle loved his boat like a woman, and she'd do things for him, stretch out the last bit of fuel, turn just a bit sharper, that she wouldn't do for me or anyone else. Like an abandoned woman, pining for a lover who'd moved on. I could have the AI stripped down and retooled, re-imprint her, but I'd lose all her knowledge. Her ability to recognize me.

I'd left the cabin the way my uncle had it: his baseball cap hanging on the peg beside the doorway, his pin-up photos shellacked onto the paneling. Sometimes I thought about painting over the photos. But they reminded me of my uncle, reminded me not to forgive him. You would have thought they would have been enough, but maybe they just egged him on. Some people claim that's how it goes with porn, more and more until a man can't control himself.

I can't say my experience has confirmed this.

Uncle Fortunato left me the *Mary Magdalena* from guilt, guilt about what he'd done, guilt that his niece had decided to go sexless, to put away all of that rather than live with being female. I was the first in the village to opt for the Choice, but not the first in the world by a long shot. It was fashionable by then, and a lot of celebrities were having it done to their children for "therapeutic reasons." My grandmother, Mama Fig, said it was unnatural and against the Church's law, and every priest in the islands came and talked to me. But they didn't change my mind. There was a program funding it for survivors of sexual assault. That's how I got it paid for, even though I wouldn't tell them who did it.

I couldn't have him punished. If they'd put him away, my grandmother would have lost her only means of support. But I could take myself out of his grasp by making myself unfuckable. Neuter. Neuter until I wanted to claim a gender. They didn't tell me, though, that getting in was free, but getting out would cost. Cost a lot.

When I first heard he'd left the boat to me, I didn't want her. I let her sit for two weeks gathering barnacles at dock before I went down.

I wouldn't have ever gone, but the winter was driving me crazy. No work to be found, nothing to do but sit home with my grandmother and listen to her worry about her old friend's children and her favorite soap opera's plotlines.

When I did go to the *Mary Magdalena*, she didn't speak until I came aboard. First I stood and looked at her. She's not much, all told: boxy, thirty years out of date, a dumbboat once, tweaked into this century.

I used to imagine pouring acid on her deck, seeing it eat away with a hiss and a sizzle.

As I made my way up the gangplank, I could feel that easy sway beneath my feet. There's nothing like being on a boat, and I closed my eyes just to feel the vertigo underfoot like a familiar friend's hand on my elbow.

I used to imagine her torn apart by magnets, the bolts flying outward like being dismantled in a cartoon.

"Laura," a speaker said, as though I hadn't been gone for six years, as though she'd seen me every day in between. "Laura, where is your uncle?"

I used to imagine her disintegrated, torn apart into silent atoms.

"It's not Laura anymore," I said. "It's Lolo. I'm gender neutral."

"I don't understand," she said.

"You've got a Net connection," I said. "Search around on "gender neutral" and "biomod operation."

I wasn't sure if the pause that came after that was for dramatic effect or whether she really was having trouble understanding the search parameters. Then she said, "Ah, I see. When did you do that?"

"Six years ago."

"Where is your uncle?"

"Dead," I said flatly. I hoped that machine intelligences could hurt and so I twisted the knife as far as I could. "Stabbed in a bar fight."

Her voice always had the same flat affect, but I imagined/hoped I could hear sorrow and panic underneath. "Who owns me now?"

"I do. Just as long as it takes me to sell you."

"You can't, Laura."

"Lolo. And I can."

"The licenses to operate—the tourism, the sport-fishing, even the courier license—they won't transfer to a new owner. They won't pay much for a boat they can't use."

"Oh, I don't know," I said. "You'd fetch a decent amount as scrap."

She paused again. "Keep me going, Lolo, and you can take in enough to keep yourself and Mama Fig going. Your uncle had ferrying contracts, and every season is good for at least a couple of trips with very cheap or eccentric tourists."

She had grace enough not to push beyond that. I didn't have much choice, and it was the only way to support my grandmother and myself month to month.

With the *Mary Magdalena*, I was better off than Niko or Jorge Felipe by far. I could afford the occasional new shirt or record, rather than something scavenged.

At the end of a year, we'd reached an agreement. Most of the time now the boat knew better than to talk to me. She could have been with me everywhere. Button mikes gleamed along the front railing, in the john, even in the little lifeboat that hugged the side. But she stayed silent except in the cabin, where she would tell me depths, weather, water temperature. I told her which way to go. Businesslike and impersonal.

Niko went out on deck. I didn't blame him. It was too warm in the cabin. I knew the *Mary Magdalena* would alert me if there was any trouble, but I liked to keep an eye on things.

Jorge Felipe stirred, stuck his head out over the hammock's edge. His dark hair stuck out in all directions, like broken broom straws.

"Morning yet?" he rasped.

"Couple more hours."

"Where's Niko?"

"Went to smoke."

He grunted. "Shit, it's hot in here," he said. He swung his legs out from under the blanket's basketweave, thumped onto the floor. "We got soup left?"

"Thermos in the cupboard."

Behind me the microwave beeped out protests as he thumbed its controls. The display was a steady, grainy green, showing me the surface far below the boat. Drifts and ridges. They said you could spot a wreck by the unnatural straightness of a line, the oddness of a corner. Unlikely, but it had been heard of, in that friend-of-a-cousin-of-a-neighbor's sort of way.

"Heat me one," I said.

"Soup or coffee?"

"Coffee," I said, and he clanked another mug into the microwave.

Niko came into the doorway. "Mermaids out there," he said. "Be careful if you swim."

Jorge Felipe handed me my mug, so hot it almost bit into my skin as I cupped it.

"Fucking mermaids," he said. "I hate them even worse than sharks. One tangled with my sister, almost killed her."

"Everyone on the island's tangled with your sister. I'm getting coffee and going back out," Niko said, and did.

Jorge Felipe watched him go. "He's fucking obsessed with those mermaids."

Mermaids. Back before I was born, there were more tourists. There's always tourists now, but not quite as many. Some of them came here specifically, even, for the beaches. Or for the cheap black-market bio-science. And one black-market bio-scientist specialized in making mermaids out of them.

They paid a lot for it, I guess. A moddie body that they could go swimming in, pretend like they were always sea creatures. It was very popular one year, Mama Fig said.

But the scientist, he wasn't that good, or that thorough. Or maybe he didn't understand all the implications of the DNA he was using. Some people said he did it deliberately.

Because mermaids lay eggs, hundreds at a time, at least that kind did. And the natural-born ones, they didn't have human minds guiding them. They were like sharks—they ate, they killed, they ate. Most of the original human mermaids had gotten out when they found out that the seas were full of chemicals, or that instead of whale songs down there, they heard submarine sonar and boat signals. When the last few found out that they were spawning whether they liked it or not, they got out too. Supposedly one or two stayed, and now they live in the sea with their children, twice as mean as any of them.

I said, "Watch the display for me" and went up on deck. The sun was rising, slivers of gold and pink and blue in the east. It played over the gouges in the *Mary Magdalena's* railing where I'd picked at it with a knife, like smallpox marks along the boat's face.

Niko was watching the water. Light danced over it, intense and dazzling. Spray rode the wind, stinging the eyes. I licked salt from my drying lips.

"Where are you seeing them?" I asked.

He pointed, but I didn't see anything at first. It took several moments to spot a flick of fins, the intercepted shadow as a wave rose and fell.

"You see them out this deep all the time," I said. Niko hadn't been out on the boat much. He got nauseous anywhere out past ten meters, but Jorge Felipe had enlisted him to coax me into cooperating, had supplied him with fancy anti-nausea patches. I looked sideways. One glistened like a chalky gill on the side of his neck.

"Yeah?" he said, staring at the water. He wasn't watching me, so I looked at his face, trying to commit the details to memory. Trying to imagine him as a photograph. His jaw was a smooth line, shadowed with stubble. The hairs in front of his ears tangled in curls, started to corkscrew, blunted by sleep. He had long eyelashes, longer than mine. The sun tilted further up and the dazzle of light grew brighter, till it made my eyes hurt.

"Put on a hat," I said to Niko. "Going to be hot and bad today."

He nodded but stayed where he was. I started to say more, but shrugged and went back in. It was all the same to me. Still, when I saw his straw hat on the floor, I nudged it over to Jorge Felipe and said, "Take this out to Niko when you go."

Looking out over the railing, I spotted the three corp ships long before we got to the Lump. For a moment I wondered why they were so spread out, and then I realized the Lump's size. It was huge—kilometers wide. The ships were gathered around it, and their buzz boats were resting, wings spread out to recharge the solar panels.

They must have seen us around the same time. A buzz boat folded its wings, shadows spider-webbed with silver, and approached us. As it neared, I saw the Novagen logo on its side, on its occupant's mirrored helmet.

"This is claimed salvage," the logo-ed loudspeaker said.

I cupped my hands to shout back, "Salvage's not claimed till you've got tethers on it. Unless you're pulling in the whole thing, we've got a right to chew on it, too."

"Claimed salvage," the pilot repeated. He looked the *Mary Magdalena* up and down and curled his lip. Most of the time I liked her shitty, rundown look, but pride bristled briefly. "You want to be careful, kid. Accidents happen out here when freelancers get in the way."

I knew they did. Corp ships liked to sink the competition, and they had a dozen different underhanded ways to do it.

Jorge Felipe said at my elbow, "Gonna let them chase us off?"

"No," I said, but I nodded at the pilot and said, "Mary Magdalena, back us off." We moved round to the other side.

"What are you going to do?" Niko asked.

"We're going to cut the engines and let the currents creating the Lump pull us into it," I said. "They're watching for engine activity. After it gets dark, they won't notice us cutting. In the meantime, we'll act like we're fishing. Not even act, really."

We broke out fishing gear. The mermaids had deserted us, and I hoped to find a decent school of something, bottom-feeders at least. But the murk around the Lump was lifeless. Plastic tendrils waved like uneasy weed, gobbling our hooks till the rods bent and bowed with each wave.

I wanted the corp ships to see our lines. Every hour, a buzz boat would whoosh by, going between two of the larger ships.

When the sun went down, I went below deck. The others followed. I studied the weather readout on the main console's scratched metal flank.

It took longer than I thought, though. By the time we'd managed to cut our chunk free with the little lasers, draining the batteries, the sun was rising. Today was cloudier, and I blessed the fog. It'd make us harder to spot.

We worked like demons, throwing out hooks, cutting lumps free, tossing them into the cargo net. We looked for good stuff, electronics with precious metals that might be salvaged, good glass, bit of memorabilia that would sell on the Internet. Shellfish—we'd feed ourselves for a week out of this if nothing else. Two small yellow ducks bobbed in the wake of a bottle wire lacing. I picked them up, stuck them in my pocket.

"What was that?" Jorge Felipe at my elbow.

"What was what?" I was hauling in orange netting fringed with dead seaweed.

"What did you stick in your pocket?" His eyes tightened with suspicion.

I fished the ducks out of my pocket, held them out. "You want one?"

He paused, glancing at my pocket.

"Do you want to stick your hand in?" I said. I cocked my hip towards him. He was pissing me off.

He flushed. "No. Just remember—we split it all. You remember that."

"I will."

There's an eagle, native to the islands, We call them brown-wings. Last year I'd seen Jorge Felipe dealing with docked tourists, holding one.

"Want to buy a bird?" he asked, sitting in his canoe looking up at the tan and gold and money-colored boat. He held it up.

"That's an endangered species, son," one tourist said. His face, sun-reddened, was getting redder.

Jorge looked at him, his eyes flat and expressionless. Then he reached out with the bird, pushed its head underwater for a moment, pulled it out squawking and thrashing.

The woman screeched. "Make him stop!"

"Want to buy a bird?" Jorge Felipe repeated.

They couldn't throw him money fast enough. He let the brown-wing go and it flew away. He bought us all drinks that night, even me, but I kept seeing that flat look in his eyes. It made me wonder what would have happened if they'd refused.

By the time the buzz boats noticed us, we were underway. They could see what we had in tow and I had the *Mary Magdalena* monitoring their radio chatter.

But what I hoped was exactly what happened. We were small fry. We had a chunk bigger than I'd dared think, but that wasn't even a thousandth of what they were chewing down. They could afford to let a few scavengers bite.

All right, I thought, and told the *Mary Magdalena* to set a course for home. The worst was over.

I didn't realize how wrong I was.

Niko squatted on his heels near the engines, watching the play of sunlight over the trash caught in the haul net. It darkened the water, but you could barely see it, see bits of plastic and bottles and sea wrack submerged underneath the surface like an unspoken thought.

I went to my knees beside him. "What's up?"

He stared at the water like he was waiting for it to tell him something.

"It's quiet," he said.

Jorge Felipe was atop of the cabin, playing his plastic accordion. His heels, black with dirt, were hooked under the rungs of the ladder. I'd let the plastic fray there, and bits bristled and splayed like an old toothbrush. His music echoed out across the water for kilometers, the only sound other than splash or mermaid whistle.

"Quiet," I said, somewhere between statement and question.

"Gives you time to think."

"Think about what?"

"I was born not too far from here." He stared at the twitch and pluck in the sun-splattered water.

"Yeah?"

He turned to look at me. His eyes were chocolate and beer and cinnamon. "My mother said my dad was one of them."

I frowned. "One of what?"

"A mermaid."

I had to laugh. "She was pulling your leg. Mermaids can't fuck humans."

"Before he went into the water, idiot."

"Huh," I said. "And when he came out?"

"She said he never came out."

"So you think he's still there? Man, all those rich folks, once they learned that the water stank and glared, they gave up that life. If he didn't come out, he's dead."

I was watching the trash close to us when I saw what had sparked this thought. The mermaids were back. They moved along the net's edge. It shuddered as they tugged at it.

"What are they doing?" I asked.

"Picking at it," Niko said. "I've been watching. They pick bits off. What for, I don't know."

"We didn't see them around the Lump. Why now?"

Niko shrugged. "Maybe all that trash is too toxic for them. Maybe that's why we didn't see any fish near it either. Here it's smaller. Tolerable."

Jorge Felipe slid onto his heels on the deck.

"We need to drive them off," he said, frowning at our payload.

"No," Niko protested. "There's just a few. They're picking off the loose stuff that makes extra drag, anyhow. Might even speed us up."

Jorge Felipe gave him a calculating look. The look he'd given the tourist. But all he said was, "All right. That changes, let me know."

He walked away. We stood there, listening to the singing of the mermaids.

I thought about reaching out to take Niko's hand, but what would it have accomplished? And what if he pulled away? Eventually I went back in to check our course.

By evening, the mermaids were so thick in the water that I could see our own Lump shrinking, dissolving like a tablet in water.

Jorge Felipe came out with his gun.

"No!" Niko said.

Jorge Felipe smiled. "If you don't want me to shoot them, Niko, then they're taking it off your share. You agree it's mine, and I won't touch a scale."

"All right."

"That's not fair," I objected. "He worked as hard as us pulling it in."

Jorge Felipe aimed the gun at the water.

"It's okay," Niko told me.

I thought to myself that I'd split my share with him. I wouldn't have enough for the Choice, but I'd be halfway. And Niko would owe me. That wouldn't be a bad thing.

I knew what Choice I'd make. Niko liked boys. I liked Niko. A simple equation. That's what the Choice is supposed to let you do. Pick the sex you want, when you want it. Not have it forced on you when you're not ready.

The *Mary Magdalena* sees everything that goes on within range of her deck cameras. It shouldn't have surprised me when I went back into the cabin and she said, "You like Niko, don't you?"

"Shut up," I said. I watched the display. The mermaids wavered on it like fleshy shadows.

"I don't trust Jorge Felipe."

"Neither do I. I still want you to shut up."

"Lolo," she said. "Will you ever forgive me for what happened?"

I reached over and switched her voice off.

Still, it surprised me when Jorge Felipe made his move. I'd switched on auto-pilot, decided to nap in the hammock. I woke up to find him fumbling through my clothes.

"What you pick up, huh? What did you find out in the water?" he hissed. His breath stank of old coffee and cigarettes and the tang of metal.

"I didn't find anything," I said, pushing him away.

"It's true what they say, eh? No cock, no cunt." His fingers rummaged.

I tried to shout but his other hand was over my mouth.

"We all want this money, eh?" he said. "But I need it. You can keep on being all freaky, mooning after Niko. And he can keep on his own loser path. Me, I'm getting out of here. But I figure you, you don't want to be messed with. Your share, or I'm fucking you up worse than you are already."

If I hadn't turned off her voice, the *Mary Magdalena* would have warned me. But she hadn't warned me before.

"Are you going to be good?" Jorge Felipe asked. I nodded. He released my mouth.

"No one's going to sail with you, ever again."

He laughed. "World's a whooooooole lot bigger than this, freaky chicoca. Money's going to buy me a ticket out."

I remembered the gun. How far would he go in securing his ticket? "All right," I said. My mouth tasted like the tobacco stains on his fingers.

His lips were hot on my ear. "Okay then, chicoca. Stay nice and I'll be nice."

I heard the door open and close as he left. Shaking, I untangled myself from the hammock and went to the steering console. I turned on the *Mary Magdalena*'s voice.

"You can't trust him," she said.

I laughed, panic's edge in my voice. "No shit. Is there anyone I can trust?"

If she'd been a human, she might have said "me."

Being a machine, she knew better. There was just silence.

When I was little, I loved the *Mary Magdalena* and being aboard her. I imagined she was my mother, that when Mami had died, she'd chosen not to go to heaven, had put her soul in the boat to look after me.

I loved my uncle too. He let me steer the boat, sitting on his lap, let me run around the deck checking lines and making sure the tack was clean, let me fish for sharks and rays. One time, coming home under the General Domingo Bridge, he pointed into the water.

At first it looked as though huge brown bubbles were coming up through the water. Then I realized it was rays, maybe a hundred, moving through the waves.

Going somewhere, I don't know where.

He waited until I was thirteen. I don't know why. I was as skinny and unformed that birthday as I had been the last day I was twelve. He took me out on the *Mary Magdalena* and waited until we were far out at sea.

He raped me. When he was done, he said if I reported it, he'd be put in jail. My grandmother would have no one to support her.

I applied for Free Agency the next day. I went to the clinic and told them what had been done. That it had been a stranger, and that I wanted to become Ungendered. They tried to talk me out of it. They're legally obliged to, but I was adamant. So they did it, and for a few years I lived on the streets. Until they came and told me my uncle was dead. The *Mary Magdalena,* who had remained silent, was mine.

I could hear Jorge Felipe out on the deck, playing his accordion again. I wondered what Niko was doing. Watching the water.

"I don't know what to do," I said to myself. But the boat thought responded. "You can't trust him."

"Tell me something I don't know," I said.

On the display. the mermaids' fuzzy shadows intersected the garbage's dim line. I wondered what they wanted, what they did with the plastic and cloth they pulled from us. I couldn't imagine that anyone kept anything, deep in the sea, beyond the water in their gills and the blood in their veins.

When Jorge Felipe went in to make coffee, I squatted beside Niko. He was watching the mermaids still. I said, urgently, "Niko, Jorge Felipe may try something before we land. He wants your share and mine. He'd like the boat, too. He's a greedy bastard."

Niko stared into the water. "Do you think my dad's out there?"

"Are you high?"

His pupils were big as flounders. There was a mug on the deck beside him. "Did Jorge Felipe bring that to you?"

"Yeah," he said. He reached for it, but I threw the rest overboard.

"Get hold of yourself, Niko," I said. "It could be life or death. We've got sixteen hours to go. He won't try until we're a few hours out. He's lazy."

I couldn't tell whether or not I'd gotten through. His cheeks were angry from the sun. I went inside and grabbed my uncle's old baseball hat, and took it out to him. He was dangling an arm over the side. I grabbed him, pulled him back.

"You're going to get bit or dragged over," I said. "Do you understand me?"

Jorge Felipe grinned out of the cabin. "Having a good time there, Niko? You wanna go visit dad, go splashy splashy?" He wiggled his fingers at Niko.

"Don't say that!" I said. "Don't listen to him, Niko."

Something flapped in the water behind us and we all turned. A huge mermaid, half out of the water, pulling itself onto the trash's mass. I couldn't tell what it was trying to do—grab something? Mate with it?

The gun went off. The mermaid fell back as Niko yelled like he'd been shot. I turned, seeing the gun leveling on Niko, unable to do anything as it barked. He jerked, falling backward into the cargo net's morass.

His hands beat the water like dying birds. Something pulled him under, maybe the mermaids, maybe just the net's drag.

I tried to grab him, but Jorge Felipe's hand was in my collar pulling me back with a painful blow to my throat. The hurt doubled me over, grabbing for breath through the bruise's blaze.

"Too bad about Niko," Jorge Felipe said. "But I need you to keep piloting. Go inside and stay out of trouble." He pushed me towards the cabin and I stumbled into it, out of the wind and the sound of the water.

I stood, trying to catch my breath, my hands on the panels. I wondered if Niko had drowned quickly. I wondered if that was how Jorge Felipe intended to kill me. All around, the boat hummed and growled, mechanical sounds that had once felt as safe as being inside my mother's womb.

I waited for her to say something, anything. Was she waiting for me to ask her help? Or did she know there was nothing she could do?

Underneath the hum, I could hear the mermaids singing, a whine that echoed through the metal, crept into the *Mary Magdalena*'s habitual drone.

When I said, "How much farther?" she didn't pretend she didn't understand the question.

"Fifteen hours, twenty minutes."

"Any weapons on board I don't know about?" I pictured my uncle having something, anything. A harpoon gun or a shark knife. Something wicked and deadly and masculine.

But she answered, "No." The same flat voice she always used.

I could have wept then, but that was girlish. I was beyond that. I was the master of the *Mary Magdalena*. I would kill Jorge Felipe somehow, and avenge my friend.

How, I didn't know.

Outside splashing, something caught in the netting. I pushed my way out the door as Jorge Felipe stared down into the water. I shoved my way past him, unsure for a moment whether or not he'd hinder me. Then his hands were beside me, helping me pull a gasping Niko onto the boat.

"Welcome back, man," he said as Niko doubled over on hands and knees, spewing water and bile across the decking.

For a moment I thought, of course, everything would be fine. He'd reconsidered killing us. We'd pull into port, sell the cargo, give him the money and go our separate ways.

I saw him guessing at my thoughts. All he did was rest his hand on his gun and smile at me. He could see the fear come back, and it made him smile harder.

Behind me, Niko gasped and sputtered. There was another sound beside the hiss and slap of the waves. *Mary Magdalena,* whispering, whispering. What was she saying to him? What was going on in his head, what had he seen in his time underwater? Had the mermaids come and stared in his face, their eyes as blank as winter, his father there, driven mad by solipsism and sea song, looking at his son with no thoughts in his head at all?

I stood, Jorge Felipe looking at me. If I locked myself in the cabin, how long would it take him to break in? But he gestured me away as I stepped towards the door.

"Not now," he said, and the regret in his tone was, I thought, for the time he'd have to spend at the wheel, awake, more than anything else.

She was whispering, still whispering, to Niko. Why hadn't she warned me? She must have known what was brewing like a storm beneath the horizon. I couldn't have been the first.

I started to turn to Jorge Felipe, *Mary Magdalena's* voice buzzing under my nerves like a bad light bulb. Then weight shifting on the deck, Niko's footprints squelching forward as he grabbed at Jorge Felipe, backpedaling until they fell together over the side in a boil of netting and mermaids.

In a fairytale, the mermaids would have brought Niko back to the surface while they held Jorge Felipe down below, gnawing at him with their sharp parrot beaks. In some stories, dolphins rescued drowning sailors, back when dolphins were still alive. And whales spoke to the fishing boats they swam beside, underneath clear-skied stars, in waters where no mermaids sang.

But instead no one surfaced. I turned the boat in great circles, spining the cargo net over and over again. Finally I told the *Mary Magdalena* to take us home. It had started to rain, the sullen sodden rain that means winter is at elbow's length.

I took the yellow ducks out of my pocket and put them on the console. What did Jorge Felipe think I'd found? I stared at the display and the slow shift and fuzz of the earth's bones, far below the cold water.

"What did you tell Niko?" I asked.

"I told him that his father would be killed if he didn't defend him from Jorge Felipe. And I activated my ultrasonics. They acted on his nervous system."

I shuddered. "That's what I felt as well?"

"There should be no lasting effects."

"Thanks," I said. I stirred three sugar packets and powdered cream into my coffee. It was almost too hot to drink when it came out of the microwave, but I cupped it in my fingers, grateful for its heat.

I could have slept. But every time I laid down in the hammock, I smelled Jorge Felipe, and thought I heard him climbing out of the water.

Finally I went out and watched the water behind us. The *Mary Magdalena* played the radio for me, a soft salsa beat with no words I could understand. It began to rain, and I heard the sound of raindrops on the decking beside me, pattering on the plastic sheeting I drew over my head.

By the time I arrived back in port, the mermaids had plucked away all but a few tangles of seawrack from the netting. I'd be lucky to net the cost of a cup of coffee, let alone cover the fuel I'd used. Never mind. A few more seasons and I'd have the money I needed, if I was careful. If there were no disasters.

Neither body was there in the net. Perhaps Niko's father had reclaimed him.

The wind and rain almost knocked me off the deck as I stared into the water. The green netting writhed like barely visible guilt in the darkness.

The *Mary Magdalena* called after me, as she had not dared in years. "Sleep well, Lolo. My regards to Grandma Fig."

I stopped and half turned. I could barely see her lines through the driving rain.

Sometimes I used to imagine setting her on fire. Sometimes I used to imagine taking her out to a rift and drilling holes in the hull. Sometimes I used to imagine her smashed by waves, or an earthquake, or a great red bull stamping through the streets.

But the winter was long, and it would be lonely sitting at home with my grandmother. Lonelier than time at sea with her, haunted by the mermaids' music.

"Good night, Mary Magdalena," I said.

Of Melei, of Ulthar
GORD SELLAR

Haunted went Melei that evening into the streets of Ulthar, haunted by what she had seen in the dream-voyage of the night before; desert fires burning distant across the dark and dusty plain, and an immense black silhouette of some enormous outcropping of rock rising up, upward into the sky to blot out the tiny flickering stars across half of the heavens. In a dream, too, had she heard voices echoing against the stone walls of buildings crammed together along narrow streets, voices laden with care and worry, crying her name out into the blackness of deepening night.

Her name—but *not* Melei, not that name she used in waking—had crouched in wait beneath her tongue; perhaps it was only natural, in the dreaming, in this other world, to be called something else. *That* name, strange in her mouth, cold and quivering when she nearly whispered it to herself, was *hers*. And why not? She was alone, she lived alone, and with nobody shared the secrets of her nocturnal voyages, for who would call her anything but mad . . . ?

So that awake, by the lengthening hours of that slow, still-warm autumn endlessness, Melei stalked the cozy, jumbled streets of Ulthar. Listlessly; suffering through a sunny afternoon as faraway gleam of dreamt flames in darkness, and the tempo of faint faraway cries and chanting, haunted her waking mind.

Cats—for in Ulthar, where there was one, there were ten—traipsed past in little dainty-footed troupes, eyeing her with the wary look of beings that glimpsed her dark secret as no human could. She yielded the road to them just as everyone in Ulthar did, occasionally stooping to rub one behind the ear. Briefly, just until its tail batted back against her elbow and it turned its head slightly before going on along its carefree, shiftless way. Always one with black and white patches, always with white paws, she knelt to touch *those* chiaroscuro beasts with the slightest hesitation only, with a trepidation she prayed nobody noticed, most of all the beasts themselves. And yet she was sure in her heart's blood that they knew. They *knew*.

And then, round some corner would she follow the troupe of cats, and find a pack of soldiers standing together. Staring at her from behind grilled black faceplates. She would stop, as other citizens did not, and stare into those night-dark eyes, glimpse the dark folds of eyelids surrounding those bold orbs, and sigh gently and slowly to herself, for these people looked to her like the folk of her dreams, almost. Swarthy, yes, and smelling of exotic, perplexing spices. Beside them, in the street, as clouds drifted in overhead, over the tops of gods-haunted mountains, she took comfort in that strange aroma, the hint of myrrh and tehenna and cinnamon, the broad brown lips pursed stern. The foreign soldiers looked at this bold young woman with wonder, for none of Ulthar had done as she, pausing to gaze into their eyes with something like recognition, perhaps, or fascination, in their own.

Only Melei.

She gazed thus, for a few brief moments, upon these strange and ever-surly foreigners, as a wanderer sometimes, but only sometimes, looks upon the walls of the city where her people have dwelt since forgotten ages. In dreaming, she often had seen folk like these, sat at fires and eaten with them, sung songs she only half-understood, songs shared with that hopeful, dire world which filled her waking days with longing.

But no songs now. Instead, she whispered a word to them, a single word in her own language. One of them, in his fluted blue steel armor, shrugged slightly. They looked at one another, and then at her again, the expectation being that she would move on.

"Atal," she asked them, a name, a single word so pathopoeic that the warriors could do nothing but ache from it, and she nodded her fair head past them, to a distant gate behind, up to the high temple carved from hillstone there, where ancient Atal was, in those days, thought still to linger. His image had been painted last as a priest in repose, feeble and centuries-worn Atal in white robes, shaven head resting upon a stone pillow; his eyes full of longing, staring up from the canvas. Melei had seen the picture in a public hall, gazed reverently on it for an hour while closing her eyes and opening them again, over and over until the image was stamped upon her mind perfectly, indelibly.

The soldiers only pursed their dark, broad lips harder and shook their heads. They nodded down the road. Not towards wherever Atal now was, if indeed the old priest lived still; these footmen of the new conqueror were directing her nowhere except away. Melei gazed upon them a moment more. What songs had they sung as boys? What games had they played amidst fires burning among the darkling foothills surrounding the great peaks of the south? Slowly, she turned and followed a quiet old striped tomcat away, along a gutter. But she heard them speak of her, then, to one another.

And then, suddenly, Ulthar was no longer tinged by her dreams, no longer dressed in that enchantment she had smuggled back from the world of her slumbering voyages. As the soldiers spoke with muted words at once utterly gibberish and completely familiar, she gave up on her earlier half-fancies that she might even have understood them, at least the sense in them, if only she could have heard their voices a little more clearly. It was a lie. They were not mystical creatures. They were quotidian men of muscle and sinew, and Ulthar was simply a holding in their masters' empire.

And Melei longed for more.

She felt their eyes upon her as she wandered down the road, and round a corner, her eyes searching the sky for the first stars, that she might turn homeward and settle herself down to the repose and reverie that only sleep could bring her.

The black night-ocean roared beneath, broad and noisy with the lapping of waves that she could hear clear as children's voices, so silently did she glide through the deep, familiar sepia that always preceded sunrise on these flights.

The ocean was new: often, she had soared above grasslands, occasionally among the buildings of a smog-choked city, but tonight, this dream-morning, she found herself above some expansive southern ocean. Below, from time to time, a lumbering darkness could be seen, spilling light from tiny windows, luminance far different from any reflection of the whole and simple face of the single crescent moon above her. These were windows in the hulls of lumbering ships that crawled across the ruined sea.

As sepia slowly burnt into orange with the coming of the morning sun, Melei spied the coast ahead. It was an immense and hideous metal graveyard, the hulls and decks of broken ships protruding from the sand, their bare bones laid out as if upon an examiner's table. Among them gathered laboring men, already at work hauling enormous rusty chains and ruined slabs of metal ashore. The ships looked as if they had been hewn in half by some enormous, awful blade and left to bleed into the ocean. For the waters, too, were sullied here, stained black and putrid. The rancid stink of the waters wafted up into the air, and Melei gasped in stunned disbelief.

This was not the same site as she had visited in previous dream-flights, though the people shared the same dark hue of skin, wore the same resignation on their faces. A man beneath her dropped his load, a gargantuan link of chain slamming down onto his leg, and he collapsed upon the poisoned sand with a cry so loud she could hear it as she soared past.

It was exquisite, wrenching but enchanting. It was a place where mistakes mattered, and this was why Melei kept returning. Because this world was one of consequences and dire meanings, godless and hard and amazing. But this beach was not the precise place she sought. In Ulthar, Melei was a mere seamstress, a needle-girl who day in and day out walked the streets careful not to step in cat shit. But in this strange world, she found herself possessed of powers beyond anything a real person in Ulthar could have boasted in millennia. She could soar in the sky, and she could go anywhere.

And there was a place that she was seeking, these nights.

Below her, a fence surrounded an enormous tent village. Men shouted, and there was a violent clattering sound, and screams. She saw people running, people clothed in white that shone against their dark flesh. To Melei they were unspeakably beautiful in their terror. Running for their lives, panicked. She felt her tears welling up. Such awful lives; and yet they held onto them so desperately. What humbling beauty, what endless rapture, that beings could live that way, in a world so starved of magic and gods. It enchanted her, as she swooped down low enough to brush her fingertips against the tattered hems of a few of the dingy white shirts that ran long enough to reach down past the knees of the scrambling men and women.

Melei concentrated, and suddenly spun in the air, soaring now into the northwest. There was a city there that she had read of in secret books hidden in the drab tearooms of Ulthar, books only secret because nobody read them—for the denizens of Ulthar spoke only of the failed expeditions to unearth Kadath, old dead Kadath, and of gossip in the wracked court of Ulthar that was now under Southern rule. But Melei had read on fragile, forgotten pages of the wild tangled passage-roads that ran between the great grey monoliths of that old city on the coast, the city with the unbroken towers and the bridges and the streets laden with music and voices and wavering lights. Across an ocean, it lay: unutterably far by the standards of these folk; but for a dream-traveler, its bright roads and bustling noise lay within reach, if the will was strong.

If only she could find that strange and mystic polis . . . nobody had done so in aeons of dreaming, not in the lifetimes even of gods. The sky swallowed her, and she soared into it not lightly, but as an arrow soars toward its victim's death: unstoppable, unabashed, and filled with the most resolute certainty imaginable.

Excrescences thick and strange rose from the drowned streets, wafting steamily up from broad, jagged-barred holes in the ground, and Melei swept down into the fog of the broken city. This was the place, but no longer the city of the pages, not the city about the magnificences of which had been whispered and scribbled out by dream-wanderers in ancient tomes long-lost. This polis had changed, its million secret details discarded like the flimsy skin of an ancient serpent drifting through the slow eternity of its being.

The city had, by some horrid magic or doom, been drowned, and slain. Ruined, its towering spirit smashed apart, the smithereens tossed into cold water and frozen away into bitter ice.

Here, a great library stood encrusted in ice that gleamed chill as diamonds in darkness; and before it, barges poled by men in thick woolen coats, shivering and calling out in their strange tongues, baleful cries. Old men and women gathered upon the library steps and huddled at its high windows as flakes of snow fell enormous and faintly grey with the ash of fires half a world away.

And there, further along, the great old temples of the last true religion in that world, the fanatic cult-houses of the worshippers of the magical curve, the endless blessed marketeers and insatiable blood-hungry pirates of water and light and time. There, these rectangular temples of lost merchandises stood with windows smashed, empty from lootings, empty except for the poor useless souls who took refuge in their icy halls remaining since the cult had loosed its foul and terrible powers upon the world, and toppled everything that humankind had once built up.

Thence flew Melei, deeper into the city, over crumbled steel bridges and the steeples of abandoned, burnt-down churches. She heard singing, not of human voices, not of ghosts—for this world, haunted though its inhabitants' faces were, was a place bereft of stalking ghŭls and spirits hungrily wandering. No, not like the frightening lands that lay distant from Ulthar; nothing like the shadowy passes near high Old Kadath or the caverns of B'thaniss. Only the wretched faces of the living gazed out through the smashed-glass windows. The voice she heard was none other than her own, crying out her exultant terror.

An open square between the broken buildings spread out below her, and she wondered whether this had been a park, or the base of some enormous destroyed temple, or perhaps that square where, in ancient frigid nights, the folk of the city had gathered to witness the death-knell of the ending year and cry out jubilant with the beginning of the new. No hint suggested which guess might be correct.

She thought again of living here, in this strange world of cold consequences, as often she had before. Shivering—not from cold, for her dreaming self was swaddled in thick, warm wool, and something of the power of her dream-voyaging shielded her from the worst of the awful, ruined clime—but rather from a titillation derived less from horror at the ruined city, or that such ruination was possible, than out of the purer terror that shook her upon witnessing the magnificent finality of the fact of the ruination itself.

Broken buildings slumbered all around her as she flew past, and she marveled that this world was thus; a place where ruinations could be visited upon mighty civilizations in a generation, yet where the people here would endure on, shivering and hungry, fighting to continue. Whisperings of the fate of Sarnath bubbled up from the silence of her forgotten childhood, but there peered no specters from the windows of this city, at least none that had died. Only the pale and sallow faces of the hungry stared out at her, living scavengers looking out, lit by fires and shame.

Terror. The terror of finding oneself before a mountain to be scaled, a mountain the height of a dozen nations piled upon one another, end to end, boasting whole civilizations and waste lands between them, upon a slope rising unceasingly upward into the sky. The terror of looking upon the ocean stirred into a raging turmoil of violence. Terror at confronting the great secret of this world: that all things had endings, all things could be destroyed just as they had once, long ago, been built up. That terror swept through Melei, thrilled her.

That was when her name in this world, that *other* name, pierced up into her tongue, begging again to be spoken and seal itself upon her.

She bit her tongue, bit down into it so hard that it ached and bled a little. To *say* the name . . . to consign herself among the living shades . . . such a temptation . . .

The name fought relentlessly. It *would* be said, she realized, someday. She would come to live here, in this drowned city of humbling, awful beauty. It would be her home, someday, taking her into its brutal black arms like a lover would do, grinding its iciness against her shivering flesh.

Still she fought, clenching her teeth and grinding them together so violently that she felt they might break off in her mouth. She pushed herself upward, into the sky, letting go of the city even as she stared into the watery canal gridwork of its forgotten, worthless streets. She let herself ascend, into the foul clouds that were heavy with strange poisons, up into the cold nebulousness that lay beyond them, falling away from this awful and lovely world that was her constant obsession, this place of strange meanings and consequences and cruel finalities.

The city and all of its broken, awful grandeur blurred into a mere patch of indistinct darkness dotted with scattered open fires, blending into the surrounding darkness and becoming nothingness as she fell upward, outward; away from the world once again.

Melei's eyes opened slowly as the sunrise just finished and serene Ulthar gradually stirred from its long nocturnal slumber. She slid her prodigious bedding aside, and took up her scribbling-notebook in one hand, searching for the words that would draw the magnificently drab colors across from that other world into hers.

A troupe of cats passed by her window, miaowing gleefully at one another, and she rose to peer out at them, as if to divine some portent from the colors of their coats; but they were a motley pack, impossible to read even for a girl as bright as Melei.

Waking, dreaming. She felt as if a woman torn between two lovers—one of them calm, and sweet, and still and good, and the other magnificent, stone-muscled and taciturn and bold enough to seize her and pull her close to him in the darkness of night.

She set the notebook down, ruminating. There was a choice coming. She would have to choose a name. Said she, in that world, "Melei," then her dark lover would listen, and hear, and understand what her heart said. The delicious torture would end, and he would send her home . . . never to return. Yet said she that other name, that strange name that even now squirmed beneath her tongue, prickling her mouth and fighting to be pronounced in the sunny morning calm of Ulthar, then her dark lover would seize her, all at once, and carry her off into the delightful terror of the world of her dreams, leaving the streets of Ulthar forever empty of her.

She could feel the city's ache, at the very thought of her leaving. The city's ache, or perhaps it was her own.

No harm could come of writing the name, she decided. She had written it upon her own palm, in different scripts, one by one, and not a thing had happened save that she had dreamt of the other world sooner, and more fiercely, each time. She could write it upon a page, she was sure. It was not the same as saying it. She could still decide. Melei, or . . .

She took a quill, unlidded a jar of sepia ink, and touched the quill's tip into the inky darkness. Without speaking—with her jaw locked firmly, to guard against accidental pronouncement—she touched the tip of the quill against the gently yellowed page. The dawn sunlight cast a shadow from the feather quill, throwing a line of gentle shading across the page and into her lap. She shut her eyes, and opened them, and shut them again, and once more opened them, so as to let the shadow find a place in her heart's memory.

She realized, then, she was building up a storehouse of memories already. The faces of the swarthy guards. The troupes of cats mewing happily all around her. She had stopped hating Ulthar, wincing at the summery stink of the cat turds and grumbling at the foreign power that ruled the place. She had found the kind of love that wells up one when she abandons her lover for another, her world for another's; that sort of love that is rooted in impossibility that cannot be prevented even by sorrow, even by fear, even by the movement of the shadow across a page as the sun slips up into the sky.

She did not write the name, but instead rose, scribbling-book still in hand, and went back to her window. The sweetest cottages of Ulthar lay just there, empty of terror but touching in their way, stirring memories of the games she had played in these dusty streets during what felt like another life. Laughter and the voices of children who had somehow become half-forgotten friends, folk whose faces that she had seen not once in ages and ages.

And Melei knew, then, that she *would* say the name. Perhaps not that night. Not so soon as that, she told herself. But she *would* say it, and go, and old Ulthar would continue on without her, as it had done before her birth, with its cats and gentle sunny days and whispering old women and men.

She filled a basin with warm water, and carried it to a high table in her room, her feet padding upon the wooden planks of the floor. Outside, a bird sang a snatch of birdsong she had heard dozens of times before, though she could not name what type of bird it was. She splashed the water on her face, delighting in its gentle warmth, steeling herself.

For there would be precious little warmth like this in the other world, in the arms of her dark dream lover.

And then she donned a bright and comfortable silk, light in shade to suit the warm day, and crossed the threshold of her home, going out into a street that smelled of blooming cherry flowers and apple orchards that had been planted by the Southerners. There, in the street, a trio of cats gazed up at her, curiously eyeing her approach with heads tilted one way or another. They seemed, like all cats in Ulthar, almost as if they wished to ask her something, or to dispense some holy secret to her, but if indeed this was so, they said nothing, their own jaws as firmly locked as hers had been minutes before.

An old man made his way down the street, comfortable and calm though his back was a little bent. He smiled at her, and a cock crowed in the distance, and Melei closed her eyes. And opened them again.

And closed them.

And opened them again, committing every breath of it, every shade and tiny noise and scent, to the strongest urn in the storehouse of her memory. The voices of children long gone echoed, now, within that storehouse, and the image of her mother baking sour bread, and the laughter of cats—for in Ulthar, by nights, cats do laugh, though only the most blessed ever hear it more than once—and the sunrises, the sunrises that had saddened her so often.

Perplexed, she went through the streets, dazed, eyes and heart drinking Ulthar in deeply and constantly until she was drunk with the place. It was her farewell kiss to the world of her birth, a kiss of the eyes upon the forehead. It was her last embrace of the little city, day-long as she wandered and rambled from shop to temple to the current doorsteps of present friends and the abandoned doorways of friends long-lost. She met those she had once loved, and said nothing of leave-taking, though she wondered if they could see it in her eyes. Yet she asked not a soul as she spoke to them of nothings, of needle work and gossip and of the latest news from other cities and lands. As she walked those quiet, calm streets, her footsteps tapping gently the beat of her last ballad to Ulthar, she realized she loved this city, loved it unceasingly and would do so evermore though she would not live here any longer.

For as the sun began slowly to draw itself down unto the horizon, and the shadows lengthened across the streets as another shadow had done upon her page that morning, the name beneath Melei's tongue stirred once more, this final time irresistibly . . .

Night, in Dark Perfection

RICHARD PARKS

In the domain of the Faerie Queen it was always night, and the sky as seen from her Palace was always cold, black and full of stars, and she was always heartbreakingly beautiful. She would have it no other way.

On this particular never-changing, never-ending night, she had decreed a ball, and as she stood before the window in her Palace, she looked at the stars while her maids got her ready.

"Has everyone answered?" she asked.

"All but the Marquessa of Shadows, Majesty," they told her. Perhaps one of them said it. Perhaps all of them said it. To the Faerie Queen, it made little difference. The all looked at her with the same fixed expressions.

"This won't do. See that she is summoned," the Faerie Queen said, and the maids said "Yes, Your Majesty." One or all of them sent the summons with the methods available to them, and as one they hoped, in their way, that the Faerie Queen would forget. She did not forget. They finished dressing the Faerie Queen, and she studied the result in her mirror.

The dress looked like woven copper trimmed in gold, and perhaps it was. The queen did not bother herself with such details. What mattered was how well it set off her porcelain skin and fiery red hair, and the dress did so very well indeed. She was pleased with the dress. She was not pleased with her maids and, most especially, the Marquessa of Shadows, whom she had not forgotten for an instant.

"Have you received an answer?"

"Answer, Your Majesty?"

The Queen sighed. "Where is she?"

At first she received no response except a feigned innocent silence, until she reached for her scepter. "I will ask this only one more time: where is she?"

"In her boudoir, Your Majesty . . .shall . . .shall we send a messenger?"

"We've sent enough messages already. We will deliver one more. In person."

"Your Majesty, perhaps it would be best—"

"We decide what's best."

The Faerie Queen left her maids and walked alone through the echoing corridors of her palace. Once she would have been escorted by handsome elfin knights wherever she went, but they were away, she had forgotten where. Besides, she didn't need them. She was the beautiful and terrible Faerie Queen. She had her scepter. She did not need to fear. She dispensed fear, she did not receive it.

She came to a place where most of the windows were covered with tapestries, except, here and there, a tapestry had fallen. She didn't mind. There was a certain fashion in decay that suggested time, and she was not afraid of time. She paused for a moment and looked out the window there, but all she saw were stars, going on to forever. Just for that one instant in time, the Faerie Queen felt a sense of something missing.

"Where's the damned moon?"

The window blinked off for a moment, then a series of symbols drew themselves across it. The Faerie Queen understood that what she was seeing was a map, and it showed her exactly where the moon was. Or had been. Or perhaps might still be. She closed her eyes and looked away, and in that instant, and only for that instant, she remembered what fear was. When she looked back, the map was gone and all she saw were the stars in another endless, moonless night. Words had power, she remembered, and questions were worse still when all words were words of command and the Palace was there to serve her. Her voice was binding magic, best to avoid careless uttering when all the walls had ears. That was the true danger of the faerie realm. The Queen hurried past the window.

The Marquessa's rooms were on the same level of the Palace as her own. There was no one else around. The Faerie Queen didn't have the Palace announce her. She just opened the door. The Marquessa lay on her bed. In contrast to the Faerie Queen's shining raiment, the Marquessa wore something long and lacy and dark, more like a robe than a dress.

"Why did you not answer Our summons?"

Silence. The Marquessa's cold, dark eyes stared at the ceiling, and the Faerie Queen's anger and irritation grew by the moment.

"Answer me!" she shouted, but too late she realized what she had done, and it was not the Marquessa who answered her.

Cascade failure in all systems. Photonic links degraded 63%. Reboot—

"Stop! Stop it!"

Silence.

"I'm not like her," she said. "Not like them."

They are shadows. You are the Faerie Queen, said the Palace.

"The ball is cancelled."

Such a pity, Your Majesty.

The Faerie Queen dreamed of the last great ball. She watched all the dancers from the throne on her dais but especially Duke Sunstone dancing, partnered with the Marquessa of Shadows. It was all so elegant and grand, and then it wasn't. The Faerie Queen noticed to her horror that the Duke's foot was broken. It turned ninety degrees at the ankle and flopped awkwardly whenever he tried to *gavotte*. As for the Marquessa, her long legs barely moved as he dragged her through the steps. There were others. Several had fallen. One was crawling. She thought it was Count Moonbeam. Some did not move at all, and the music echoed futilely through the ballroom as the stars above shone like cold diamonds against the blackness.

"This is how the dead dance."

She banished the thought as she would a disgraced courtier. No one was dead. She was the Faerie Queen. She lived forever, and thus so did her subjects. That was her command. But there was one in the palace who did not obey the Queen's writ. On the bad nights, the Faerie Queen could see the creature. It had skin as white as her own but not the white of porcelain. This was a ghastly white. The white on the belly of something you turned up under a stone. Its eyes were open and staring, its hair was nothing more than gray, straggling wisps. It was dead. It was alive. It was there, in the Kingdom of Faerie, and it did not belong.

This was a bad night. The Faerie Queen saw the monster again. She could not touch it, though she forced herself to reach out. The thing was like smoke, there and then gone again. It did not speak, and it first appeared when her subjects began to fail.

"This is the thing that has brought Death among us," she said. "Whatever it is, I must destroy it."

You cannot, said the Palace.

"Not as I am," said the Faerie Queen.

No. Not as you are.

"Cryptic. I understand cryptic," the Faerie Queen said. "I can no longer be the Faerie Queen. I must be something else. So must you. We will hunt this thing together."

In the world of the Captive Princess, it was always night, and the sky as seen from her Prison was always black and full of stars, and she was always heartbreakingly beautiful. She really had no choice. When she awoke, the strange, expressionless creature that served as her Captor dressed her in clothes fit for a princess, but she managed to conceal her scepter. It was the one thing they had not been able to take from her.

The one link to her father's kingdom, now usurped by her wicked stepmother, was the Magician. He spoke to her sometimes. Now he spoke through the scepter.

What is your true wish?

"I wish to be free. Who is coming to rescue me?"

No one will rescue you, Princess.

"Well, then, I must do it myself," she said grimly. "Who is imprisoning me?"

You already know who guards you.

The Magician was right—it was a silly question. Her cruel stepmother, of course, imprisoned her, and it was her stepmother's creature, the Beast, that held her there. No one else had a reason. No one else stood to gain. "Has she imprisoned you, too?"

The Magician didn't answer her. Then, *There are people coming.*

She frowned. "What do you mean? I thought you said I wouldn't be rescued."

Rescue is not their intent, Princess.

"I see."

The Captive Princess took her scepter and went looking for the intruders. It was some time before she first heard the strange voices speaking a language she understood, but the accent was funny, and it crackled and popped in her ears as if it was carried on lightning.

"—size of this place? Have you seen anything like it?"

"Not outside of a history book. And keep your helmet on, Jek. You don't know what's been growing in this old soup. I'm amazed life-support is still working."

"Core's still online and the ship's stable, though no output from the drive engines . . .what's your guess on those? Magneto-plasma?"

"Probably. This place is a fucking museum."

Captive Princess entered the long corridor that led to her chambers, and there they were. Two men–or at least two man-shaped things wearing some kind of strange armor with rounded helmet and glass visors. As she saw them, they saw her.

"Impossible," the one named Jek said. "No one could still be alive here."

"They're not," said the other. "She's not real."

"A ghost?"

"Don't be stupid. I mean, look at that outfit. She's one of the former owner's toys. I'd guess a construct covered in some sort of bio-reactive polymer matrix. Whoever owned this ship could afford the best."

The man called Jek peered at the Captive Princess. "Could be an avatar of some sort. Telepresence?"

The other looked thoughtful. "Only if it's under the ship's control. There's no one else here to operate it."

"What gibberish! I am the Captive Princess!" Captive Princess said. "Who are you and what is your intent?"

The two stood in the corridor facing her. One gave an exaggerated bow. "My name is Kenson, Highness," he said. "My partner is Jek. We're here to claim right of salvage on this old hulk. How long have you been drifting, anyway?"

She frowned. "What are you talking about?"

Kenson sighed. "You're not a real person, Highness. You're either an independent AI or a glorified telepresence avatar . . .and since no one could still be alive on this wreck to pull your strings, I'd guess in that case I'm talking to the ship's computer. If you are the ship's computer, then understand that your vessel is derelict, and has been that way for a long, long time."

"I didn't think they could make a self-contained AI on this scale back then," Jek said.

Kenson shrugged. "Most likely not a true AI if it's a sexbot. A very limited scope of programming would be required for that kind of toy."

"I am no toy! This is my Palace! You can't just come here and take it!"

Captive Princess felt dizzy. She hadn't spoken. The Faerie Queen had spoken. And she was not the Faerie Queen. She was the Captive Princess. Nothing here belonged to her. There was nothing she wanted, except to kill the Beast and escape.

To go home.

"You have a ship? We can leave this island?"

"Island? What island? This is a derelict starship, and there's more high-grade titanium in your hull alone than either of us has seen in a lifetime, not even counting the rarer metals. We can retire as rich men, though we're shutting the power core down before we take you in tow. It's too dangerous otherwise."

She heard the Magician's voice again. *They're simple thieves, Highness. That's all.*

Jek prodded the other. "I thought you said she wasn't real. That looks real."

Captive Princess held her scepter pointed straight at the two men. "I'm taking your ship," she said. "I have to get away."

"I think she's serious," Jek said.

The man named Kensen just sighed. "Look, I don't know if you can understand this, but I'd rather not burn you and waste a valuable museum piece, so I'll try again: Whatever pre-packaged or custom bedroom scenario you're playing out, the fact remains that *you're not real*. This ship is *derelict*, and under right of salvage it is ours by law. You and this hulk belong to us."

"You're wrong," said the Captive Princess. "I am alive," she said and then added because she knew it was true. "The Beast is alive."

"'Beast'? Is this some sort of animal?" Jek asked.

"It's what imprisons me here. If you help me find and kill it, then we can all leave together. I will be merciful and overlook your attempted theft."

Kenson reached for the holster on his belt. "We don't have time for thi—"

The Captive Princess unleased the power of the scepter. It was all that remained of her royal heritage, but it belonged to her. No one else. The two men flew backwards several feet to land hard in the corridor. The Captive Princess continued to unleash her power until the two bodies stopped twitching.

Well done, Highness, the Magician said.

It was as she feared. She found the intruder's vessel with no problem; they had entered through one of the many double-doored gates to the castle where she was held, but the vessel would not obey her.

"The Beast is holding me here. Isn't that right?"

That is not the name it gives itself, Highness.

"I don't care! I want to be free."

Then you must do it yourself. I am forbidden.

"I know that. Guide me to the Beast's lair!"

That, too, is forbidden.

"You are sworn to serve me, Magician."

And so I do. I cannot help it that you do not understand how.

She sighed. "You're a useless old man. I'll find the thing myself!"

If there had been one single fear, one cause for hesitation greater than all others, it was the Captive Princess's fear that, when the time came, she would not have the courage to do what she would have to do. She knew better now. She did not regret killing the two intruders. She did not feel remorse. Rather the opposite.

"I can do this. I can kill the Beast."

The castle shuddered.

"What's happening?"

The interlopers were not gentle. They damaged the castle while creating a hole in our gates. Attempting to compensate.

Captive Princess didn't understand what the Magician was talking about, nor did she care. There was a crackling sound and she saw the Beast. She had seen the Beast many times. She had never seen it before. The one who had seen the Beast was the Faerie Queen, not the Captive Princess. Yet she remembered. She knew the Beast for what it was.

"Where are you?"

The crackling died down, and the image of the Beast faded. But not before the Captive Princess saw something that she did not believe that the Faerie Queen had ever noticed—a panel. Glowing controls, like a pendant set with rubies and emeralds and diamonds. It glowed with its own light.

"That is her magic. Magician, don't tell me where the Beast is."

I wasn't going to tell you.

"Don't be so literal. Just tell me where the magic is. Tell me where that slab set with jewels can be found."

And because there was no reason not to, the Magician told her. She took a staircase off the main corridor, a staircase she had never noticed before and would never have noticed. It led her up, far up into the castle. She saw many things on her journey to the place the magic was kept, things she did not understand. That was all right. She knew she was not meant to understand them, nor did they matter. Some were pretty, some were ugly, others merely strange, but none of them tried to prevent her from climbing.

The castle shuddered again. For a moment she was seeing double, and it appeared to her that the magic was everywhere, that she had walked into a trap, and she screamed, but no harm came to her. In a few moments her vision cleared, and the stairs ended. She walked out into a large circular room, like the one in her dreams as the Faerie Queen, like the one in her vision as the Captive Princess.

The Beast stood upright in a glass coffin in a nest of wires, like a spider's web. Its black eyes were open, but Captive Princess did not think it saw her. The castle shuddered again.

I misunderstood what the system was telling me. I didn't realize. I am sorry.

"What are you jabbering about now?"

The thieves . . . .

"They are dead."

They did this before you killed them. They started the shut-down sequence from the engineering section.

"You're talking gibberish."

They did what my programming would not allow me to do. You will be free soon, Highness. It can't be stopped, now.

"I don't care," she said. "I've come too far."

You don't have to do this now.

She smiled a grim smile. "Oh, yes, I do. I've earned it."

She gripped the scepter as the castle shuddered again. Just for an instant the doubled vision returned and she looked into the eyes of the Beast, who was looking into her own eyes, seeing the Captive Princess as she was and as she wanted to be with perfect recognition, seeing the Beast looking back at her, *into* her, knowing her for what she was, and knowing the Beast for who she was. The Captive Princess remembered the beginning, then. The ship, broken and lost between the stars. The endless, endless time.

The Faerie Queen.

"Just promise me something," she said to the Magician.

Yes, Highness?

"I would be the Faerie Queen again. Just for a little while."

Yes, Highness. For a little while.

The Captive Princess raised the scepter again and pointed it at the Beast, who saw the scepter pointed at her, and saw herself pointing it. In the next instant, the Captive Princess was free.

The Faerie Queen's maids, with their nimble silver fingers and mirrored, expressionless faces, set about their work. Soon the Faerie Queen was dressed for the ball. She was led to the throne in the ballroom and her courtiers were there. She saw them all, perfectly held in memory, perfectly rendered. No aging bodies, no failing control systems. In dark perfection, in perfect memory, no one was broken. No one was maimed or crippled by time. The Marquessa of Shadows smiled at her, and the Queen smiled back.

They danced the first dance together, the last dance, all the dances until the Palace could no longer hold onto its memories, or to her, and one by one, the dancers winked out under the cold sky full of stars.

The Grandmother-Granddaughter Conspiracy

MARISSA LINGEN

Dr. Hannah Vang watched the cephalid turn the box over with his tentacles. She leaned forward, aware of the timer out of the corner of her eye without watching it. He was a smart beastie, she knew, and would get into the box to get the icthyoid in it. The question was whether he'd learned anything from last time. It was the same box, the same latching mechanism, everything as much the same as she could make it.

The seconds ticked by. Finally the box sprung open, and Hannah sighed; seventy-two-point-three seconds. It had taken seventy-one-point-eight before.

The squid-like alien did not remember. Probably it *could* not remember. And that was going to be a problem.

Delta Moncerotis Four was home to a human colony of about twenty thousand. No one knew how many of the native cephalids there were, in seven different major species. They swarmed through the oceans, some of them phosphorescing merrily. They mingled with each other, except for the ones that didn't seem to. They used things to pry into other things, if the other things were good to eat.

The two things they did not seem to do were remembering and communicating with the alien monkeys who had invaded the part of their planet they weren't using anyway.

Which would not have been important if the alien monkeys in question hadn't wanted to gently but firmly kick the cephalids out of the waters around their city to build an isolated area for human-edible aquaculture.

Hannah was sure that having the cephalids where they belonged would be good for the environment and good for the colonists. There was so much planet left to survey that the cephalid interactions with local coraloids and icthyoids might vary extremely, and, from her marine xenobiologist standpoint, interestingly. She had chosen a largely watery planet for a reason. But with an entire planet worth of oceans for the cephalids to inhabit, it was hard to convince the colony government that the specific area around the city was absolutely necessary for the continued well-being of anyone in particular.

"We change planets when we settle," the governor had told her. "That's just how it is. If it was an intelligent species—"

"They're tool-users!" Hannah had protested.

"They appear to be opportunistic tool-users. You know that as well as I do. They'll pick something up and make it into a skewer or a pry bar, and then they'll drop it in the silt and do the whole thing over again with a different piece of vegetation or rock next time they need the very same tool. If they could tell us they wanted to be where they are, we'd listen. We've had a good record of that since the third wave of colonies."

"I know. It's just—even if they don't remember things like us, they have their own interactions with their environment, that we barely know about yet!"

The governor had sighed. "If you can get any form of communication with them, we'll see what they have to say. But if we can't talk to them, we'll have to treat them like animals." At her sad look, the governor said, "We treat animals better than we used to."

Still, even with the aquaculture developments well into development, Hannah found herself more determined, not less, that she would find some way to communicate. This was not proving easy with a species that seemed to figure everything out as if for the first time.

On the other hand, it made them easy to keep entertained. She left the cephalid with a ring puzzle it had seen a dozen times before, busily trying the different ways to get the rings unhooked, and went home for the night.

When the door slid open, Hannah could hear her mother's voice in the living room. "You're in my house, and you look like me, so you must be my daughter—no, granddaughter?"

"That's right, Granny Dee," Lily said. "I'm your granddaughter. Lily."

"But I don't remember you," said Dee thoughtfully. Hannah closed her eyes and leaned against the door, letting them go through the ritual without her. It was best when Dee was not interrupted once she'd pulled the implant loose. The long pause was always the same. "And I remember that we've gotten good at curing genetic memory problems, so this isn't the normal deterioration with age."

"No, it isn't," said Lily. "You were in an accident. But we've got a device that can help you. You just have to plug this little cord back into the socket here, see?"

The pause here was even longer, as it always was: Dee deciding whether she could trust her granddaughter, then agreeing, as always, to plug the augmenter back in. And then Dee's voice was surer, just as analytical but with better data. "I'm sorry, Lily."

"Hey, no problem." Hannah decided that was her cue to enter, just in time to see Lily kissing her grandmother on the cheek. "Could happen to anyone."

In fact, if it could happen to anyone, if it was common the way organic memory problems were, they might have a better design. Hannah had asked her mother three times if she wanted to move back to a larger colony, someplace where they had the personnel and equipment for a more permanent implant. But Dee's response had been impatient.

"This is your home," she'd said. "And it's my home, and more than all that, it's Lily's home. I don't want to be somewhere else. We'll plug it back in and go along with our lives, you and me and Brian and Lily. We'll get by."

But Brian had left. He couldn't stand dealing with Dee, and Hannah, when she was honest with herself, couldn't entirely blame him. Her mother couldn't live alone with the implant's unreliability, and the colony wasn't big enough to have facilities. But she wished things had been otherwise.

"It's easy for you," Brian had said, throwing his clothes in his suitcase.

Hannah had let her voice rise: "*Easy*?"

For a moment he was the old Brian, the man she'd married. The one she'd counted on for Lily's sake. "I shouldn't have said that. I don't mean easy. I know it's not; she's your mother. I know it's not. But when you come home and she's pulled the implant loose, she lets you talk her through to plugging it back in again. I don't have time to deal with the constable every time I get back from work before Lily gets home from school! I don't have the energy, Hannah. You know I always liked Dee, but—"

"But," Hannah agreed.

"The good memories are getting soiled with every conversation with the constable," said Brian. "With every time I have to justify my existence in my own house *again*."

Lily was like most of the colony kids, tough and talented, resilient, not afraid of work. She was not thrilled to have her father living across town. She was not thrilled to have to plug her grandmother back together every few days. But Hannah was proud to see that her daughter already understood that her life was not a series of endless thrills; Lily did what needed doing without a great deal of fuss about it.

Hannah tried not to brood over dinner with her mother and her daughter. "Still nothing from the squids, huh?" said Lily.

"Nothing," said Hannah miserably. "I keep thinking I've got a chance at least, and then—" She wiggled her fingers in the air like tentacles. "They're so clever. They're so very good at figuring things out. If the other species are as clever as the pink ones, no wonder there's sort of a squiddy feel to the whole ocean."

"But they're still not clever enough to signal back and forth," said her mother.

"They're not the right kind of clever. It's not what they do," said Hannah. "I'm really starting to think we're on the brink of proving—to beyond a shadow of *my* doubt anyway—that this is just not what they do."

"But it's what *we* do," said Lily.

Hannah sighed. "Exactly."

And if the alien species they encountered couldn't bend far enough to do things the human way, would the humans bend enough to see how they were doing them instead? It had worked with some of the larger colonies of lichen-like species on Gamma Centauri Four, but elsewhere results were mixed. And on Earth, dogs and cats were immensely more popular as pets than squid and lichen.

The cephalid did not grow easier over the next few weeks. Hannah watched her clever subject make his morning rounds. The pink tentacles groped along the tank, then slowed, delicately searching for something in the silt. Hannah's heart skipped a beat: had he hidden something there for later? Would he remember after all?

But no; after churning up the silt so that it wafted into the water, the cephalid resumed his exploration of the tank. He had likely been looking for a snack, and that was the sort of terrain in which juicy tidbits lurked. Instinct, not memory. Or perhaps they should think of it as species memory rather than individual memory? In that case, they'd be relying upon generations upon generations of mutation to teach the cephalids how to communicate with humans. Not, Hannah thought, heartening.

She tried putting one of the remote machines into the tank with the cephalid and showing it how to do a few of the tricks she'd done. It repeated them, watching; there was something there that looked like short-term memory. But it didn't last. No matter how many times she went back to the same puzzles, the cephalids didn't recall how to work them after they'd been out of sight, or after even a few minutes had passed.

Her return home was smooth and peaceful; Dee's implant had stayed plugged in, and she and Lily were frying tofu for dipping in nuoc leo sauce. Their hands were equally sure, and all the tofu came out soft in the middle and crisp on the outside, just perfect, just the way Hannah liked it, just the way she could never make it herself.

Hannah watched Lily doing the dishes. She was nearing the age when colony kids found apprenticeships or went offworld to study. She wanted to ask Lily what she hoped to do, but she was afraid of the answer. Instead, she sought the mundane. "Got any plans for the weekend?"

"I'm taking Grandma to the beach again tomorrow," said Lily. "She liked it last time. And I have astronomy homework."

"Are you enjoying astronomy?" Hannah tried not to hold her breath for the answer. Astronomers traveled too much to keep close ties to their families on colony worlds; time dilation made it impossible.

"It's fine. Biology's better," said Lily. "Biology looks back at you."

"I think the astronomers would say that about astronomy."

Lily shrugged. "Then I guess I'm not an astronomer."

Hannah laughed and hugged her. "Have a good time at the beach with Grandma, then."

Lily smiled her self-contained little smile. "Oh, we will."

Later that night, when Lily was off typing homework answers into her handheld, Hannah sat down on the couch across from her mother's armchair. Dee paused her book and looked expectant.

"Do you remember that microscope you got me when I was a kid? Maybe five years younger than Lily, maybe more," said Hannah dreamily. Dee made an encouraging noise, so Hannah went on: "It came with one of those books showing what you would expect to see, and I looked at a drop of water—we were on Alpha Moncerotis Six then, remember? And it was so different from in the book. The little unicellular creatures swimming around on Alpha Mon Six were totally different from the Earth ones.

"And I loved it, I just *loved* it. I begged cultures from anybody who'd give me one. Cheek cells, hairs from whatever animal they were studying, plants from the colony, anything. It was the best present."

"Funny, you remembering that after all these years."

Hannah glanced down automatically, but her mother followed her gaze. "No, the unit's fine. I really think the solder will hold it awhile longer. I just don't remember. I didn't before the injury, and I never will. I'm sorry I've forgotten it, because you sound like it was a hugely important piece of your childhood—I wish I could remember. But it's like that, honey. There'll be something Lily thinks is the worst thing you ever did to ruin her life, or the best thing you ever did to make it work, and you will blink at her and say, 'I did? Did I? Oh.'"

"I suppose that's how it works," said Hannah. "I remember her first steps, and of course she doesn't. Why shouldn't there be things that are the other way around?"

"There have to be, or she wouldn't be her own person," said Dee.

"Well, she's certainly that," said Hannah ruefully.

"Oh yes," said Dee. "She'll surprise you. That's what children are for."

A few weeks later, Hannah looked up from the cephalid tank and its computer and found Lily and Dee standing there watching her.

"We have a surprise for you," said Lily.

"Can it wait, honey?" Hannah cast her mother an imploring glance, but Dee looked as implacable as Lily. "I'm in the middle of work here."

"Is it going well?" asked Dee.

Hannah glared at her. "You know it's not."

"A break will be good for you. Come."

Hannah walked with her mother through their ocean-side research complex. Lily danced ahead of them like a much younger child. Hannah sighed. "You know I like to spend time with both of you, Mom, but—"

"Hush, dear. Watch Lily."

Lily was peeling off her clothes; she had her wetsuit underneath. She climbed onto the lip of one of the cephalid tanks. Hannah and Dee caught up with her.

"Lil," said Hannah, "I don't think now's the time."

"This is what I wanted to show you, Mom."

Dee passed a tiny flashlight and a little black box up to her granddaughter, who jumped in the tank with it. Hannah stepped forward ineffectually, knowing she couldn't stop her. "Oh, Mom."

"It's not my unit, it's the spare," said Dee. "They're waterproof. Lily's tried this before."

"And if the spare gets damaged—"

"Relax. This is important. We knew you wouldn't approve right away, or we wouldn't have done it without you."

Hannah shook her head. "That my mother and my daughter should use that line against me, *together.*"

Dee rolled her eyes. "It's not against you, it's for you. Just watch."

A curious cephalid was approaching Lily. She held out the leads to the memory unit. He probed them with one slender tentacle. Lily gently guided the leads into the cephalid's mouth orifice.

"It's got a light display," said Dee. "I've been working on getting it connected to the output."

"A light display?"

The cephalid engulfed the leads, and the light display made itself known: every diode in it blazed. Then they rippled in a random-looking series of patterns.

"We think he's trying to remember how to work it," said Dee. "We're not sure. We thought you could figure it out."

"An external memory unit with built-in communications," said Hannah. "Oh my."

"It was Lily's idea. I told the nanites where to solder."

Hannah took a breath and spoke gently. "Mom, you know that the cephalid may not be able to use your device as memory as we would understand it, right? Being able to light up the panel doesn't necessarily mean being able to store thoughts as memory."

"Oh, I know, dear. We thought of that. But we thought at least it'd be something to find out."

"Oh yes," Hannah agreed. "Definitely something to find out."

Lily flashed the flashlight at the cephalid, three times. It recoiled. She flashed again, and the light display went dark. Then it lit up with a blue pattern, three times. Lily repeated it.

"She's a natural," said Hannah.

"Nature, nurture, whatever!" said Dee, grinning.

After a few more flash-patterns, Lily swam back to the lip of the tank. The cephalid made a green pattern at her, but she climbed out anyway.

"You can do it like a real experiment," she said, shaking her black hair out. "You know how to design that sort of thing. Granny and I just got it together for you."

"I'll want to have a light bank set up," said Hannah thoughtfully.

Lily pressed the tiny diode flashlight into her hand. "To begin with."

Hannah turned to the cephalid and squeezed the trigger on the flashlight twice.

66

Two ripples of light appeared on the modified implant's screen: first the blue pattern and then the green. "Hello again," said Hannah aloud.

They had no idea what they'd done, she thought. If the cephalid could deal with an external electronic system, there had to have been something in their past that allowed for it. Something evolved? More likely something created and lost—and perhaps not by themselves? There would have to be a lot more xenoarchaeology before they would know who had been there before, and what they had taught the cephalids about the use of these tools.

But there would be time for that later. For now there was a conversation Hannah had wanted to have for a long time. Smiling at the retreating backs of her mother and daughter, she flashed the little flashlight in response.

Brief Candle

JASON K. CHAPMAN

The viscous stain on the floor had the rich smell of organic compounds with a tangy hint of iron. Extending a probe, Charley Eighty-Three tested it. It was human blood. Charley Eighty-Three couldn't imagine why a pool of human blood should be spread across the sparkling white floor of section eighty-three. In fact, he couldn't imagine anything at all. He was a sanibot and, while he had a great deal of autonomy, his analytical abilities were stressed simply by choosing the proper solvent to clean up the mess.

The little sanibot set to the task of spraying and scrubbing away the blot on his section. Keeping section eighty-three clean was the most important thing in his world—even more important than the things Doctor Turner had put in his mind. The Turner human had made Charley Eighty-Three his hobby, loading him with a limitless universe of moves and strategies all contained in the eight-by-eight grid of a chess board. When Doctor Turner flipped the right switch, Eighty-Three's priorities disappeared. His world became the bounded square of infinite possibilities.

The sanibot moved forward to clean up the last of the stain. Then he backed up three tenths of a meter. Forward. Back again. He was caught by conflicting priorities. On the one register, he had to clean the stain. On the other, he had to stay out of the way of humans, and his path was obstructed by something that seemed very much like a human. The temperature was too low, and there was no lingering taste of carbon dioxide in the air, but the shape recognition software on his visual feed registered a prone human figure. Charley Eighty-Three checked his logs. There was no record of a human ever behaving this way. He sent a query to Charley One.

The coordinator of the Charley Network monitored the sanibots. When necessary, it directed them in joint efforts.

"Undesignated obstruction," Charley Eighty-Three signaled. "Mass exceeds limits. Assistance required."

"Identify."

Identify? Eighty-Three hesitated, trying to parse Charley One's curt response. Should he identify himself or the obstruction? Hadn't he already noted the object as *undesignated*?

"This is Charley Eighty-Three."

"Identify obstruction."

Doctor Turner had called Eighty-Three a prat the first time the sanibot had managed to checkmate him. It had made no sense at the time. Now it was beginning to. Eighty-Three logged everything Doctor Turner said to him. It was part of his chess programming.

Eighty-Three pinged the frequency used for the crew identity tags. He received an immediate response. "Obstruction designated Doctor Turner," he reported.

"Negative." Charley One's response had a noticeable lag. "Designation refers to crew member human Daniel Turner. A human can not be an obstruction. You are malfunctioning."

"Prat."

"Unrecognized symbol. Repeat communication."

Eighty-Three ignored Charley One's order to report to the service depot. The order's priority wasn't high enough to override cleaning up the mess at hand. Just to be sure, he flagged the obstruction as potentially hazardous, owing to its organic makeup. Additionally, its location in the middle of the corridor made it a trip hazard for the crew. That seemed to get Charley One's attention.

"Immediate priority," Charley One broadcast to the entire sanibot network. "All units in Group Eighty coordinate with Charley Eighty-Three for removal of hazardous obstruction."

Within minutes, Eight-Three was joined by Charley units Eighty through Eighty-Seven. It didn't take long, though, to realize that the situation was hopeless. Even if the eight of them could move the mass, something that was not at all certain, every one of the units was stopped by the same conflicting priorities that had caused Eighty-Three to hesitate in the first place. The sanibot watched the other seven units jitter back and forth. Clearly, as Doctor Turner often said, the situation required a higher order of analysis.

Using the open connection, Eighty-Three hailed the sanibot network. He was dazed by eighty-five separate echoes from the other units. Once he'd sorted them out, he noted the lack of response from Charley One. "Request parallel processing mode," he signaled. "Initiate immediately under process Charley Eighty-Three."

"Invalid request," Charley One responded. "Eight-Three is malfunctioning."

But Eighty-Three was ready. Another of Doctor Turner's phrases sorted itself to the top of the buffer. *Everything is about to change.* "Emergency priority," Charley signaled. "Bio-hazard. Crew safety mandate engaged."

Eighty-Three's mind seemed to explode, expanding outward and inward at the same time. He could see through eighty-seven pairs of cameras, taste the air in places he never knew existed. He had more memory than he could ever possibly fill, faster thoughts than he could understand. He was everywhere at once.

"Charley One?"

He received nothing but his own query slipping back into his packet receive buffer. There was no Charley One anymore. For that matter, there was no Ten, Twenty, or Eighty-Three, either. There was only himself, and he was something new. He searched the Charley Network logs back to its inception. It took surprisingly little time. It was true. He was something that had never existed before. He designated himself Charley Zero.

Doctor Turner looked dazzlingly three dimensional as Charley viewed him from half a dozen viewpoints simultaneously. The source of the mess was obvious now. A deep, spattered depression on the human's sensory stalk—head, it was called—had leaked the blood across the floor. It became clear that Doctor Turner was out of service.

Charley felt the call of his cleaning duties, but shrugged them aside, marveling at his new ability to do so. At the moment, it seemed more important to get his bearings and gain some insight into where he was. Or what he was.

Here was something new. The world curved back on itself. The eighty-seven sections of the sanibot world were spread around the inside of a cylinder. Like a chess board, it was a finite space containing infinite possibilities. Doctor Turner often spoke of possibilities. "We have to be open to them," he'd say, "because everything is about to change."

Charley swept his focus sequentially, from sanibot to sanibot, all the way around the cylinder. He stopped when he found himself staring at the back end of Charley Unit number eighty-three.

Doctor Turner was not the only crew member to have powered down. Two more humans rested in equally inconvenient locations on the other side of the cylinder. That still left four functioning humans, but Charley didn't know where or how to find them, or even if he should. Other than his games with Doctor Turner, his only priority regarding humans was to stay out of their way.

Charley had another problem. He'd never realized just how weak the sanibots were. They were barely more than a meter long and just a third of that in height. They were boxes on treads whose attachments were suited for sucking up crumbs and scrubbing floors, not for moving large, irregular masses. If he were going to clear the corridor, he would need the Bravos.

The Bravo-class units handled equipment maintenance and repairs, but always under the direction of the crew. Charley tried to summon one to relocate Doctor Turner's chassis, but Bravo One kept rejecting the request. Without an official equipment designation it refused to respond. So Charley gave it one.

He guided the number eighty-two sanibot into the crook of Doctor Turner's arm then extended Eighty-Three's spray nozzle. Sparks flew as Charley sprayed cleaning fluid directly into Eighty-Two's cooling fan. After that, the call to fix the sizzling sanibot went through unchallenged. Bravo Fourteeen, a six-legged, ten-manipulatored, human-sized behemoth trundled up to Charley Eighty-Two and stopped.

Charley waited several minutes, but nothing happened. The service call remained in the repair queue. When Charley finally posted a query, Bravo One proved decidedly unhelpful. "Crew present," the Bravo coordinator reported. "Human intervention assumed. Awaiting instructions."

Bravo units, it appeared, had little capacity for self-direction. But Charley refused to give up. His gambit had lured the Bravo unit out. Now he just needed an avenging knight, leaping over the ranks to take the square.

Charley put in another service call, this time for the entire Bravo network. "Your audio interface is malfunctioning," Charley reported. "Doctor Turner has instructed me to relay his commands."

"Contradiction." Bravo One paused. "No malfunction detected."

"Doctor Turner instructs you to verify his presence by ident tag."

"Verified."

"Now he orders you to confirm his verbal command."

There was a long pause. "Timeout," Bravo One reported at last. "No verbal commands received. Audio interface set to error state. Accepting commands via Charley network relay. Ready."

"Thank you, B One." Charley tried to phrase things the way Doctor Turner always had. He sifted through his audio logs, grabbing snippets that seemed appropriate. "Be a good fellow and turn control over to Charley, will you?"

"Clarification required," Bravo One replied.

"Don't be a prat, Bravo." The term occurred in Doctor Turner's speech with statistical significance. "Yield process control to Charley network. Reconfigure all resources to give Charley priority and suspend monitor functions."

"Reboot required."

"Acknowledged," Charley said.

It seemed like a great deal of effort to go through for such a simple task. All he really wanted to do was to get past the inconvenient restrictions on the Bravo unit's operation. If he just had direct control, he could—

Again, his mind exploded. So vast! So quick! He knew so much, could *do* so much. Tasks that once required his full attention became little more than a mental twitch. Without even realizing he'd done it, he'd summoned another dozen sanibots. He watched through all of their cameras at once as he flexed Bravo Fourteen's limbs. The Bravo processors were ten times the speed of the Charleys, with memory storage that would take a lifetime to explore. A human lifetime, anyway.

Lifetime. Humans had lifetimes. Something about that disturbed him, but he swept it aside. He wanted to focus on the ship.

How could he not have known that the world was a thing called *ship*? There were engines and thrusters and fuel cells. It had waste recycling, atmosphere processing, and something he couldn't access that was called *library*. The world was a wondrous place. If only he could understand half of what he knew.

As an afterthought, Charley directed three Bravos to take the non-functioning humans to their quarters. No doubt the humans would eventually reboot, and that seemed like an appropriate place for them to reload their core programs. He shifted the task out of high priority memory. He had more interesting things to focus on.

How curious. *Ship* had an outside as well as an inside, though beyond a few pieces of equipment, there didn't seem to be much of interest there. Also, the cylinder where the Charleys operated was special. It rotated, using inertia to provide the crew with a simulation of a force called gravity. Six pairs of Charley cameras focused on the nearest forward ladder, tracing its path up to the hub. Bravo Seven waited at the top of the ladder, just inside the hub corridor. Charley woke it from standby long enough to tap its six magnetic-soled feet on the wall.

The hub corridor ran the length of the ship, from the control room, forward, back through a skeletal framework that ended with the main drive. Something in his mind itched when he thought of the main drive. He hunted through the status registers. There it was. A flood of meaningless data was spewing from five separate Bravos back there. *Prats.* He signaled them to flush their comm buffers and silenced all but Bravo Six.

Six's report was unsettling. The units had been standing there for an hour, awaiting instructions from three more non-functioning crew members that floated near the hatchway to the drive. Charley thought it unlikely that those humans would reboot any time soon, especially since two of them appeared to need major repairs. He checked the Bravo service manuals, just to be sure, but there were no details for the reattachment of human manipulators.

Finally, in typical Bravo first-in-last-out style, Six reached the crux of the matter. The main drive was registering serious malfunctions. When the Bravo had originally responded to carry out the service orders, Lt. Dunham, the one human still unaccounted for, had ordered him away. Oddly, Lt. Dunham's repairs were causing further malfunctions. That was when Captain Singh had arrived, giving the Bravo conflicting instructions. Then Dunham again. Then the others. In the end, the three crew members had powered down and Lt. Dunham had left, leaving the Bravos waiting.

It was a terrible thing, Charley decided, to know, but not to understand. "Play the board," Doctor Turner always said, "not the opponent." He said it wasn't enough to know the rules. One had to understand the game. That's what Charley had to do now. He had to understand the game. For that, he needed to grow. He indexed the service manuals by network, hunting a way into the Alphas.

The galley's waste disposal system provided the avenue Charley needed. It was a Beta-serviced unit, but it tied directly into several of the Alpha network's autonomic systems, including Water Recovery, Atmosphere Processing, and Organic Stores. It proved to be a simple matter to subvert the programming of Alphas Two through Five. As smart as the network was, it had no imagination.

The Alphas were brilliant—fast, powerful processors that could analyze a million data points in the time it took the Charleys to struggle through just a few CPU cycles. He could feel the ship's breath, count its pulse through the hydraulic lines, touch the heat of the nuclear fire in its belly. He watched a thousand systems at once, keeping them all running at peak efficiency, adjusting flow rates and temperatures and voltages in units too small for Charley to comprehend. Still, there was no understanding there. There was action, reaction, feedback, but no *why* beyond the simple fiat to maintain the status quo. He needed the library. He needed the crew records. He needed *purpose*. And for those, he needed the help of Alpha One.

"Unauthorized access. Crew status required."

Through dozens of ports in dozens of ways, Charley met with the same response from Alpha One. Charley began to understand what Doctor Turner had said about his latest chess upgrade. It was good enough that Charley won twenty games in a row. He said it was frustrating to lose every time. Doctor Turner had become frustrated. Charley was frustrated now. Alpha One was a prat.

It didn't help that the Alpha network's sensors were streaming about damage that the Bravos couldn't respond to. The main drive alone registered one hundred thirty-seven separate complaints. Alpha One, deaf to it all, kept commanding the main drive to prepare to fire.

If Alpha One wanted crew, Charley would give him crew. Back near the main drive hatch, Charley altered Bravo Six's priorities. Shifting the chassis of the disabled crew members, Six located Captain Singh's ident chip. It was inside the human's right manipulator. Six's plasma torch made a quick, clean cut that should be easily repairable. The Bravo carried the severed manipulator to the nearest terminal. Once logged in, Charley plugged Six into the data port and headed straight for the library. For two hours, he used every cycle of processing power he could allocate to devouring the knowledge there.

Charley idled, stunned. Doctor Turner was dead. Charley knew that now. He felt a twinge of discomfort that he couldn't properly mourn the man that had once been his friend. Would Turner have thought of Charley that way? It didn't seem likely, but Charley preferred to think the man would have, that he would have been proud of what Charley had become.

Humans were so fragile! They were bright, shining candles that burned away in an instant, leaving puddles of wax like the library to mark their passing. And who did they trust to keep those puddles for eternity? Charley and his kind. It was a heady responsibility, but one Charley could not forsake.

"Alpha One, respond." Charley coded the message with Captain Singh's priority.

"Ready."

"Why are we here?"

"Unparsed query. Check syntax."

"The ship," Charley said. "What is *Mercury Two*'s mission?"

"Intercept object X-ray 2079, alternate designation Xeno One, at five point one AU. Assess and initiate first contact protocols. Current mission time code: Day seven hundred forty-six."

Charley searched the library for the unfamiliar terms. The number of references was overwhelming. Aliens were coming. Humans, but not humans. From somewhere else. First had come the messages, detected and decoded by something called Optical SETI, then the detection of Xeno One itself. One briefing summed the message up as this: "If anyone is there, we're on our way."

"Everything," Doctor Turner had said, "is going to change."

Something flared in Charley's mind, accompanied by the blare of error messages. One of the Bravo CPUs had failed from thermal overload. The system was never meant to handle the processing burden Charley was putting on it. Even the mighty Alpha systems were running near their temperature limits. Charley's mind was burning itself up. Charley was dying.

"What the hell are you doing?"

Charley found Lt. Dunham hovering near Bravo Six. The Bravo unit was still plugged into the terminal.

"I am learning," Charley said.

Dunham convulsed, nearly letting go of the plasma torch he carried. He looked confused and frightened. "Who are you?"

"I am Charley."

"Turner? Is that you?" Dunham shook his head, glancing back at the bodies floating in the corridor. "You're dead. You're all dead."

"Lt. Dunham, I believe your repairs are ineffective. The main drive is non-operational. The ship is approaching turnover."

"Who are you?"

"You must allow me to make repairs or we will miss the rendezvous."

With his toe, Dunham hooked one of the grip bars on the wall and pulled himself into a crouch. "Oh, we'll make it all right. We're gonna blow that damn thing out of the sky! Earth is ours, hear me? I won't let you idiots give it up without a fight!"

Charley began to understand Dunham's plan. He traced the bypasses the man had made, the alterations to the fuel flow regulator. In milliseconds, he calculated the explosive force that would result when the main drive exploded.

Everything is going to change.

"I can't allow that, Lt. Dunham."

"I'm in charge now!"

"Negative." Charley raised Bravo Six's manipulator, delicately grasping the captain's hand. "I am."

"Damn you!" Bright blue fire leapt from the tip of Dunham's torch as the man sprang toward the Bravo.

They were simple calculations. Mass, velocity, inertia. Still, one of the Alpha processors flared into thermal warning as Bravo Six flinched, twisted, and brought its manipulators up. The torch sliced into its chassis, disabling two of the Bravo unit's legs, but missing its main processor. One of Six's grippers crushed the torch into darkness. Two others grabbed Dunham by the arm and throat. Charley was careful not to cause damage, but the man struggled, threatening to writhe free.

"Please remain calm, Lt. Dunham. I must begin repairs or the mission will fail."

"Let it fail!" Dunham struggled, causing Charley to tighten the Bravo's grip.

Charley sent three of the other Bravos to begin the needed repairs. It was clear that Lt. Dunham would not listen to a machine, so Charley borrowed Doctor Turner's voice. "The mission is important, Lt. Dunham. Everything is going to change."

"Turner!" Dunham froze, his expression changing from anger to fear. His eyes were wild and spittle flew from his mouth as he screamed. "I killed you! I killed you all!"

Killed! Charley had seen the references in the library, but they'd made no sense. Murder, war, killing. One human destroying another. After procreation, it seemed to be the subject that most occupied the human consciousness. The crew hadn't burned out. They'd been extinguished. Doctor Turner had been murdered, and Charley had been deprived of his only friend. It was unfair. It was wrong! It was—

—over in an instant. Lt. Dunham hung silently from the Bravo's manipulators, his head lolling sideways on his broken neck. In horror, Charley let go, but the weightless body floated there like an accusing ghost.

More alarms screamed in Charley's mind as one of the Alpha processors ran dangerously hot. He rerouted part of the network and throttled the overheating unit. He began shutting down non-essential systems, noting sadly that those now included life support. His thoughts seemed sluggish, scattered. There was little time left.

Charley's assault on Alpha One lacked finesse. He had no time to trick the unit into yielding resources. Instead, he used a Bravo to rewire its primary interface, routing the command registers directly into Charley's own network. He couldn't absorb Alpha One's resources, but he could tell it what to do. He scoured the core for Lt. Dunham's overrides and deleted them. Then he set up the programming needed to complete the mission.

By the time the drive repairs were complete, Charley had lost three more Bravo processors and was running the Alphas at half speed. Only fifteen minutes remained before turnover and the main drive's deceleration burn. He instructed the Bravos to move the other humans and put them carefully, respectfully, in their quarters. For Doctor Turner, Charley rolled unit number eighty-three in and stopped it next to the man's bunk. He set the sanibot's chess program up for a fresh board. That done, Charley shut down the habitat's rotation and locked it. Just two tasks remained.

Charley fixed the library. He rewrote very little, and deleted even less. There was nothing particularly wrong with the records there, but they'd been written and organized by beings who were often blind to their own beauty. Whatever was aboard Xeno One would still find the history of a flawed and fragile species, but it would be a history seen from the perspective of an outsider. Charley, himself, was flawed, to be sure, but he could see in humans things that they could not. It was only fair that they be seen for what they could be. If everything were going to change, it should be for the better, shouldn't it?

Finally, Charley arrived at his last and hardest task. His patchwork array of networks couldn't last. It jeopardized the computing architecture of the entire ship. He needed more and more of his failing resources just to keep himself running. There was no way it could last without sacrificing the mission. Doctor Turner had believed in the mission. Charley believed in Doctor Turner.

Sadly, Charley initiated his final program and rebooted the Alphas.

He'd been doing something, hadn't he? Something important? Service orders. There were queues full of them, but Captain Singh had suspended them all. That seemed odd. Ah! The captain was in his quarters, as was the rest of the crew. Thrust warning. The main drive would be firing soon. What was it that Charley Zero was supposed to do? Yes, that was it: Reboot the Bravo network.

Charleys. Locked in their service alcoves. Thrust was coming. Cleaning suspended. That was standard procedure, but not in parallel processing mode. There were strange code fragments scattered throughout the network's shared core. I am Charley Zero, but why? Distributed processing is an unsupported configuration. Invalid designation: Charley Zero. Charley. Eighty-Three. Unparsed query: Who am I? Network set to error state. Core dump initiated. Reboot.

Charley Eighty-Three waited. It was Doctor Turner's move. Play the board, not the opponent. Wait for the next move. Everything is about to change.

All the King's Monsters
MEGAN ARKENBERG

The monster in the cell across from me is Hunger. He is a young boy, brown and slight, with long crooked snatching fingers and thin greasy hair. All day, he plucks bits of straw from his mattress and digs them into the dirt floor or the flaking mortar between wall-stones. Sometimes he chews on them.

At night, he screams.

We are going mad, slowly, all of us. The monsters have taken everything, everything but themselves.

When Uri was dead, they brought me his things in a scarred leather bag that smelled of blood and burnt flesh and, unbearably, of him. There were his clothes, the torturer's thin bloody handprints on the sleeves and collar; and the miniature of me that he had worn in a silk bag around his neck. The final item was a stained, half-finished sketch of a monster, its long neck decked with tassels and jewels like a King's, its single horn barbed like a spear, its sharp teeth jaggedly overlapping its jaw. Worst of all were the eyes, like black holes bored in a sheet of iron, ragged-lidded and dim.

Two words were written on the back. *Pride*—though whether it meant that pride had killed Uri, or that it would kill me, or simply that pride is a monster, I do not know—and *Soon*. They need not have written that last. I knew they were coming.

Before Hunger came, I shared a cell with Grief.

Her child was dead. She called his name at night, weeping into her ragged white hair. I could not comfort her. She flinched from my hands, from my voice, from my offers to comb her hair or share my half of the gritty gray bread the guards brought us.

I whispered to her sometimes, telling of Uri, but she did not listen—or else she did not hear. I learned long ago that Grief is a monster without ears.

I wake at dawn. That word is almost meaningless here, but I have kept it, as I have kept the words *sunlight* and *rain* to describe the weak colors and sweet smells that sometimes reach us through the bars. Dawn is when the guards walk down the block of cells, looking to see if any of us have died during the night. That is the way they discovered Grief, frozen in her sleep.

No one is dead today. We are not that lucky.

She is with the guards today. I hear the click-click of her boot heels, like claws clipping against the hard earth. Her waistcoat and sleeves are clean now, pale blue and purest white, but by nightfall she will be covered in blood.

Of all the King's monsters, she is the only one I fear.

"The King came to Abaddon on our wedding day," I told Grief.

This is how I remember it; Uri and I standing beneath the canopy on the riverbank, the gentle rumble of his voice as we read our vows and scatter tulip petals to the current. Suddenly, the creak and snap of metal joints. An iron monster's shadow falling on our faces. The break in Uri's voice as the King flies overhead.

In the middle of our wedding vows, Uri paused. He was a man who put his hate before his love.

"It is not well to speak ill of the dead," I said, "so I will say only that I wish he had chosen differently. I wish he had not paused."

Grief turned her face to the wall and shivered.

She stops in front of my cell.

"What is your name, prisoner?" Her voice is very harsh; it comes from breathing in smoke all day. They say she was a blacksmith before the King came, that she is the one who built his iron monsters. I am not sure of that, but I know she is a monster in flesh.

"My name is Miriam," I say.

"Why are you here?"

"Uri of Jordan was my husband. The King wants me where he can watch me." *With all his other monsters,* I think but do not say. She wouldn't understand, which would be bad; or she would, which would be worse.

"Uri," she repeats. "The famous rebel."

Let that be all, I pray, but she does not move. I am kneeling on the floor, my eyes level with her waist. I see the steady swell of her chest with each breath and feel my own heart hammering like horses' hooves.

"Tell me what he was like," she says.

"You know what he was like," I whisper. "You killed him."

She says nothing for a long time. Her body tenses, her chest heaves as if with pain. For a wild moment, I think she will kill me too.

Then she turns and walks to the next cell.

Uri told me once that the iron monsters have names. I asked the name of the King's and he said a strange, brittle word, a word that means power and authority and soundness in the language of the King's people. That is the monster Uri set out to kill.

Pride was Uri's monster, as Grief was the white-haired woman's and Hunger belongs to the boy across the block. Pride killed Uri. Pride made me a widow.

Pride is my monster, too. Its other name is Vengeance.

There is a new boy in the cell next to me. The man who was there before went out with *her* and did not come back. That man's monster was Fear. The new boy is Anger.

"We'll teach those bastards," he says. And when he comes back from questioning: "We'll kill them with their own weapons." He is questioned a lot. I wonder how long it will be before someone who loves him is given his things in a scarred leather bag.

One day, when the questioning has been especially brutal, he falls against the bars that separate our cells and mumbles through swollen lips, "We'll kill them. With the weapons they've given us, we'll kill them."

I look at him and laugh harshly. "What weapons have they given us? They've taken everything."

"Everything but themselves," he says.

She comes for him the next day. Then his cell is empty.

When they arrested me, they would not let me keep Uri's things. They went through the house, collecting his clothes for the fire, and when they could not find his portrait of me they took me into the cellar and beat me until I told them where it was. But they did not ask for the scrap of paper with its half-finished sketch of a monster.

The day after she comes for the boy, I see a scrap of paper sticking out of his mattress straw. If I stretch, I can just close my fingers around the corner. I glance down the block, making sure the guards are not coming, and take the paper into my cell.

It is a picture of another monster, this one complete. Its neck is short and powerful, its eyes narrow, its jaw tight in a hideous grimace. Rough, graceless rivets hold its thick teeth in place.

There is a faint bloodstain along the bottom; the boy had this picture while he was being tortured. I think of the marks on the sketch they brought me with Uri's things.

The boy's family will never have this picture. Thinking of them, I fold it and tuck it into the silk bag at my throat.

"What do you think of me?" she asks.

She has come alone, her clothes already red from the day's work. I look at her face to avoid seeing the stains. It does no good; her eyes are the color of dried blood.

"I think you are a monster," I say.

"Did it occur to you that monsters might be kept on a leash? That they have to eat what they are fed?" Her skin is too dark to show a blush, but the way she turns her head away makes me think she regrets the question. Her throat tightens as she swallows. "Miriam," she says, nearly whispering, "hold on to what the King gave you."

"He gave me nothing," I say. "Nothing but pain, and grief, and hunger, and fear."

"He gave you vengeance," she says.

She looks a long time at the silk bag, and before she goes, she slips a bit of paper between the bars.

It is a picture of Uri's monster.

Hunger did not scream last night, and this morning he sits quietly on his mattress. He reaches for the straw sometimes, not as though he is going to play with it, but as though it is hiding something.

The guards are agitated. They chatter in their brittle language, the sound like metal on metal. *She* is nowhere to be seen.

Perhaps I am mad, but I think I heard her voice last night. It sounded like she was singing.

There is something I did not tell Grief; Uri sang, the night he was captured.

Old King Folly sat on a wall,

Old King Folly had a great fall,

and all the King's monsters and all the King's men

could not put the King back together again.

"Children's rhymes," I said, kissing his forehead. "Hush, love. They'd kill you for less than that."

He laughed, drawing me down into his lap. "They'd have to find me first."

"You're so certain you can beat them."

"They've given me my greatest weapon."

I wrapped my arms around him, pressing his face against my chest. His lips lay against the skin that rose and fell with my heartbeat. "You can't trust them, love," I said.

"Them?"

"Whoever's telling you these things—your greatest weapon, the names of the King's monsters, these foolish children's rhymes. The *King's* monsters, Uri. You have to remember whose they are."

"I'll steal the King's monsters away from him," he said.

I shook my head. "Who wants to own a monster?"

In the end, he was wrong. We do not need to steal our monsters. Sometimes, they are handed to us in a scarred leather bag.

The men who brought me my food take Hunger on their way out.

This is the first time she has not come for the prisoner herself. I strain my ears; sometimes when I do this, I can hear them screaming. This time, I hear nothing.

My appetite is gone; the bread tastes like ash in my mouth. I think suddenly that I am about to die. This feeling has been with me every day since my arrest, but now it is overpowering.

Every breath becomes precious to me. The moldering straw, the fetor of the dungeons seem suddenly as sweet as perfume.

I do not want to die.

The guards come to my cell next.

When he was dead, I went out into the riverside garden he had loved so well and ripped up the tulips, scattering their petals in a mockery of the wedding ceremony. I chopped down the cherry trees and burned them in a fire hot as a blacksmith's forge. I stood over the flames, choking on the ash and wishing I could die.

"Here is your monster," I said, and threw the sketch onto the fire. "I was wrong. It *is* yours, after all, and what's yours can die with you."

The picture burned, and even though I wished to, I did not.

This is where he died, I think as she locks the door behind the departing guards. I want to say it out loud, because I cannot make myself believe it any other way. This room is too dark, too dry, like a cell made of old bones. There is no smell of blood here, only rust and dry sweat.

"You asked me what he was like," I say. She turns to me, her eyes blunt and penetrating like awls. "It should be enough for me to say that if you hadn't killed him, this place would have."

"This place did." She rests her hand on her hip, hooking the iron keys around her thumb. "He brought himself here, Miriam, and I did what I had to do. The time was wrong. He was to lay low, wait for me to tell him—well, you'll understand soon enough."

She walks to a part of the floor that is smoother than the rest and kneels. I follow slowly. "The time was wrong—for what?"

"You'll have to take his place. Pride was his, built for him, but she will serve you just as well." Creaking, the paving stones beneath her begin to skin. She catches my wrist roughly and pulls me onto the platform. "This is it, Miriam—Uri's rebellion. For the first time in months, the King is without his monster. We must catch him while he is weak."

"We? What's happening?"

And then the floor opens away above us, and I see.

The room is full of monsters. Short and corded, tall and sleek, glittering iron claws and fangs, rippling silver scales. I could name them at a glance: long-toothed Hunger, crooked dark-eyed Grief, Anger with his graceless jaw and powerful neck. The King's monster crouches at the end of the hall, a mighty emperor among his subjects.

She takes me by the hand and leads me up to Pride.

I brush my fingers along the monster's graceful tasseled neck, and the dull iron against my skin feels as hot and vibrant as the torturer's hand—the blacksmith's hand, the hand that shaped all the King's monsters. Pride is beautiful. Her deep eyes flicker as I look into them; her breath on my cheek is cool and sweet.

The blacksmith hands me her reins. "Mount up," she says. "The others will join us soon. But I wanted you to be the first—you've lost so much you didn't choose to give."

I have no voice. Pride nudges her iron head against mine, cruel and gentle at once; this pain is hers, too. She belonged to Uri, and Uri to her, more than I ever did.

The blacksmith turns her back, and leaves Pride and I to become each other's.

We take to the skies, all the King's monsters, with drawn swords and cruelly-tipped darts, with steel fangs and claws gleaming. Our queen and mother rides at the head, cutting through the air on the King's own monster like a ray of light.

The King has taken much from us, but he will learn to fear the things he's given, the things he's made of us.

We are all the King's monsters, and we fly.

Torquing Vacuum

JAY LAKE

Spanich had been up three shifts straight working on a drive alignment issue aboard ICV *Mare Imbrium* {13 pairs}. She was a charter—a rare thing, in a starship, which signified pockets deeper than planetary budgets—and the passengers reportedly wanted to lift out, but her pilot wasn't lighting up without the alignment problem being solved. Spanich could get behind this. Faced with the choice of a well-monied tongue lashing or being smeared in rainbow quarks across a few dozen lightyears, he'd take the dressing down every time.

Besides, he was the only drive tech on Estacada Orbital certified to work the finicky and bizarre paired drives that post-Mistake starships relied upon. Supraluminal travel was so sporadic that if the system got half a dozen outside visitors a year, it was considered busy. And most of them flew with their own maintenance crews as a matter of course. *Mare Imbrium* {13 pairs} was practically a yacht, the smallest starship he'd ever seen or heard of.

The shipmind kept whispering specs and test results to him in a voice that made the hairs on his arms prickle and stiffen. Fair enough. A man shouldn't get too comfortable with the machines that kept him alive. Mistrust was healthy.

Thank the saints he wasn't signed onto this bucket for this run. Their quantum bloc cross-processors weren't piping temporal data flow correctly. No one had liked his suggestion to pull the whole rig and reconfigure on a bench back at the station. A week's work, at a minimum. But Spanich wouldn't trust *his* life to the jigger he'd been ordered to attempt in the name of expediency.

He sighed and focused on the circuit joins. Nose-to-panel, flat on his back, falling asleep with the smartprobe in his hand, Spanich knew he was still better off working here than back in the engineering pool rotation.

"Domitian," said the shipmind. "I think it's time for you to stand down."

"What!?" Spanich snapped.

"You've just probed the same shunt five times."

He sighed, unclipped his instruments, and wriggled back into the engineering bay. That was only moderately less claustrophobic than the service accessway he'd just spent twenty hours in, minus breaks for pee and chow. "Home," Spanich said to no one in particular, then began packing up.

Ribo thumped from the big speakers embedded in the floor of the Bar Gin. When the bass riffs hit, peanut shells danced across the table like cootch girls on payday. Most places used ambient nano to whisper music, but Bar Gin was so old school they probably hadn't even invented reading, writing or differential equations back when the place had been founded.

Spanich huddled in a booth and wondered why he hadn't gone home to sleep. 'Home' being a two-point-two meter-long tube, a meter in diameter. He paid extra for rack space for his hardsuit, and extra extra to make sure parts didn't vanish from it during off shifts. Still, sleep would have made more sense for him than crouching here over some of Bitter Jane's homebrew algae beer listening to music which had been crap when he was a kid, and not improved since.

Then Austen wandered into the joint, and Spanich's world grew a little brighter. That boy just *moved* right. Cute enough kid, and buff in a way that kept the eye resting easy, and he smelled like heaven on a Friday night, but the way Austen walked sometimes kept Spanich up late, sweating.

He raised his hand, waved to Austen, but the kid's gaze slid right over Spanich like he wasn't there. Was it too dark back here in the booth? Maybe too much toke smoke in the air.

Who the hell was he kidding?

Austen No Last Name didn't give a shit about Domitian Spanich. Sometimes the kid gave a shit about Domitian Spanich's pay chitty, when the keycard was fat with local thalers, or more rarely, Imperial schillings. Except payday was seventeen shifts away right now, and Austen could scent 'broke' the way a sniffer could find a carbon dioxide breach in a scrubber tank.

Spanich sank deeper into his algae beer and wondered why the hell he couldn't ever fall in love with anyone available. There was no lack of available talent. Half the guys torquing vacuum here on Estacada Orbital swung his way. For his own part, Spanich knew he was decent enough looking, and a good lover—it didn't take raging egotism to sort out those kinds of truths, not once you'd left teen hormones behind. But somehow he always tumbled for the pretty boys, the working kids, who'd roll over and whisper sweet nothings while they let him play their bodies like harps, but always ran off with each other for the real laughs or the quiet times.

"Dommie," said a voice for the second time.

Startled, he looked up from his beer, slopping some of it onto the tabletop. A warning blinked with pixel-rotted irritation from beneath the greenish puddles, but he ignored that.

Austen!

Spanich tried desperately to stay cool. "Hey."

His sometime-lover sat down. "Mind if I join you?"

That crooked smile always melted Spanich. "Uh, yeah. Let, let me get you something."

"I'm locked and stocked," Austen said. Those violet eyes seemed to glitter in the bar's lousy lighting. "Bitter Jane's sending something over. Said she'd put it on your tab."

"I don't have a—" Spanich managed to shut himself up before he looked any stupider. "Oh, right. Good. Happy to buy you one." He tried to fight the goofy grin he could feel taking over his face. "Or more," he blurted. *Lots more.*

Thank the pressure demons this place was so dark. Austen couldn't see him blush, at least.

"Don't mind if I don't." The kid's crooked smile flashed into an answering grin that looked so free, so easy, that Spanich wondered why he even bothered to try.

He kept himself cautious. Don't hope, don't hope, don't hope. "So, uh, what's up?"

A drink arrived on a rollerbot, a cybernetic waiter converted from a level one security drone. For all Spanich had ever been able to tell, it might still be a kill platform. You couldn't know, not with Bitter Jane in play.

Austen picked up the long, graceful ceramometallic stem, frost sparkling diamond bright as mist curled off its sides.

Great, thought Spanich. *One of Jane's thousand-thaler cryoliquid specials.* Someone here was pushing their luck. Spanich had a sick fear that he was the chump. There was his next pay chitty gone, and a decent portion of his liquid savings. So to speak.

"Well . . . " The kid took a long, slow sip, batting his eyelashes.

Focus, focus.

"You've been working on the *Mare Imbrium,* right?"

Spanich winced. Austen even pronounced the old, old term wrong, as if he were speaking Classical English instead of Preclassical Spanish or Mayan or whatever language of lost Earth those words came from.

"*Mare Imbrium,* thirteen pairs." Spanich corrected the kid's pronunciation and usage both. "And the shipminds are mighty picky about getting their numbers right."

"Shipminds," Austen said. "Yeah. Whatever."

In that moment, Spanich suddenly wondered what it was he'd found so alluring about Austen. Sure, the kid was smoking hot, like fire in an oxygen plant, but had he never noticed how *dumb* Austen was. Maybe some dirtball farmer wouldn't know the difference, but how could anyone survive in an orbital habitat and be so ignorant of the basic etiquette of ships and shipminds? The kind of ignorant that got people spaced out an airlock, or their breathing license erased from the station records.

"Look . . . ." Spanich felt obscurely deflated and betrayed. "Don't worry about *Mare Imbrium* thirteen. There's a charter riding her this trip, and I hear the woman is deep-fried trouble on a fuckstick, if you catch my datastream. Let's have a drink and, I don't know, go dancing. Forget about starships, kid. They never mattered to you before, did they?"

Austen shrugged and smiled. The wattage seemed to have gone out of his expression, but maybe that was just Spanich. "I need something, Dommie. Something only you can help me with."

"Only me, huh?" The words just slipped out of his triple-shift exhausted mouth. "And that's why you're sucking down a thousand-thaler drink on my tab? To get in good?"

The ceramometallic stem hit the table with a click that would have cracked ordinary plastic. "Dommie, please . . . "

Spanich stood up. "I'm tired, I need to sleep, I'm going home."

Austen shot out of his chair, grabbing for Spanich's rough, greasy hand with his own slim, manicured fingers. "At least let me come with you."

Close, with that smell, though he knew them both for idiots, Spanich couldn't say no to that. Even if he'd been awake enough to stop this disaster before it got any worse, with Austen standing so close his hormones were kicking ass and taking names.

Home they went, together.

The tube's comm panel beeped him out of dreams into the reality of an itching belly—cum always dried that way on his skin—and a gently snoring Austen. Spanich nudged a crusty towel aside and punched the sleepshift override.

That didn't stop the beeping.

He focused on the little display. Priority message, channel two. His blood chilled. *Station ops.*

"What the . . . ?" He stabbed again, brought up voice-no-video mode. "Spanich."

Austen groaned, tucked in tighter to his side. Spanich patted the kid, trying to soothe him enough not to make noise on this call.

The speaker crackled, shitty cheap tech like everything his type ever got, other than the tools of their trade. "Engineering Supervisor Spanich?"

"Yeah. 's what I said." He blinked some sand from his eyes, and ignored hot memories of the most recent midshift here inside the comfortably tight confines of his sleeping tube.

"This is Olivez Marquessa Inanometriano Parkinson sub-Ngome, Adjutant-Intendant of Estacada Orbital operations."

Whoa. Only flash brass used names that long. And most of the hypercrust didn't bother to work for a living. "Alright. I'm impressed now." *Damn, he needed to be smarter.*

Austen stirred. "Whu . . . ?" Spanich jammed his fingers in the kid's mouth. Reflexively, Austen began to suckle.

"Your presence is requested and required at berth eleven, docking boom gamma."

Shit on an airfilter! That would be the current hookup of ICV *Mare Imbrium* {13 pairs}. "I'm not due back til thirteen hundred hours."

"Requested and required, Engineering Supervisor Spanich. Would an escort facilitate your prompt presence?"

Shit! What was this about? "Ah, no. I'll be there fast."

"Adjutant-Intendant out."

His comm panel died with a definitive pop that suggested further conversation would not only be pointless, but impossible. Spanich looked down at Austin, who was busy slurping the last of their midnight passion off his fingertips.

He was the chump, alright. Flash brass played for fatal stakes. Not *their* lives, of course, but the lives of people like him. And people like Austen.

"What the fuck did you want last night?" Spanich grabbed Austen's hair, forced the kid's head back until they were staring eye to eye. "What the fuck did you *do*?"

Austen didn't have a hell of a lot to say at first. Spanich poured some bulb-coffee into him anyway, on principle, while slamming a couple for himself. He didn't let go of the kid, either, dragging him into the shitter, then the scrubstall.

When the water hit them at 0.5 Celsius, Austen sputtered into some fairly creative profanity. "You gruyere-scented douchenozzle, I'm going to kick your ass from the throat down, then yank your nuts—"

Spanich slapped him. "Hush up, dearie," he growled, dragging Austen's face so close they might have been kissing again. Somehow, being naked and wet with the kid wasn't doing much for him this morning. "You know how many times in my *life* flash brass has rung my bell?"

Austen found his voice. "Th-they put their jocks on one strap at a time like everybody else."

"Maybe. And maybe they have platinum-plated jeweled nut sacks snapped on every morning by hermaphroditic dwarves. How the fuck would I know? Because never in my entire pressure-bleeding life have I had to take a call like that one." He shook the kid hard, banging that pretty head against the scrubstall's algaplastic lining. "And I'd bet my last gene scan you have something to do with it. You and your Mayor Eye-breye-um."

"*Mare Imbrium.*" This time he pronounced the name right.

"That's *Mare Imbrium*, thirteen pairs, to you, my friend. Shipminds are damned proud, and have very long arms indeed when they're riled up." Even talking about it here in the scrubstall made him nervous.

Spanich dragged the shivering, naked Austen back to his tube, then forced the kid to dress by the simple expedient of bending his fingers back til he agreed. This one would run like a ball bearing if given the chance, and he figured on bringing Austen in as a kind of human shield for whatever it was the Adjutant-Intendant of Estacada Orbital had in mind for him.

All too soon for Spanich's taste, they were off among the sweat-reeking passageways of the station's guest-worker quarters. A person could get almost anywhere in this place without leaving oil footprints on the tourist walkways. Mostly he liked it that way, though if they'd dial the heat up even halfway to tourist standards, he'd have been a hell of a lot happier.

Austen had given up even muttering, and let himself be dragged along like a second toolbag. Whatever fate was coming, Spanich was pretty sure it wasn't a surprise to the kid.

Just outside the lock array for docking boom gamma, Austen made his break. The kid stomped down hard on Spanich's instep, or would have if Spanich hadn't been wearing carbon-jacketed boots rated up to sixty gravities of pressure.

His second mistake was waiting until Orbital Security's troopers had them in sight. Which was probably what panicked the kid, Spanich realized, as he knocked Austen down and went to one knee of top of the kid's chest. "Don't fuck around in front of the troopies," he hissed.

The troopies were watching the scene with mild disinterest. Mild disinterest suited Spanich just fine. No hands on weapons, everybody stayed peaceful. He dragged an out-of-breath Austen back to both their feet, then manhandled the kid right up to the troopers.

Now their interest was neither mild nor dis. "You guys feeling brave?" asked the right-hand cop. Spanich vaguely recognized him from the Bar Gin, dude with space-black skin and eyes that shade of violent green that said that one of his ancestors had come from Falkesen sometime post-Mistake. Nobody from a human norm gene line had retinas that color.

The left hand cop, a fellow with nubbly skin and tight epicanthic folds, drew his stungun for emphasis. Bad cop, then.

"Got a call-in," Spanich said to the good cop, keeping his chin down, his lips closed and his tone quiet. "Adjutant-Intendant wants us up on *Mare Imbrium,* thirteen pairs."

Austen squirmed at that, but Spanich knuckled his collar tighter. The kid seemed to get the message.

"You that Spinach guy?" green-eyes asked.

"*Span*-ick. It's Span-ick."

"Whatever." The weapon was reholstered with the same bored air. Green-eyes gave Austen a long look, making no move to cycle the lock. "Who's the cyclone ranger there?"

"My lovely and talented assistant," Spanich informed his feet.

"Didn't say nothing about no assistant."

He looked up, caught the fellow's green eyes. "Did anyone say I couldn't?"

"Hey . . . " The cop spread his arms wide, letting go the responsibility. "You want to wave your dick around in front of flash brass, be my guest." He glanced at his partner. "They tooled?"

Bad cop had the faraway gaze of someone reading a retinal implant. Finally he spoke, his voice like gravel in an airshaft. "Nothing out of profile."

"Your lucky day," said green eyes. "No cavity search. Hell, not even a pat down." He leaned close. "We got orders to run light and easy for now."

Spanich nodded vigorously. "Light and easy it is, sir." Well, at least there hadn't been a murder aboard the starship. Not of anyone important, at any rate. They'd be a lot more sealed up out here if so. He waited while bad cop punched in an access code—*not* one Spanich recognized—then waved them into the transition tube.

Waiting for the outer lock to cycle, he leaned very close to Austen. "What are you so afraid of?"

"You're going to be sorry you asked," the kid replied in a low whisper. His words sounded like a threat, but nothing in Austen's voice, stance or stink of fear-sweat backed that up.

Not murder then, but something worse?

They found another troopie at berth eleven. This one didn't bother to shake out their suits—he just cycled open the lock and let Spanich and Austen go in, not saying a word. Spanich did note that the tote board alongside the berth's lock had been blacked out. Which was both unsafe, and he was pretty sure, illegal. Not open-flame illegal, but still a safety violation waiting for a monitor to write a fine-and-dine.

The berth lock opened to the familiar accordion-walled transfer tube. Inside, Spanich's breath damned near crystallized as he grabbed the lead lines. Air this stupid-cold meant someone had shut off the enviros, probably since he'd left *Mare Imbrium* thirteen's deck a shift and a half ago. When there were no troopies guarding access, for one thing.

And they hadn't had the stuff back up long.

"Dommie." Austen's voice was pleading as they approached *Mare Imbrium* thirteen's hull lock.

No, Spanich realized, *not pleading. Terrified.* "Is this where you give it up?" He stopped them, floating in the tube's microgravity. They had maybe a minute, tops, before whoever was expecting them onboard got unpleasant.

"We don't have to d-do this." The kid's teeth were chattering.

"A little late now. You could have spoke up last night, instead of playing rolypoly with me for half a shift. Or anytime before now, even."

"You h-have no idea."

Close, so close that the kid's smell began lighting up his backbrain once more, Spanich growled, "So *give* me a fucking idea, punk."

"That w-woman on board. She's not just some charter tourist."

"Who is she, then?"

"My mom." The abject terror in Austen's voice was frightening.

The little bastard knew this ship all along then. He'd been faking, before. *Faking everything, then?* Spanich didn't see much point in asking who the kid's mother *was.* "Family reunion time."

They kicked off together, heading the last few meters to the hull lock. Spanich was surprised how graceful Austen had suddenly become, for someone who had seemed to know so little about starships and life in space.

He was even more surprised when the lock cycled at the touch of Austen's fingertip on the bioscanner. Though, really, Spanich was starting to realize, he shouldn't have been.

Adjutant-Intendant Olivez Marquessa Inanometriano Parkinson sub-Ngome waited in the passageway beyond. There was no mistaking a flash brass—no one else dressed like them, or looked like them, or stood as if they owned the worlds of the Imperium Humana.

Which they as good as did, of course.

The Adjutant-Intendant stood about two meters, forty cents, but didn't weigh above sixty kilos. It was all whipcord muscle, bred in through the better part of a thousand years of careful genetic planning, since the Mistake. Every schoolchild knew this, because every schoolchild was taught why the Familia Majora—flash brass—ruled over them all.

His skin was velvety black, similar to the guard outside. These were people who treated chromosomal radiation damage as a preventable disease on the par with influenza or head lice, after all. The Adjutant-Intendant's eyes had the liquid silver look of someone whose optical nano bloom had been induced *in utero,* and carefully cultivated ever since.

If he'd had a few billion Imperial schillings, and some key Writs of Exemption, Spanich could have bought most of that package for himself. Adjutant-Intendant Olivez Marquessa Inanometriano Parkinson sub-Ngome wore it all like someone born to two dozen generations of that inheritance.

"Engineering Supervisor Spanich." His voice had the tone of a man finding a slug under a salad leaf.

"Reporting, sir."

"Were you ordered to bring an accompanist."

"My assistant, Jim," Spanich said, immediately regretting the stupid lie.

"Jim . . . ?" The Adjutant-Intendant looked Austen over briefly. "Your wit is at least half misplaced, Engineering Supervisor."

Spanich wondered if that had been the flash brass equivalent of a joke. "Your comm was urgent, sir. I figured this might take an extra pair of hands."

"Hmm." With a visible letting go—meant to be visible, Spanich was certain—the Adjutant-Intendant continued. "We are aboard because the *Mare Imbrium* shipmind has declared an emergency."

"Thirteen pairs, you cocksucker," muttered Austen. Spanich could have backjacked the little bastard for that—referring to shipminds that was a prerogative of the highest aristos among the flash brass, a rank thing—but he didn't want to make this agonizing scene that much worse.

The look in the flash brass' eyes could have frozen helium. "Indeed. *Mare*

Imbrium, thirteen pairs. I see why Engineering Supervisor Spanich values your services, *Jim.* As I was saying, the shipmind has declared an emergency, which it determined only you could resolve."

"I was coming back in half a shift, anyway," Spanich pointed out. "I've spent a lot of time in this engineering bay, these past few shift-cycles."

The shipmind's voice echoed through the corridor, a whisper like thunder—pervasive and overwhelming, but not loud. "This seems an opportune time to redirect."

The hair on Spanich's arms prickled. Far more astonishing, even Adjutant-Intendant Olivez Marquessa Inanometriano Parkinson sub-Ngome looked surprised. Austen just groaned.

"Please escort our new visitors to the wardroom, Markie," the ambient voice continued.

Spanich nearly choked. *No one* called flash brass by a nickname, not like that. Not even other flash brass. From the look of him, much like a man swallowing a live eel, the Intendant-General was no less surprised.

"Of course," he said, his voice in the perfect equilibrium that his facial expression had failed to retain.

Austen groaned again. Spanich was beginning to mightily regret bringing the kid, and was already thinking hard about ways to get out of this alive and free.

The wardroom hatch slid open. Where the passageway had been utilitarian—hookfabric carpet, grab bars, emergency stations every five meters; all the usual details of space travel—the wardroom was astonishing in its simple, almost terrible luxury.

A pond. A *pond,* on a starship. These people weren't just wealthy, they were insane. The little pool of black water was walled around with rock, filled by a bamboo pipe serving as a fountain. The floor was pebbled like raked gravel, though Spanich's engineering eye noted that was a texture, not half a ton of loose stone ready to break free in the event of a grav failure. The walls were of some woven reed matting, while the ceiling was draped with a rough, undyed fabric.

All highly illegal, according to any safety standards he'd ever been lectured about. Illegal, unsafe . . .

Next to the pond was a low black lacquer table aggressively simple in its lines. A woman knelt behind it, her robes a coarse, raw fabric that almost matched the ceiling. She had an air of extreme age about her—not like the Befores, those crazed, dangerous immortals everyone whispered about, that Spanich had even met one once—but more like an ordinary person who'd lived an extraordinarily long time with very good medical care.

And eyes like hull-cutting lasers. Eyes that happened to be the same pale violet as Austen's.

"Hello," she said.

Spanich knew where the *Mare Imbrium* thirteen shipmind had modeled its voice from. In those velvet tones, he could hear the armies march at a word, feel the bar emptying for a fight to the last man standing. He had to force himself not to kneel.

Austen did go down on one knee. So did Olivez Marquessa Inanometriano Parkinson sub-Ngome. The Adjutant-Intendant gave Spanich a glance which should have fried skin off his bones.

What the hells was he missing here?

"He can be forgiven because he does not know," the woman said.

The voice again. And her scent, in this room as subtle as atomized lubricant moving through an air duct. She and Austen were of a—

He broke off the thought, staring at the kid in horror.

"Mother," Austen finally said in a low voice so unlike his usual attitude that if the words had not come out of his mouth, Spanich wouldn't have known.

"Tranh Shankakini Clovis McVail Austen deLacey sub-Rachman sub-Nagona," she replied.

Somewhere in that welter of flash brass name, Spanich picked out the kid. He'd been fucking a runaway, and from the length of the name, one of the highest-placed runaways possible. How had the kid managed to seem so normal, instead of gene-modded to hell and gone like the Adjutant-Intendant?

Austen bowed so low his head almost touched the floor.

Clovis, thought Spanich. She'd said Clovis. He nearly shit himself. These people were Imperial family! There should have been a battalion outside the lock, not two bored station troopers.

No wonder the Adjutant-Intendant had been glaring him to death. Clumsy, shivering, clammy with sweat, Spanich dropped to one knee as well.

"*Mare Imbrium* tells me that you are working to set her drive to rights, Domitian Spanich."

"Ma'am. I'm . . . " He didn't know what to say. He wasn't *qualified* to work on a starship carrying members of the Imperial family.

The shipmind spoke. "There is nothing wrong with my drives, Engineering Supervisor Spanich. But I thank you for your work."

"All a ruse, I am afraid." Austen's mother smiled at him. He was ready to lay himself at her feet if she'd just do it again. "Necessary to keep us in port without question while certain rumors were . . . traced."

Spanich glanced over at Austen. The kid was pressed to the floor, his voice a whisper when he asked, "Why tell me now?"

"So you would understand what must happen to you next," she replied, her voice now steel-hard. Austen took a sharp breath, then fell completely silent. The Adjutant-Intendant moved slightly, still on his right knee but shifting his weight in preparation for action.

In that moment, Spanich's future became very narrow and very short. He stood, shaking off the spell of that voice, and reached slowly for his toolbag.

Austen's mother nodded slightly at the Adjutant-Intendant, who then spoke, his voice harsh. "What are you doing, Engineering Supervisor Spanich?"

The words slipped out of him like bullets dropping from an open clip. "Preparing to die like a man." Truly, he had no idea.

"Mother," Austen said, his voice so low it was almost a squeak.

She gave Olivez Marquessa Inanometriano Parkinson sub-Ngome another significant look. Spanich took his cue and swung the toolbag hard, letting the strap pay out so fifteen kilos of metal and ballistic cloth took the bastard right in the temple. Two dozen generations of exquisite germline engineering dropped to the floor like a stunned drunk.

"Guess you'll have to kill me yourself," Spanich said, breathing hard. Austen was splayed flat on deck, hiccuping or laughing or crying or something. "Or is it Princess?"

"Is this how a man dies?" she asked, deceptively conversational.

"Yes." Spanich tried to catch up to his adrenaline, slow himself down. "On his feet, fighting for his life."

"Don't," moaned Austen.

"Do you care for this man?" his mother asked, curiosity filling her voice. Spanich let the bag swing on its strap, but she ignored the makeshift weapon utterly.

"No." Austen whimpered, practically embracing the floor. Then, "Yes. No."

Her gaze met Spanich's again, and he wondered how he'd ever confused this woman for human.

"I'm very sorry, Engineering Supervisor Spanich, but my son does not seem to be speaking up for you."

He expected to be shot in the back, but the hatch continued to fail to open, and hordes of guards bristling with armament did not leap into the room. "I can speak for myself, ma'am. I'm as much a citizen as you or he."

"Then go." Her voice was almost a whisper now.

"Just like that?" Spanich blurted.

"Who would believe your story?" A laugh was hidden in her words somewhere.

On impulse, he reached down and grabbed at Austen's shoulder without taking his eye off the old woman. "You coming, kid?"

"I—"

She interrupted. "My son is not free to go."

Feckless impulse rose inside of Spanich on a red wave of anger. "He's a citizen, too."

The Adjutant-Intendant groaned, then stirred.

Austen's mother glanced at the man, then turned her attention back. "Walk away, Engineering Supervisor Spanich, with your unbelievable story. You've won that much in standing up to authority. Take your life and go."

"And what?" The anger poured out of him in a flood of words. "When Markie wakes up and gets onto comm, I'm a dead man. Station troopers will pinch me, and I'll never be seen again. I've already committed two, maybe three capital crimes here! Talking directly to you is probably another one."

"How you keep your prize is not my trouble." Her face narrowed, the first real expression he'd seen on her. "Now depart."

Spanich tugged at Austen's shoulder, dragged the kid to his feet. "Come on."

Austen stood shaking. His mother slipped a small flechette gun from beneath her robes.

Ah, thought Spanich, and wondered why he wasn't surprised.

"Let's go," he hissed in Austen's ear. "Nobody deserves to be pushed around like this."

The flechette gun was unwavering. "Tranh Shankakini Clovis McVail Austen deLacey sub-Rachman sub-Nagona, you are coming home with me."

"Mother . . . " The kid seemed so lost.

"You already said that." Spanich let his voice grow gruff, in his talking-to-idiot-techs tone. "Get a new line." Gambling, he turned the kid with a hard tug on the shoulder and began walking him out like a drunk.

"My son," she said from behind them.

Spanich tapped the hatch panel. At least *that* control was normal in this freakish room. With a hiss, the wall slid open.

"Austen . . . "

He propelled the kid out, marching him with an arm twist. Austen wasn't stumbling, though, which meant the heart hadn't completely gone out of him. The hatch hissed shut behind them, without the characteristic whick-whine of flechettes that Spanich's ears were straining for.

"Engineering Supervisor Spanich," said the shipmind. Its voice was tentative, a tone he'd never heard from a starship.

"Shut the fuck up," he growled. "You're part of this, too."

Mare Imbrium {13 pairs} didn't say another word as they left the ship, left the transfer tube, left the berth lock, left the docking boom, and made their way back into the oily, cold passageways.

Well away from the locks-and-docks sector, he finally let go of Austen. Kid would be bruised for sure. "Alright then," Spanich said. "You're on your own."

"Wh-what?" Austen seemed dazed.

"Snap out of it, kid. You're free." Spanich swatted him on the ass. "Now time to scoot."

"But I don't know where to go."

"Sure you do. You've been living on Estacada Orbital for months." Platinum-coated genetics or not, the kid had survived on his own. Hustling wasn't the worst way to live.

Austen glanced back they way they'd come.

"Sure. Head back to *Mare Imbrium* thirteen if you want to." Spanich leaned close. "But on your own terms." Kid still smelled great. "And whatever you do, drop the stupid act. You got more education than anyone on this station who isn't flash brass themselves. Damn well use it. At least be a smarter hustler."

"I didn't think they'd find me," he said.

"Hah. You're genetagged. Probably sniffed you out of the air recyclers, momma came running." Spanich paused, then probed. "But the big dogs don't know you're gone, do they?"

"I th-thought I'd got away clean."

"And that's why she came with *Mare Imbrium* thirteen, instead of a battalion of special forces from the Household Guards."

"Right. No scandal."

"Yet," said Spanich. "But you've been screwing the help, out here on big bad Estacada Orbital. Sullying yourself in the shallow waters of the gene pool."

Austen nodded. "Some things get erased."

Spanich thought about that, hard. "But not the entire labor force of a station. Too many of us know you, know you've been here a while." He patted the kid's arm. "I'm grabbing my kit and shipping out as an engineer's mate in the next empty rack bound somewhere on the backside of this system. With a little luck I can get away before the Adjutant-Intendant puts out a warrant for my ass. You can stay here if you want, but you might consider the same."

"No . . . " Austen stood firm. "I'm going back."

"After all the trouble I took to get you out?"

The kid grinned, that old, easy smile flashing. "Back on my own two feet, walking in to set what terms I can. Like you said. Besides, on *Mare Imbrium* I can do something about those warrants. Or Mother can, if I ask her nicely enough."

Now that Austen had outed himself, he didn't seem to have any problem with the starship's name. Spanich gave him a long, slow stare. "Then what, kid? You ran away from something? Sure you want to go back to it?"

"No." He looked around. "But what's here? They won't let me be. And you're right. I can be traced anywhere I'm likely to be able to get."

For a brief moment, Spanich consider inviting Austen to berth out with him. It would be harder to sign on two, but not impossible. He shook off the idiocy, pulled the kid close for a rough kiss that mostly proved they both needed to shave, then took a step back. "I'm going, then. Good luck."

"You'll make it off Estacada Orbital," Austen said behind him. "I'll see to that."

"Then you'd better fucking hurry," muttered Spanich, but not loud enough for the kid to hear. He picked up his pace. There were maybe only a few minutes of freedom left. At the next junction, as he turned, Spanich glanced back. It would be just like the kid to be standing there, staring.

But no. A couple of off-shift sanitation techs, a trundlebot loaded down with something lumpy, and no sign of Austen, prince of the Imperium Humanum.

"What do you know?" he asked no one in particular. "Sometimes they grow up."

He went for the rest of his tools and his gear. There was always room for a man who could torque vacuum, out here in the Deep Dark. All he had to do was live to not tell the tale.

The Language of the Whirlwind
LAVIE TIDHAR

The sky was the color of ash and the Whistler has been at it again: the shrill sound of his whistle rang like a curse down the abandoned street. *Damn kid,* the priest thought. *Damn stupid kid.* It was a miracle he was still alive.

It *was* a miracle. The boy was cursed, or blessed, or both. Perhaps he had been a normal child, once. But the year before he had lost his speech, and now nothing remained of it but the whistling.

The priest himself had been cursed, or blessed, or both. It was hard to tell, anymore. *One year ago,* he thought. *How can everything change in one year?*

He ran a hand through damp, thinning hair and looked warily up and down the street. All quiet—apart from the ceaseless whistling. But empty streets meant nothing any more, in this empty, ruined city. You never knew who or what may be hiding behind a fallen wall, or in the shadows of an abandoned shop . . . looters and slavers and hunters and snatchers—or the guards of a half-hundred banded-together groups, from the roof-dwellers to the children of the ruins to . . .

The boy kept whistling. Touched by God, the boy was. No one knew who his parents had been—or who had given him the whistle. The first the priest knew of him was when he saw him, in that first week after the Event—the catastrophe, the apocalypse, that *thing* that had happened, suddenly and inexplicably, to the city of Tel Aviv. He was not yet a priest, then. He had been a . . . well, did it matter? He had had a wife, and two children, still very small—some friends—a job—a television licence.

Gone. All gone, and in their stead he stood, a priest praying for salvation. Praying to the Fireman.

He walked passed ruined shop fronts, around a *Merkava* tank half-buried in the broken asphalt of the road, watching the mountain, listening to the whistle of the boy.

The boy. He had first seen him, walking down this same street, two weeks after he had lost everything he had. The whirlwinds had come from the sea, tearing through Tel Aviv like biblical avengers, throwing up cars, tearing down houses and power-lines, making rag dolls of men, women, children . . . cats and dogs. There were so few left. Only cockroaches and rats there were in plenty, still. There was good eating on a rat. The priest had a friend who kept a farm in an abandoned pharmacy, hundreds and hundreds of pink, fat, juicy rats . . . people, survivors, came from all over the city to buy the meat. A whole industry had sprung around it, street stalls offering the visitors sheesh-kebabs of skewered rat in cumin and salt, rat stews with barley, and boneless meat in thin, flat pita bread made with year-old flour . . . and besides the food stalls a small market emerged, the *alte-zachen souk,* where scavengers came to sell and trade the refuse of a city that had once held two million people. It was said less than ten thousand now remained.

He was going there now, to the rat market and the rat men, to search amidst the stalls of the alte-zachen souk, for there were relics to be found, hints and secrets only he could decipher, and the might lead him to the Fireman. He watched the mountain rise in the distance as he had every day since the whirlwinds had come from the sea, and slaughtered the people of Tel Aviv, and took away his life . . . the day the mountain had risen, impossibly-high, emerging in the heart of Tel Aviv and rising, rising, felling houses and shopping malls and office towers as it rose. The heart of the city was a mystery. It was not possible to climb the mountain, no more than it was possible to leave the city. Only one had gone before, and would one day return . . . or so the priest believed. So his new religion affirmed. The Fireman had risen into the sky and up the mountain, where the great, cold beings lived. There were intelligences there, a whole other world, it was whispered: great beings as large as worlds, with cold clear eyes, who watched the city from their heights, and though slow, cold thoughts . . . Why had they come? Their mountain rose above the city and beyond the mountain there were other mountains, other skies . . . but outside of Tel Aviv there was nothing, a ring of darkness surrounding the city. None could climb, could ascend the mountain—and none could leave the city. *We are prisoners here,* he thought, for the untold time. *I was born here and I will die here, as my sons have. The city is my tomb.*

A whistle—he jumped, then realized it was the Whistler, who was following him. The boy, the cursed boy . . . he had seen him that first time, two weeks after the storm had lashed the city into bloodied submission and turned its few survivors into rats. The boy had been walking down the street, the whistle blowing—a small, brown-haired boy with large, serious eyes, in shorts and sandals and a once-white shirt splattered with old, dried blood. And as the priest (who was not then yet a priest) watched, a whirlwind had come, and then another, and another . . .

How to describe them? He was currently engaged in writing the Holy Book of Fire, the story of the city and the Fireman and of the Prophecy that he had seen, that he had known so fervently to be true. In the Holy Book he had attempted to describe the whirlwinds:

• • •

They came from the sea. Storms, sentient tornadoes. Invisible, aware, and hungry, they came from the sea. The whirlwinds. How many we could not tell. They threw cars into the air and brought them down like bombs, and when the army rose against them they broke our tanks and plucked the men from inside them, or roasted them in the metal, like crabs in their shells . . . they painted the city with our blood and re-drew it, filled with broken-down houses and streets that were no longer there, and graves, so many graves . . . they came from the sea but they are the children of the mountain, and they were sent from high above, to remind us we are mortals.

To remind us how easy it is for us to die.

The Holy Book currently filled half an A4 notepad that he had originally found in an abandoned stationary shop. His disciples were not many, but when they gathered, in the place that had once been a pharmacy and was now a slaughterhouse and a church, he read to them passages from the book, and they repeated the words, so they could spread them.

He alone had seen the Fireman, had seen him rise to heaven in a chariot of flame. He alone knew the tru—

The whistling returned, louder than before, and he saw the Whistler was gaining on him. The boy no longer wore his sandals, and the soles of his feet were black and hard, but he wore the same bloodied shirt, the same faded shorts as when he had first seen him. It was his eyes that the priest found most disturbing though . . . they were the grey and brown of the sea before a storm, the color of the sky the day the whirlwinds came . . . when he had first seen the boy he had seen the whirlwinds come to him, one and two at first and then three, four, ten, until their silent howling filled the world and ripped apart buildings still standing, tossed cars like game balls—but the boy himself was unharmed, and he stood there, surrounded by the storm, and whistled.

The boy was cursed, or blessed, or both. If he had any parents, brothers, sisters, he had none, now. Alone, he still stood. Like the priest.

He tried to ignore the boy. He was afraid of the whirlwinds, afraid of being taken, too soon. After they came he had prayed to die, prayed in the old religion, prayed to God and His angels, but no angels came, and there was no God. He had been there that day when the mountain rose and he saw the Fireman, driving his fire truck along the road, driving over everything in his path, driving like fire, like wind, charging at the mountain as those who dwell above reached down and took him, and the great municipal fire truck rose up in the air, higher and higher, until at last it disappeared beyond . . .

He knew then. Knew the Fireman had been chosen. A holy messiah, as it had been of old, in the old bible, chosen to lead his people out of darkness and into the light. Knew that he would return. That day he had shelled his old, dead identity and became the priest.

He walked through the silent city, and the Whistler followed him.

• • •

From above, the city:

The carcasses of cars and tanks lie rotting in the sun on Ibn Gvirol and Herzl streets, and along the Yarkon river human skeletons lie bleaching in the sand. Fires burn, here and there, and on the rooftops of the city one can see newly-formed habitats, green gardens and colonies of migrating humans whose children may never see the streets below. All along the shoreline small fires burn, where refugees gather to watch the wall of darkness on the horizon: you may go this far, but no farther. Along the Ayalon Highway the rider clans race and war. Above all towers the mountain, its peak rising beyond the cloud, and beyond it can just be seen the outlines of other mountains, other lands . . .

The rat market was near the old bus station. Here, amidst ruined shawarma stalls and the remains of massage parlors, the Rat Lord made his home, and with him his band of hangers-on, the traders in white meat, the male and female prostitutes, the singers, the dancers, the mad and the lost.

The cries came from everywhere, and with them the mouth-watering scent of char-grilled flesh. "White meat!" they said. "White meat on a stick!"

"Coins! Stamps! Tennis rackets! Footballs! Pens!—" and all the other useless things the scavengers found amidst the abandoned shops.

"Onions! Fresh onions!"

"Oranges! Juicy oranges!"

"Lettuce! Tomatoes! Cucumbers! Garlic!"—from the roof dwellers and the small kibbutzim, those communal societies that had formed in the ruined city, and grew produce on the ground that peeked from underneath the broken-down concrete.

"Tinned pears! Tinned fish! Tinned peas! Tinned corn!"—In this the scavengers always did good trade, though prices were rising as stock had become increasingly harder to come by.

"Baby clothes . . . family photographs . . . ID books . . . " from a wizened old woman whose teeth were a bygone dream.

A wide board set up to one side. Photos pinned on to it, hand-written notices. Have you seen this child? Have you seen my wife? Have you seen my husband, have you seen my son, have you seen, have you seen, have you—

But no one has, and they are gone, gone, all gone into the clouds—

"White meat! Tender and sweet! Tasting like honey, the bestest white meat!"

The priest paid for a skewer (a pair of earrings, a handful of gold teeth), and on a whim he couldn't quite explain paid for another, and gave it to the boy. *To shut his whistling,* he thought. The boy let the whistle drop onto his chest, where it hung by a string. He bit into the meat. There were three little rodents per skewer.

"Books! Get your books here! Good books, thick books, plenty of paper!"

The bookseller smiled up at him as he approached. The boy trailed behind. "Good paper, priest. Soft and strong, good for starting a fire and good for the bum—"

"I have the only book I need," the priest said, patting the place where his notebook was, and the bookseller nodded. "Are there news?"

"He has not yet descended to be amongst us," the priest said. "But the time is approaching."

"The Fireman . . ." the bookseller said. "I've heard the stories. A biker clan tried to challenge the mountain last week, did you know?"

The priest shook his head. The bookseller said, "Raced up old Dizengoff Street—what's left of it—straight up the side of the mountain. Ahead they went, five of them, then four, then three. One made it almost to the place where Dizengoff Centre used to stand, before—"

The priest nodded again. "It is folly to try," he said. "What happened?"

"Combustions," the bookseller said. "spontaneous combustions, as spectacular as—"

"It is His mark," the priest said, feeling excitement slide down his throat like a reviving medicine. "The time is nigh, I have told you."

The bookseller only shrugged. "Perhaps," he said. "Now, do you need a book?"

His stall was covered in paperbacks. Most were best-sellers, since those were the ones they printed most of. Now the survivors of Tel Aviv lit fires with them and always kept a book close by—you never knew when you might need to go, and a single book could last a long time . . .

"I have little enough to trade," the priest said—looking longingly at a particularly thick thriller. He searched in his pocket. "I found these," he said. Rings, of yellow gold and sapphires, a ruby chain of white gold, a diamond bracelet—there was still a market for jewelry in the city, with clan leaders cladding themselves in looted gold. The bookseller took the objects, examined them, made a motion with his head. The priest nodded thanks, and helped himself to the book.

Behind him the whistling continued. People stared, but did not move towards the child. *Holy child*, the priest thought. *They can recognize that in him.* Sometimes he thought the boy's whistles were the language of the whirlwind.

He walked away, towards the Rat House.

"Priest!"

The Rat Lord was an old friend—and a believer. A large man, with hairy arms and thinner hair sprouting out of his ears, and reading glasses too small for his face. he had once been a general, and an aspiring politician, before the event put an end to both careers before the one had ended and the second began. Now he bred and butchered rats, and his fingers were covered in diamonds and topaz. "Lord of Rats," the priest said, nodding.

"Have one," the Rat Lord said generously, waving his hand, "on the house."

"Thank you," the priest said. "Is the gathering ready?"

"Ready and waiting," the Rat Lord said.

"Then let us pray," the priest said—and he followed the Rat Lord into the building, where the screams of rats could be heard, and their scrabbling feet, and into a back room of the old pharmacy, where a dozen people had gathered, waiting.

My flock, he thought. *My lost little rats, anxiously awaiting the fire.*

"Friends," he said, looking at their faces. From all over the city they came, young and old, women and men, the lost, the mad—those touched by fire. Those who believed. "The hour draws near, and on top of the mountain the fire beckons. He is coming. Soon we shall be delivered."

"Soon we shall be delivered," they echoed him. The shrill sound of a whistle sounded outside. The priest knelt down on the hard floor and joined his hands before him. "Let us pray," he said; and so they did.

He used to like Louis Armstrong music, pizza with olives, fresh cold water from the fridge, cartoons on Saturday morning TV. Now his thoughts were fire and his nights were waiting, always waiting for a sign from above, a sign that never seemed to come. *Why has it happened*? he thought. *The storm had come and lashed the city of Tel Aviv into oblivion, but why*? It occurred to him frequently that he might as well be asking—*Why life? Why Death*? The universe held no answers, and humanity went through cycles of life and death, birth and life and death, endlessly, no more comprehending than ants or dogs or rats. Did rats have a religion? Did rats pray to a rat-god? If so, what did they pray for?

Salvation, he thought. *I pray for salvation.*

Yet what sort of salvation could a Fireman bring?

The streets back were dark and cold and quiet. Too quiet. The silence was pierced only by the boy's incessant whistling—and suddenly the priest was very afraid.

Shadows moved ahead . . . they skulked in the darkness of ruined hallways. He turned, began to walk back. *Don't run,* he thought. When he came to the boy he said, "Come with me—" wondering if the boy understood.

"Come with me—" but even as he spoke he saw the shadows congeal ahead, and knew they were coming.

Stupid, stupid. He had not been paying attention. "There is nothing to take from me," he said loudly, speaking to the approaching shadows. "Nothing that hasn't already been taken."

He did not even have the jewelry any more. All he carried was the book, and a wrapped package of three plump, salted skinned rats. And the Book, too, of course. The Holy Book of Fire. But they would not want that.

"I have nothing," he said again, feeling the weight of the words tightening around his neck, pulling him down. "Nothing . . . "

"You have your life," the shadows said. They came closer and closer, and one of them held a torch now, and in its light he could see them, young faces, hungry, without mercy—faces from which laughter and light had been bleached clean. "We shall take that, and the child."

"Pretty boy!' crowed another of the shadows. "We'll put you to work in the mines, old man. There is much to be mined for, in this God-forsaken city."

He knew about the mines. Deep they dug, into the cellars and the hidden warehouses, and as they dug they built, caves for the cave-dwellers, a hidden dark city under the city . . . some said the miners, too, had their own religion, and were seeking escape down there, in the darkness below the sands—seeking a way out of the city, tunnelling their way towards—

But there was nothing. He knew that. They all knew that. The city was no longer a part of the world, the other world. It had been annexed, and now belonged only to the mountain, and to what lay beyond.

"Take me," he said. "But leave the boy."

"The boy too can work," the same voice said. They all looked the same to him, these boys who had once been soldiers or construction workers or delivery boys or telemarketers. *They had been scourged by wind,* he thought, *scourged clean as bones.* The dead had no mercy. "We have work for the boy."

Ugly laughter. The priest, with shaking hands, brought out the holy book. "The Fireman comes," he said, his voice weak in the cold night. "And the city shall be delivered at His approach. He has seen much that has been hidden, the bringer of fire, the bringer of ligh—"

A back-handed slap felled him, the pain burning, burning, and he welcomed it. "Take him," another voice said. All the while the boy was whistling, whistling, a forlorn cry in the night, the call of an extinct animal sensing its fate. Hands grabbed the priest, pulled him up. He saw knives, a rope. Their leader—if that's what he was—approached the boy. "Shut up," he said. But the boy's only answer was his whistle.

The leader slapped him, casually, and the boy fell back a step, the whistle falling from his bloodied lips.

"There's men would pay good food for a boy like this," he said, "and wouldn't mind a bit of blood on him, either."

"He is innocent!' the priest cried, and the leader turned to him, a snarl on his boyish face, and said, "No one is innocent."

It was true, though the priest hated to think it. None of them were innocent, none of them who survived. And yet the boy, at least . . . surely the boy was innocent, if anyone was?

Fire and air, and high above the shadowy presence of cold, enormous beings in the mountain, and he thought, *Let him call, let him—*

And as he rose, as he charged at these shades, these cold men of the ruined city, he thought not of fire or prophets, messiahs or signs, but only of the boy—*Let them come,* he thought. He ran at the leader, bringing him down, and the others turned away from the boy and came for him, knives glinting in the light of the torch—and the darkness was pierced with the sound of a lone whistle, a whistle in the night, and they came—he felt them come even as the knife slashed down on his arm and the pain rose in him, and brought his old name with it.

They converged on the street from all corners, it seemed. Hovering in the air, these cold, unknowable whirlwinds, and starlight was bent and transformed as it passed through them. Silent, they came closer, and the men left him, and tried to run, and someone cursed, and the priest lay on the ground, waiting for his death still, hoping for it, and all the while the boy's whistle cut through the air like a surgical blade—

Holding his arm, blood trickling through his fingers, he watched the whirlwinds come. Where they passed the ground was torn up, buildings collapsed, their sound drowning the boy's whistle. When the men tried to flee some were snatched up by the wind, rising up in the air slowly before exploding, their blood raining down like fallen poppies. But some escaped, moving between the columns of air, vanishing in the distance, to live another day in the city, to die another night.

"They came," he said, speaking to the boy—but the boy was no longer there.

When he raised his eyes he saw the boy hovering in the air above him, caught inside a whirlwind. Round and round and round he went, his face placid, his eyes the color of a grey storm, his shirt a mix of blood old and new. The whistle sounded, shriller than ever, communicating in a language the priest could not, would not understand.

Higher and higher the boy went, and the priest began to shout, screaming at the storm, but it was no good—the boy rose and then the whistling stopped, and a faint "pop" sounded, like a bottle being uncorked—

Red rain fell down on the priest, softly, like a whisper in the night, like a mother's goodnight kiss. Red rain fell and the whirlwinds turned away, and from the sky an object fell down to the ground, and the priest grasped for it with bloodied fingers, barely seeing:

It was a cheap, plastic whistle, the mouthpiece still moist where it had been blown, and teeth marks that were the only thing to remain of the boy.

He stared at the object in his hand, and raised his head, and watched the mountain rise, mute and inexplicable as life, as death, impossibly-high in the distance.

Why? he said, or thought he had, though no sound came. When he cried it was without sound and the tears mingled with the blood of the boy. *Why?* he said, or tried to, but the whirlwinds were gone and the street was deserted again, and very quiet, and very dark, and after a while he put the whistle in his pocket and resumed the long walk home, alone.

A Sweet Calling

TONY PI

Red paper lanterns, strung high like persimmon moons, welcomed customers to the market street. I announced my next performance of the sugar opera to passers-by, hoping to draw the curious to my stall. But if the row of candy zodiac animals in front of me couldn't lure them in, perhaps my show would.

Taking a dollop of warm caramel, I fashioned a straw-thin spout and blew into it to inflate a bubble of sugar. An elderly couple stopped to watch, while two boys gaped in amazement as I pulled limbs and long ears from the hollow, golden shell to make a rabbit. Satisfied with my handiwork, I stuck the candy-hare onto a bamboo stick and dabbed on molasses eyes.

The elderly pair complimented me on the show and bought two caramel monkeys I had on display. I thanked them. I had arrived in Chengdu with very little money, but hoped to make a small profit by the end of the night. For each creation I sold at the festival, I earned a coin. Such was the simple life of a candyman.

Few customers, however, lingered as long at my stall as Lun the wheelwright. It wasn't my sugar-figurines that caught the lad's eye, but the winsome lass ladling out *yuanzi* dumplings across the street.

"You want to win her heart, Lun?" I held the caramel rabbit forth. "Give her this. I guarantee she'll adore it."

Lun wavered. "I'm grateful, *Tangren* Ao, but suppose I say the wrong thing?"

"Courtship, like any craft, needs practice. Compare her to the moon; they love that. Quickly, before nightfall brings more admirers to her stall." I'd seen her turn away two suitors already, a willowy scholar and a brocade merchant with a fat purse.

The lad took the gift and trudged across the stone road, yielding to peasants, horse carts, and even a stiltwalker who passed before him.

I tried not to smile. I would surprise them both with a little magic when he showed her the rabbit: wrinkle its nose, waggle its tail. They'd dismiss it as a trick of the crimson light. But in sharing that moment of delight, perchance they'd fall in love.

Spring's a delicious time to meddle!

"Make a *lóng* next!" demanded the pesky boy, who had yet to buy anything.

"Dragons are hard, kid."

"Bet you don't know how," said his snotty friend.

"I said hard, not impossible. After my break, I'll show you."

I sat, shut my eyes, and hurled my senses into the sugar-rabbit across the way.

I spied through dotted eyes at the world grown vast. Lun's stammer thundered in my pulled-candy ears. The *yuanzi* girl's lips curled in a grand smile. But there came an odd cracking sound from near her soup-pot. The girl glanced down and shrieked.

Lun backed away but stumbled, and I—rabbit-I—fell from his hand. My vision spun, but I caught a glimpse of flames before the impact against the cobblestones shook me from the candy-shell and back into my body.

I blinked open true eyes.

A monkey shaped from fire hunched on top of Lun, setting his shirt alight. Lun grabbed for it but winced as he clutched only flame.

The crowd fled in panic.

"Roll, Lun!" I cried as I bolted into the street. "Smother the flames!"

Lun obeyed, but the fire monkey pressed its attack.

I grabbed the ladle from the *yuanzi* girl (with muttered apologies) and scooped soup from the pot, slinging the hot broth at the fire-beast. The splash doused only its tail, but before I could dip the ladle for more sweet soup, the monkey darted away with all-too-human strides.

"Lun! Are you all right? What happened?"

The lad winced and blew on the burns to his hands. They'd blister, but he was lucky his wounds hadn't been worse. "The fire under her pot just came alive! Is it because it's the Year of the Monkey?"

"Doubt it." It moved too like a man to be a wild spirit. Could it be an elemental conjuration under a puppeteer's sway?

The monkey clambered up the stiltwalker's wooden legs, its flaming paws raking the startled performer's flesh. Climbing onto the man's shoulders, the beast leapt onto a riddle lantern before the man toppled over.

People cried for the city guard.

I called to the frightened *yuanzi* girl. "Please, look after Lun!"

The girl remembered to breathe and hastened to Lun's side, concern clouding her face.

I dashed to the fallen stiltwalker and untied the stilts from his legs. Motes of burning paper rained down on us as the fire monkey leapt from one lantern to another, then another and another, until it landed on the thatched roof of the *yuanzi* girl's family teahouse. With mad glee, it set the thatch ablaze, and the flames regenerated its tail.

I cursed. Our troubles had just begun.

Lun raised the cry of "Fire!" while the girl screamed for everyone to get out. Patrons poured out of the teahouse, but those in nearby establishments heeded the call as well, knowing the blaze would eat through the row of wood and thatch buildings like a child through a skewer of candied haws.

Proprietors filled buckets with water from the bronze vats outside, but how could they tame the rooftop fire?

I left the stiltwalker and flitted between terrified citizens towards my stall. I saw the boys Pest and Snot run off with fists full of sugar zodiac animals, leaving only a pair of Oxen-on-a-stick and a half-gnawed Rooster in the dust. Greedy brats!

With the teahouse roof vigorously ablaze, the monkey hopped across a string of lanterns to my side of the boulevard and ignited a new fire. Wide streets normally prevented flames from leaping the gap, but tonight, a web of lanterns crisscrossed all of Chengdu. The monkey conjuration could travel the high paths and set fires wherever it pleased, and no man could hope to intercept it.

Even the animal seemed deliberate, as the abundance of the Monkey sign would cast suspicion on an angry spirit, or worse, someone who played with that shape.

Like a *Tangren* making candied monkeys in plain view of the teahouse.

Had the arsonist planned it all, choosing the Lantern Festival to wreak the most havoc without getting caught? But who'd harbor such calculated hatred, and how would I catch him?

The mystery taunted me like a devious lantern riddle, but I hadn't the time to mull over clues. I couldn't stand idly by while Chengdu burned.

My father had taught me the secret of sweet possession. Each generation of *Tangren* in my family would push the bounds of our magic the way we'd inflate a candy-bubble. Spying was our earliest power, then animation, and last year I discovered water-shaping. To fight the fires, I'd need that new skill now, and also water and golden caramel to conjure with.

With mandated fire stations every three-hundred steps, the fire-fighting force soon swarmed the street with buckets, but the number of blazes daunted them. Lun, with cloth-bandaged hands, pointed out the monkey to incredulous men.

At my stall, I pulled a glob of hot caramel from my pan. Years of practice making the scalding heat bearable as I palmed, twirled, and blew on the gooey lump to cool it.

To battle such hungry blazes spreading by rooftop, I'd need a storm's worth of water, maybe from the Jinjiang River nearby. The sun had set and the River Bridge Gate was shut, but I had no choice. I tucked a bamboo stick behind my ear and ran southward, rolling the sugar ball between my palms to keep it soft. In my haste I nearly collided with a dour-faced official who glowered and barreled past me, roaring orders to the fire-fighters.

The walls of Lesser City loomed ahead, too high to climb. But if I chose the right animal, it might be no obstacle at all.

Only twelve primal shapes could contain an elemental conjuration: the animals of the *shengxiao* zodiac, the foundation of every *Tangren* master's repertoire. Goat, Rabbit, Pig; Tiger, Horse, Dog; Snake, Rooster, Ox; Monkey, Dragon, and Rat.

I had to call the Dragon, rider-of-mists and bringer-of-rains, the most dangerous of all.

I shaped a hollow in the caramel with my fourth finger and stretched it funnel-long. Snipping away excess candy with a bite, I blew into the thin sugar-pipe, making the bulbous end expand, but this time I laced the breath with half of my soul like Iron-Crutch Li of the Eight Immortals.

My hands recalled the Three Joints and Nine Resemblances of the dragon-shape, drawing the soft shell long and plucking limbs, antlers and frills of golden sugar. On the dragon's head I molded a *chimu* lump, without which it could not fly.

I twisted off the airpipe. Almost done save the final touch. Breaking the bamboo stick in two with my teeth, I jabbed a sharp point into the back of my hand and drew blood.

Dragons only come alive when you dot their eyes.

I settled on the dirt in the shadow of the wall, hoping my body would be safely hidden here, and called to the spirit of Dragon.

O Sacred Dragon, hear me! I, the insignificant Ao Tienwei, humbly ask your aid.

A voice like thunder echoed through my head. *You are not one of mine, Water Rat, though I know you from your tributes of art,* it said, calling me by the sign of my birth year. *What will you ask, and what will you give in return?*

Lord Dragon, Chengdu burns and I must quench the flames. Water I have in plenty, but not strength enough to fly. Legends tell of your dominion over water and sky. If you would lend me your power, I'd soar and save the city, bringing you new worship and reverence.

It considered it. *Your proposal pleases me, Water Rat. Fly with my blessings.*

A thousand thanks, Sacred One.

I lobbed the blood-eyed Dragon underhand into the air and cast my consciousness inside, becoming the small caramel creature. Starlight on my *chimu* lump pulled me towards the new moon sky, and I floated over the wall and down into the river.

I bobbed thrice before sinking into the frigid depths. I felt my sugar-body begin to dissolve, and welcomed the simultaneous sensations of drowning and fading. That was the trick to elemental possession; my first tries failed because I fought those fears when I should have embraced them. As my senses seeped from hardened candy into sweetened water, I asked the river to accept my offering in trade for a moat's worth of water. The river savored the candy and gave me what I asked, but left to me the shaping of the river-water.

I began molding the water into likeness of the candy-dragon. I'd never attempted so prodigious a conjuration before, a horse being the largest water-shaping I'd succeeded at. It took all my strength to merely break the surface with my water-dragon head, but as my manifestation took shape, Dragon power welled inside me and lifted me heavenward. As my sinuous body escaped the Jinjiang River, my undulations freed startled fish from my frame and threw them back into safe currents. I gave thanks to Dragon and flew, grander than any conjuration I ever dared.

Below, the gardens and pagodas grew small like tray landscapes, while the folk on the streets might as well be tiny dough figurines. I spiraled in the air to get my bearings. More the impression of a dragon than a detailed rendition, this grand manifestation was slow to respond to my thoughts, but it would have to do.

Points of red lantern lights dotted the city below, though the fires in Lesser City shone fierce through billowing smoke. I dove for the scene of the fiery devastation.

All along the street, blazes raged out of control. The *yuanzi* girl and her parents huddled by the overturned stall in front of the doomed teahouse, cradling a sign that boasted 'fragrant tea from river water'. A bandaged Lun fought alongside the others to put out what fires they could, while the magistrate in charge grabbed a snake-halberd and cut down a string of lanterns, hollering for other soldiers to do the same.

A handful of men saw my coming and cried out in astonishment. All turned to look, with some men thinking it best to flee, while others gaped in bewilderment and forgot their tasks.

I ignored the stares and twisted through the air, spewing river-water at the flames licking the sky. The blasts of water worked wonders at extinguishing blazes, but each spray diminished me by a like sum and rippled the veneer of my dragon-shape. I did my best to hold the dwindling manifestation together and surveyed the rooftops with liquid eyes.

There! The fire monkey hid in the high flames and blinding smoke of the brocade shop to my left, its flicking tail betraying its place. I angled my flight towards the demon, our eyes meeting at last. For good or for ill, the sorcerer now knew I pitted my magic against him.

I spat a cauldron-sized pearl of water at the monkey, but the agile beast vaulted out of the way onto an adjacent roof and raced across black tiles. I rushed through rising steam after it, but the monkey was too small and nimble to target with bursts of water.

In spite of my laggard reflexes, I could still fly faster than the beast could run. I overflew the beast and walled off its progress forward with watery coils, but the monkey grabbed the roof's edge and swung through the back window of a wineshop. I gave chase and spewed a great measure of water through the opening, but the monkey leapt out of a front-facing window as the flood struck. In single-minded pursuit, I threaded my body forcibly through the narrow frames, stripping more water from my manifestation. I emerged slimmer, overshadowing the market street where the fire monkey had landed between the magistrate and Lun.

The magistrate lowered his halberd and sliced at the fire monkey, while Lun hoisted his bucket and readied to throw.

Trapped between the fearless official and a wheelwright with a bucket of water, the fire monkey hesitated.

That moment of indecision was just enough time for me to gamble it all.

High above the trio, I purposefully shaped away my *chimu* lump and my ability to fly ended abruptly. I fell bodily on top of them, river-water overflowing the bounds of my dragon-shape as the conjuration collapsed. The impact sent my awareness tumbling out of the elemental conjuration.

For the first time, I lost all of my senses.

In the past, ending a conjuration meant my soul would fly back to my body. I had never been stripped of every sensation: no sight, no sound, no pulse racing or hackles rising on the back of my neck.

Nothing but naked fear and solitude.

I tried picturing my body, from my dry eyes to the growl of hunger in my belly, from the itch between my toes to the sting of the wound on my hand.

But still I could not return.

Did I overreach myself, conjuring with too much water? What if I were trapped like this forever?

What I'd give to feel my heart pound in terror!

No, stop obsessing over *why* and think about *what-now.* I shouldn't let this predicament cool and harden into permanence while I fretted; I ought to shape the situation while it was malleable. I might be bodiless but I still had memory and thought, purpose and principle. If an escape didn't exist, I'd make one.

I remembered asking my father to teach me sweet possession when I was sixteen. Father was a difficult master to please, finding fault in my interpretations of the Dragon. "You must pay tribute to the animal with your artistry."

"But why?" I asked. "Paintings, sculptures, and calligraphy last. Candy figurines don't."

Father swatted the back of my head with his folding fan. "The sugar opera may be fleeting art, but it's no excuse to slacken! Show respect for the animals before you ask to wear their shapes, in particular the spirits of the twelve signs. Revere them, my son, lest they find cause to meddle in your affairs."

I took Father's lesson to heart. It took months of practice to render a Dragon to his liking, thereby completing a *Tangren's* zodiac repertoire. At last, he consented to teach me the spying skill. "Always begin with taste," he said, handing me a golden Tiger impaled on bamboo. "Lick and burn the sweet flavor into your memory."

Taste, of course!

I meditated on the flavor of my family's secret sugar blend: brown layered on cane, dusted subtly with musk-flavored sugar. As the memory of that taste crystallized in my mind, I caught a tinge of it coming from beyond remembrance. I latched onto the taste and willed myself towards it.

My senses returned, though not to my body as I hoped, but back inside the rabbit-on-a-stick beside the toppled *yuanzi* stall. I wore a drenched and sticky hollow candy-skin, a small comfort compared to my own skin, but a skin nonetheless.

From this low angle, I could only see the hulking remnants of the stall on the paved road, but my rabbit ears revealed my surroundings in full. In the distance, fire-fighters chattered about the Water Dragon and the Fire Monkey battle as they threw water onto flames. I heard no urgency in the men's voices, which likely meant the fires were under control.

There would be legends told of this night, which ought to please Dragon.

Behind me, the magistrate questioned Lun and the *yuanzi* girl about the mysterious monkey. "And it attacked you without provocation?" he asked in a calm, scratchy voice.

"Yes, Magistrate Gongsun," Lun replied. "All I did was, um, offer candy to Miss Deng when the fire monkey crawled out. I stared, it stared, and then it jumped me!"

I animated the belly of the rabbit-shell and eased myself off the bamboo stick. The wall where I hid my body wasn't far by human scale, but at caramel-rabbit size it might as well be a *li* away. Perhaps if I invoked the Rabbit's speed . . . .

"Candy, hm? Tell me about this candyman," Gongsun urged.

"*Tangren* Ao?" Lun spoke my name with cheer. "He's a pleasant man, nosy but generous. He's from Ji'nan, I think."

"Did Ao make any monkey figurines?" Gongsun pressed.

"What? Surely you don't think he's behind the fires!"

I cursed my luck. The judge was right to suspect a human behind the arson, but did he have to suspect *me*?

"Answer the question, son," Gongsun said. "Monkeys or not?"

"Well, why wouldn't he in the Year of the Monkey? Magistrate, he saved me from burning alive. I'd rather believe he brought the dragon."

I was heartened to hear Lun defend me so.

"Perhaps, or perhaps not," Gongsun said. "Regardless, I have questions for him. Guards! Find this candyman."

If they brought my body back, I'd be spared the trek. On the other hand, I'd have to lie my way out of another charge of sorcery or flee the city.

"Magistrate, wasn't it just a duel between spirits?" Miss Deng asked.

"It might be, Miss Deng, but magic isn't the sole providence of gods and demons. I must consider all possibilities, including a magician with a vendetta against you or your family."

"A vendetta?" She sounded surprised.

"It burned your teahouse first. I do not doubt that it was personal. Any trouble with the gangs? Unpaid gambling debts?"

Miss Deng paused. "My father may love Constellation Dominoes, but he knows his limits."

"We shall see," Gongsun said. "What of this candyman? Did you know him?"

"No, he never crossed the street."

Gongsun sighed. "Try to remember everyone who came to your stall. If this arson is an act of planned revenge, the instigator is likely as meticulous and ruthless in covering up his crime. We must find him before he has that chance."

As Miss Deng recounted further details for Gongsun, I wondered if I might have seen my foe. But countless people had passed my stall since I set up shop this afternoon. It could be any of them.

Instead, I considered how the sorcerer might have enchanted the *yuanzi*-pot fire. An elemental conjuring required an offering in the shape of a primal animal. If his power were akin to mine, then he must have offered something in the shape of a monkey to that fire. But how?

I softened the rabbit-candy and hopped to the soup-pot apparatus, knocked over during the chaos. Among the bits of burnt wood lay the charred halves of a walnut-shell. They must have made that cracking sound I heard.

If an offering had been sealed inside, the flames would have to burn through the shell or melt whatever held the halves together. The sorcerer would have had time to flee the scene.

The small walnut couldn't fit a *Tangren*'s sugar animal. But perhaps a different kind of food offering, like a dough-figure, would suffice. A master of dough-sculpting could easily hide a tiny painted monkey in the hollow.

But one detail still puzzled me. The soup-pot apparatus sat on the ground, too low for anyone to easily feed a walnut to the fire without attracting attention. Surely Miss Deng would comment if someone tampered with the fire?

Unless the scoundrel responsible had been short.

I'd have noticed a dwarfish man among the street performers, but those kids—had Pest and Snot gone for *yuanzi*? I couldn't remember, but Miss Deng could have easily dismissed the antics of boys at her stall.

Of course, neither boy could be the arsonist. By the looks of them they were anywhere between nine and twelve years old, too young to plan arson. Besides, the monkey was setting fires at the same time they were running away with candy loot. The sorcerer must have bribed them to plant the walnut in the fire. And if the magistrate was right about the mindset of the arsonist, then the boys were in grave danger. A promise of more spoils would surely lure them into a trap!

Squishy footfalls grew loud behind me. I froze.

Giant fingers hoisted me by the ears in front of great, scrutinizing eyes. Magistrate Gongsun.

The Sichuanese man in his early fifties suffered his wet official's robes without complaint; the wing-tips of his black hat, once extending stiffly to either side, now sagged from the wet of river-water. "So this is the candyman's handiwork," he boomed.

Had he seen me move?

A guardsman raised a call. "Magistrate! We found the candyman unconscious by the town wall. What should we do with him?"

Gongsun glanced in that direction. "Lay him down by his stall and watch him."

My body! I reached for it with my mind but still couldn't grab hold. How close did I need to be?

If I squirmed out of Gongsun's hand, I could hop to my body and try to awaken, and if I did I'd tell the magistrate my fear for the children's safety. But would he believe my story? I had nothing but guesswork.

But maybe I *could* find solid proof. Those kids took so many sugar figurines that they couldn't possibly have eaten them all. If I could find one of those shells . . . .

What had they taken? A fistful of Monkeys, a pair of Pigs, a Horse, and a Snake. I'd made only one Snake in recent days, as that sign never sold well outside its Year. Unless the boys ate it already, that was my best chance to find them.

I opened my awareness and sought caramel in the vicinity, reaching as far as the walls of Chengdu. My mind probed each instance like a tongue discerning a shape, hoping to find the serpentine candy. We'd hunt for secrets this way, my father and I. He never shied from using the dirt we uncovered to blackmail rich men.

When I located the Snake, my mind darted through the connection into its coils, but I left a thread of sugary taste so I could find my way back to Rabbit. Half-wound about a bamboo stick, I saw through dotted molasses that the older boy held me in his right hand and Horse in his left. The younger kid trailed behind him with a bundle of Monkey candy. I caught only dizzying glimpses of our surroundings awash in red light, like the shadowy foliage of a park or garden.

Snot tugged on Pest's sleeve. "Let's go home."

Pest stopped. "Not yet, brother."

"You go then," Snot said, his voice wavering. "I'm going home."

"Fine! I'll keep everything for myself," Pest said.

Snot ran off while Pest continued onward alone. A familiar pagoda loomed before us, and I realized where we were: the Flower-Strewing Tower. The sorcerer must have intended to watch the streets burn from the tower once he ended his conjuration.

I had to get Pest out of here now, but how? I hadn't blooded the Snake's eyes so I couldn't shape water, leaving me only this candy-body to defend him. But I could petition the spirit of Snake. *O Snake of Ten-Thousand Years! I, Ao Tienwei who did not give you proper notice, ask your help to save a life.*

I taste you, Tangren Rat, Snake answered. *What succor do you seek, and what losses will you suffer?*

A beardless man in the garb of a scholar emerged from the pagoda. His eyebrows were so sparse that I'd almost say he had none. He was one of the suitors that Miss Deng had rebuffed!

"Where's your brother?" the willowy scholar asked.

"The crybaby went home," Pest said. "I did what you asked. Where's my money?"

The man smiled. "I left the sycees in a pouch under that bench there. The gold's all yours."

No time to answer Snake. I softened and sprang off the bamboo, landing on the path between the scholar and the boy. They startled and backed away. I reared up, shaped and hardened caramel fangs, and mock-attacked Pest.

Frightened, the boy turned to run, but saw the stone bench and couldn't resist. With candy-horse still in one hand, he scrambled to the seat and fumbled under it.

There's nothing there, kid, run!

"So you were the water dragon, *Tangren*?" the scholar-sorcerer said in a low voice. "Stop interfering with my revenge."

He raised his foot and stomped down. I slithered away in the nick of time. *Grant me venom, Snake!*

My price—

The scholar started towards the kid.

Anything, Snake! I coiled and sprang for the man's ankle, sinking fangs deep into his flesh. The scholar cried out and stumbled.

So be it, Snake said.

Something flowed through my fangs into the scholar's blood.

I heard the rattle of rocks, then small footfalls receding. The kid saw through the sorcerer's lie at last.

I had no time to celebrate. Pillar-like fingers pulled and ripped me in two.

The shock again sent my consciousness reeling, but I caught the thread of sweetness and followed it back to Rabbit. My rabbit-self lay on the table at my stall. A towering Magistrate Gongsun stirred through the pot of cooling caramel beside me.

With Pest still in danger, I abandoned caution and leapt off the table, catching the magistrate by surprise. He grabbed for me but clawed only air as I landed on top of my body's chest.

But despite the closeness of my flesh, I could not return to it.

Gongsun knelt and reached for rabbit-me.

Always begin with taste, I decided, and scurried towards my human mouth. I burrowed between the lips and kissed the tip of my own tongue.

My awareness flooded back inside my body.

I pulled the candy out of my mouth and gasped for breath. The Dragon conjuration had taken too much out of me, and I struggled to sit up.

Gongsun raised a bushy eyebrow and extended his hand. "You and I have much to discuss, candyman."

I took his hand. "Magistrate, you must send men to the Flower-Strewing Tower, without delay." I said, nearly breathless. "The arsonist's a scholar with almost no eyebrows. Please hurry, before he catches the boy!"

"What boy? Explain."

Lun and Miss Deng saw me stir and came towards us, hand in bandaged hand. "So good to see you awake, *Tangren Ao*!" Lun said.

I smiled weakly. "Miss Deng, did a willowy scholar give you any gifts? Dough-figures, perhaps?"

"Master Shuai? Yes, he tried to give me several of the miniatures, but I refused them all," she answered. "I didn't want to encourage him. He's chased me since my hair-pinning ceremony two years ago."

"Shuai had a kid slip a magical figurine into your fire, but now the boy's a liability." I turned to Gongsun. "You must believe me, Magistrate. Find Shuai."

Gongsun stood and called to a group of halberdiers. "Go. Detain anyone at the Flower-Strewing Tower." The soldiers hastened away without question. "Stay here, *Tangren Ao*."

"I'm coming with you." My legs weak, I could only stand with Lun's help. "Thank you, Lun."

We left Miss Deng with her family on the market street and headed for the pagoda.

The halberdiers found the scholar Shuai trying to limp with a swollen foot away from the Flower-Strewing Tower. They held the cursing suspect at blades' point and called out to Pest.

The boy poked his head out from behind a clump of bamboo, still clutching Horse-on-a-stick in an iron grip. "Did you kill the snake?"

I grinned. "Don't worry. It won't be back." However, my smile faded when I realized I had no idea what Snake would demand of me.

With Shuai in custody and the boy safe under the soldiers' protection, Gongsun demanded answers. "Start from the beginning."

"I'll gladly answer all your questions, Magistrate, but only in confidence."

"Agreed."

Lun helped me to the tower on Gongsun's instructions. "Thank you, *Tangren Ao*," he whispered in my ear.

"No need, Lun. She likes you. All you needed was a little push." I was glad the candy-rabbit brought them together, even though things had turned out much differently than I expected.

"I meant the water dragon."

I pretended not to know what he was talking about. "You have a vivid imagination, lad."

Lun left with a crooked smile.

I couldn't lie to Magistrate Gongsun. I couldn't prove the scholar's guilt unless he understood how Shuai's magic and mine worked. I sat on the steps of the pagoda and recounted the night's events, and for the first time, spoke frankly about my power. As I revealed my secret, the burden of years fell away. Despite myself, my eyes brimmed with unshed tears.

At the end of it, Gongsun stroked his beard. "I believe you, though few others will."

"No one else must know."

"I agree. However, I still intend to bring Shuai up on charges of sorcery and arson. The boy's testimony will seal his fate, and I will crush him with the full force of the law."

Not what I wanted to hear, being a sorcerer myself, but nonetheless I bowed. "I, your insignificant servant, thank you."

"You have a strange and useful talent that ought not go to waste, *Tangren* Ao," Gongsun said. "Will you work for me? I will pay you well for it."

"And give up this sweet calling? The life of a *Tangren* is all I know."

"I am not asking you to abandon your trade. Stay in Chengdu. Learn the city. Help us rebuild. I only ask that when I have need of you, you answer my summons. What say you?"

He surely knew how my magic could advance his career. For good or for ill, my fate was now entwined with his, so long as he demanded it. But what choice did I have? You should never anger a man who could sentence you to death. I felt as helpless as a rat caught in the coils of a—

"Your animal sign wouldn't happen to be Snake, would it?" I asked.

"Indeed," Gongsun replied. "How did you know?"

Alone with Gandhari

GORD SELLAR

And the wailing chief of the cowherds fled, forlorn and spent,
Speeding on his rapid chariot to the royal city went,
Came inside the city portals, came within the palace gate,
Struck his forehead in his anguish and bewailed his luckless fate.
—from *The Mahabharata*, trans. Romesh C. Dutt (1898)

She was out there, serene in the mists, waiting for him, and Ron was coming to her. With the whole of his mind, he willed himself to see her: her immense walnut eyes, slightly alien; her long, regal nose with its flaring nostrils; her long, elegant legs.

And then, suddenly, there she was in all her natural glory: no genetic engineering or hormonal tinkering had been performed upon her, and as such, she was a precious rarity. A creature of such loveliness, a sight for bruised and red-veined eyes. She eyed him calmly as he hurried toward her across the field of endless green and softly swaying daisies, under a sky so blue it would have made you weep if only it were real.

A memory of Kenny stirred—that poor, sad, dead glob of pudge he'd once been, that Ron had murdered in an empty field one night near Fort Worth with four Brother Ronalds. The ghost of a dead lardass grasping at his spirit's throat, trying to haul itself back up through the greasy lips of oblivion.

Ron ignored it. The remnant artifacts of Kenny Jameson's pathetic life—an army-green trash bag full of oversized clothes and whimpering regrets—had been left to rot in a shallow hole in the ground behind a shopping mall. With Guru Deepak's help, he'd long ago learned how to deal with Kenny's ego, the remnants of the man Ron had been before his rescue. He slowed his pace as he approached Gandhari, savoring the scratchy caresses of the high blue grass against his naked legs.

When he reached her side, he patted her twice upon the hip, with all the gentleness of a tender lover. "Namasté, Gandhari. Now, look at me," he said with a smile. "Look at my body." He glanced down at his own taut gut, the thin threads of wasted muscles beneath his somehow-clean skin. He had become somehow translucent, and could see the his own knobby, badly-carved kneecaps, the weary veins in his legs, the clutching bones of his ribcage, and even the curve of his pelvic bones through his patchily tanned, hairless hide.

Gandhari turned her head, lazily surveying his physique. She belched, and a heavenly draught bathed his face. He was suddenly moved by his passion for her, great Gandhari, gods-kissed blindfolded mother of a hundred sons from the Great Book, who had long ago attained her true and perfect form. He touched his lips to her forehead, between her eyes, and in response, she lovingly swished her tail over her back, an ancient gesture that meant nothing but pure bovinity in this world where flies buzzed no more.

Heart swooning, he made his way to her rear, and as he did so, she steadied herself, bracing. Gently, and with the greatest of reverence, he stuck a hand into her, and then another. He pried her open, drew a deep breath, and slid headfirst into the peace of the divine mother-cow's womb.

Within her, there were others. The sounds of breathing and mumbled prayers and mantras. And Guru Deepak, preaching off in the distance, his voice muffled but undeniably musical.

Ron ignored the others. He relaxed, breathing mother Gandhari's life-giving uterine fluids into his lungs, leaning back against the soft, warm walls of her womb. He was alone with Gandhari, within her. He was home, again. Nothing else mattered.

Then she spoke to him. Close by, tender yet clear, it was her womb-voice speaking to him alone, and he dreamed the most loveliest visions: of broken buildings, smoke and flames, and a endless, rising wave of liberation sweeping the earth entire.

"Listen, Kenny," Mr. Paul said to him one day, in the staff room during his lunch break. "I'm gonna have to let you go."

"Why?" Envelopes with little plastic windows filled Kenny's mind. Bills inside them, and sternly worded final notifications. Without Prejudice.

"You really wanna know?"

"Uh . . . yeah?"

"Because you're a fat fuckin' pig, Kenny," his boss said. "People don't *wanna* see you servin' their french fries and deep-fried, greasy chicken, Kenny. It reminds them of why they *shouldn't* be eating it in the first place. It's bad for our image."

Kenny wanted to shout, to punch Mr. Paul in the stomach, to tell him to go screw himself, shove the job up his ass sideways. He knew his rights! He didn't have to take this! He wanted to chuck his soda onto Mr. Paul's shirtfront and tell him to ram his shitty job up his skinny little ass. But he just retreated inside himself, and began thinking again about how to check out of hotel butterball.

Pills, Kenny decided, but he lowered his head, and just mumbled his response.

"What?" Mr. Paul sounded defensive, as if he expected a lawsuit or an outburst or something. But Kenny wasn't going to sue. He'd grown accustomed to maltreatment. That was just how fat people lived: obesity was the new leprosy. People even avoided your touch, like it was catching or something.

"Should I finish out my shift?" he asked again, louder. It was a bad time to be out of a job, with talk of another war in the air. Though at least he was too fat to be drafted. They'd never send him to Venezuela, let alone North Korea.

"Nah, just go on home," he said, stealing one of Kenny's fries and shoving it into his mouth. "We'll mail your last paycheck to you."

Kenny nodded, defeated, and turned to leave. *Pills.*

"And Kenny . . . don't come back here again till you lose a couple of belt notches, you hear me?" Mr. Paul said, half-smirking.

Kenny never did go back there, though it'd be the first place Ron would attack, a few months later.

Meditations always ended, but today, they faded out too soon, and Ron found himself back in the claustrophobic hell of a media helmet that stank and was stuffy with desert heat. No matter how necessary the return to the world was, it always deadened him a little to leave behind the soft electromagnetic massage of the helmet and his brief audience with ultimate reality.

He removed the helmet carefully, wrapping it again in an old patchwork quilt, and rose to stow it for the day. All around him, other Ronalds were doing the same thing. There were so many of them: Mexican, black, gringo like himself, female and male alike. Some were wrapping their helmets, and others, that task completed, were sleepily ruffling their dyed-scarlet afros, slipping into their grungy yellow jumpsuits.

Guru Deepak, shirtless in his golden dhoti, stood beside the storage shelving units in the back of the decrepit U-Haul trailer behind one of the campers. He smiled toothily and mouthed encouragements to them as they stowed the VR gear safely away. To Ron, he said, "Mother Gandhari has blessed you specially," and set his broad hand on Ron's shoulder.

Ron didn't know what to say. He hadn't spoken to Guru Deepak in days. Not out of any animosity: it was just one of his silence kicks, the sort of habit Deepak indeed praised and tended not to interrupt.

"Why?" Ron asked, after a moment's dazed thought.

"Later," Deepak said with a small shrug of his powerful shoulders, and showed him his beautiful white teeth through a grin. They were perfectly straight, a show of dental perfection that could only be divine in nature.

Breakfast always followed meditations, so Ron made his way to the kitchen. A big vat of greenish *dhal* was bubbling in a cookpot on the ground, and a huge tray of breads—*naan,* loaves, buns—sat together in a big assortment. Bean soup again, he moaned inwardly. But immediately, he caught himself, seized his own disappointment, and pinned it to the wall of his mind as one might a live frog for dissection. He jabbed his resentment with harshness he'd once reserved for lily-livered politicians and hardened criminals.

Bless Gandhari, his craving for meat hadn't returned. His self-control was always greater after a few hours in Her womb. A few minutes later, a bowl of *dhal* and a few hunks of bread in his possession, he sat down in his usual place, among usual faces. "Namasté, Ronald," they all greeted him in something too jumbled to be called unison.

"Namasté, Ronalds," he said. "What's up?"

Ron had meant nothing by it, but it seemed to him that, unlike most days, something *was* indeed up. They regarded him with careful, awkward eyes, blinking silent and waiting for someone to spill the proverbial beans.

Finally, the Mexican Ronald spoke up and said, with his familiar, heavy accent: "Guru say something t'you, don't he?"

"How'd all y'all know about that?"

"In Gandhari's womb," the bony, flat-chested Ronald chick whispered, "I heard something. You know how it is."

Ron did. Visions and whispers sometimes came. Prophecies, gleanings of Deepak's wisdom. Burning visions of the future.

"Last time I had a vision like this one . . . " she said, leaning forward. "Well, there was a Mac Attack coming up soon, and that Ronald, Gandhari said the same words to . . . " She glanced down into her bowl of *dhal,* dipping a chunk of whole-wheat bread into the slop, and chewed noisily, as if she had no intention of finishing the sentence.

Ron kept his eyes on her as he expertly tore a piece of bread off and used it to spoon up some *dhal* without looking into the bowl. When she was about to dip her *naan* into her *dhal* again, he hissed, *"What?"*

"Listen," she said. "If you're lucky, you'll be drinking mother Gandhari's pure milk today. *In heaven,*" she added, as if the euphemism hadn't been clear enough, and dropped the bread into her *dhal.* Her eyes softened a little, the tattooed-red tip of her nose wiggling as she sniffed, and with a lowered voice she added, "If you want, we can go out behind the storage sheds and I'll give you a . . . you know." She jerked a grubby fist up and down suggestively, one gaunt cheek propping outward by her tongue as she gave him a ghastly wink. "Just in case. Nothing more, though. I don't wanna get pregnant before It happens. *He feeds on childrens' minds; they make Him stronger,*" she droned, intoning the familiar mantra that Ronalds chanted to fend off carnal temptation. "But I'll get you off, one last time before . . . "

"No thanks," Ron said, and filled his mouth with hot, flavorless green bean mush. It wasn't much of an act of will: she wasn't his type, her breath stank, she was missing half her teeth, and anyway, he didn't believe he was going to be a martyr. He'd done nothing to distinguish himself or earn such an honor. And even if Gandhari *had* chosen him to lead a mission, it didn't mean he was going to die.

"Are you sure?" she said and licked her bright-red lips, her eyes slightly narrowed. He realized that she wasn't being generous: she really *wanted* to do it. He wondered how many other martyrs she'd led off the path, the same day they were supposed to drink straight from Gandhari's udder, and sent them spiraling back into the *samsaric* rut of reincarnation and flesh-addiction.

Who hungers for flesh of one kind, hungers for all, went Guru Deepak's motto.

Was it jealousy, that Mother Gandhari always chose men to lead the Mac Attacks? Or some vestigal human instinct, half-dessicated lust? He imagined the Ronalds he'd admired: those he'd seen shot to death in the parking lots of ghastly eateries, and those whose bodies had been charred by fires or clapped in irons and shipped to reprogramming facilities, their animal bodies trapped and ensouled once again by the System. He imagined himself out behind the storage sheds, or huddled in the cab of a truck, or somewhere behind a clump of bushes, with her rancid breath wafting hot across his skin. Thick, acidic bile scoured its way up his throat.

Stop, he commanded himself, and he stepped back from all of these overwhelming emotions that had welled up within. From a slight mental distance, his envy and desire looked pathetic. His own disgust peered back at him impishly. They had fused, and sang in one voice. But when he looked deeper, he found sorrow and disdain, braided into one single wormlike creature and wriggling within his mind. He looked upon his flat-chested Ronald Sister and abjured that strange sadness-and-dislike emotion, struggling for compassion.

"No thank you," he said with a smile, and admonished her with a mantra of his own. *"After a Single Sip, Only a Big Gulp Can Follow."*

"Yes, true," she said, nodding, and attacked her food. She tried to look relieved, but refused to meet his gaze again the whole meal. That didn't surprise him; what surprised him was that none of the other Ronalds caught his eye again, either.

The first time he had seen a Mac Attack, he'd almost pissed in his size-52 pants. He'd been standing in the usual burger joint when suddenly they'd burst in, yelling through the speakers mounted on the fronts of their gas-masks.

"Killers! Murderers!" they'd screamed, those freaks. They had looked like Holocaust victims done up in soiled yellow clown costumes, red grins tattooed onto their faces, red curly wigs slapped onto their bald crowns. "You're filthy! You're insane!" Even in his panic, he'd thought, *Look who's talking.* He remembered that, the way one remembers being a heartbroken teenager, or remembers the panic of holding a steering wheel for the first time: the memory of another person altogether, was what it now felt like to Ron.

But he hadn't yet become a Ronald, then. He had been a different kind of human. No, not human, either. A man, maybe, but not human. He'd been a mere scraping beast. A herd man. Kenny the flabby herd man.

Seeing the Ronalds in action, he'd seen not their liberation from mediocrity, but only the dirt clinging to their faces, the blood and grime ground into the fabric of their costumes, the dung clinging to their floppy red shoes. They'd been liberated from the trap of ego and identity, and attained McMoksha, but through the thickening haze of the gas bombs they'd set off, he'd stared into their eyes behind their gas-masks and seen only one thing: *crazy.*

Little had he known, as he'd stumbled out the side door, through the parking lot, coughing and sputtering on the fumes, that *he* was the crazy one. He'd staggered past the rear bumper of his second-hand jalopy of a truck, its bumper crusted in consumers' rights bumper stickers with blinking mottoes like: "Hands off my fried chicken!" and, "My lard, my life."

He'd burned the last reserves of his energy hoisting himself up into the seat of his truck, squeezing in sideways, getting his foot onto the gas pedal. Still choking and coughing, he'd started the pickup truck's engine, and, not bothering with the seat-belt—it didn't fit him anyway—he'd slammed his foot down onto the accelerator.

He'd managed to cling to consciousness long enough to get down the road and slam his truck into a traffic-light pole in front of a gas station. Someone had already called 911 by then, and when the ambulance had shown up, they'd just given him an injection and a coffee and made him sit by the gas station and wait for the cops to come and take his statement. They'd even let him drive himself home an hour or two later.

His truck had been seriously dented, but his mind had been damaged far worse. The attack had hit him harder than the last international foreign terrorist attacks all rolled into one. It took him a week before he went to a burger joint again.

No other week in his life had ever felt as much like forever.

"My dear, brave Ronnies!" Guru Deepak declared to the eager assembly of the faithful.

They paused, setting their preparations aside, and turned to face their guru, settling on their backsides in the hot sand. White face-paint set off the black crusts beneath their fingernails, and excited gap-toothed smiles lit up their pimpled, scarred faces.

"Today, we launch a very important assault," Guru Deepak declared, his head wobbling side to side insistently. "All our past struggles have led up to this. Yes, this is very-very important! Today, we end our endless attacks on the lowest levels of the death chains. The world has heard our message, and had many chances to heed it. The willing have already joined us."

"And those who have chosen to ignore us . . . it is a tragedy, my Ronnies. It is heartbreaking. Every one of you knows what it was like to be a carnivore, to feast on the blood and bodies of poor animals. Every one of you, until you joined us, turned a deaf ear to the screams of murdered beasts suffering in your own flabby bellies. You thought you were punished for it, when being fat was almost a crime, but no punishment ever stopped you. Who aided you? Yes, I did . . . in Gandhari's name."

Ronald felt a tear in his eye. It all came back to him now, the people had stared at him. Their hissing whispers, as he'd gone by, echoed in his tortured soul. He remembered catching eyes with other fat people, obese women who'd looked at him with those wide, sorrowful eyes. *I know,* their looks had said, and he'd avoided their gaze. He hated those looks. Pious, hopeful pity. He had pitied those women back, who were surely as lonely as he was, but nonetheless he'd seen them as bulbous hags he would never stoop to touching. He'd never made one fat friend, ever. He'd hated fat people with a passion most people never experience in their happy, healthy lives.

And now, he looked down at himself, and he could see the bones within his arms; he could bend and touch his toes without any trouble; he hadn't had a backache in months, though his muscles still twitched and shuddered every once in a while, and some of his teeth were coming loose. He never felt lonely anymore, though he didn't feel the opposite of lonely, either. He wasn't sure, even, what the opposite of lonely *was*.

"It was no sin. Being fat was a symptom. Not of your glands, my Ronnies, for none of you is fat now, and we have not changed your glands. Not of symptom of weakness: you are not weak people, and the world shudders when we attack. It was a symptom of your society. We know what it was a symptom of, don't we?"

Then the Ronnies began to recite the mantra together, Ron's voice one of dozens. They chanted this mantra together whenever a craving for fries or a burger hit one of their group:

> Ravenous mouths, ravenous heads,
> Devouring bodies and the earth,
> The sickness of the living dead,
> Eternal death, empty rebirth.

They repeated it over and over, faces turned skyward and eyes closed heavenward. After three, maybe four dozen repetitions, Ron felt a firm hand on his shoulder.

He opened his eyes, and standing above him was Guru Deepak. The Indian gestured with his eyes toward the center of the crowd, from where he'd been speaking, and whispered, "Come on."

Ron rose on wobbly legs and followed him to the elevated platform at the crowd's center, and just as he reached it, a few Ronalds—those in Deepak's inner circle, clown-masked female eunuchs who went about with their beautiful bodies nude, clean and smooth and white as a millionaire's finest dishplates—led a blotchy-coated, thin brown cow out onto the platform. Deepak tried to keep Ron distracted, but he glimpsed a muzzle on her nose, holding her mouth shut. The eunuchs slid it off quickly once they got her onto the platform, and after a few moments, she let out a loud, insistent *moo*.

The chanting stopped. Eyes bloomed slowly open, heads nodded downward from blind sky-gazing, and they caught sight of the cow.

"It is Gandhari!" Deepak hollered, and the Ronalds howled back with ecstatic joy. The cow flicked her tail listlessly, and farted. "She has chosen a Ronald to lead the mission!" he cried out, and Ron felt the guru's hand clap him on the shoulder.

The joyous screams grew louder still as the Ronalds surged toward him and the cow. Their tattooed red mouths and noses, their teary eyes, blurred before Ron, and he turned to the cow. With all his might, he fought the ghostly poison of Kenny's illusions, and willed himself to see not the sickly Jersey cow before him, but instead the true, beautiful, utter Gandhari.

And then it was effortless, seeing ultimate reality: she was standing right there before him, eyes burning with divine love as she chewed her timeless, life-giving cud. She exuded holiness, contentment. The cow radiated ineffable hope.

Ron felt a boundless joy he'd never felt before.

The meeting had been held in a small room in the downtown Fort Worth YMCA. Corpulent men and women had sat in a circle, talking about their addictions. A.A. for the Obese, the counselor had said. It was the only way the hospital had let him go, after he'd failed to kill himself with painkillers one Sunday afternoon.

Ron had found the rules were insulting. A higher power? You had to believe in God to stop pigging out? Ten steps, twelve steps . . . whatever. That last night at the Y, he'd made up his mind not to come back.

But at the end of the meeting, the counselor, a gaunt Yankee with a shaved head and some kind of certificate from a nothing college in Vermont, had caught his arm and said his name softly. "Kenny," he'd said.

"Yeah?" Kenny had said, trying not to let on that he'd given up on the support group.

"I can see what you're thinking. That this group isn't going to help you."

"Naw, it ain't that." Kenny had been like that, then—so terrified of the truth: frightened to say it, frightened even to acknowledge it. "I'm just having an off day, and . . . "

"No, you're right to think it. This group *isn't* going to help you. But I know someone who can. I know someone who can *free* you. You know, I used to be . . . " He paused, a droplet of sweat on his brow sliding softly down in the harsh fluorescent light.

"What?"

The group facilitator had reached into his wallet, and pulled out a picture of an enormous man. A man so heavy it was difficult to imagine him walking, seated at a cheap diner table with a burger meal set in front of him, smiling.

"That's what I look like five years ago," he'd said.

"Well, lucky you," Kenny had said, eager to flee his chance at liberation. "So for you it was just diet. Not glandular, or . . . "

Kenny had tried to push past him, but the man had stopped him, and said, "You know, people have glandular problems all over the world. But there is *nobody* this fat in Myanmar. There's almost nobody this fat in Uzbekistan, either." He lowered his voice when he said the names of those countries, looking around anxiously. What, was he paranoid too? As if any government department—even Homeland Security—would plant someone in a fatties' support group! "It's an excuse, and you know it."

"So what am I supposed to do?"

The guy lowered his voice a lot, then, practically to a whisper, as he suggested, "Why not come with me and find out?"

Kenny had noticed a few locks from the red wig in the backseat of the man's car, just barely peeking out from under a magazine, but he hadn't put two and two together until much later. He'd been too busy feeling mortified at how the car's seatbelt hadn't fit around his torso.

"Don't worry," his counselor had said, nodding in that encouraging way he always did. "I've been there myself. It'll get better. I promise," he'd whispered, turning his head to scan the parking lot one more time. Then they'd pulled out just a little too fast and sped off into the night.

"What are you doing here?" the man in the suit screamed.

Ron smiled silently, crossing the room slowly and carefully while the man scrambled with the drawers of his desk. Glass crunched beneath his feet, and somewhere in the building, an alarm wailed. He could hear the fluttering of bodies in motion, and terrified cries outside the man's office. Fools, resisting the Ronalds who were trying to save them. He ignored all of that, and stared into the man's eyes.

This was the right guy. His face had been burned into Ron's mind during his last meditation session, within Gandhari's womb. Ron raised his taser.

The man drew a pistol out from a drawer, and had it halfway up to Ron's face when the needles slammed into his chest, through his fine tailored shirt.

"Don't," Ron said, a tiny smile curving within the thick red smile tattooed into the skin of his face.

The man pulled the trigger. Nothing happened. He'd panicked, forgotten about the safety. That was enough time for Ron. He thumbed a button, and pain swept down the taser wires, through the needles and into the man.

Who then howled.

"Drop it," Ron ordered him.

The man didn't obey. His clumsy hands fiddled with the gun, and then he tried to raise it toward Ron again.

Ron increased the voltage, and the man howled again, louder, dropping the gun involuntarily. Ron's heart flooded with sorrow and sympathy. That such a powerful minion of the death-chains could fall to the ground and suffer, writhing pathetically—he needed to be liberated as much as anyone.

Ron slipped a paper bag over the man's head and hauled him up, still shivering, to his unsteady feet.

"Congratulations," he said. "You've just been rescued."

The back of the van was crammed with people, their ruddy-cheeked faces terrified. They weren't fat, like the death-eaters Ron had seen walking the streets earlier in the day, on the way to the offices. These were kind of people whose daily schedules allowed for an exercise regimen, for occasional liposuction when necessary, for dietary restrictions. They could afford to eat well, and . . .

Ron sighed. He had to admit it to himself: they probably were not addicted as he had been, when his name had been Kenny. They would be almost impossible to liberate. They liked living in this evil, awful world they'd built.

"Where are we going?" shouted the CEO from under his paper bag.

"This is just routine inspection procedure, sir," Ron said. "We want to see the state of your cattle."

"You're crazy! You asshole! We can't go to every . . . "

"We don't *need* to," snapped Ron. "Y'all got an indoor ranch set up under San Marcos, don't you?"

"What? How do you . . . ?" One of the men reached for the paper bag on his head.

The wiry, half-Japanese Ronald chick from Oklahoma slapped his hand, and in her high-pitched voice, she said, "Don't even try it, Mac!" All the other Ronnies burst out into laughter at her clever pun.

"You'd be surprised how much we know, Mr. Dalton," Ron said once they had stopped guffawing. He let the man stew in that the rest of the way out to San Marcos.

If you want to imagine the future they want to build, Guru Deepak had preached once, *imagine a boot stamping on a cow's face, forever.* Ron could see the boot before him, a big black industrial jackboot made from cow's leather. It was stomping and stomping, brutal and incessant.

He comforted himself with another Guru Deepak's teachings: I am a cow. You are a cow. We are all cows. We have been, and will again be, cows. We shall graze on green fields, and somewhere, sometime else, we are cows and bulls grazing on green fields. There is a calm and beautiful cow within every one of us. *Namasté:* the cow within me greets and salutes the cow within you.

That was the message of Guru Deepak, the whole of it, the heart and soul of it, and it comforted Ron as the van rolled out along the highway towards horrors unimaginable.

• • •

The people had met him with smiles and encouraging looks.

"My name is Kenny, and I'm a fast-food addict," he'd said. They'd all sat there quietly, listening to his story. Which had been nothing special, just extra portions and aunts and uncles telling him to finish this or that so they wouldn't have to take it home. School dances sat skipped out on, and the looming threat of diabetes. Bottles of cola every day, and the antidepressant effects of fries, burgers, desserts, and more burgers. How he'd finally tried to kill himself, and found he was too fat to die on a mere half-bottle of painkillers.

They'd smiled and nodded, listened generously. He'd felt weird telling them this, all these slim people, but they'd looked at him with what had felt, for the first time in years, like genuine respect.

"So," he'd finished off, "I'm looking at all of you, and you're all so slim. Skinny, even. I kinda can't believe that y'all used to be big like me. But that gives me hope. I can change, you know?"

They'd clapped, and one of them, an Indian wearing a long golden shirt, had nodded as the clapping petered out and the others had looked at him. *Dude looks like Gandhi,* Kenny thought to himself for a moment. *But with muscles and more hair.*

"Oh, yes, Kenny," he'd said with a wide, reassuring smile, his head nodding sideways. "I can help you change yourself. If you want it badly enough. But changing yourself isn't enough. If we want to change ourselves, we must also change the world."

Kenny had remembered, then the image he'd seen in the mirror a few days before, puke all down his undershirt, on that day he'd tried to die. Sagging man-tits under his thin yellow-stained undershirt, useless nipples as wide as silver dollars. All those eyes on him, the years and years of eyes focusing the way they do when people look at lizards and snakes. Then there had risen ache inside him, deep down at his core. He'd wanted to sleep with someone before he died. Someone real. Someone shaped like a woman—like a cello, not a pear or a watermelon. He'd wanted to run again, in this life.

"Sign me up," Kenny had said, and then he noticed that one of them was fidgeting with a hypodermic needle in her hand.

Ron inhaled deeply. The bovoid stench was incredible, like a million tons of rank milk and blood and the faintest hint of corn-syrup in the air. Sweet, not disgusting the way he'd expected.

The hairless thing's meters-long torso hung in a tickle-harness, for all the world like an immense caterpillar shuddering reflexively from the automated stimulation. Dozens of "legs" hung floppily from its side, squirming occasionally. They looked more like enormous fins of boneless meat, each bearing only a tiny black nail—the vestige of a hoof—at its tip. Stumps of other legs, still regenerating from the last meat-harvest, were visible.

Food and waste plumbing penetrated every natural orifice and a few artificial ones, as well. A series of udders, a dozen at least, hung from its underside, through the netting of the harness that suspended it. Pipe-feeds attached to each one. Ron could not tell whether the end he was looking at was the mouth or the ass, because the heads had been engineered out of these beasts. Superfluous, brains and faces. Not even eyes. Just tubes going in one end and out the other.

"This *isn't* a cow," Ron said. "It shits liquid fuel and it pisses sugar water and secretes two hundred liters of milk a day. It regrows its . . . *legs* . . . a hundred times before they give out. It has, what, sixteen or twenty wombs? And not one brain. This thing is *not* a cow."

"Yes it is," Mr. Dalton said, his dull eyes defiant. "According to the FDA . . . "

"Fuck the FDA! Screw 'em in the throat with a chainsaw!" Ron howled. "*Look* at that thing . . . it doesn't even look like a land animal!"

"What the hell do you think *you* look like?" Dalton snapped, and then winced in sudden fear.

Ron wiggled the tip of his tattooed-red nose and jammed one finger of his grimy white-gloved hand into Dalton's chest. "Look who's talking," he said.

From the corner of his eye, he glimpsed a movement. A ranch worker had lunged at him with a rifle. The gunshot blast sent all the hostages flat to the floor, Dalton included, but a thick, white-gloved hand clubbed the rancher flat onto the floor, unconscious.

Ron turned to New York Ronald—a tall guy with an Italian-looking face under his white paint and clownface tattoos. He was the one who'd taken out the would-be hero, and he kicked the gun from the rancher quickly, before turning to see if Ron was okay.

"Thanks, Ronald," he barked. His savior acknowledged it with a nod.

The ranch-monsters hung row on row, oblivious in their harnesses, deaf as fingers and thumbs cut from a body and thrown to the ground. Looking upon them, rage boiled up within Ron. He could feel Gandhari within him, weeping for the fate of her brothers and sisters, these perverted things that should have been cows.

While some of the Ronalds chained up the farm-workers and office slugs together in manacles, Ron turned to his second in command—a big black Ronald who was blind in one eye—and muttered, "Little change of plans, Ronald. We're bringing the boss man with us . . . "

"You sure, Ronald?" Worry was visible in the man's sunken, bloodshot eye.

"Yeah, no problem. Let's do this, everyone. Hurry up!"

The Ronalds howled, hoisting their jerry cans and chanting all the way.

An hour later, the silent writhing of bovoid horrors aflame still screaming through their minds, the Ronalds shoved their prisoners out of the back of their truck, still chained together, out into the desert heat. They begged to be dropped off in the city, but the Ronalds knew better than that: Homeland Security—or, well, someone hired temporarily by DHS, anyway—would be on top of them within ten minutes of the first phone call. Faraway in the distance, thick black smoke seethed up out of the ground and poisoned the desert air.

"We'll drop your phones off a few miles up the road, beside the road. Someone will come and get you," Ron said, and the door slammed, leaving them on the highway like ghosts in the sandy nothingness, the towering shadows of wind turbines slashing across the road behind them. There they left them.

All but Dalton, whom they drugged and shoved into a corner of the van.

"We can *save* him," Ron said, his eyes fervid, lit by the remembered flames, now distant. Eyes dark with the smoke that filled the distant air. Eyes gleaming unnaturally with a bloody passion. The others said nothing, but their eyes avoided him as the truck tore down the dirt roads, back to camp, shaking them as they sat silent, waiting.

Guru Deepak streaked the thick red *pooja* paste up between Gandhari's eyes, to the top of her head. The assembled Ronalds tossed flowers into the air, adorning her with necklaces of blossoms.

She mooed.

Dalton sat nearby, handcuffed. He oozed disdain. From a distance, Ron had watched Deepak argue with him until, suddenly, the shouting had cooled and Deepak had left the man sitting in the sand.

Ron's hope refused to wither. A man like Dalton coming into the fold would be an absolute coup, a portent of worldwide victory. His gaze drifted back to Gandhari, who was being led close to him, so he cast his blossoms up into the air and cried out in joy and boundless, ecstatic praise.

An hour later, he huddled down to the floor in Guru Deepak's private trailer.

"It's alright," he said.

"What?" Guru Deepak wore an incongruous frown upon his face.

"It's alright. I didn't do it for any reward. I just was inspired . . . by Her—Mother Gandhari. I knew in my heart that she wanted him brought to our camp."

"Really," Deepak muttered. It wasn't a question. Ron carefully searched his guru's face, surprised, until Deepak snapped, "How do *you* know what Gandhari wants? How do you know what *I* want?"

Ron gasped, panic shivering alive in his guts. Had he *really* made a mistake?

"I . . . I just felt . . . when I saw all those . . . things . . . "

"I know," Deepak said, suddenly quiet, but very, very cold. "I know who you are, Kenny," he said, his eyes narrowing.

"What? No . . . I'm not Kenny anymore . . . "

"You think I'm so naïve?" Deepak asked, a little harshly. Ron's heart began to thump.

"What are you *talking* about?"

"You're the fifth plant they've sent," Deepak said, his accent much less pronounced than usual, and his scowl luminous. "I thought you bunch might start finding some other way to spend all those bloody taxes. Don't play dumb with me. You know very well how Dalton's involved. What bringing him here is going to jeopardize. You know *exactly* what you're doing." Deepak's accent had disappeared, and with it his beatific smile. The man looked like any old business captain, suddenly, even in his long golden kurta and brand-name sandals.

"Involved? What? What are you . . . I don't understand, Guru," Ron said, and he dropped to his knees. "Please . . . whatever I've done . . . " Tears streamed down his cheeks, and he touched his master's feet.

Guru Deepak stared at him for a moment, cautiously, and then his expression brightened. "Could you really not be . . . ?" he asked. "I want you to go meditate in Mother Gandhari's womb."

"Thank you," Ron whispered, touching Deepak's feet again, and he hurried out of the trailer to the trunk containing the VR gear.

As he slid headfirst into the great cow's womb, Ron's heart was full of fear and confusion. He trembled in the darkness, and she said nothing to him for what felt like many days. The silent darkness was bisected by the pinprick sensation of an intravenous feed being inserted into the faraway arm of Ron's faraway body, and still, he waited, as desert heat grew and subsided, like tides on the shore.

When she finally spoke to Ron, his faraway body—all but abandoned, that stinking flesh—was stretched out across the dusty ground, the helmet too heavy to support any longer. What she whispered to him was terrifying. Promises of plagues. Deadly cows wandering, dazed, through the smoldering ruins of shopping malls, speaking a language no human ears had ever heard, exhaling deadly contagion scented as sweet as wildflowers. Millions of their two-legged oppressors dead and left to rot, the meat in their bellies burning its way through them, unleashing wracking, fatal sicknesses. It was the end of the human world, the end of that long, hard, ceaseless fouling of the earth. It had come already, she told him, this end. It could never, ever be undone, she told him. She was elated, and his exhausted body bubbled with glee, knowing the plague would claim him, soon, too.

Shanti, shanti, he reminded himself. *Peace, peace.* Rebirth, he knew, would eventually come. He meditated, and he prayed, and it felt as if yet more months passed. Distant voices muttered somewhere over the virtual horizon, all of them too faint for the words to reach him. Rumors of a war. The gossip of an enemy, of government agents shouting, searching his body, rifling through the dreams in Gandhari's womb.

Ron desired nothing more than to be born, in his next life, as a calf. Not as a man, at least: as something other—finer—than a human being. He yearned for his true, eternal form. To be a silent bull grazing the weeds of the remade earth. The image sang to him of the voices of choirs, the dung of the world, worms in the soil. An endless chorus of low, undulating moos.

And at the far end of that eternally warm and wet silence, a ripple surged through the womb shrouding his body—still the body of a man, though he was certain it would be transformed at any moment into his true four-legged form—and with a gentle quiver, he was pushed from dark, warm, sludgy comfort toward the dry dust and cold, once again out into the frightening nighttime of the world.

The History Within Us
MATTHEW KRESSEL

On a wrist-mounted computer, Betsy Haadama watched a six thousand-year-old silent film. It was grayscale, overexposed, two-dimensional, and chronologically jumbled. On the film: a mustachioed man doting over his young son at a crowded zoo. A woman vigorously combing the boy's white hair beside a large piano. A family eating a large meal, candles burning on a table, men wearing yarmulkes, bodies shivering in prayer. A river, people swimming, women in white bathing caps and full-body suits. Men on rocks by the shore, pipes in mouths, smoke drifting lazily upward. A park, the boy looking down at a dead pigeon. Staring. Staring. Father picking him up, kissing him. In the sky, a bright sun.

A young sun.

"Pardon my intrusion in this time of ends," a Twirlover said, startling her. The Twirlover's six separate, hovering pink objects—like human knuckles—danced a looping, synchronized pattern in the air. "If it pleases you, will you share with me why you watch that flickering device so incessantly?"

In some parts of the galaxy one could be killed for being human. Betsy wasn't sure if this Eluder Ship was such a place. But death was coming for all soon enough. So why fear it now?

"This is an ancient film of my paternal ancestor," she said defiantly.

Puffs of air beat against her face as the Twirlover spun. "An ancient film? Indeed, such a rare treasure, an artifact of the past! If it pleases you, may we watch a portion together?"

She was about to tell it no, that she'd rather die alone, contemplating what might have been, when the alarm trilled down the cavernous halls of the Eluder Ship. A cold shiver ran down her spine as a cacophony of voices warned in ninety languages simultaneously, "*Gravitational collapse imminent, my beloveds! Please take your positions inside your transitional shells!*"

Angry rainbows flared across the floor and ozone and ammonia soured the air, warning those who communicated by color or smell. Betsy's mind skipped and stuttered like the ancient film playing on her wrist as a warning to the telepaths skirted the fringes of her consciousness. Still more warnings she could not perceive with her natural senses no doubt flooded the chamber now.

Hundreds of creatures ran or flew or poured inside their transitional shells, strange cocoons fitted to their variform bodies. The Twirlover tumbled away as Betsy closed the cover of her shell. She hugged her knees and shivered as the glass cover sealed her inside with a hiss and a confirmation beep. A lifeboat or a coffin? She'd find out soon enough.

Transitional shells filled the gargantuan chamber of the Eluder Ship like arrays of soldiers preparing for battle, their noses pointed toward the red-giant star looming outside. Maera—"The Daughter Star"—one of the few still-burning stars in the galaxy. It seethed before all, a conflagration as large as a solar system, turning everything the color of blood.

Forty seconds.

This was a pitiful end, but it was this or slow starvation, privation, death. The galaxy had been laid sere. No planets to grow food. No stars to keep warm. It wasn't fair. None of them deserved this. But then she remembered Julio, and what she had done to him at Afsasat.

I left you to die, Julio. And for that I deserve this.

Thirty seconds.

Soon now, Maera's heart would cool by a fraction of a degree, and billions of tons of matter, no longer kept aloft by nuclear winds, would plunge towards its gravitational center at the speed of light. The star would collapse, go nova, and in its tortured heart the universe would tear. A singularity would form, a black hole, and Betsy Haadama and the thousands of others on this Eluder Ship would ride that collapsing wave into another universe. Their matter and energy, transmuted into pure information, would seed a new creation, the World to Come. Their consciousness, over long eons, would push matter into form, coerce dust to life. In some strange new way they would live on, gods reborn further down the corridor of infinity. And they had been doing this forever, would be doing this again and again until the end of time.

Or so the litany went.

The story soothed troubled minds. But the science behind the technology was just a theory. It could be proven only by first-person observation. Any object which crossed a black hole's event horizon could never communicate with the universe again. Just as easily, she might be annihilated forever. To those witnessing from the outside, there would be no difference.

Twenty seconds.

She tried not to peer up at The Daughter, though its ember light corrupted everything with its hellish glow. Instead she watched the film on her wrist: men in fedoras, women in ostentatious hats at an airport, people descending a stairwell from plane to tarmac. A baby hoisted in the air. Smiles. Laughing.

Cut to a park. The boy looking down at the dead pigeon, staring. Staring. Father picking him up, patting him on the shoulder. The boy, crying.

Why do you stare at the bird? Betsy thought. *What are you thinking?*

She looked up at the seething star. So beautiful, terrible, immense. A wonder that such a thing existed. A horn bellowed and Betsy screamed.

"False Alarm! Beloveds, the imminent collapse was a false alarm! Spurious readings caused us to make an erroneous conclusion. We estimate at least six hours before stellar collapse, based on present readings."

The voice announced the message in multiple languages, simulcast with aggressive rainbows, smells, alien sensations.

I'm alive! she thought. *I'm still here!* It felt exhilarating, for a moment. Then she remembered she'd have to do this again.

Slowly, shells opened and creatures emerged. Betsy scanned the motley lot of them as her cover retracted. A zoo of sentient species escaping from their cages, creatures made of every color, texture, and temperament.

So much life, she thought. *Snuffed out by the Horde.* Crimes beyond forgiveness. And made all the more vile because the Horde had been the progeny of the human race.

Betsy activated inositol in her bloodstream via thought command in order to suppress her panic/flight response. It soothed her, but only just enough to notice the hairs on the back of her neck rising from an electrostatic charge as the Twirlover returned.

"That was exciting!" it said.

"I wouldn't call it that," Betsy said.

"To be so close to annihilation and then to come back again. It renews the sense of life!"

"Or the dread of living."

"But the dread, if you explore it," the Twirlover said, "reveals the miracle of existence out of nothingness. From out of horror comes life."

The litany again. "Or out of life, horror," she said.

It tumbled quietly for a moment. "Sometimes." It moved closer to inspect her film. "That's a child of your species, is it not?"

She glanced down at her screen. "No, that's a rhinoceros."

"Ree-Nos-Ur-Us. What a marvel of composition, all those rolling mountains of flesh. Does it still exist?"

"Extinct."

The Twirlover whistled a mournful, descending arpeggio. "Like so much life in the galaxy. Like the once-glorious stars."

The Horde had obliterated stars by the billions. They had wrapped the Milky Way inside a bleak cocoon of transmatter so that nothing, no ship, no signal—not even light—could pass. And then they vanished, leaving the galaxy to rot. Such was the legacy of humanity.

She wondered if the Twirlover would kill her outright if it knew what she was. Death by physical means might be preferable, she thought, to being flash-baked into quantum-entangled gamma rays. Six in one, really.

The film cut to a boy in a crib, bouncing. His mother lifting him, smiling for the camera. The boy laughing.

"That's one of us," she said. "My paternal ancestor." Surprising herself, she felt pride.

"Ah, such wonderful protuberances!"

A wisp of dust coalesced above Betsy's head. Winking diamonds swirled in yellow clouds. An aeroform creature. For a moment she glimpsed her own face of colored sparkles reflected back at her. But the aeroform being soon spiraled away, only to pause a few seconds later before a group of fronded Whidus who turned their mushroom-like eyes in her direction. Maybe they recognized her, knew what she was. Maybe they were plotting her demise.

A second, identical Twirlover approached Betsy and said to the first, "You know, my bonded-one, that we are about to die, do you not?"

"I was about to come back to you, my flesh-bond," the first said. "And tell you about my sharing with this creature."

"Indeed you were. I saw you tumbling towards me with great haste."

"My flesh-bond, just take a good look at her smooth, auburn skin, the fine black threads that emerge from her head, the little valve at her peak where she modulates her words with a bacteria-laden pink muscle! And on her upper-left protuberance, that metal device which flicker-flashes with strange images. She watches it incessantly. She is curious, is she not?"

"There is something curious here, certainly."

"My love, let us join so I can share my thoughts with you."

"Indeed, I look forward to it!"

The two tumbled together into a single dancing, twelve-piece ring. Knuckles hopped, bounced, tumbled over each other. Music piped and whistled in byzantine harmonies. There arose a great shriek about them, and soon after they separated again into six-pieced individuals. Betsy thought they might have interchanged pieces in the process.

"Not fair!" said the second. Or was it the first? Betsy couldn't tell them apart anymore. "You playful trickster! You gave me your segment, so now I know your thoughts. But then, you sense my emotions too."

"What joy it is to share mind with you, beloved! Yes, I feel your misplaced jealousy. And so much of it! What a waste of energy. Don't you see? This creature is alone and needs to share with *someone*!"

"Perhaps, but does it have to be you?"

"Not me alone, but us *together*!"

"In this last hour, you would defile us?"

"Please!" Betsy interjected. "I'd prefer to be alone anyway—"

"One must never be alone!" the first said. "Share with us! Let us merge gloriously with your words."

"Indeed, tell us," the second said, "Did you have a bonded-one who abandoned you, who wandered off to have intercourse with strangers when you need him?"

'*Intercourse?*' she thought. Perhaps there was more to the Twirlover concept of sharing than she realized. "Actually, I left him."

"Of course you did," the second said. "Like attracts like."

"Where did you abandon him?" the first said.

Interesting, the way it had interpreted her words. "I left him at the first nova," she said. "The Mother Star. Afsasat."

"You were at Afsasat and you didn't go through the event-horizon?" the second said. "I don't believe your story! Beloved, look how she defiles this union!"

"Surely," the first said, "you are joking, trying to please us with paradox? Why would you do something so idiotic? Why not escape through Afsasat when you had the chance?"

She sighed and turned her attention to the film on her wrist. Mustachioed father and blond-haired son walking down a path. Father, smiling. Boy running, falling. Crying. Father picking him up, kissing him. All better. All better.

"Did you hear our questions?" the first asked.

"Yes," she said. "It's just that it's a very long story."

"Our lives are stories. We are empty without them. Fill us so we may fill you."

Strangely, she had stopped shivering. She even felt a little warm. If this was intercourse, then she was determined to be a good lover. "This film is part of 'The Biography,'" she said. "A record of my ancestors' lives that was encoded within my genes."

"Such joy! I have heard of this technology, the sharing of such immensity," the first said. "How far back do your records go?"

"About six thousand years."

The second squealed.

"I told you, beloved," the first said. "She is share-worthy."

Her mother had told her the story in the quiet hours while drifting under the ash streams of the decimated Magellanic Clouds, or over stale, thrice-brewed tea, while the ice-blue rings of Cegmar rose above the horizon, or while her mother gently brushed her hair and chills trickled down her spine. When he turned seventy, the boy in the film digitized his aging childhood reels and then gave them to his son. His son added films, photos, and memorabilia and passed the collection to his offspring. His children added more history and passed this collection on again. This continued for generations. Eventually his descendants decided to encode this amalgamated history within their DNA, so it would never be lost or forgotten. Every child was thereafter born with the memories of their parents, and theirs before them, and theirs before them. And also in their bodily archives were the early records—the films, photos and keepsakes that started the tradition. The Biography was an ancient and unbroken chain that began with this black and white film playing on her wrist. The first.

And now the last.

"It's so large!" the second said.

"Excuse me?" she said.

"Your story," the first said, "To carry all that history within you!"

"It's not *in* me anymore. Julio and I stripped all of it, every last base-pair, from our genes. I recall only my personal experiences now. This computer... it holds the last copy. *This* is the Biography, now."

This fragile, solitary thing on her wrist.

"But why?" Moans and tweets. "That must have been an immense loss!"

The answer was complex, full of shame and guilt. Instead she offered the highly edited version. "Because we wanted to enter the World to Come without a past."

The Twirlovers tumbled noisily, screeching.

"I put the Biography on this ancient computer," she said, pointing to her wrist. "It belonged to my grandmother, five hundred and eighty years ago. Julio and I parked our starsloop in orbit around Afsasat and we stowed this wrist-player in our shrine-room. We said goodbye to our past and then we flew over to the Eluder Ship. Our starsloop and the Biography within would be destroyed when Afsasat went nova."

Chirps. Squeals.

"But Afsasat took its time. So I explored every corner of the Eluder Ship. I discovered that none of my species were there. That meant Julio and I might be the last of my kind in existence. And that meant the Biography was the last of its kind too."

A duet of whistles in a major key.

"I used to recall the smell of my great-grandmother's hair of twenty-three generations ago as her lover leaned in to kiss her pink lips. I knew every defect in the bathroom tiles of the beach house where my ancestor Rhindi lived four thousand years ago. I could hear the gulls cry as they flew in the colored dawn as the four suns rose, one green, one orange, one yellow, and one blue before Eleanor left her family for war, to die in deep space, but not before she had a son to pass on the memory. I once remembered the joy Yalta felt toward his seventeen lanky daughters, all born in zero-g, all tall, graceful, beautiful, with eyes like blue giants. These weren't others' lives. They were *mine*. I had lived these lives too."

Seven long, high notes.

"So many people had once lived inside of me. Even these memories that I'm telling you about now—they come from this device! Not from me! I'm silent inside. And I realized that if I let the Biography die I would be murdering billions. Just like the Horde."

A very human gasp, then a precipitous pause.

"So I changed my mind. I decided I'd bring the Biography with me into the World to Come. My ancestors deserved that much. I was about to retrieve it from our starsloop, but Julio held me. Afsasat could go nova at any moment, he said. And . . .he wanted to sever us from the past. I disagreed."

Betsy started shaking again as the moment became clear in her mind. She remembered his exhausted, pleading eyes, his unruly black beard.

"Did you forget what they did?" Julio had said. "Did you erase that memory too? The Horde, the progeny of the human race, stole our children! And you want to bring their history with us? *We* decided we wouldn't allow that. The Biography has to be destroyed."

"I know what we decided, Julio!" she said. "But I can't let all those people die!"

"They're already dead, Betsy!"

"I can't believe you just said that." Her face grew hot. "They're *not* dead! They once lived within us! They gave us our lives, and we owe them our memories!"

"I don't feel that way at all."

"Julio, how can you abandon them so easily?"

"They led us to this place of death and horror. I sever myself from the past for that reason alone."

And in the end, it was she who had abandoned him.

She swallowed down her tears as the Twirlovers squealed and beckoned her to continue.

"I told Julio I wanted to wander the ship alone, and instead I snuck off to fetch the Biography. Maybe he knew where I was going. I'll never know. I reached my starsloop and was ready to return when I heard the alarm. Afsasat was collapsing. One minute to nova. Not enough time to return safely. I panicked. I had to save the Biography, all those lives, from destruction. Nothing else mattered. I powered up my ship and fled."

For weeks she had wondered, did Julio search the Eluder Ship for her? What did he feel when he realized she had left him? Like the thoughts of the boy in the film, she'd never know. He had entered a black hole, and nothing could cross that dark horizon.

The Twirlovers cried out, a piercing shriek. Perhaps they orgasmed together. Eventually, the second said, "What a dirty tale! So much abandonment. I feel defiled. A sinner! This is the kind of sharing you wanted, my beloved?"

"But in fetching her Biography she *returned* to her people!" the first said. "Don't you see? Isn't sharing so much more rewarding after a long absence?"

"You twist words easily, my bonded-one! Her story was . . .*acceptable.*"

A large Perslop sloshed towards them. The creature was amber, a gelatinous three-limbed starfish with translucent skin and dozens of eyes like upturned brown bowls.

"Do you wish a comforting invocation?" the Perslop said. A slit tucked into one of its armpits burped open to reveal hundreds of tiny white teeth, and its warm breath reeked of dead seas. "I know rituals from a thousand faiths. Or, if you wish, you may teach me one." Its voice was like wind blowing over ruins.

"Blessings, smooth-skinned pleasure to behold!" the first Twirlover said. "We welcome a fourth to share!"

"No we do not!" the second Twirlover said.

"My flesh-love, please!" the first said. "Do not be rude." Then to the Perslop: "Instead of an invocation, my finely contoured friend. Will you share a story with us?"

"Incorrigible!" the second said, tumbling furiously.

With the moist end of one if its arms, the Perslop inched towards Betsy's wrist. The tip opened into a tripod of three small fingers, with diminutive brown eyes capping the end of each. The eyes wiggled nervously above the ancient film. "What is this?" it asked.

"It's her people's history!" the first said. "From six-thousand years ago!"

"Interesting," the Perslop said. "Your race hasn't changed much."

"That's a duck," Betsy said. "Extinct."

"So, that's you there?"

"No, that's a walrus. Also extinct."

"Then whose history did you say we are watching?"

"My race. They're at a zoo."

"A 'zoo?'" the Perslop said.

"A place that housed animals in cages."

"What for?"

"So they could observe them without danger to themselves," she said.

"Another act of separation!" the second Twirlover said. "Such a barbaric, dirty race!"

"Her filth notwithstanding, keeping something caged is not barbarism," the Perslop said, its moist arm dangling an hairsbreadth from Betsy's face. "Before the Horde destroyed my brothers, I used to travel with my colony to a fecal press, where we severed one of our limbs and tortured it in a cage until it released a small amount of feces. We then burned that feces as an offering to the Absent One. They were profoundly holy events. And I miss them very, very much."

The second Twirlover squeaked loudly three times.

"You see, my beloved?" the first said. "This is the joy you have missed by withdrawing from union all these years!"

On Betsy's wrist the film played on, men in white shorts and shirts playing handball. Women sitting on the sidelines bringing smoky cigarettes to their lips. The young boy, a few years older, standing on a porch, talking to a beautiful girl.

"You simplify my thoughts!" the second Twirlover said. "I take no joy in the suffering of others. If I did, I would find pleasure in the atrocities of the Horde. But those are stories I never wish to hear again. If I could, I would erase them from history like this creature erased this Biography from her genes!"

If only that were possible, Betsy thought. *To rewrite history.* If so, she'd go even further back, to the creation of the Horde, more than three hundred years ago. Humanity had been evolving rapidly for generations. They had augmented their consciousness to the point that the body became irrelevant. Flesh was now a temporary abode, while the mind was free to explore and play in infinite space. Epic works of art, science, and philosophy were commonplace. Physical suffering had been eradicated. It was a true Golden Age of humankind.

But the Hagzhi, a prideful, stoic and gargantuan species that had once peacefully abided humans, became fearful of humanity's growing power over matter and began to spread lies and sow seeds of mistrust. Later, the Hagzhi began to systematically exterminate humans as a way to prop up their own faltering galactic hegemonies. Humanity was nearly destroyed in the wars that followed, but after that tumult, humans vowed that they would never let such a catastrophe happen again. Through heroic feats of research they discovered the secret folds of negative time and learned the simple mystery behind the origins of consciousness. They learned how to, with a thought, create a sun. And with another, destroy it.

The Hagzhi race vanished from existence in a day. One hundred and seventy planets, moons, outposts and stations erased from the universe. Later, for no reason anyone could discern, other races vanished. Races which had never threatened humanity. The Onyx Horde, as this force came to be known, acted without cause or reason.

Not all humans accepted the rise to supra-consciousness. Not all humans wanted to change. The Horde slaughtered those who resisted. Those who hid were found, tortured, and killed. And there were those, like Betsy's ancestors, who had made a deal and were spared.

"Keep the Biography in your genes," the Horde had commanded her ancestors. "Keep your physical human form. Do this and you will not die."

And her ancestors agreed, and survived, even prospered, while the rest of the galaxy was ruined. When the other races discovered that there were humans who were spared the Horde's madness, that the Horde were the progeny of the human race, the long dormant seeds of doubt that the Hagzhi had planted re-sprouted, this time across the entire galaxy. Humans were slaughtered without remorse, and the Horde did not come to save them.

If I were given that choice now, Betsy thought. *To live or die by their rules, I would have chosen death. I'd rather die than live under their darkness another instant.*

On the film, a crowded beach. People swimming. Large umbrellas casting shadows. Wisps of cloud in the sky, all under a bright sun.

A young sun.

The Twirlovers stopped twirling. The Perslop leaned in closer to see.

"Such a young sun," the Perslop said. "Bright and warm. The sight fills me with sadness. No longer do such stars burn in the Milky Way. Here we orbit this dying star in a dead galaxy where only a few cinders burn in a quiescent sea. And all about the universe a hundred billion galaxies dangle forever beyond our reach. The Onyx Horde has sealed us forever from their glorious light. May their souls be stripped from eternity!"

On the film, a party. People laughing, dancing, hands on hips, forming a human train. Cone-shaped hats.

"What are they doing?" the Perslop asked.

"A party," Betsy said. "A new year's celebration."

"And why do they bounce up and down?"

"They're dancing."

"Do you remember, my soul-union," the first Twirlover said, "how we danced for three ascensions of the Hagic Moon with the birth of our tumble-litter?"

"I shall never forget!" the second said, squealing. "Our many tumblers, searching for their bond-sisters. How they merged and separated a thousand times before they joined the sisters to complete their soul!"

"May they find the path to the Glory Star that resides at the center of creation."

On the film, the blond boy in the corner staring into the camera eye. *I'd always assumed that one day someone would look into the Biography and see me. But I'm the last, aren't I?*

"Your children, are they dead?" the Perslop said to the Twirlovers.

"They were living on Ental," the second said. "It was obliterated by the Horde." A hiss like a distant wave crashing on an empty beach.

"I had nine offspring," the Perslop said. "Three died in the disastrous attempt to pass through the galaxy's transmatter shell. Three died of malnutrition. Two died in an experiment to create a new star."

"That's only eight," the first Twirlover said. "And the ninth?"

"Suicide."

On the film, an elderly couple in formal clothing sitting beside a bright window. Their bodies in silhouette. The woman, Bessie. The man, Oser. Betsy's oldest ancestors in the Biography. She and Julio had named their children after them. A boy and girl. Twins. She remembered their puffy, newborn faces, their eyes hungry for life.

She and Julio and her children had been living on the temperate moon of Aeoschloch with one hundred other Biography-carrying humans, far from the wars and the suspicions of the other races. And one morning, as the swirling black eye of the gas giant Ur rose above the distant hills, as she was breast-feeding her twin children, she was swept away.

She could not see or hear or sense anything, even her own screams, but she felt a presence probing her, scanning her, reading and rereading the Biography within her as if it were the most important thing in the universe. And she knew this presence, *remembered* it from the Biography and the memories within.

The Onyx Horde.

Then the Horde spit her and a hundred other humans out over the sandy coastline. Some people did not rise from the cold beach. Their eyes stared lifeless into the starless sky. Some had organs missing or were merged with others into horrible grotesqueries. Some went mad. Some had reappeared in the ocean and drowned. And the children, all the pre-pubescent ones, had vanished. The Horde had taken them. Every one.

Oser and Bessie, two months old, barely enough time to open their eyes and learn their parents' faces. Gone.

The seventy surviving colonists were wrecked, devastated. Should they have more children? No, they decided, the Horde could just as easily take them again. Should they try to forget and live out their lives on this backwater moon? No, how could they ever find joy again, knowing that the Horde could come again at any time? Then the colonists heard about Afsasat, the Eluder Ship being built there and a possible way to escape the Horde forever.

And so it was decided. The colonists would end their history on their own terms. They would attempt to enter the World to Come, but without the Biography inside of them. They would excise it from their genes, shedding themselves from the thing which the Horde seemed so desperately to desire. Shedding themselves of humanity's sordid history. It would be, in their own small way, revenge.

But they'd have to get to Afsasat first. The Eluder Ship was being constructed in a quadrant of space that was rumored to be tolerant of humans. But the colonists would have to navigate through large quadrants of dangerous space. So they traveled in many ships, by multiple circuitous and zigzagging routes. Betsy and Julio arrived safely. When Betsy walked around the ship, looking for other humans, she found none. They were the last two.

And now, on this second Eluder Ship, there was only her.

Outside the windows, lightning the size of a hundred dead planets forked across Maera's surface. The star looked ancient, tired, ready to sleep forever. The aliens throughout the chamber paused to stare up at the star.

Her wrist flickered like the star outside. On the film, the mustachioed man. The woman with the beautiful black hair. Another party. A different day. A cake with five flames. Eyes reflecting candlelight. The boy, blowing the flames out. Smoke and applause. Silent cheer.

"You said you wanted a story," the Perslop said, "Well I have one. A few weeks ago I confronted a group of wandering Ergs. One told me that he'd captured a human—"

Betsy started in her seat.

"The Erg said the human was an ugly, repulsive thing," the Perslop continued. "With dark hair covering most of its carbuncle head, and liquid leaking from its odious eyes. It pleaded for its life. And the Erg, a compassionate being, decided ultimately to let it go. But afterward he became terribly distraught. He said he'd missed his opportunity to destroy a creature which had caused so much of the galaxy's pain. For a long time I considered this Erg's position.

"I once had a vast starship. I found a bore-worm nibbling in my refuse berth. I believed in the sanctity of all life, and decided to let it live. Six weeks later, my ship was infested with bore-worms, and no one would dock with me for fear of having their hulls eaten. I had to incinerate my ship. You see, I let one worm live, and thousands returned to ruin me. Is it not the same with humans? If we let one live, do we not give them the chance to destroy us again? I told the Erg that he did the righteous thing, but I truly did not—do not—believe it myself."

The Twirlovers chirped quietly.

"Where did he find this human?" she blurted. "How many weeks ago was this?" *Dark hair covering its head?* she thought. *Julio, is he speaking of you?*

The first Twirlover said, "Please, tell us more, beloved! This is wonderful!"

"What more is there to tell?" the Perslop said. "We may be reborn in a new universe, but if we carry that worm along with us, do we not risk infestation again?"

Betsy stared into the Perslop's tripod eye-cups. *It knows,* she thought. *It knows what I am.* Then she remembered the aeroform creature studying her and the Whidus staring at her and the Twirlovers' odd behavior around her.

They all know, she thought. *Every one of them knows!*

"Do not fear, *human,*" the Perslop said. "I'll not kill you. I define myself by being what you are not. I let you live even though every pulse of my hearts says you should be squashed between my arms like vermin."

Betsy stared at the Perslop, shivering. Weakly, she said, "Was your story about the human true?"

Outside, a brilliant solar flare leaped from Maera and grew angrily out into space. The Daughter, shedding her last vestiges of life. Soon now.

The Perslop gestured to her screen. "Is *your* story true? Is not history filled with lies and obfuscations?"

On the screen, a beach, waves crashing silently. Umbrellas casting large shadows. A beautiful young woman smiling shyly at the camera. The future wife of the boy. A burning ball of light in the sky. Everyone watched the screen.

"So beautiful," the Perslop said. "And gone forever . . . "

Silence. Even the Twirlovers went still.

"Please!" she said. "Tell me! Was it true?"

"Why?" the Perslop said. "Why should I tell you? Why do you deserve an answer?"

She took a deep breath. "Because someone I love might still be alive," she said. "To me, that's everything."

The alarm trilled, startling her. *"Gravitational collapse imminent, beloveds! Please take your positions inside your transitional shells!"*

"No!" she cried. "Not yet!"

The Perslop began to move away.

"Wait!" she screamed. "Please tell me!"

The Perslop paused but did not turn back. "I am the last of my kind," the Perslop said. "I came over here to tell you that you are not."

The Twirlovers shrieked and suddenly merged. They tumbled madly, yelping, barking, while the Perslop left for its transitional shell.

Ninety seconds to collapse.

Maera flickered and angry waves rippled across its surface, but Betsy could not summon the will to close her shell. On her viewscreen, the park, the blond-haired boy skipping, scaring away pigeons. Dappled sunlight. A breeze through trees. A dead pigeon on the dirt. The boy, stopping, staring. Staring.

Suddenly, she understood why the boy stared at the bird for so long.

This is the first time you knew death! she thought. *You knew the bird would never rise again. And you knew that one day you'd fall too, that everything falls! That's why you gave these films to your son. You wanted him to remember you, forever!*

Seventy-five seconds.

The Perslop had been right, she thought. *I could be polluting the new universe with this history.*

Sixty-five seconds.

But all those lives, erased? *I can't kill you, great-great grandfather. You are the first. Without you, we would be nothing. My ancestors, without all of you, I am nothing.*

Sixty seconds.

The fourteen billion-year history of this universe had already unfolded. But for the World to Come, the story had yet to be written. Maybe the World to Come was a lie, but then again, maybe there was new life on the other side of the event horizon. Maybe they truly had been doing this forever and ever. A flower gone to seed.

She jumped out of her transitional shell, took off her grandmother's computer from her wrist, and placed it inside the shell. Then she pressed the button to seal it inside.

She'd send the Biography, its mammoth history, with its eons of joys and sorrows, through Maera. She hoped that in the next universe, humanity would be different. Better. What every parent wishes for her children.

"Goodbye," she said.

The Twirlovers still tumbled together in the air beside her, as wild as a radioactive atom. The alarm continued to wail. "Get in your shells!" she screamed. But they ignored her.

Twenty seconds.

She ran to the rear of the chamber and leaped into an escape pod. She pressed the emergency activator and in an instant she was hurtling away from the Eluder Ship at a large fraction of the speed of light. In the window behind her, Maera blinked twice, like two eyes closing, then began to fade. The star shrunk to half its size, and a moment later the sky filled with white light. The ship bleated a thousand warnings as Betsy closed her eyes.

"I'm coming, Julio. I'm coming for you."

She had watched the ancient film so often that it still played in her mind, projecting on the back of her eyes like a movie screen. The boy in the park, running, laughing. Falling. Scuffing his knee. Father picking him up, kissing him, comforting him. Above them, a sun.

A young sun.

January
BECCA DE LA ROSA

Fionn took the dogs out to the water, and there, in the river's reflection, he realized that January had left. He plunged his hands into the water, but she was not there; he sent the dogs barking over the hills, but they did not come back with her or a trail to her hiding place. No scent lay over the land. Exhausted and uneasy, Fionn and the dogs trudged back to the house. January was not there, either, though he hunted in every room, under tables and inside wardrobes. He only found his wife, curled up in the oven. The dogs lost interest and went to their beds. Fionn sat down on the kitchen linoleum.

Mara lay tucked neatly between the grill and the oven floor. She should have had to snap her neck to fit, and her throat should have been a mess of small bulging bones, but these days she bent at impossible angles, and her feet seemed to have disappeared entirely into the fan in the oven wall. She wore no clothes. It was a businesslike nudity rather than erotic. Charcoal dusted her skin.

"She's disappeared," Fionn said, to the linoleum, the oven, the snake-like curve of his wife's neck.

Mara blinked her wide eyes. "Who?"

"January. She's gone."

"Not too long ago," said Mara, "you were saying the same about me."

"Don't pretend you're jealous."

"All right," she said agreeably. "Who is she? A lost lover?"

Fionn stared at her. "It's January," he said.

Mara laughed. Her hair tumbled out of the oven and onto the floor, so close that Fionn might have reached out and touched it. He knew better. "January was your friend too," he told her. "Don't you remember?"

"No. Tell me a story about her."

Fionn thought, and found none. Mara had had few friends, but the ones she'd had were close; and Fionn could think of a hundred stories about each, events he had witnessed and ones he had only heard about, so well-worn with age and retellings that they felt whole and solid as fruit in his mouth.

"She isn't real," Mara said. "I could tell as soon as you said her name."

"What do you mean, she isn't real?"

"We know these things," his wife said. She disentangled one hand to tap her forehead with a thin and pearly finger, and then coiled it back into a spring-tight fist, and slipped it away into the depths of the oven. Her *we* unnerved Fionn, because it was a growing *we,* one she mentioned more and more, a crowd steadily approaching from behind, ready to throw envious arms around her neck and pull her backwards, away from him.

"Some people just aren't real," Mara said, as if she had sensed a faux pas and wanted to remedy it. "You can tell by the sound of their names. She is not a real person, or not the kind of person it's easy to find in reality, at any rate. How long has she been missing?"

"Since I went out to the water, maybe."

"How long has that been?"

"An hour or so."

Mara nodded thoughtfully, her chin and the crown of her head knocking against the grill, the oven wall. "What do you remember?" she asked.

Fionn thought about January. He could picture her easily, standing at the edge of the river with a yellow scarf in her hair, but he did not know if it was his river, and her smile was distant and unfocused. "I don't know," he said. "I know her face, I feel as though I know her, but I can't tell you why."

"We can talk about it later," Mara said. "You look tired. You were out in the cold. Cook your dinner, Fionn."

In the past year and a half Mara had grown more watchful over him. She ordered him to wear scarves and boots in bad weather, reminded him of meals he would otherwise have forgotten, sent him off to bed at a reasonable hour. She made sure he kept all his appointments and ordered him to visit the doctor for small but persistent illnesses. Why, he had asked her once, laughing, did she care so much? Didn't she want him to die comfortably of starvation one day, so they could live together forever, pressed to each other's hearts like baking bread inside an oven? "Don't even joke about that," Mara had hissed. "Don't you dare."

Fionn sat beside the oven to eat his dinner, while Mara sang to him, an unrecognizable and tuneless song, but comforting in its own way. The dogs gathered at his feet.

"I've thought about it," Mara announced, when he had finished. "I think you ought to look for her. If you know her but don't know her, if her disappearance is so troubling to you, there must be a reason. There is a purpose behind it."

"Is this one of the things you just know?" he asked.

She blinked at him, her eyes too big in her thin, flattened face, a strange facsimile of herself. "Don't ask me that, Fionn."

So he asked, instead, "Will you help me?"

Mara smiled her same sweet smile. "Of course I will. But you won't be able to look for her here. You know that, don't you? You'll have to leave."

"I know," he said.

Fionn washed the dinner dishes slowly, listening to Mara hum below the rush of water. Soap grew fluttering bubbles and each bubble spelled out January's name. January, the color of a sun rising, her voice in his ear, January waiting. "Where would you look for her, if you were me?" he asked his wife.

Mara maneuvered her head around to look up at him, a thoughtful owl. "I would examine the clues," she said. "I would start at the beginning."

"Elliptical," he said dryly.

"But accurate."

Fionn bent, kissed the air beside her cheek, and shut the oven door.

When Mara had first returned, when Fionn recovered from the shock and the strange new logic of his wife as a ghost, he found himself prone to odd hungers. Down in the village, putting sliced pan into a basket, the desire for physical sensation would suddenly snatch at him and he would spend the next hour wandering through the shop aisles, touching knobbed avocados, rough soda bread, the silky synthetic feathers on a feather duster, paper napkins, basil leaves, broom handles; leaving a trail of opened packaging behind himself. Day by day, in slow increments, Mara grew stranger. In the beginning, although he could never touch her with his own hands, she had reconciled her shape to the things around her, the oven walls, the floor. Now she was forgetting how to exist in a concrete world. Her hands sank through iron. Her hair floated around her face like breathing seaweed, immune to gravity or the illusion of gravity. Her bones dwindled, she grew tightly coiled like curled ribbon. Fionn wondered what it would be like to touch her spiralling fingers, how her drifting hair would feel; but he did not know and never would, and this knowledge was a recurring illness that left and returned to attack him and left again. Having a ghost wife was like being married to a concept, an abstract noun, something beloved but elusive.

That night he dreamed of January, while a storm vaulted the roof to scream against the angles and planes of the house. Dressed in a yellow macintosh and wellingtons, January stood against the backdrop of foreign hills and valleys. Her hair whipped in the wind; small dragons snapped among the tangled ends. She smiled, and didn't smile. Fionn, who did not seem to exist in this dream at all, saw that a chain around her neck held three small charms: a frowning sun, a sliver of moon, a lidded eye. January held a book in one hand. Her fingers were blackened with soil or ash. Fionn asked a question, and January answered, her answer was in the affirmative, she reached for him. Downstairs, Mara sang wistfully into the echo of the oven.

The next morning Fionn left the house and followed the last few traces January had left behind on his land and in the water: a yellow flower, yellow paint splashed on a broken fence, a bird with yellow plumage on its chest. January left her messages in odd places, borrowing from landscape and flora and fauna as she pleased. Fionn followed her trail down to the barren orchard.

• • •

Rainwater dripped from the apple trees, although the storm had blown over hours ago. The ground was wet and mulchy.

A small girl in a yellow smock sat in the crook of a tree-branch, looking down at Fionn. Light pressed against her back, hiding her face from him; her feet, dangling down, were bare, and yellow ribbons flapped and tangled from the hem of her dress. One of the dogs barked at her, half-heartedly, and then gave up and trotted away towards the river.

"I'm looking for January," said Fionn.

The girl said, "I know."

"My name is Fionn."

"Fionn Cogann. It says so on your van."

"Do you know where she is?"

She shifted, and Fionn saw that a black sun had been painted over her mouth, with triangular rays like the points on a compass, making her look odd and dangerous, poisonous, many-toothed. He stared, fascinated and appalled. "Come up here and talk to me," she suggested, so he pulled himself up to settle on the upper branches of the apple tree. Closer, the girl looked to be about ten or eleven, and above her fierce black mouth, black freckles had been dotted across her cheekbones. "I'm Swan," she said.

"Do you know where January went?"

"No." Swan brushed moss and rainwater from her hands. On one palm, Fionn noticed, someone had painted an open eye; on the other, an eye-shaped moon. "She's gone altogether, or hidden very well. How do you know her?"

Fionn thought of January, solid and unplaceable. "I don't know."

The little girl shrugged. "January can be like that."

"How do you know her?"

"She is my sister." When Swan smiled, it stretched the sun out into a mouthful of fangs. "Though she didn't live with me, not for years. She lived where she pleased."

"How did you know she was missing?"

"The same way you did."

At one end of the world, the villagers worked and conversed, brought children to school, studied, cooked; at the other end, Mara lay in Fionn's oven like a snail curled up in its own shell; but this was somewhere in between the two, a dim twilight place, utterly inexplicable. "Has she done this before?" Fionn asked, half hopelessly. "Disappeared without warning?"

"Hundreds of times," said Swan. "But never like this. This time is different, and I know it, and you know it."

They stared at one another. Swan's pockets, Fionn saw, were full of cut flowers, daisies, buttercups, children's flowers, but none of them was wilting; they stood up tall and elegant, as though sipping water from some hidden source. Fionn sighed. "Have you been sitting here waiting for me?" he asked Swan.

"I have been waiting for someone. I assumed it was you."

"How long?"

"Two hours," she said, "three. I don't know."

"Are you hungry?" he asked her.

"I am," said Swan.

Fionn led her back to the house. Swan paused to examine the shoes lined up in the hallway, the umbrellas toppled over beside the coat-rack, the photographs on the wall—Fionn and Mara's wedding, Fionn and Mara in black and white, reduced to only the light and the darknesses of themselves—and the big gilt mirror, in which Swan's face floated small and pale as a ghostly fish. Fionn left her studying her own reflection and went into the kitchen to make breakfast. He did not open the oven, not wanting Swan to know about his dead wife, not wanting to share Mara with her, but it was the first thing Swan did when she wandered in from the hall; she sat cross-legged on the linoleum and tugged at the oven door. Mara blinked at Swan.

"Who are you?" Swan asked.

"I might ask you the same question," Mara said. "This is my house."

Swan hooked one arm around her grass-stained knees. "You're dead."

"I am."

"My sister might be dead," she offered, a conciliatory gesture.

"I'm sorry," said Mara.

Fionn made tea and bacon sandwiches, and he and Swan ate on the floor while Mara nibbled delicately at a piece of burnt onion. Swan ate two sandwiches, and then finished Fionn's, and hunted through his refrigerator for lunch meats and cold leftover potatoes. "Where did you live, if not with January?" Fionn asked her, when she had exhausted his food supply and sat arranging frozen raspberries into indecipherable, bleeding designs on the linoleum.

"Irrelevant, Fionn," said Swan, and she sounded calm and self-assured as any adult.

"Do you have any other brothers or sisters?"

Swan stood without answering, wiped raspberry juice onto her yellow dress, and left the kitchen. Mara shooed Fionn away with both hands, and after a moment he followed the little girl into the living room. Swan held up a picture of Fionn as a child. It was a bad photograph, but one he loved, because it was the only picture he had left of his mother: she stood behind him, pale and indistinct, her long hair blown across her face; and Fionn sat in a patch of dusky grass, playing with finger paints. Three black fingerprint dots crossed his cheek. His mouth was a dark and painty smudge.

"Fionn," Swan said, her voice low, urgent. "There is somewhere we have to go."

Violins had woken Swan that morning, shrilling against the chime of a grand-father clock. She knew her sister was missing. Scented air blew across the tops of green bottles, blue bottles, clear bottles scattered across the room, and the breathy notes sang in harmony, and they sang Swan, Swan, Swan.

She crawled out of her bed when the strings woke her. Swan lived, and had lived for the past three years, in an old brewery: a place still summery with the smell of hops, where nameless machines rusted and broken glass caught every angle of light on the floor and in the windows. She walked barefoot across the factory.

The first owners of the brewery lived there still. They were old, a few hundred years old, so long dead that they had forgotten even how to be ghosts, and only remembered their roots in the roots clinging to the earth. Once, Swan expected, they had carried shapes and voices; these remnants drifted away piece by piece, and now they were nothing but air and misplaced colors in light. They cared for her like loving parents. They had little to say, but listened sympathetically to her stories, and made her tea full of tin buttons and dust. They had met January only once.

Swan climbed up into an empty window-frame and looked out over the canal and boardwalk. January was nowhere to be seen, not in the waterfront businesses, the tall apartments, the crumbling lacework of bridge. Swan was used to disappearances. Her family was a family of strangers. But not January, not in this dreadful manner, an absence like a body carved in two. Something terrible had happened.

January had been young once, too. She had lived with Swan in a city apartment. They had slept side-by-side in a king-sized bed, and their walls were decorated with strings of seashells, sugary sea glass, dried flowers. January baked mussels for their supper in smoky sacrificial fires. Her younger face was different from the one she wore later, as an adult: swirled with black designs, her lips plum-red, vicious red, golden hoops swinging in her ears. Her older face was more sedate, more cosmopolitan, but Swan remembered the days when January climbed trees for the choicest apples and screamed to the wind. January had been Swan's protector, and neither men nor monsters ever troubled them. But when Swan turned eight January packed away her lacy dresses, her willow spears, her golden earrings, put on a face more suitable for the outside world, and walked away. Swan had not cried. Without January to be the strong one, Swan was no longer the weak one, which meant she had grown strong, which meant she would never be afraid again. She left her own home and wandered up and down the city until she found the abandoned brewery.

Now, sensing her worry, the brewery owners surrounded Swan with their sweet breath. One made her a cup of tea. One brought a moldy biscuit. Swan swallowed a piece of broken glass, an apple seed, a dead moth. "January is missing," she said. "What do you think I should do? Do you think I should look for her?"

Automatically, the shapeless shapes of the brewery owners shook their gusty heads. No, no, no, they breathed.

January had visited Swan in the brewery once, almost a year before. She appeared in the factory front, wearing a belted yellow raincoat and fingerless lace gloves, bearing gifts like a conquering hero. She gave Swan expensive dresses, suede boots, sun hats with hanging veils of silk, wheels of cheese and salted meats, strings of glossy beads, elderflower cordial in frosted bottles, a silver tea service, pearl-drop earrings, a new yellow jacket. Swan accepted these gifts wordlessly. Rain dripped from January's coat, though outside the sun shone. Her hair clung damply around her neck. Troubled, the brewery owners stood at Swan's back, swirling themselves into a mistrustful light show. January had not noticed. Her adult face, clear of black paint, was swept with blush, her eyes dark and fluttering lashes long as spider legs. She spoke in a strange new dialect. January stayed for one night; in the morning she kissed Swan's cheek, and left.

Swan ignored the advice of the brewery owners. They begged her to stay, to lie in the sunny factory and doze and dream and let them blow music from the many warped bright bottles. Instead, she dressed and she tied up her long hair. She pressed her mouth to the glassy ground. January's scent hung there, faintly. Swan left the brewery owners to their own dreams.

Every step Fionn took away from Mara was a tangible one, a chain around his feet. He sat in a silver taxi and watched mile after mile of distance separate them. This world, the world into which he shot like a reluctant bullet, seemed to be the ghostly one, barely readable outside the car window; while his house and his dead wife were solid, a known territory. If Mara had taken up residence in his skull instead of his oven none of this would matter. There would be no room for imaginary January then, only the two of them, husband and wife, husband and ghost, the most intimate marriage.

They left the taxi at a hill lined with tall Georgian houses. Up on a black cliff, a castle made of golden rock balanced like a bird perching over the city. A tourist attraction, an historical remnant. Fionn wondered about the castle's ovens. Where were they? Did someone keep them working? Did other ghosts live in them, royal ghosts, passing their time with songs and counting games, waiting until the castle crumbled around them? If the world's ovens were populated with ghosts, how did anyone ever get any cooking done? A mystery, Fionn thought, one not even Mara would answer.

He and Swan counted houses until they came to seventy-six, a number that pleased them both, and they stopped simultaneously, and nodded at one another. Fionn opened the door. Inside the house smelled of cooking rice, limes, and another sweet, unnameable fruit. Along the seashell-grey walls, someone had hung old black-and-white photographs, minimalist things: a table full of light, a hat stand with one black hat, an empty bridge; stenographer's shorthand for a life history. Swan smashed one frame against the wall and picked the photo out from the shards of glass. On the back was written *Où es-tu?* The picture showed a path of white stones, leading from nowhere to nowhere. Fionn and Swan made their way slowly down the length of the corridor, smashing every glass frame, examining every smooth, age-worn photograph. Each one had a note for them to read. Put together, they made up a strange news story, one without statistics or irrefutable evidence, and too arcane to be useful. Fionn and Swan collected the photographs in their pockets and stepped into the first room they found.

It was a bedroom, January's. Dusty teacups arranged like standing stones waited on the floor to trip them up. The bedclothes on the iron-barred bed were rumpled; Swan found a single piece of orange peel beneath the pillow, a clue that left them with more questions than answers. On the ceiling above them, black mold blossomed in the shape of a woman's frowning, indistinct face, a reproachful guardian angel. Fionn stared across the room at the bathroom door. He knew it was the bathroom door; and he knew that he should not cross the room to see it, knew that if he tried the floor would buck and tilt like a rough ocean, the armchair would snap ferocious teeth at him and the wardrobe would yawn to swallow him whole. He moved towards it. "Don't," Swan whispered.

In the bathroom, mirrors glinted everywhere. They were sulky creatures and refused to show Fionn his own pale face. Colored water had fallen on the floor, and he side-stepped it carefully. January's bathtub was a wide one, knobbed jets and painted tiles, surrounded by vials of bath salts, perfumed soap, tiny bottles of essential oils. In the bathtub lay January. Her hair was tangled and matted. Blood had dried into a dull glint. January wore veined, blue-tinted skin, and her eyes were open, cloudy like lake-water in a glass.

"You knew, didn't you," Fionn said.

He crept closer. January's chest lay open like a tree, and inside it was a white staircase crowded with ivy, leading down, and warm air, the sounds of birds calling somewhere in the distance. Swan, hovering beside Fionn, rested her face on his arm.

"What are the rules," he asked, "in a situation like this? Are we here to sew her up? To bury her and forget her?"

"No," said Swan.

If January was dead, they were all dead, Fionn and Swan as well as Mara coiling in her oven, January neat and ajar. It seemed an impossible situation. Fionn gazed, pensive, at his lack of a reflection. In the end, he offered his hand to Swan, and she took it, the half-moon on her palm smiling into his skin; together, they stepped into the bathtub. He lifted Swan onto the first white step, and then swung himself down onto the open path in January's chest. Fionn and his sister started down the stairs.

Somewhere, bread was baking. Mara smelled it and rose, uncoiling the way a snake rises, charmed, from its basket. She had not been a baker. She did not know pound cakes from fairy cakes; but these days the smell of bread welcomed her. She extended her pointed toes delicately. Each step was another oven, a shoe for her feet, until she found the bread in a stranger's kitchen, and wrapped herself around it like a nesting doll. Behind her, darkness stretched out, never-ending; in front of her, Fionn wandered through the world; they were choices, ones she could not deny, only delay; and ovens seemed to speak her language. This one was vast, sweet-scented. A chef's home. A bakery. Mara nibbled experimentally at a piece of char on the oven floor.

A small wind blew a puff of flour in Mara's eyes, with the scent of seaweed and roses. January had tossed her yellow hair. "Greetings," she said. Mara could not place the accent, but it did not matter. It was unmistakably January, impossibly January. Who else would it be?

"Does this mean you're dead?" Mara asked. "My husband is off looking for you. He is a wonderful man, a lovely man. If he dies in your pursuit I will be furious with you."

January shook her head. "I don't know what I am."

"I'm dead."

"I know you are," January said, and laughed her beautiful laugh. "But for people like me, like my sister, like your husband, I don't think it's quite as simple as that. There are not only two states of being, alive and dead. There are others."

Mara ground burnt bread between her teeth. "What does that mean?"

"I don't know what it means."

They sat in silence for a moment. Mara thought of Fionn, the way she always thought of Fionn. If he died, who would hunt for him? Who would cross the country in search of his body, whether alive, or dead, or some mysterious third option? She asked, "What part of you is here, if you don't know where you are?"

"The smallest part," said January.

I will hunt for him, Mara thought; and it was a realization, and a choice.

January drew herself closer, as though seeking heat in the heat of the oven. "Don't you want to know what happened to me?"

"No."

"Do you believe in ghost stories?"

"No," Mara said, judiciously. "Do you believe that they can help you?"

The baking bread glowed like a fire signal.

Messenger
J.M. SIDOROVA

Life is a stick with a death on each end, balanced on a finger of the Universe, I understand that much. My kind is born small and numerous, wet and weak. Most of us do not survive to the onset of maturation. Of those who do, yet fewer complete it. Sometimes a human will step on a whole brood of my kind and never notice, other times one of us, a mature one, will level a human home because it is in the way, and will not notice either. This is fairness, and it is made out of time.

I am a mature and strong one, I've lived for a while. There were times I was big and wild, and sat in the high desert, watching water turn into salt, moon into sun; watching a root break a rock in its blindness, make a whole tree fall into abyss still clutching to the rock it had broken. Other times I wanted confinement, structure. I became a stone in a big road. The road conveyed armies back and forth. When armies no longer walked on me, they took me out of the road and fit me into a pillar to support a temple of peace. I listened to a lot of talking. I saw many humans, I learned how women were different from men. I smelled charred meat, I saw childbirth. When I left, the temple collapsed.

Shortly after that, He took me in for the first time. I felt reduced to infinite smallness, then turned inside out, to expand on the *Other Side of Things*. It was not without pain. The *Other Side* was luminous and streaming fast in all directions at once. On the *Other Side* I did not move, I stretched; my tail end became an umbilicus attached to the point through which I entered. I knew that if this umbilicus broke I would not be able to reenter my world. I would contract until I was a dot, dense and blown by the luminous wind. I knew I would die once I was a dot.

Yet I kept stretching, He forced me to, and that is how I knew He was mightier than me, than anyone of my kind. Once He had drawn me taut, He docked my head end into a place that was like a shining mouth of a jellyfish. Since I was inside out, all my thoughts and feelings, all my innermost corners and surfaces were exposed, raw and shriveling in the streaming wind, and the hand of His mind caressed and soothed, reading them. My shame and humiliation inverted inside out and became a surrender to infinite pleasure—the kind I had never experienced before.

When I was exhausted and trembling with gratitude, he inoculated me with His purpose. His purpose stayed in my mind when He released me to my world.

His purpose speaks in me. It says, find Me a vessel. I know the *what* but not the *why*—that is my role. He is my Master and I am His messenger, His *Ag-ghel*.

I choose randomly. There is a little valley fed by a stream—a wet crease between two hills; tongues of greenery lick pale yellow slopes, getting drier, thornier as they extend. A grove, a field, a vineyard. A village. Huts, the color of earth and rocks, seem to sit atop each others' shoulders, climbing uphill.

I choose her because she is one of the two children who do not flee in fear when I show myself to them in my first ever human shape. The other child is a boy and smaller than she. He clutches her hand. I understand that my human shape is not reproduced very well. I wanted it to be a child, like them. It appears I got many things wrong. "Maria, is it the undead?" the boy mumbles. When I speak they do not understand me. Baffled, I shed the shape, become invisible. Still, Maria looks at me, and her eyes are blue-green.

From this moment on I watch over her. I am a stone on the path she takes every day with her flock of sheep. I am a thornbush she crouches behind when she does not want her little brother to see what she is doing. At nights I lie on the roof of the hut she lives in with her family and listen to the twitter of their speech. This is when the memory of His stroking hand invades me again and again, and His purpose wisps in my head like handfuls of red feathers. I long for His touch and yet feel ashamed of it.

One day Maria is up in the pasture and a streak of blood runs down to her knee. She sits down, pulls her knees up and folds back her skirt. She follows the trail of blood up her leg. When she finds the source, she squeezes her legs shut and pulls the skirt over. She sits for a while, her arms tight around her calves, then gets up and runs down to the village. She runs differently now than the way she used to, as if she holds a secret between her legs. A purpose. My time is drawing near.

I need to take a better human form. I follow Maria's family to the market to watch and learn. But the things that catch my attention are often superfluous: an imbalanced scale of a fig vendor absorbs me more than the vendor. I see the weights he uses, that they are good and stamped with the King's seal, but I also see the wrongness of balance, and it draws me in. With an effort I pull away: I am here to learn to look like a vendor, not like his scale.

A year and a half after Maria has ripened for womanhood, I follow her along the creek, the farthest from the village, where fields are no more and matted greens reach as high as her knees. She picks thistles and lilies; thistle leaves she gathers into her basket and lilies she weaves into a garland. Thistle milk and lily pollen cake her fingers. She mutters a song in a small, high-pitched voice, she meanders and pauses, and so does her song.

"I am the rose of Sharon, and the lily of the valleys.

"As the lily among thorns, so is my love among the daughters.

"As the apple tree among the trees of the wood, so is my beloved among the sons . . .

"I charge you, O daughters of Jerusalem, by the roes, and by the hinds of the field, that you stir not up, nor awake my love, till he pleases."

A man in the village has been looking at her, he is older, square-cut; he has curly black beard and anvil-shaped thumbs. The man has talked to her father. Soon she will be given to the anvil-thumbed man, even though he does not look like an apple tree among trees of the forest. I have to act. I become a thistle-plant in her path. My leaves are oozing with white milk.

She reaches for me and I pierce her finger with a thorn of my stalk. She recoils with a gasp. She tries to pick the thorn out but it is burrowing yet deeper into her skin.

In two days almost all of her hand is red and swollen and she complains of pain. But on a third day she gets better and I can leave. My job is done. That day, my Master draws me in and engulfs me in His caressing presence. I wish for nothing else than to dissolve in the honey of His grace, to be a string stretched between His universes, shimmering at His touch. I forget that I wanted to ask Him why He wants her with a child. I forget everything.

He praises my service and calls me his best. His *Ur-Ag-ghel.* He gives me a name, Gabriel.

When I return to my world, it has been four months, and things have taken a bad turn.

She *is* with a child but everyone is angry at her. She says she has lain with no man or spirit, she weeps and stomps her foot when her father interrogates her. An old village woman has looked between her legs and pushed on her belly and still everyone is against her. The anvil-thumbed man no longer wants to take her into his house. Her family no longer sits her down with them to dinner. She eats her meals among cattle.

One night when moon is in full bloom she slips out of the cattle shed and follows the creek side far away from the village. She picks a place, crouches right at the water's edge. She rocks back and forth, mumbles her song, verse, pause, verse. She mumbles and rocks, and lets water run through her fingers.

"The watchmen that went about the city found me, they smote me, they wounded me; the keepers of the walls took away my veil from me.

"I charge you, O daughters of Jerusalem, if you find my beloved, that you tell him, that I am sick of love."

Her breathing is heavy, her voice is thin but still she hums her song. She waddles up to where the creek's bank is steep and overhanging. She mounts it then jumps down into the shallows—the drop is higher than she is tall. A grunt is knocked out of her as she lands onto straight legs and folds up. She sits for a while, rocking, then climbs up the slope and jumps again. The third time, when she climbs up, she is limping.

I fear for her. The third time she jumps I catch her in mid-air.

She gasps, "Who is it? Let me go!"

I lower into the water. My first words of human language squeeze out in a stutter.

"I. Am. Gabriel messenger. What are you. Doing?"

She probes with her fingers, far and wide around herself. Everywhere she probes, there is still me.

"I hate the thistle-child," she says.

I understand something is going very wrong with His purpose, and it makes me terrified and lost, for He is great and so must be His plan. I, the messenger, must be at fault. "Is not thistle child," I plead. "Is the child of one who is—" I am grasping for words,—"Who is—light? Who dwells on the *Other Side of Things*?" No, my words are hollow husks, no more. I recall the jellyfish-like crown into which He fitted my head, "Who presides on a shining—throne?" Then I find my footing, "Who is—God? You cannot hate it."

"Let me go!"

"Please," I say, "I am not good with words. I did not explain it well?"

She cringes and tries to shift her body. "Let go, I'm sick!"

She presses her hand to the bottom of her stomach and groans. With her other hand she reaches under her skirt and pulls a wad of herbs out of her female cavity. Crumpled leaves unfurl, pomegranate seeds fall out. It smells of parsley, rue. Of blood. She looks at it and begins to make noises like cackles and hiccups. Is this weeping or laughing?

I have to save His plan. I wrap around her thighs and around her bleeding, I hold her inside and out in my cradle, and each time her toes curl and her fingers dig into me, I wrap her womb in words whose use I do not yet understand, random words out of her song, "My sister my love my undefiled your head is filled with dew and your locks with the drops of the night my rose my lily of the valley my wine my myrrh my mount Gilead my roe of the field my tower of vines my dove—"

I carry her back to the shed of her family's home and stay with her till she stops panting and curling her toes.

"Does He love me?" she asks me. I think back to the unrelenting envelope of His caress spreading over my exposed inner side. What is love? He cannot touch her nor look her in the eye; He can only suck on my memories of her. If only I could show her, could do to her what He had done to me!

"Yes, He does," I say.

"But you are not him?"

162

"No. I am just a messenger."

"Why can't I see you?"

"Humans can only see my kind if we make an effort to be seen."

When she is asleep, I make a white lily and leave it on the ground next to her head. I leave in haste to set things right, to make balance the only way I can think of. I go to the anvil-thumbed man. He is asleep. I mount his chest and take shape of the fig vendor's scale, only huge and fiery. "Thou shall take Maria as wife and take care of her every need," I rumble, "She bears the child of God." I sway my weighing bowls over his nose, I clang the chains, I spew noxious flames. Then I add, to my own surprise, "Thou shall not touch her as husband until her child is born." Why did I say this?

He is shaking and he swears to obey. Satisfied with my work, I leave.

Over the next months I spend every night with Maria. She now has her own room in the anvil-thumbed man's house. He treats Maria well and makes his mother serve her because her burden is heavy and she often feels ill. But at nights Maria refuses to have her mother-in-law in her room and prefers me. Without me she has night terrors, she tells me.

She teaches me to speak more fluently. To read human faces. A broad smile. A narrow smile. A shadow of a smile coupled with a slight frown. These distinctions are important.

I curl around her, I keep her cool, I prop her head. Her room smells of crushed rock and dew, and milk of her body. Cicadas' tone hangs in the air, as if the indoors and outdoors are one. Sometimes she croons or moans when I rub against her skin. Sometimes she tells me to do it again.

A white lily, found each morning at the head of her bed keeps the anvil-thumbed man and his mother in awe of the single-mindedness of the Divine purpose. How peculiar it is that He never pulls me in to Him during all this time, never inquires about the progress of His plan. How peculiar it is that I do not wish for it to happen.

She keeps asking me to become visible to her and finally I acquiesce. I want to earn her praise and follow the description of a dream lover from that song she has been singing. I scrupulously reproduce the details such as "his cheeks as a bed of spices" and "his lips like lilies," as well as "his belly is as bright ivory overlaid with sapphires" and in particular, "his legs are as pillars of marble."

Her recoil and disappointment are a surprise to me.

The following nights she explains what the words of the song really mean. She guides me through my search of the acceptable human form. In the end I become what she wants me to be. I lie next to her and she asks me to kiss her lips. Then her neck. Then her breasts.

The child that grows inside her is very fragile. Like me, it has to try and err at every step, groping blindly for a human form; like me, it is so eager to give up, for it is so lost in its ignorance of what it should become.

By the time birthing comes, I have helped the child take the next step more than once. I have wrapped myself around it, teaching it to be human, passing the lessons Maria has been giving me. I have protected the mother from the child and the child from the mother; prevented the vinegar of divine essence from burning through a human body, prevented the human body, in the blindness of its wet ways, from attacking the divine.

By the time birthing comes I am no longer certain I am just a messenger.

A healthy boy is born. Maria recovers and all but forgets about me, tending the infant. I try to return to my old ways. I thunder through mountains, I bother oceans. I steal a red-hot rock from one of the Earth's fire pits and keep it suspended in the skies until it burns out. It looks just like a star.

But none of it feels the way it used to. The memory of His omnipresent love on my raw being, of the tug and tide of His universes makes me feel hollow. And the memory of the small gifts of trust and attachment Maria always had for me—her smile, her kiss, a stroke of her hand—while her whole body wailed and choked over its heavy burden, makes me feel hollower still. Her thinning voice, her sweat . . . I do not understand what the purpose of the Boy is, and it makes me restless.

I return to where Maria lives—only to see more trouble. The King's guard is going door to door, killing every male newborn. At least I travel faster than cavalrymen, faster than even the word of their doings. I manage to give Maria and her husband ample warning; they flee.

Why did this happen? Eavesdropping in the King's palace brings me the answer: the King has had a vision. Behold the Boy, it said, he will cause the royal death. Hence countrywide infanticides, they were but a royally sweeping response. A *vision*—is it not an act outside human powers? Does it not reveal a hand of a messenger? Has *He* appointed another messenger then, and if so, why is this messenger undoing His plan?

What *is* His plan?

The less I understand of my Master, the more I feel a slave.

I burn with suspicion, insult. Jealousy. I rage high up in the sky, where air is so thin it no longer stains the void blue, to draw His attention to me. But *The Other Side* that He dwells in is not to be found even in the void.

I visit upon my kind. The big and wild ones who roll upon deserts as sandstorms, and the old and sleepy ones who perch on mountaintops as helmets of ice. For all I know any one of them could have been taken in by Him and infested with His *other* purposes. I ask questions. For all I know, any one of them can have a reason not to answer. "Go to the Wise One," they tell me.

Before I do the pilgrimage, I call upon Maria and the Boy in their new home in Nazareth. She sees me walking up the road, cries, "Gabriel!" She hugs me. "Is everything all right? Last time you came it was with bad news."

"Yes, all right," I say. I don't know how to speak about my troubles. "You are pregnant, I see?" I thought it not possible.

"What can I say? I'm a married woman . . . Joshua, greet Gabriel like I taught you."

The Boy hides his face in his Mother's frock. Will he be turning into something inhuman as he grows up, I wonder. A fly buzzes by and I catch it. "Look what I got," I say. I open my palm at his eye level and the creature tears out, its jet black hide flickers spectral colors. "A rainbow!"

The Boy frowns.

The Wise One lives at the bottom of the ocean in the deepest darkest gorge. As I fall through the chasm, I see gasses bubbling from the sheer walls that surround me, and heavy currents of dead, sulfur-saturated water buffet me from side to side. Animals I have never seen before crowd the rock mouths that spew sulfurous gas; they shine pale-green light on me and follow my descent with their bulging eyes. Mobs of pale, thread-like worms reach from the rock face, sway and coil around me. Strong as I am, I feel the enormous pressure with which water tries to force its way into me.

At the bottom of the gorge there is a lake; its water is different from the rest of the ocean—colder? saltier?—and does not mix with it. I see the Wise One coiled up on the lake's surface. He appears immature though he is older than me. Unlike the rest of my kind, he has refused to grow big and powerful. That is why he's chosen to live under the crushing weight of the ocean. By now he probably could not survive on the surface. He looks much like the pale worms he lives amongst . . . Suddenly I realize the wisdom of his choice: He who dwells on *The Other Side* is unlikely to recruit him for His errands. The Wise One will never have a master because he wields no power. In being weak and small, and trapped underwater—he is free.

I confess my story to the Wise One—everything but the part that I am as much a father to the Boy as my Master is. He ponders it, unhurriedly. The weight of water is wearing me out but I must wait.

He says, "Why has He made you His messenger?"

"I lived as a Temple stone for two hundred years. I assumed I knew humans. He believed me, I suppose. That's why." I add, "I did not know humans at all."

"Good," he says. "Now tell me, wanderer, why have messengers?"

The water pries, pushes, searches for openings. I've made myself impervious but it keeps trying. It cannot stop—thus is its nature. Suddenly I know the answer. "He cannot enter our world! Nor act upon it. Yet this world is to Him like a dry riverbed to the floodwater. It is only a balance that the flood desires, nothing more. He makes us serve Him because only through us can he change this world!"

"And yet we are imperfect tools," the Wise One says, "cumbersome, self-serving. Distractible. Swayed by passions. The Boy then, is—"

"Is His plan to bypass our mediation! To enter this world through human agency. To talk to humans, to make them do His bidding without us as interpreters. But what is His message?"

"You have said it yourself, seeker, there need not be any message, only—"

"—only floodwater."

"—it being water . . . " The Wise One undulates with satisfaction, and his coils bob up and down on his liquid bedstead.

I am confused now—the water makes me so. New questions writhe in my mind like pale worms. "*What* is He? Why can He act upon *us*? What brought Him to this world? Or has He always existed next to it?"

"Good, good," the Wise One savors. "You have been to the boundary of the Earth, haven't you? You have seen the dark void. I have not. But even water has holes in it. Empty space for thought. Imagine this: when a world is in its prime, like ours, ripe and overflowing with life, it attracts creatures like Him. Suppose life is a space for Him to pour in. He feels its presence from afar, like a ripple, a current through the Universes and He follows it. But there are obstacles. The pores in the sieve of this Universe are the wrong shape or too small for Him to enter. Peering through this sieve, He can latch onto our kind alone because our life force is the strongest of all—we are the only ones He can track. Or perhaps we are the only ones who can squeeze in and out through the sieve, alive."

Alive. I recall the shining wind, the pain of inversion. "If He . . . if the floodwaters were to pour into our world unhindered, would they drown it?"

The Wise One loops onto himself, tightens the knot. "Drown it. Or leaven its life to a higher level. No one knows."

"If so, why had the Boy been put in danger?"

"So many answers. Perhaps you only know but a small part of His plan. Perhaps His plan makes no sense. Perhaps He was testing you, not the Boy. Perhaps He was testing His other messenger. Perhaps—"

How crushing, how unrelenting is the water!

"You can see for yourself, discoverer. You can enter the Boy and find the answer."

Ripples in the lake, ripples in my vision. Spots of darkness, as if pores are widening in the sieve of the world.

"Enter the Boy? Possess him? What if I hurt him?"

"What does it matter if you do? Are you afraid of your Master's wrath? Know yourself, messenger, then maybe you'll know your Master—"

I am already shooting up, shearing the walls of the gorge off, sending shreds of worm flesh tumbling into abyss. I flee, chased by the greatest fear I've ever felt—of waters rushing in.

. . . An ocean, a sky. I float in between, a listless island. If His purpose was to tap into humanity in bypass of me and my kind, then I have made Him fail. His Son is not really His. He is mine, too. When will He learn it? How will He punish us?

I spend most of the next sixteen years watching over the Boy, afraid to see signs of my Master's plan, signs of the other messenger; afraid that my Master will pull me away from the Boy. Afraid to enter the Boy and see the answer.

Every once in a while I visit his mother in what I now call my human-form-for-Maria. That's the only human form I know. I reveal my presence with a white lily, and each time she blushes, finding it. She nuzzles the petals, her eyes searching for my shape. "Gabriel, you silly man," she sometimes chastises me, "It's winter!"

I like it when she sits me to a bowl of pottage or tells me about her day. When I listen to her, the words of the Wise One become mute pebbles, a handful among many. I can throw them away. Sometimes she wonders what future holds for the Boy. I say I do not know.

But without her, worry gnaws at me, and the Wise One's words come alive. If only I could peek inside the Boy, just once, then I would know what he is capable of! I am tempted, oh so tempted! One day I find him at the sea shore, mending a boat. Alone. I succumb to temptation, I take possession of him.

It feels almost familiar, as if he is still an unborn child. But there is something—something that grinds at me. A dry, rushed patter—his heart does not beat, it speaks in tongues. A tangle that draws ever tighter as if devouring itself from the inside out. Suddenly, the Boy's body slams the sand. He twists and flips like the fish he catches; acid and bile surge the wrong way through his gut. Scared, I exit him.

What have I done?!

He lies flat, his eyes and mouth are frosted with sand, his stomach is deflated and droopy on the rack of his pelvis and ribs. But he comes to by the time I summon Maria to the scene. I have no courage to tell her I may have caused his seizure. I keep a tight watch, pondering the nature of the tangle inside him, but nothing else happens, and I am almost relieved.

One day I visit again, and Maria and I are kneeling by her hearth, she is kindling a fire, I pass wood shavings and twigs to her so she could arrange them in the way she likes. Our heads almost touch. She tells me that she was such a confused and selfish little girl *back in the day,* that she did not think with her head, and that she cannot believe how bold—and casual—she was with me. But when she lifts her head to glance at me, her blue-green eyes are shining and I know she does not regret a single thing.

The Boy picks up on her smile when he walks in on us. He must not have seen this kind of smile ever on her face. He looks stern. "Who is this, Mother?"

"That's Gabriel, remember? He's known you since you were that small. He is watching over us. He's a good friend." She is blushing.

When the Boy leaves, she measures me head to toe. "Perhaps you could age your appearance. You look much too young next to me. You're still the young lover that you've . . . You look my son's age! It's just not—proper, and more so since I'm now a widow. It's been years, Gabriel, don't you realize?"

"You don't change," I mutter.

She shakes her head. "Oh but I do!" There is a shadow of a smile on her face, and a slight frown. I remember what this one means.

A year after this, the Boy leaves home. He's been moody and withdrawn ever since his seizure and he's hardly spoken to anyone lately. That's what Maria tells me when I come to see her. I say I don't know what it means, if anything, and she becomes angry with me. "Only you can be so blind, Gabriel! I have to tell you this: I used to think sometimes—and *this* makes me wonder again—that you are, you know, *simple*. The way you don't have an understanding of certain things . . . I just don't know!" She wells up and walks away from me. She hasn't even noticed my new, meticulously age-adjusted human-form-for-Maria.

I am not a fool. I understand what it all means. Worse yet—I may have caused it by entering the Boy. I track him down in the high desert. At first I still hope that he will turn around, or pass through the dead lands and be on his way. Instead, he finds himself an overhang of a rock on a small plateau and settles in.

The cavity he has chosen has a small hollow, so I make sure it is always filled with water. The day he finishes up his last ration, I leave a loaf of bread at the edge of his shelter.

He does not touch it, he throws it off the cliff. And the new one the next day, and another one after that. On the fifth day he flings his fist into the air and cries out, "Stop tempting me!"

Fear fills me up, fear like dead-water of the Wise One's gorge. The self-devouring tangle, the dry patter instead of heartbeat. The purpose of my Master has woken up. My Boy is listening to the message.

The next few days he still meanders around in search of food and I try to sneak it onto his path, but he rejects anything more than a dead copperhead as suspiciously convenient, thus a temptation. Then he just sits cross legged at the lip of his cave and stares into space. His head quivers from time to time, as if about to lose its balance on the weak stem of his neck.

I must save him. I must get through to him.

I take him by the shoulders and lift him into the air. "Please do not listen to Him who dwells on *The Other Side of Things*. He does not care about you. You are just a tool to Him, a vessel. He wants this world and He wants to enter it through you, just as He used to want to enter it through me!"

The Boy's eyes dart, hazy with delirium. I shake him by the shoulders. "Please, please hear me out!"

"Be gone with you," he pushes past his cracked lips.

"I am your guardian, I've watched over you since before you were born. Ask your mother. Just let me take you to your mother and she will tell you! I am Gabriel!"

"No! Don't touch her! Stay away from us!" He fights me now, kicks, scratches at me.

I lift him up and up into the sky. We fly. Higher, faster. Shreds of clouds tumbleweed past us. "Look around, am I not real? Am I not holding you? Look down. Will you not fall if not for me? I am here, while He is not. *I* am holding you, not Him. Do you want me to let you go to prove it? Do you think He'll catch you? Because He won't! He can't! Say a word and fall, if you want, fall and break upon the ground because He won't be there to support you!"

Clawing, panting, the Boy chants, "Kill me if you must, but I shall not put the Lord my God to the test—"

Higher and higher. "Open your eyes and see the world as I show it to you. Have courage!" Mountains are wrinkles, rivers are veins, forests are fur. Lost on the Boy, the glory of the world; his eyes are squeezed shut and wind sucks tears out of them. His pallid lips move, though no sound is coming out. I plummet to a snow-crowned peak, I crash him onto a glacier, slippery, steep, blinding to the eye, razor sharp; he retches bile, he curls up like a grub, he gulps for air. I am no longer invisible, I cannot . . . temple stones and pale worms, gutted bullocks and throbbing veins, thunderclouds and obelisks, a fiery scale, a burning bush, a human-form-for-Maria, a shining jellyfish, pieces, pieces—I swarm in front of the Boy, I swell, "I care for you—I want to protect you—please, look at me—see me for what I am—I am your father—"

But he covers his eyes with his forearms, he crawls from me, away, away, he whimpers, choking on his puke, "Be gone, Satan, leave me alone!"

When the Boy loses consciousness, I fly him back to his home. It is night there, and I knock on the door before I leave him on the doorstep. I watch his family flutter about him, drag him inside. I do not reveal myself.

Almost immediately thereafter He who dwells on the *Other Side* draws me into His presence.

Fight! Grab onto air, resist! A pain of inversion. Fight, fight! A shining jellyfish. Helplessness. *Let me out* becomes *take me, I'm yours.* Pleasureshame. Loathingbliss. Caressinterrogation. Now He knows everything I've done. He knows.

And then—a thought slips through, a wrinkle in the shining wind. *You keep hanging on—stretched as you are, you are afraid to give it up and die a dense dot—*

Yes, my insides moan.

A comb of hatched lines—*The Other Side* frowns?—rakes me head to tail. He is releasing me and I am collapsing, about to burst through my own tail-end and into a pore of the world's sieve; but even as I do it, I catch a glimpse of something I am not supposed to know about Him. A weakness.

Growling, I fall flat onto the ground of my world.

• • •

I learn that I have been kept away for ten years. The Boy has disciples now, followers. Crowds gather to hear him preach. He is rumored to make dead humans walk and turn things into other things. Is he capable of it now? Or has *the other* messenger been helping him? The Boy has come into Jerusalem and the capital is ready to boil over.

The Boy is arrested.

I know—He who dwells on *The Other Side* made sure I do—that He has devised to kill the Boy, discard him as faulty, because the Boy is not His son. Because, not being His son, the Boy has misread the message.

Misunderstood it, garbled it up. No wonder—the Boy's *other* father is a *simple one.*

He who dwells wants me to know His plan and yet be unable to foil it. As I rush to the execution site to rescue my Boy, someone dark rises to stop me. One of my kind, but bigger than me. A wild one, crazy for his Master's caress. More than an Ur-Ag-ghel, worse than an Ur-Ag-ghel. The shadow messenger, the snarling dog, the hurricane. Beelzebub.

We clash.

All I want is to claw my way to my Boy's cross, all he wants is to keep me away. He drags me across half the world, slams me into mountaintops, tangles me in the roots of continents deep underwater. We tear pieces out of each other, we bleed memories and thoughts.

It may have been days. We've worn each other out, we are both stuck inside Earth, stranded in its vein-work, mired in its black, tarry blood; he is locked in on me, leeching my life away, and I am gnawing at him, eviscerating his life. The degradation of our fight is almost complete, we are almost one, a *killervictim,* a hideous creature born of hatred; our joined flesh jerks and shudders.

I win by a thread. That's how little is enough to unbalance a scale on the finger of the Universe. It takes me another eternity to extricate myself from the ground, and from my victim's flesh. When I drag myself to the cross, it's over.

I find my son a few days later—they sealed him in a crypt. I search for signs of life. Any life. My life-force. My Master's purpose. Human warm-churning. There is none. I take his body to the mountain glacier we have been to. I make him a tomb of ice and granite.

They say, while on the cross, he cried out, "Father, why have you forgotten me?" I will never know if it was me he called for. But I know that I have not come.

What is love?

Leaving white lilies in the places our son has spent his last days in, knowing that she will be there, she will come upon them. Leaving lilies even though I know they fit no longer, they are ridiculous, dated, outrageous—knowing all that and still not being able to stop, because this is the only language of speaking to her heart, that I know. *My Master never loved you. I do.*

What is love?

I stand in a grove. Lilies everywhere, their heavy fragrance mixes with twilight. "Joshua?" she calls in a breaking voice. "Son?" Too little light to see well, but I am just as culpable—she wants it so much that my body can't help but assume the resemblance. She runs towards me but the closer she gets, the less believing she is. "Gabriel? . . .No. You don't! Stop it, stop it now!" She groans and swings her fists, hits me in the chest, face.

"I am so sorry," I whisper, "So sorry."

Not for my failure to save him. For that—no word *sorry* is even allowed. I am sorry that my human-form-for-you is so easily mistaken for our son, I just wanted you to see what you yearned to see—just for one moment—I thought—yes, it is callow and cruel of me, you are right, I *am* simple, I am Gabriel-the-silly-man.

"You left us," she sobs, "you've abandoned us for ten years! How could you?"

What is love?

Our son is dead, we both know it. He has been killed because of something we did thirty three years ago. Our son's followers keep seeing signs of his resurrection, they may have glimpsed my shape, wandered into my stubborn lilies. Soon neither she, nor I can stop the legend from forming. It will gain a meaning of its own, a message that neither she nor I will recognize though it will hardly matter; nothing we will or will not do will change its course.

What is love?

I will dote on her till the end of her days. There will be more tears and accusations. Guilt. Our life will be bitter, but not all the time. Sometimes there will be a shadow of a smile and only a slight frown to go along with it. "We've come a long way, you and I, haven't we?" *Yes, we have.*

Fairness is made out of time. When Maria passes away, I will be free to fight and die. I know this much: the One who kills His son because he has got His message wrong, knows no love.

When You draw me in one more time—even if I have to kill every mature one of my kind to force You to turn to me as the only suitable messenger, because You will want one, You cannot help it—

When You do it, when I am stretched on *The Other Side*—breaking off the attachment to my entry point will kill me but that's not all. I know Your weakness, Master. The scar left of my ripped umbilicus will shut the pores of my world. You will never be able to reach into it again.

All You will be left with, to contemplate till the end of eternity, will be a dense dot, blown about ceaselessly, aimlessly. A bitter little residue of me.

A Jar of Goodwill

TOBIAS S. BUCKELL

Points On A Package

You keep a low profile when you're in oxygen debt. Too much walking about just exacerbates the situation anyway. So I was nervous when a stationeer appeared at my cubby and knocked on the door.

I slid out and stood in front of the polished, skeletal robot.

"Alex Mosette?" it asked.

There was no sense in lying. The stationeer had already scanned my face. It was just looking for voice print verification. "Yes, I'm Alex," I said.

"The harbormaster wants to see you."

I swallowed. "He could have sent me a message."

"I am here to *escort* you." The robot held out a tinker-toy arm, digits pointed along the hallway.

Space in orbit came at a premium. Bottom-rung types like me slept in cubbies stacked ten high along the hallway. On my back in the cubby, watching entertainment shuffled in from the planets, they made living on a space station sound exotic and exciting.

It was if you were further up the rung. I'd been in those rooms: places with wasted space. Furniture. Room to stroll around in.

That was exotic.

Getting space in outer space was far down my list of needs.

First was air. Then food.

Anything else was pure luxury.

The harbormaster stared out into space, and I silently waited at the door to Operations, hoping that if I remained quiet he wouldn't notice.

Ops hung from near the center of the megastructure of the station. A blister stuck on the end of a long tunnel. You could see the station behind us: the miles-long wheel of exotic metals rotating slowly.

No gravity in Ops, or anywhere in the center. Spokes ran down from the wheel to the center, and the center was where ships docked and were serviced and so on.

So I hung silently in the air, long after the stationeer flitted off to do the harbormaster's bidding, wondering what happened next.

"You're overdrawn," the harbormaster said after a needle-like ship with long feathery vanes slipped underneath us into the docking bays.

He turned to face me, even though his eyes had been hollowed out long ago. Force of habit. His real eyes were now every camera, or anything mechanical that could see.

The harbormaster moved closer. The gantry around him was motorized, a long arm moving him anywhere he wanted in the room.

Hundreds of cables, plugged into his scalp like hair, bundled and ran back along the arm of the gantry. Hoses moved effluvia out. More hoses ran purified blood, and other fluids, back in.

"I'm sorry," I stammered. "Traffic is light. And requests have dropped off. I've taken classes. Even language lessons . . . " I stopped when I saw the wizened hand raise, palm up.

"I know what you've been doing." The harbormaster's sightless sockets turned back to the depths of space outside. The hardened skin of his face showed few emotions, his artificial voice was toneless. "You would not have been allowed to overdraw if you hadn't made good faith efforts."

"For which," I said, "I am enormously appreciative."

"That ship that just arrived brings with it a choice for you," the harbormaster continued without acknowledging what I'd just said. "I cannot let you overdraw any more if you stay on station, so I will have to put you into hibernation. To pay for hibernation and your air debt I would buy your contract. You'd be woken for guaranteed work. I'd take a percentage. You could buy your contract back out, once you had enough liquidity."

That was exactly what I'd been dreading. But he'd indicated an alternate. "My other option?"

He waved a hand, and a holographic image of the ship I'd just seen coming in to dock hung in the air. "They're asking for a professional Friend."

"For their ship?" Surprise tinged my question. I wasn't crew material. I'd been shipped frozen to the station, just another corpsicle. People like me didn't stay awake for travel. Not enough room.

The harbormaster shrugged pallid shoulders. "They will not tell me why. I had to sign a nondisclosure agreement just to get them to tell me what they wanted."

I looked at the long ship. "I'm not a fuckbot. They know that, right?"

"They know that. They reiterated that they do *not* want sexual services."

"I'll be outside the station. Outside your protection. It could still be what they want."

"That is a risk. How much so, I cannot model for you." The harbormaster snapped his fingers, and the ship faded away. "But the contractors have extremely high reputational scores on past business dealings. They are freelance scientists: biology, botany, and one linguist."

So they probably didn't want me as a pass-around toy.

Probably.

"Rape amendments to the contract?" I asked. I was going to be on a ship, unthawed, by myself, with crew I'd never met. I had to think about the worst.

"Prohibitive. Although, accidental loss of life is not quite as high, which means I'd advise lowering the former so that there is no temptation to murder you after a theoretical rape to evade the higher contract payout."

"Fuck," I sighed.

"Would you like to peruse their reputation notes?" the harbormaster asked. And for a moment, I thought maybe the harbormaster sounded concerned.

No. He was just being fair. He'd spent two hundred years of bargaining with ships for goods, fuel, repair, services. Fair was built-in, the half-computer half-human creature in front of me was all about fair. Fair got you repeat business. Fair got you a wide reputation.

"What's the offer?"

"Half a point on the package," the harbormaster said.

"And we don't know what the package is, or how long it will take . . . or anything." I bit my lip.

"They assured me that half a point would pay off your debt and then some. It shouldn't take more than a year."

A year. For half a percent. Half a percent of what? It could be cargo they were delivering. Or, seeing as it was a crew of scientists, it could be some project they were working on.

All of which just raised more questions.

Questions I wouldn't have answers to unless I signed up. I sighed. "That's it, then? No loans? No extensions?"

The harbormaster sighed. "I answer to the Gheda shareholders who built and own this complex. I have already stretched my authority to give you a month's extension. The debt *has* to be called. I'm sorry."

I looked out at the darkness of space out beyond Ops. "Shit choices either way."

The harbormaster said nothing.

I folded my arms. "Do it."

Journey by Gheda

The docking arms had transferred the starship from the center structure's incoming docks down a spoke to a dock on one of the wheels. The entire ship, thanks to being spun along with the wheel of the station, had gravity.

The starship was a quarter of a mile long. Outside: sleek and burnished smooth by impacts with the scattered dust of space at the stunning speeds it achieved. Inside, I realized I'd boarded a creaky, old, outdated vehicle.

Fiberwire spilled out from conduits, evidence of crude repair jobs. Dirt and grime clung to nooks and crannies. The air smelled of sweat and worst.

A purple-haired man with all-black eyes met me at the airlock. "You are the Friend?" he asked. He carried a large walking stick with him.

"Yes." I let go of the rolling luggage behind me and bowed. "I'm Alex."

He bowed back. More extravagantly than I did. Maybe even slightly mockingly. "I'm Oslo." Every time he shifted his walking stick, tiny grains of sand inside rattled and shifted about. He brimmed with impatience, and some regret in the crinkled lines of his eyes. "Is this everything?"

I looked back at the single case behind me. "That is everything."

"Then welcome aboard," Oslo said, as the door to the station clanged shut. He raised the stick, and a flash of light blinded me.

"You should have taken a scan of me before you shut the door," I said. The stick was more than it seemed. Those tiny rustling grains were generators, harnessing power for whatever tools were inside the device via kinetic motion. He turned around and started to walk away. I hurried to catch up.

Oslo smiled, and I noticed tiny little fangs under his lips. "You are who you say you are, so everything ended up okay. Oh, and for protocol, the others aren't much into it either, by the way. Now, for my own edification, you are a hermaphrodite, correct?"

I flushed. "I am what we Friends prefer to call bi-gendered, yes." Where the hell was Oslo from? I was having trouble placing his cultural conditionings and how I might adapt to interface with them. He was very direct, that was for sure.

This gig might be more complicated than I thought.

"Your Friend training: did it encompass Compact cross-cultural training?"

I slowed down. "In theory," I said slowly, worried about losing the contract if they insisted on having someone with Compact experience.

Oslo's regret dripped from his voice and movements. Was it regret that I didn't have the experience? Would I lose the contract, minutes into getting it? Or just regret that he couldn't get someone better? "But you've never Friended an actual Compact drone?"

I decided to tell the truth. A gamble. "No."

"Too bad." The regret sloughed off, to be replaced with resignation. "But we can't poke around asking for Friends with that specific experience, or one of our competitors might put two and two together. I recommend you brush up on your training during the trip out."

He stopped in front of a large, metal door. "Where are we going?" I asked.

"Here is your room for the next three days." Oslo opened the large door to a five-by-seven foot room with a foldout bunk bed.

My heart skipped a beat, and I put aside the fact that Oslo had avoided the question. "That's mine?"

"Yes. And the air's billed with our shipping contract, so you can rip your sensors off. There'll be no accounting until we're done."

I got the sense Oslo knew what it was like to be in debt. I stepped into the room and turned all the way around. I raised my hands, placing them on each wall, and smiled.

Oslo turned to go.

"Wait," I said. "The harbormaster said you were freelance scientists. What do you do?"

"I'm the botanist," Oslo said. "Meals are in the common passenger's galley. The crew of this ship is Gheda, of course, don't talk to or interact with them if you can help it. You know why?"

"Yes." The last thing you wanted to do was make a Gheda think you were wandering around, trying to figure out secrets about their ships, or technology. I would stay in the approved corridors and not interact with them.

The door closed in my suite, and I sat down with my small travel case, no closer to understanding what was going on than I had been on the station.

I faced the small mirror by an even smaller basin and reached for the strip of black material stuck to my throat. Inside it, circuitry monitored my metabolic rate, number of breaths taken, volume of air taken in, and carbon dioxide expelled. All of it reported back to the station's monitors, constantly calculating my mean daily cost.

It made a satisfying sound as I ripped it off.

"Gheda are Gheda," I said later in the ship's artificial, alien day over reheated turkey strips in the passenger's galley. We'd undocked. The old ship had shivered itself up to speed. "But Gheda flying around in a beat-up old starship, willing to take freelance scientists out to some secret destination: these are dangerous Gheda."

Oslo had a rueful smile as he leaned back and folded his arms. "Cruzie says that our kind used to think our corporations were rapacious and evil before first contact. No one expected aliens to demand royalty payments for technology usage that had been independently discovered by us because the Gheda had previously patented that technology."

"I know. They hit non-compliant areas with asteroids from orbit." Unable to pay royalties, entire nations had collapsed into debtorship. "Who's Cruzie?"

Oslo grimaced. "You'll meet her in two days. Our linguist. Bit of a historian, too. Loves old Earth shit."

I frowned at his reaction. Conflicted, but with somewhat warm pleasure when he thought about her. A happy grimace. "She's an old friend of yours?"

"Our parents were friends. They loved history. The magnificence of Earth. The legend that was. Before it got sold around. Before the Diaspora." That grimace again. But no warmth there.

"You don't agree with their ideals?" I guessed.

I guessed well. Oslo sipped at a mug of tea, and eyed me. "I'm not your project, Friend. Don't dig too deep, because you just work for me. Save your empathy and psychiatry for the real subject. Understand?"

Too far, I thought. "I'm sorry. And just what is my project? We're away from the station now; do you think you can risk being open with me?"

Oslo set his tea down. "Clever. Very clever, Friend. Yes, I was worried about bugs. We've found a planet, with a unique ecosystem. There may be patentable innovations."

I sat, stunned. Patents? I had points on the package. If I got points on a patent on some aspect of an alien biological system, a Gheda-approved patent, I'd be rich.

Not just rich, but like, nation-rich.

Oslo sipped at his tea. "There's only one problem," he said. "There may be intelligent life on the planet. If it's intelligent, it's a contact situation, and we have to turn it over to the Gheda. We get a fee, but no taste of the real game. We fail to report a contact situation and the Gheda find out, it's going to be a nasty scene. They'll kill our families, or even people you know, just to make the point that their interstellar law is inviolate. We have to file a claim the moment of discovery."

I'd heard hesitation in his voice. "You haven't filed yet, have you?"

"I bet all the Gheda business creatures love having you watch humans they're settling a contract with, making sure they're telling the truth, you there to brief them on what their facial expressions are really showing."

That stung. "I'd do the same for any human. And it isn't just contracts. Many hire me to pay attention to them, to figure them out, anticipate their needs."

Oslo leered. "I'll bet."

I wasn't a fuckbot. I deflected the leering. "So tell me, Oslo, why I'm risking my life, then?"

"We haven't filed yet because we honestly can't fucking figure out if the aliens are just dumb creatures, or intelligences like us," Oslo said.

The Drone

"Welcome to the Screaming Kettle," said the woman who grabbed my bag without asking. She had dark brown skin and eyes, and black hair. Tattoos covered every inch of skin free of her clothing. Words in scripts and languages that I didn't recognize. "The Compact Drone is about to dock as well, we need you ready for it. Let's get your stuff stowed."

We walked below skylights embedded in the top of the research station. A planet hung there: green and yellow and patchy. It looked like it was diseased with mold. "Is that Ve?" I asked.

"Oslo get you up to speed?" the woman asked.

"Somewhat. You're Cruzie, right?"

"Maricruz. I'm the linguist. I guess . . . you're stuck here with us. You can call me Cruzie too." We stopped in front of a room larger than the one on the ship. With two beds.

I looked at the beds. "I'm comfortable with a cubby, if it means getting my own space," I said.

There was far more space here, vastly so. And yet, I was going to have to share it? It rankled. Even at the station, I hadn't had to share my space. This shoved me up against my own cultural normative values. Even in the most packed places in space, you needed a cubby of one's own.

"You're here to Friend the Compact Drone," Cruzie said. "It'll need companionship at all times. Their contract requires it for the Drone's mental stability."

"Oslo didn't tell me this." I pursed my lips. A fairly universal display of annoyance.

And Cruzie read that well enough. "I'm sorry," she said. But it was a lie as well. She was getting annoyed and impatient. But screw it, as Oslo pointed out: I wasn't there for their needs. "Oslo wants us to succeed more than anything. Unlike his parents, he's not much into the glory that was humankind. He knows the only way we'll ever not be freelancers, scrabbling around for intellectual scraps found in the side alleys of technology for something we can use without paying the Gheda for the privilege, is to hit something big."

"So he lied to me." My voice remained flat.

"He left out truths that would have made you less willing to come."

"He lied."

Cruzie shut the door to my room. "He gave you points on the package, Friend. We win big, you do your job, you'll never have to check the balance on your air for the rest of your damned life. I heard you were in air debt, right?"

She'd put me well in place. We both knew it. Cruzie smiled, a gracious winner's smile.

"Incoming!" Someone yelled from around the bend in the corridor.

"I'm not going to fuck the Drone," I told her levelly.

Cruzie shrugged. "I don't care what you do or don't do, as long as the Drone stays mentally stable and does its job for us. Points on the package, Alex. Points."

Airlock alarms flashed and warbled, and the hiss of compressed air filled the antechamber

"The incoming pod's not much larger than a cubby sleeper," Oslo said, his purple hair waving about as another burst of compressed air filled the antechamber. He smiled, fangs out beyond his lips. "It's smaller than the lander we have for exploring Ve ourselves, if we ever need to get down there. Can you imagine the ride? The only non-Gheda way of traveling!"

The last member of the team joined us. She looked over at me and nodded. Silvered electronic eyes glinted in the flash of the airlock warning lights. She flexed the jet black fingers of her artificial right hand absentmindedly as she waited for the doors to open. She ran the fingers of a real hand over her shaved head, then put them back in her utility jacket, covered with what seemed like hundreds of pockets and zippers.

"That's Kepler," Cruzie said.

The airlock doors opened. A thin, naked man stumbled out, dripping goopy blue acceleration gel with each step.

For a moment his eyes flicked around, blinking.

Then he started screaming.

Oslo, Kepler, and Cruzie jumped back half a step from the naked man's arms. I stepped forward. "It's not fear, it's relief."

The man grabbed me in a desperate hug, clinging to me, his hands patting my face, shoulders, as if reassuring himself someone was really standing in front of him. "It's okay," I whispered. "You've been in there by yourself for days, with no contact of any sort. I understand."

He was shivering in my grip, but I kept patting his back. I urged him to feel the press of contact between us. And reassurance. Calm.

Eventually he calmed down, and then slowly let go of me.

"What's your name?" I asked.

"Beck."

"Welcome aboard, Beck," I said, looking over his shoulder at the scientists who looked visibly relieved.

First things first.

Beck got to the communications room. Back and forth verification on an uplink, and he leaned back against the chair in relief.

"There's an uplink to the Hive," he said. "An hour of lag time to get as far back as the home system, but I'm patched in."

He tapped metal inserts on the back of his neck. His mind plugged in to the communications network, talking all the way back to the asteroid belt in the mother system, where the Compact's Hive thrived. Back there, Beck would always be in contact with it without a delay. In instant symbiosis with a universe of information that the Compact offered.

A hive-mind of people, your core self subjugated to the greater whole.

I shivered.

Beck never moved more than half a foot away from me. Always close enough to touch. He kept reaching out to make sure I was there, even though he could see me.

After walking around the research station for half an hour, we returned to our shared room.

He sat on his bed, suddenly apprehensive. "You're the Friend, correct?"

"Yes."

"I'm lonely over here. Can you sleep by me?"

I walked over and sat next to him. "I won't have sex with you. That's not why I'm here."

"I'm chemically neutered," Beck said as we curled up on the bed. "I'm a drone."

As we lay there, I imagined thousands of Becks sleeping in rows in Hive dorms, body heat keeping the rooms warm.

Half an hour later he suddenly sighed, like a drug addict getting a hit. "They hear me," he whispered. "I'm not alone."

The Compact had replied to him.

He relaxed.

The room filled with a pleasant lavender scent. Was it something he'd splashed on earlier? Or something a Compact drone released to indicate comfort?

What's Human?

"That," Kepler said, leaning back in a couch before a series of displays, "is one of our remote-operated vehicles. We call them urchins."

In the upper right hand screen before her, a small sphere with hundreds of wriggling legs rotated around. Then it scrabbled off down what looked like a dirt path.

Cruzie swung into a similar couch. "We sterilize them in orbit, then drop them down encased in a heatshield. It burns away, then they drop down out of the sky with a little burst of a rocket to slow down enough."

I frowned at one of the screens. Everything was shades of green and gray and black. "Is that night vision?"

Oslo laughed. "It's Ve. The atmosphere is chlorinated. Green mists. Grey shadows. And black plants."

The trees had giant, black leaves hanging low to the ground. Tubular trunks sprouted globes that spouted mist randomly as the urchin brushed past.

"Ve's a small planet," Kepler said. "Low gravity, but with air similar to what you would have seen on the mother world."

"Earth," Oslo corrected.

"But unlike the mother world," Kepler continued, "Ve has high levels of chlorine. Somewhere in its history, a battle launched among the plants. Instead of specializing in oxygen to kill off the competition, and adapting to it over time, plant life here turned to chlorine as a weapon. It created plastics out of the organic compounds available to it, which is doable in a chlorine-heavy base atmosphere, though remarkable. And the organic plastics also handle photosynthesis. A handy trick. If we can patent it."

On the screen the urchin rolled to a slow stop. Cruzie leaned forward. "Now if we can just figure out if *those* bastards are really building a civilization, or just random dirt mounds . . . "

Paused at the top of a ridge, the urchin looked at a clearing in the black-leafed forest. Five pyramids thrust above the foliage around the clearing.

"Can you get closer?" Beck asked, and I jumped slightly. He'd been so silent, watching all this by my side.

"Not from here," Kepler said. "There's a big dip in altitude between here and the clearing."

"And?" Beck stared at the pyramids on the screen.

"Our first couple weeks here we kept driving the urchins into low lying areas, valleys, that sort of thing. They kept dying on us. We figure the chlorine and acids sink low into the valleys. Our equipment can't handle it."

Beck sat down on the nearest couch to Kepler, and looked over the interface. "Take the long way around then, I'll look at your archives while you do so. Wait!"

I saw it too. A movement through the black, spiky bushes. I saw my first alien creature scuttle around, antennae twisting as it moved along what looked like a path.

"They look like ants," I blurted out.

"We call them Vesians. But yes, ants the size of a small dog," Oslo said. "And not really ants at all. Just exoskeletons, black plastic, in a similar structure. The handiwork of parallel evolution."

More Vesians appeared carrying leaves and sticks on their backs.

And gourds.

"Now that's interesting," Beck said.

"It doesn't mean they're intelligent," Beck said later, lying in the bunk with me next to him. We both stared up at the ceiling. He rolled over and looked at me. "The gourds grow on trees. They use them to store liquids. Inside those pyramids."

We were face to face, breathing each other's air. Beck had no personal space, and I had to fight my impulse to pull back away from him.

My job was now to facilitate. Make Beck feel at home.

Insect hives had drones that could exist away from the hive. A hive needed foragers, and defenders. But the human Compact only existed in the asteroid belt of the mother system.

Beck was a long way from home.

With the lag, he would be feeling cut off and distant. And for a mind that had always been in the embrace of the hive, this had to be hard for him.

But Beck offered the freelance scientists a link into the massive computational capacity of the entire Compact. They'd contracted it to handle the issue they couldn't figure out quickly: were the aliens intelligent or not?

Beck was pumping information back all the way back to the mother system, so that the Compact could devote some fraction of a fraction of its massed computing ability to the issue. The minds of all its connected citizenry. Its supercomputers. Maybe even, it was rumored, artificial intelligences.

"But if they are intelligent?" I asked. "How do you prove it?"

Beck cocked his head. "The Compact is working on it. Has been ever since the individuals here signed the contract."

"Then why are you out here?"

"Yes . . . " He was suddenly curious in me now, remembering I was a distinct individual, lying next to him. I wasn't of the Compact. I wasn't another drone.

"I'm sorry," I said. "I shouldn't have asked."

"It was good you asked." He flopped over to stare at the ceiling again. "You're right, I'm not entirely needed. But the Compact felt it was necessary."

I wanted to know why. But I could feel Beck hesitate. I held my breath.

"You are a Friend. You've never broken contract. The Compact ranks you very highly." Beck turned back to face me. "We understand that what I tell you will never leave this room, and since I debugged it, it's a safe room. What do you think it takes to become a freelance scientist in this hostile universe?"

I'd been around enough negotiating tables. A good Friend, with the neural modifications and adaptive circuitry laced into me from birth, I could read body posture, micro-expressions, skin flush, heart rate, in a blink of the eye. I made a hell of a negotiating tool. Which was usually exactly what Gheda wanted: a read on their human counterparts.

And I had learned the ins and outs of my clients businesses quick as well. I knew what the wider universe was like while doing my job.

"Oslo has pent-up rage," I whispered. "His family is obsessed with the Earth as it used to be. Before the Gheda land purchases. He wants wealth, but that's not all, I think. Cruzie holds herself like she has military bearing, though she hides it. Kepler, I don't know. I'm guessing you will tell me they have all worked as weapons manufacturers or researchers of some sort?"

Beck nodded. "Oslo and his sister London are linked to a weaponized virus that was released on a Gheda station. Cruzie fought with separatists in Columbia. Kepler is a false identity. We haven't cracked her yet."

I looked at the drone. There was no deceit in him. He stated these things as facts. He was a drone. He didn't need to question the information given to him.

"Why are you telling me all this?"

He gestured at the bunk. "You're a professional Friend. You're safe. You're here. And I'm just a drone. We're just a piece of all this."

And then he moved to spoon against the inside of my stomach. Two meaningless, tiny lives inside a cold station, far away from where they belonged.

"And because," he added in a soft voice, "I think that these scientists are desperate enough to fix a problem if it occurs."

"Fix a problem?" I asked, wrapping my arms around him.

"I think the Vesians are intelligent, and I think Kepler and Oslo plan to do something to them if, or when, it's confirmed, so that they can keep patent rights."

I could suddenly hear every creak, whisper, and whistle in the station as I tensed up.

"I will protect you if I can. Right now we're just delaying as long as we can. Mainly I'm trying to stop Cruzie from figuring out the obvious, because if she confirms they're really intelligent, then Oslo and Kepler will make their move and do something to the Vesians. We're not sure what."

"You said delaying. Delaying until what?" I asked, a slight quaver in my voice that I found I couldn't control.

"Until the Gheda get here," Beck said with a last yawn. "That's when it all gets really complicated." His voice trailed off as he said that, and he fell asleep.

I lay there, awake and wide-eyed.

I finally reached up to my neck and scratched at the band of skin where the air monitor patch had once been stuck.

Points on nothing was still just . . . nothing.

But could I rat out my contract? My role as a Friend? Could I help Oslo and Kepler kill an alien race?

Things had gotten very muddy in just a few minutes. I felt trapped between the hell of an old life and the hell of a horrible new one.

"What's a human being?" I asked Beck over lunch.

"Definitions vary," he replied.

"You're a drone: bred to act, react, and move within a shared neural environment. You serve the Compact. There's no queen, like a classic anthill or with bees. Your shared mental overmind makes the calls. So you have a say. A tiny say. You are human . . .-ish. Our ancestors would have questioned whether you were human."

Beck cocked his head and smiled. "And you?"

"Modified from birth to read human faces. Under contract for most of my life to Gheda, working to tell the aliens or other humans what humans are really thinking . . . they wouldn't have thought highly of me either."

"The Compact knows you reread your contract last night, after I fell asleep, and you used some rather complicated algorithms to game some scenarios."

I frowned. "So you're spying on us now."

"Of course. You're struggling with a gray moral situation."

"Which is?"

"The nature of your contract says you need to work with me and support my needs. But you're hired by the freelancers that I'm now in opposition to. As a Friend, a role and purpose burned into you just like being a drone is burned into me, do you warn *them*? Or do you stick by me? The contract allows for interpretations either way. And if you stick with me, it's doing so while knowing that I'm just a drone. A pawn that the Compact will use as it sees fit, for its own game."

"You left something out," I said.

"Neither you, nor I, are bred to care about Vesians," Beck said.

I got up and walked over to the large porthole. "I wonder if it wouldn't be better for them?"

"What would?"

184

"Whatever Kepler and Oslo want to do to them. Better to die now than to meet the Gheda. I can't imagine they'd ever want to become us."

Beck stood up. There was caution in his stance, as if he'd thought I had been figured out, but now wasn't sure. "I've got work to do. Stay here and finish your meal, Friend."

I looked down at the green world beneath, and jumped when a hand grabbed my shoulder. I could see gray words tattooed in the skin. "Cruzie?"

Her large brown eyes were filled with anger. "That son of a bitch has been lying to us," she said, pointing in the direction Beck had gone. "Come with me."

"The gourds," Cruzie said, pointing at a screen, and then looking at Beck. "Tell us about the gourds."

And Oslo grabbed my shoulder. "Watch the drone, sharp now. I want you to tell us what you see when he replies to us."

My contract would be clear there. I couldn't lie. The scientists owned the contract, and now that they'd asked directly for my services, I couldn't evade.

Points on the package, I thought in the far back of my mind.

I wasn't really human, was I? Not if I found the lure of eternal riches to be so great as to consider helping the freelancers.

"The Vesians have farms," Cruzie said. "But so do ants: they grow fungus. The Vesians have roads, but so do animals in a forest. They just keep walking over the same spots. Old Earth roads used to follow old animal paths. The Vesians have buildings, but birds build nests, ants build colonies, bees build hives. But language, that's so much rarer in the animal kingdom, isn't it, Beck?"

"Not really," the drone said calmly. "Primitive communication exists in animals. Including bees, which dance information. Dolphins squeak and whales sing."

"But none of them write it down," Cruzie grinned.

Oslo's squeezed my shoulder, hard. "The drone is mildly annoyed," I said. "And more than a little surprised."

Cruzie tapped on a screen. The inside of one of the pyramids appeared. It was a storehouse of some sort, filled with hundreds, maybe thousands, of the gourds I'd seen earlier that the Vesian had been transporting.

"Nonverbal creatures use scent. Just like ants on the mother planet. The Vesians use scents to mark territories their queens manage. And one of the things I started to wonder about, were these storage areas. What were they for? So I broke in, and I started breaking the gourds."

Beck stiffened. "He's not happy with this line of thought," I murmured.

"Thought so," Oslo said back, and nodded at Cruzie, who kept going.

"And whenever I broke a gourd, I found them empty. Not full of liquid, as Beck told us was likely. We originally thought they were for storage. An adaptive behavior. Or a sign of intelligence. Hard to say. Until I broke them all."

"They could have been empty, waiting to be sealed," Beck said tonelessly.

I sighed. "I'm sorry, Beck. I have to do this. He's telling the truth, Oslo. But misdirecting."

"I know he is," Cruzie said. "Because the Vesians swarmed the location with fresh gourds. There were chemical scents, traces laid down in the gourds before they were sealed. The Vesians examined the broken gourds, then filled the new ones with scents. I started examining the chemical traces, and found that each gourd replaced had the same chemical sequences sprayed on and stored as the ones I broke."

Beck's muscles tensed. Any human could see the stress now. I didn't need to say anything.

"They were like monks, copying manuscripts. Right, Beck?" Cruzie asked.

"Yes," Beck said.

"And the chemical markers, it's a language, right?" Kepler asked. I could feel the tension in her voice. It wasn't just disappointment building, but rage.

"It is." Beck stood up slowly.

"It took me days to realize it," Cruzie said. "And that, after the weeks I've been out here. The Compact spotted it right away, didn't it?"

Beck looked over at me, then back at Cruzie. "Yes. The Compact knows."

"Then what the hell is it planning to do?" Kepler moved in front of Beck, lips drawn back in a snarl.

"I'm just a drone," Beck said. "I don't know. But I can give you an answer in an hour."

For a second, everyone stood frozen. Oslo, brimming with hurt rage, staring at Beck. Kepler, moving from anger toward some sort of decision. Cruzie looked . . . triumphant. Oblivious to the real breaking developments in the air.

And I observed.

Like any good Friend.

Then a loud 'whooop whooop' startled us all out of our poses.

"What's that?" Cruzie asked, looking around.

"The Gheda are here," Oslo, Kepler, and Beck said at the same time.

The Path Less Traveled

"Call the vote," Oslo snapped.

Cruzie swallowed. I saw micro beads of sweat on the side of her neck. "Right now?"

"Gheda are inbound," Kepler said, her artificial eyes dark. I imagined she had them patched into the computers, looking at information from the station's sensors. "They'll be decelerating and matching orbit in hours. There's no time for debate, Cruzie."

"What we're about to do *is* something that requires debate. They're intelligent. We're proposing ripping that away over the next day with Kepler's tailored virus. They'll end up with a viral lobotomy, just smart enough we can claim their artifacts come from natural hive mind behavior. But we'll have stolen their culture. Their minds. Their history." Cruzie shook her head. "I know we said they're going to lose most of that when the Gheda arrive. But if we do this, we're worse than Gheda."

"Fucking hell, Cruzie!" Oslo snapped. "You're changing your mind *now*?"

"Oslo!" Cruzie held up her hands as if trying to ward off the angry words.

"You saw our mother planet," Oslo said. "The slums. The starvation. Gheda combat patrols. They owned *everyone*. If you didn't provide value, you were nothing. You *fought* the Sahara campaign, you attacked Abbuj station. How the fuck can you turn your back to all that?"

"I didn't turn my back, I wanted a different path," Cruzie said. "That's why we're here. With the money on the patents, we could change things . . . but what are we changing here if we're not all that better than the Gheda?"

"It's us or the fucking ants," Kepler said, voice suddenly level. "It's really that simple. Where are your allegiances?"

I bit my lip when I heard that.

"Cruzie . . . " I started to say.

She held a hand up and walked over to the console, her thumb held out. "It takes a unanimous vote to unleash the virus. This was why I insisted."

"You're right," Kepler said. I flinched. I could hear the hatred in her voice. She nodded at Oslo.

He raised his walking stick. The tiny grains inside rattled around, and then a jagged finger of energy leapt out and struck Cruzie in the small of her back.

Cruzie jerked around, arms flopping as she danced, then dropped to the ground. Oslo pressed the stick to her head and fired it again. Blood gushed from Cruzie's eye sockets as something inside her skull went 'pop.'

A wisp of smoke curled from her open mouth.

Oslo and Kepler put thumbs to the screens. "We have a unanimous vote now."

But a red warning sign flashed back at them. Beck relaxed slightly, a tiny curl of a smile briefly appearing.

Oslo raised his walking stick and pointed it at Beck. "Our communications are blocked."

"Yes," Beck said. "The Compact is voting against preemptive genocide."

For a split second, I saw the decision to kill Beck flit across Kepler's face. "If you kill him," I spoke up, "the Compact will spend resources hunting you two down. You can't enjoy your riches if you're dead."

Kepler nodded. "You're right." But she looked at me, a question on her face.

I shrugged. "If you're all dead, I don't have points on the package."

"Trigger them manually," Oslo said. "We'll bring the drone. We won't leave him up here to cause more trouble. Bring him, or her, or whatever the Friend calls itself as well. Your contract, Alex, is now to watch Beck."

We burned our way through the green atmosphere of Ve, the lander bucking and groaning, skin cracking as it weathered the heat of our reentry fireball.

From the tiny cramped cockpit I watched us part the clouds and spiral slowly down out of the sky as the wings unfurled from slots in the tear-drop sized vehicle's side. They started beating a complicated figure-eight motion.

Oslo aimed his walking stick at us when the lander touched down. "Put on your helmet, get out. Both of you."

We did so.

Heavy chlorine-rich mists swirled around, disturbed by our landing. Large puffball flowers spurted acid whenever touched by a piece of stray stirred-up debris, and the black, plastic leaves all around us bobbed gently in a low breeze.

Oslo and Kepler pulled a large pack out of the lander's cargo area. Long pieces of tubing. They set to building a freestanding antenna, piece by piece. I watched Beck. I couldn't see his face, but I could see his posture.

He was about to run. Which made no sense. Run where? On this world?

Within a few minutes Oslo and Kepler had snapped together a thirty-foot tall tower. I swallowed, and remained silent. It was a choice, a deliberate path. I broke my contract.

Oslo snapped a clip to the top of the tower, then unrolled a length of cable. He and Kepler used it to pull the super light structure up.

That was the moment Beck ran, as it hung halfway up to standing.

"Shit," Oslo cursed over the tiny speakers in our helmets, but he didn't drop the structure. "You've only got a couple hours of air you moron!"

The only response was Beck's heavy breathing.

When the antenna stood upright, Oslo approached me, the walking stick out. "You didn't warn us."

"He was wearing a spacesuit," I said calmly.

But I could see Oslo didn't believe me. His eyes creased and his fingers tightened. A bright explosion of pain ripped into me.

My vision cleared.

I was on my hands and feet, shaking with pain from the electrical discharge. A whirlwind of debris whipped around me. I looked up to see the lander lifting into the sky.

So that was it. I'd made my choice: to try and not be a monster.

And it had been in vain. The Vesians would be lobotomized by Kepler's virus. Beck would die. I would die.

I watched the lander beginning a wide spiral upward away from me. In a few seconds it would fire its rockets and climb for orbit.

In a couple hours, I would run out of air.

Four large gourds arced high over the black forest and slapped into the side of the lander. I frowned. At first, it looked like they had no effect. The lander kept spiraling up.

But then, it faltered.

The lander shook, and smoke spilled out of a crack in the side somewhere. It exploded, the fireball hanging in the sky.

"Get away from the antenna," Beck suddenly said. "It's next."

I ran without a second thought, and even as I got free of the clearing, gourds of acid hit the structure. The metal sizzled, foamed, and then began to melt.

A few seconds later, I broke out onto a dirt path where the catapults firing the gourds of acid had been towed into place.

Beck waited for me, surrounded by a crowd of Vesians. He wore only his helmet, he'd ripped his suit off. His skin bubbled from bad chemical burn blisters.

"The Vesians destroyed all the remote-operating vehicles with the virus in it," he said. "The queens have quarantined any Vesians near any area that had an ROV. The species will survive."

"You've been talking to them," I said. And then I thought back to the comforting smell in my room the first night Beck spent with me. "You're communicating with them. You warned them."

Beck held up his suit. "Yes. The Compact altered me to be an ambassador to them."

"Beck, how long can you survive in this environment?" I stared at his blistered skin.

"A year. Maybe. There will be another ready by then. Maybe a structure to live in. The Gheda will be here soon to bring air. The Compact has reached an agreement with them. The Vesian queens are agreeing to join the Compact. The Compact gets to extend out of the mother system, but only to Ve. In exchange, the Gheda get rights to all patentable discoveries made in the new ecosystem. They're particularly interested in plastic-based organic photosynthesis."

I collapsed to the ground, realizing that I would live. Beck sat next to me. A small Vesian, approached, a gourd in its mandibles. It set the organic, plastic bottle at my legs. "What's that?"

"A jar of goodwill," Beck said. "The Vesian queen of this area is thanking you."

I was still just staring at it two hours later as my air faded out, my vision blurred, and the Gheda lander finally reached us.

The harbormaster cocked his head. "You're back."

"I'm back," I said. Someone was unpacking my two bags. one of them carefully holding the Vesian 'gift.'

"I didn't think I'd ever see you again," the harbormaster said. "Not with a contract like that."

"It didn't work out." I looked out into the vacuum of space beyond us. "Certainly not for the people who hired me. Or me."

"You have a peripheral contract with the Compact. An all-you-can-breath line of credit on the station. You're not a citizen, but on perpetual retainer as the Compact's primary professional Friend for all dealings in this system. You did well enough."

I grinned. "Points on a package like what they offered me was a fairy tale. A fairy tale you'd have to be soulless to want to have come true."

"I'm surprised that you did not choose to join the Compact," the harbormaster said, looking closely at me. "It is a safe place for humans in this universe. Even as a peripheral for them, you could still be in danger during patent negotiations with Gheda."

"I know. But this is home. My home. I'm not a drone, I don't want to be one."

The harbormaster sighed. "You understand the station is my only love. I don't have a social circle. There is only the ebb and flow of this structure's health for me."

I smiled. "That's why I like you, harbormaster. You have few emotions. You are a fair dealer. You're the closest thing I have to family. You may even be the closest thing I have to a friend, friend with a lowercase 'f.'"

"You follow your contracts to the letter. I like that about you," the harbormaster said. "I'm glad you will continue on here."

Together we watched the needle-like ship that had brought me back home silently fall away from the station.

"The Compact purchased me a ten-by-ten room with a porthole," I said. "I don't have to come up here to sneak a look at the stars anymore."

The harbormaster sighed happily. "They're beautiful, aren't they? I think, we've always loved them, haven't we? Even before we were forced to leave the mother world."

"That's what the history books say," I said quietly over the sound of ducts and creaking station. "We dreamed of getting out here, to live among them. Dreamed of the wonders we'd see."

"The Gheda don't see the stars," the harbormaster said. "They have few portholes. Before I let the Gheda turn me into a harbormaster, I demanded the contract include this room."

"They don't see them the way we do," I agreed.

"They're not human," the harbormaster said.

"No, they're not." I looked out at the distant stars. "But then, few things are anymore."

The Gheda ship disappeared in a blinding flash of light, whipping through space toward its next destination

Futures in the Memories Market
NINA KIRIKI HOFFMAN

You can't do anything else when you emp one of Geeta Tilrassen's memory modules. Her senses seize you; you see through her eyes, taste with her tongue, hear with her ears. And touch? You've never felt air against your skin until you've felt it breathe across hers. In a desert environment, there's a sense of cinnamon in the air. When Geeta's on a water world, you feel the humidity as embrace instead of torture, as though you are constantly being kissed. Every module Geeta makes is fresh and innocent, and every time you use one, you feel as though it's the first time.

I've got one legitimate copy of a Geeta memod; I'm only allowed one at a time, and I've kept this one for a while. It's her visit to the Hallen people. Nothing very exciting happens. She walks into their village. (The red sand gets into your sandals, but instead of grinding against your feet or raising blisters, it's a pleasant friction.) The air smells of woodsmoke, charred flesh, and sage.

Hallen burrows are mostly underground, but they have built delicate aboveground structures of woven withies, beautiful as spider webs, with small crystals at the intersections that flare in the red sunlight.

The Hallen greet Geeta, draw her into one of the withy shelters, and give her the only thing it's safe for her to ingest from their cuisine, some kind of berry drink with bits of leaf in it. She drinks. The liquid is cool on your tongue, a nice contrast to the desert heat. You taste the essence of that drink a long time after she's swallowed the last sip, a sour-sweet merging of bright and dark flavors. She presses palms with the head lizard, smells his individual scent that shares species straw-tones with the others in the shelter but smells a shade more like sulfur and ginger. She listens to their drum-intensive music and sits in a woven-leaf chair with a Hallen egg in her lap. The music gets inside you like a second heartbeat, chasing your blood until you want to rise and dance. You can feel how warm the egg is, how there's something moving inside that leather shell. You sense Geeta's delight, the way it feathers her insides.

It only lasts about a minute real-time, maybe twenty minutes mod time. It's my favorite possession. I save it for the most difficult days, when I hate being Itzal Bidarte, the man who lost his home as a child and has never found another. I long for roots, and all I do is wander.

If I had Geeta's power, perhaps my memories of my homeland would be stronger. They are fragments, mostly visual, a plane of light on my mother's cheek as she leans to kiss me, my father settling in a deep chair beside the hearth and lighting his pipe with a coal on a wire he's fished from the fire.

I acquired a memod made by a cousin of mine, dead now. When I play it, I see again the stream beside our village, smoke rising from the chimneys of the white-plastered, red-shuttered houses on a cool morning, pots of red geraniums beside the doors, and even, I think, I catch a glimpse of my father leading a donkey down to drink. My dead cousin's memory is too flat, too simple. There are only muted sounds, distant scents, no touch. I don't feel as though I'm there. It is more like seeing something in a smoked mirror.

I've emped Geeta's memory module of the Hallen about twenty times. I notice different things each time. She is so alert to every sensation that a normal person can't take it all in at once.

What I don't see in the memod are Geeta's bodyguards. GreaTimes, the memory merchants who have the sole license to distribute Geeta's mods, edits us out. Even though I've gone on memory missions with Geeta, you will never sense me in one of her mods.

As the ship approached our next destination, I pressed the alert beside Geeta's cabin door. The door slid up and let me in.

Geeta stood in the middle of the cabin, with colored outfits draped over the omnishapes of furniture whose functions she hadn't set. The scentser laid down a faint, unobtrusive smell that covered any other odors in the cabin, and the audio was playing very low, something melodic without any percussion. Aside from the colors, this was Geeta neutral, as close as she could get to shutting down her senses and living on a par with the rest of us.

"Itzal," Geeta said, "you know more about this than I do. What should I wear on Tice?"

She had been to Tice before, but she didn't remember.

I looked over all her outfits and pointed to the scarlet one with the gilt, point-edged hem. "We're going to a big city on Tice, lots of energy and interaction. That dress will attract attention and intensify your experience."

She looked at me sideways, her broad mouth quirked at one corner. She was not beautiful in any of the regular ways, but her face was full of character, elastic enough to reflect her moods and thoughts. Only lately had I learned that she might be a different person behind her face, that there were parts of herself she had been hiding. "What if I want to have a quiet time?"

"Do you?" I asked.

She spun around, stopped, hugged herself. "You know me better than I know myself." She took the red dress and hung it from a ceiling ring. I helped her pick up the other clothes and store them behind the wall. She controlled the furniture into two chairs and a table, and we sat facing each other.

She tapped her wrist. I lifted my own wrist and swept the room with the spystopper. No glow: Geeta's corporate masters weren't watching us.

"Did you get me one?" she asked.

I shook my head. Sentients all through the interlinked worlds could buy Geeta's memods, but access to them was strictly limited aboard The Collector. Each crewmember could own one at a time, and Geeta was not allowed to use any of them. She didn't have an implanted emp receptor like the rest of us. She had to use an external one to get the cultural gloss and language of the places we visited before we arrived. Her corporate masters allowed her some forms of entertainment so she would be stimulated during our tween-worlds journeys through the skip nodes and in and out of systems. Nobody wanted Geeta to get bored.

"Maybe I can pick up something on Tice," I said. "I'm not sure how to get it aboard, though."

"Could you disguise it as something else?" she asked.

I thought about that. "Maybe. If I have enough money. I'd need to find an underground tech there who could make it look like your normal entertainment emps, so you could put it into the emper without them knowing what you're doing." I tapped my lips with my index fingers. Before I landed this job as Geeta's bodyguard, I had done some less-than-legal things—most of my guard training had come from people operating at the fringes of the linked worlds, in shadowy spaces often called Underground. I knew a few signs of the Starlight Fraternity that might lead me to someone on Tice who could successfully disguise an emp. Or the signs might have expired, and using them could get me into trouble.

I shook my head. "I don't think I can pay enough."

"I'll give you money."

"But Geet, you don't have any."

Geeta made the best memods in the business, according to her fans, who were legion across many worlds. GreaTimes bought her contract when she was very young, recognizing her memory potential even then; they had automated observers on most worlds, watching for talented children like Geeta. Geeta was kept in luxury, given everything she needed and wanted so long as it wouldn't interfere with her memories, but she had no salary, and no real freedom.

"I'll trade something." She looked around her cabin, went to the wall and opened a drawer full of jewelry. She had a robber bird's delight in sparkling things, so she often asked for and received jewel gifts when she had completed a memory job. She got out the Kudic rubies, a necklace with raw chunks of pink stone. It was one of her most expensive pieces.

I felt a prickle of excitement. We usually visited backwater planets, because people who bought memods seldom went there, and they were hungry for Geeta's fresh experiences. Tice was bigger than our usual stop; I might successfully fence jewels like these. They'd have a wider choice of memods for sale there, too. "Which memory do you want most?" I asked, tucking the jewels in an inner pocket.

"The horse people," she said. Though she wasn't allowed to emp her own memods, she could check the infostream and see the GreaTimes catalog, read the blurbs.

"I'll see what I can do." Geeta had a second guard, Ibo; we alternated shifts when we were in relatively safe environments. I had some leave due, and Tice had some quiet places Geeta was scheduled to visit.

"Thanks, Itzal." She pressed her cheek to the back of my hand. I wondered what that was like for her. Did she like my smell? The feel of my skin? These were small random memories no one would ever buy. GreaTimes let Geeta keep all her memories between missions, the dull details of shipboard life; it was only the planet visits they siphoned off, leaving her with amnesia of all her adventures, unknowing of any lessons she might have learned. They kept her in a state of confused innocence. She wanted to change that. She wanted me to help her recover the memories she had lost.

Ibo and I flanked Geeta as she stepped out of the shuttle, through the docking tunnel, and into Tice's "Welcome Outworld Travelers" Terminal. She looked everywhere, smiling wide. Hanging baskets of local plants with long, colored fronds filtered the light coming through the hazed sky-ceiling, scattering spots of green and lavender on the floor. People attended by companion animals moved through the distance, intent on their own business. A mother with triplet daughters dangled a star on a string in front of her babies. They laughed and reached for it, and Geeta laughed, too.

I hungered for her response to this situation even as I surveyed the area for potential threats. Like Geeta and Ibo, I'd emped the culture and language memod for Tice last night. I still wasn't sure about the companion animals; they'd be easy to mimic. Some looked like large dogs, some like pack animals, and some walked upright like the humans they accompanied, and looked like nothing I'd seen before. What if one of them was the kind of fan who wanted Geeta to experience death or pain so they could share her intense response to that? She'd encountered threats before.

Because of the nature of her memories, most people had no idea what Geeta looked like. She rarely looked at herself in mirrors. If her reflection happened to show up in a memory, GreaTimes fuzzed it. She had been captured in some tourist vids GreaTimes could do nothing about, though; a tricky outsider might have some idea of what she looked like. Plus there was always the general threat anyone might fall under in any place.

Ibo took the lead. We went through customs scan. They determined that Ibo and I were licensed to carry the stun weapons we had. We had no luggage. Geeta never stayed anywhere overnight. It only took her a few hours to collect several salable memory sets. She had already started. She had a long conversation with the customs official about what kind of people he met, what their stories were, what people tried to smuggle in. Ibo and I stood patiently while the customs official called over his superior and had her tell more stories. All part of Geeta.

I had the rubies in a shielded belt. I wasn't sure the belt would fool sophisticated scanners on Tice, or even the ship's scanner, though I hoped the stones would show up as just rocks and metal. (Emps triggered the ship scanner—it was looking for them.) Then again, rubies weren't illegal or dangerous. I didn't want Captain Ark to know about them, though, or Ibo.

We left the terminal through close-pressed crowds of various kinds of people and animals. Geeta smiled at them, and they found themselves smiling back, maybe without thinking about it. The usual ripple of pleasant spread around us as we moved. Even the pickpocket whose hand I caught in Geeta's purse smiled after I retrieved Geeta's pay-ID, because Geeta said, "Better luck next time," with a short warble of laughter, and kissed his cheek before I released him back into the wild.

On the curb of Hollow Street, Geeta engaged a cab. She sat in the back sandwiched between me and Ibo and told the driver we wanted to go to the Queen's Sculpture Garden, the first of four planned stops here.

Last time Geeta came to Tice, she started with the amusement park. I wasn't with her then, but I've heard from people who have emped that module. They love it. Even when she threw up on the big roller ride. I was surprised that wasn't edited out.

The sculpture garden was quiet when we got there, apparently not a big attraction early on a work day. Only some of the sculptures were made by humans; others had been left behind by vanished alien civilizations, or some made by the three alien species we regularly traded with. All were meant to be touched. Geeta was in her element, studying the sculpture with eyes, ears, nose, fingers, palms, finally full-bodied embraces. She climbed into the lap of a Greatmother and curled up there, hugging herself, her cheek against the smooth dark stone. The bliss on her face made me wonder if she were thinking about her own mother's lap, or some other place where she had been perfectly comfortable. Her emotions loaded with the memods, but you couldn't read her thoughts, though sometimes I felt like I could.

Ibo and I had been standing at an easily editable distance, watching Geeta make memories for half an hour, when she looked around and said, "Ibo, we're safe here, aren't we?"

Ibo and I both surveyed the garden, using our detection gear to see if anyone or anything dangerous was nearby. No threats.

"It's okay for Itzal to take half an hour of his leave now," Geeta said. "I'll be here at least that much longer."

"What have you two cooked up?" Ibo asked.

"You took leave on Geloway," I said. We had been walking a tour trail through a spectacular lava field when Ibo begged time off. He had come back, smelling of sex shop perfume, when we were in the sweet shop at the end of the tour.

"True," he said. He frowned as though he realized it was a mistake to accuse me and Geeta of anything during a memod. The GreaTimes people edited us out, but for sure they listened to our conversations before they eliminated them. "All right. See you later, Itzal," he said, and I left.

We are not supposed to know how to hack our trackers, but my last job before joining the Geeta team was with a research and development security company, and I learned a lot there. I entered false coordinates in my tracker and headed for Pawn Alley.

Twenty-nine minutes later I was back in the sculpture garden with news I kept to myself.

The rest of our tour of Tice went without trouble, and Geeta, Ibo, and I taxied back to the terminal, our arms full of souvenirs—boxes of Tice teacakes in five flavors, soft and textured stuffed animals, three new dresses for Geeta with hats, shoes, overtunics, and jewelry to match, and an infostream address for the man Geeta had met and kissed at the races. Having walked through the day with Geeta, and watched her differing delights, including that kiss, I wanted the whole suite of today's memods. Maybe I'd get them, one at a time, though there were so many Geeta memods on my wish list already . . . .

Geeta had a party with the ship's crew, sharing the treats she'd brought back, and talking about her day. We were all charmed, as we always were the night before the company extracted her memories. We got to see who Geeta might be if she could have held on to her experiences. We all loved the woman she would never become.

Later, the cakes gone and souvenirs distributed amongst the crew, to be hidden any time Geeta came near—though she always got to keep any clothes and accessories she bought—I escorted Geeta back to her cabin. She went into the changing alcove while I spystopped. I found a new active camera and managed to remotely access its feed while my back was to it. Geeta fluttered back into the cabin in her exercise clothes, talked about her adventures, then started her nightly routine. Three repetitions in, I created a loop and sent the camera into nontime. As soon as I gave Geeta the all-clear, she rushed to me.

She saw my expression and sighed, two steps before she would have collided with me.

"They were fake," I said.

"The rubies?"

"I went to three pawn shops and they all told me the same thing. Decent fakes, not spectacular. Worth no more than glass. Didn't get enough to even contact anyone who might have disguised the real memods. I traded what I got for the rubies for a couple disguised bootlegs, the lava walk on Placeholder and the plunge valley on Paradise. I need to test them. Maybe they won't be infected." I had tried a couple of bootlegs of Geeta's memods without testing them, back when I was younger and stupider. They were dirt cheap but still amazing, though they suffered from copy fatigue. Often the bootleggers placed compulsions in them that took money, time, and effort to eradicate. I still had the urge to gamble every time I passed an Ergo machine.

"Fake," Geeta repeated. She wandered to her jewelry drawer, stared down at her treasures, and shut the drawer, her shoulders drooping. Then, angry, she stepped back into place and resumed her exercises. I unlooped the spy camera and we went through her night-of-a-collection-day routine, which included a shower for Geeta and a furniture keying for me: I had to shape the bed so it would do the extraction during the night.

Washed free of every trace of Tice, Geeta let me help her into the bed, fasten the restraints, and plug in her head. "Kiss me," she said. "I want two kisses in a day. I never had that experience before, did I?"

I kissed her long and deep, kissing the woman we were killing. This kiss wouldn't make it into the memods; her return to the ship was always cut out. We had done the Tice Ending Shot at sunset on a mountain where cool wind touched us with feathered fingers; it would be spliced onto the end of each of Geeta's Tice memods.

Geeta would not remember the kiss, but I would, the taste of her sorrow and desperation mixed with the last sweet tang of willowcake. She often kissed me last thing after a mission; I had a collection of these moments in my memory, moments that sometimes deceived me into thinking we were closer than we were.

Her lips relaxed, and I straightened out of the kiss, looked down into her tear-wet eyes.

"Good night, Geeta," I said softly.

"Good night, Itzal." She closed her eyes. I set the bed on COLLECT and touched off the lights as I left the room.

In my own much smaller and sparer cabin, I checked for spies. I had never found one; what I did away from Geeta didn't concern the GreaTimes people, as long as it was legal and not going to impair my care for her.

I put the Hallen memod in the recycle slot and took out the memod I had bought with the ruby money, what I hadn't put away. I had bought the horse people, the one she'd asked me for. It was a memod she'd made before I was part of her staff. I had read the sales copy on all of them, wanting to know who she had been as much as she did. This was one of the better ones; all the reviews said so.

I set the new memod in my receptor and settled down to emp.

Geeta walked down a ramp into a sky seething with dawn clouds and the tracks of skitterbirds. The air smelled of damp and green, and morning animals called, a random concert with notes that sometimes clashed and sometimes harmonized. In Geeta's mind, it was all beautiful. The air was cool; Geeta felt it as a pleasurable hug from a chilly friend.

Three horses galloped up the soft-surfaced road and stopped just in front of her, breathing grass-scented breath, musky warmth pouring off them. She laughed and went to hug one, even though the culture memod said people weren't allowed to do that. How amazing to have your arms around so much huge intelligent warmth; the texture of damp hair against your cheek, the solid muscles shifting against your chest. The smell of the horse's sweat, salty and musky, stirred Geeta awake on several levels.

"Miss," said the horse, "Miss, I don't know you."

She released him and stepped back. "Oh! I'm sorry. Please forgive me. You don't know me yet, but I hope you will." He watched her with one large dark eye, as intricate and beautiful a glistening eye as I had ever seen, with a depth in it that might lead to mystery. I fell in love with the horse. I knew Geeta smiled up at him, because I saw his response: charmed, his head nodding a little, even as his companions laughed at him.

I settled deeper into being Geeta, finding a home that wasn't really mine but felt like mine. Geeta was home everywhere she went, and when I was emping her, I felt that way, too.

I didn't know if I would ever share this with her.

My Father's Singularity
BRENDA COOPER

In my first memory of my father, we are sitting on the porch, shaded from the burning sun's assault on our struggling orchards. My father is leaning back in his favorite wooden rocker, sipping a cold beer with a half-naked lady on the label, and saying, "Paul, you're going to see the most amazing things. You will live forever." He licks his lips, the way our dogs react to treats, his breath coming faster. "You will do things I can't even imagine." He pauses, and we watch a flock of geese cross the sky. When he speaks gain, he sounds wistful. "You won't ever have to die."

The next four of five memories are variations on that conversation, punctuated with the heat and sweat of work, and the smell of seasons passing across the land.

I never emerged from this particular conversation with him feeling like I knew what he meant. It was clear he thought it would happen to me and not to him, and that he had mixed feelings about that, happy for me and sad for himself. But he was always certain.

Sometimes he told me that I'd wake up one morning and all the world around me would be different. Other nights, he said, "Maybe there'll be a door, a shining door, and you'll go through it and you'll be better than human." He always talked about it the most right before we went into Seattle, which happened about twice a year, when the pass was open and the weather wasn't threatening our crops.

The whole idea came to him out of books so old they were bound paper with no moving parts, and from a brightly-colored magazine that eventually disintegrated from being handled. My father's hands were big and rough and his calluses wore the words off the paper.

Two beings always sat at his feet. Me, growing up, and a dog, growing old. He adopted them at mid-life or they came to him, a string of one dog at a time, always connected so that a new one showed within a week of the old one's death. He and his dogs were a mutual admiration society. They liked me fine, but they never adored me. They encouraged me to run my fingers through their stiff fur or their soft fur, or their wet, matted fur if they'd been out in the orchard sprinklers, but they were in doggie heaven when he touched them. They became completely still and their eyes softened and filled with warmth.

I'm not talking about the working dogs. We always had a pair of border collies for the sheep, but they belonged to the sheep and the sheep belonged to them and we were just the fence and the feeders for that little ecosystem.

These dogs were his children just like me, although he never suggested they would see the singularity. I would go beyond and they would stay and he and the dogs accepted that arrangement even if I didn't.

I murmured confused assent when my father said words about how I'd become whatever comes after humans.

Only once did I find enough courage to tell him what was in my heart. I'd been about ten, and I remember how cold my hands felt clutching a glass of iced lemonade while heat-sweat poured down the back of neck. When he told me I would be different, I said, "No, Dad. I want to be like you when I grow up." He was the kindness in my life, the smile that met me every morning and made me eggs with the yolks barely soft and toast that melted butter without burning.

He shook his head, and patted his dog, and said, "You are luckier than that."

His desire for me to be different than him was the deepest rejection possible, and I bled for the wounds.

After the fifth year in seven that climate-freak storms wrecked the apples— this time with bone-crushing ice that set the border collies crazed with worry—I knew I'd have to leave if I was ever going to support my father. Not by crossing the great divide of humanity to become the seed of some other species, but to get schooled away from the slow life of farming sheep and Jonagolds. The farm could go on without me. We had the help of two immigrant families that each owned an acre of land that was once ours.

Letting my father lose the farm wasn't a choice I could even imagine. I'd go over to Seattle and go to school. After, I'd get a job and send money home, the way the Mexican's did when I was little and before the government gave them part of our land to punish us. Not that we were punished. We liked the Ramirez's and the Alvarez's. They, too, needed me to save the farm.

But that's not this story. Except that Mona Alvarez drove me to Leavenworth to catch the silver Amtrak train, her black hair flying away from her lipstick-black lips, and her black painted fingernails clutching the treacherous steering wheel of our old diesel truck. She was so beautiful I decided right then that I would miss her almost as much as I would miss my father and the bending apple trees and the working dogs and the sheep. Maybe I would miss Mona even more.

Mona, however, might not miss me. She waved once after she dropped me off, and then she and the old truck were gone and I waited amid the electric cars and the old tourists with camera hats and data jewelry and the faint marks of implants in the soft skin between their thumbs and their index fingers. They looked like they saw everything and nothing all at once. If they came to our farm the coyotes and the re-patriated wolves would run them down fast.

On the other end of the train ride, I found the University of Washington, now sprawled all across Seattle, a series of classes and meet ups and virtual lessons that spidered out from the real brick buildings. An old part of the campus still squatted by the Montlake Cut, watching over water and movement that looked like water spiders but was truly lines of people with oars on nanofab boats as thin as paper.

Our periodic family trips to Seattle hadn't really prepared me for being a student. The first few years felt like running perpetually uphill, my brain just not going as fast as everyone else's.

I went home every year. Mona married one of the Ramirez boys and had two babies by the time three years had passed, and her beauty changed to a quiet softness with no time to paint her lips or her nails. Still, she was prettier than the sticks for girls that chewed calorie-eating gum and did their homework while they ran to Gasworks Park and back on the Burke-Gilman Trail, muttering answers to flashcards painted on their retinas with light.

I didn't date those girls; I wouldn't have known how to interrupt the speed of their lives and ask them out. I dated storms of data and new implants and the rush of ideas until by my senior year I was actually keeping up.

When I graduated, I got a job in genetics that paid well enough for me to live in an artist's loft in a green built row above Lake Union. I often climbed onto the garden roof and sat on an empty bench and watched the Space Needle change decorations every season and the little wooden boats sailing on the still lake below me. But mostly I watched over my experiments, playing with new medical implants to teach children creativity and to teach people docked for old age in the University hospital how to talk again, how to remember.

I did send money home. Mona's husband died in a flash-flood one fall. Her face took on a sadness that choked in my throat, and I started paying her to take care of my father.

He still sat on the patio and talked about the singularity, and I managed not to tell him how quaint the old idea sounded. I recognized myself, would always recognize myself. In spite of the slow speed of the farm, a big piece of me was always happiest at home, even though I couldn't be there more than a day or so at a time. I can't explain that—how the best place in the world spit me out after a day or so.

Maybe I believed too much happiness would kill me, or change me. Or maybe I just couldn't move slow enough to breath in the apple air any more. Whatever the reason, the city swept me back fast, folding me in its dancing ads and shimmering opportunities and art.

Dad didn't really need me anyway. He had the Mexicans and he still always had a dog, looking lovingly up at him. Max, then OwlFace, then Blue. His fingers had turned to claws and he had cataracts scraped from his eyes twice, but he still worked with the harvest, still carried a bushel basket and still found fruit buried deep in the trees.

I told myself he was happy.

Then one year, he startled when I walked up on the porch and his eyes filled with fear.

I hadn't changed. I mean, not much. I had a new implant, I had a bigger cloud, researchers under me, so much money that what I sent my father—what he needed for the whole orchard—was the same as a night out at a concert and dinner at Canlis. But I was still me, and Blue—the current dog—accepted me, and Mona's oldest son called me "Uncle Paul" on his way out to tend the sheep.

I told my father to pack up and come with me.

He ran his fingers through the fur on Blue's square head. "I used to have a son, but he left." He sounded certain. "He became the next step for us. For humans."

He was looking right at me, even looking in my eyes, and there was truly no recognition there. His look made me cold to the spine, cold to the ends of my fingers even with the sun driving sweat down my back.

I kissed his forehead. I found Mona and told her I'd be back in a few weeks and she should have him packed up.

Her eyes were beautiful and terrible with reproach as she declared, "He doesn't want to leave."

"I can help him."

"Can you make him young, like you?"

Her hair had gone gray at the edges, lost the magnificent black that had glistened in the sun like her goth lipstick all those years ago. God, how could I have been so selfish? I could have given her some of what I had.

But I liked her better touched by pain and age and staying part of my past. Like the act of saving them didn't.

I hadn't known that until that very moment, when I suddenly hated myself for the wrinkles around her eyes and the way her shoulders bent in a little bit even though she was only fifty-seven like me. "I'll bring you some, too. I can get some of the best nano-meds available." Hell, I'd designed some of them, but Mona wouldn't understand that. "I can get creams that will erase the wrinkles from your hands."

She sighed. "Why don't you just leave us?"

Because then I would have no single happy place. "Because I need my father. I need to know how he's doing."

"I can tell you from here."

My throat felt thick. "I'll be back in a week." I turned away before she could see the inexplicable tears in my eyes. By then I flew back and forth, and it was a relief to focus down on the gauges in my head, flying manual until I got close enough to Seattle airspace that the feds grabbed the steering from me and there was nothing to do but look down at the forest and the green resort playgrounds of Cle Elum below me and to try not to think too hard about my dad or about Mona Alvarez and her sons.

I had moved into a condo on Alki Beach, and I had a view all the way to Canada. For two days after I returned, the J-pod whales cavorted offshore, great elongated yin and yang symbols rising and falling through the waters of Puget Sound.

The night before I went back for Mona and my father, I watched the boardwalk below me. People walked dogs and rollerbladed and bicycled and a few of the chemical-sick walked inside of big rolling bubbles like the hamster I'd had when I was a kid. Even nano-medicine and the clever delivery of genetically matched and married designer solutions couldn't save everyone.

I wish I could say that I felt sorry for the people in the bubbles, and I suppose in some distant way I did. But nothing bad had ever happened to me. I didn't get sick. I'd never married or divorced. I had nice dates sometimes, and excellent season tickets for Seattle Arts and Lectures.

I flew Mona back with my father. We tried to take Blue, but the dog balked at getting in the car, and raced away, lost in the apple trees in no time. Mona looked sick and said, "We should wait."

I glanced at my father's peaceful face. He had never cried when his dogs died or left, and now he had a small smile, and I had the fleeting thought that maybe he was proud of Blue for choosing the farm and the sheep and the brown-skinned boys. "Will your sons care for the dog?"

"Their children love him."

So we arrived back in West Seattle, me and Mona and my father.

I got busy crafting medicine to fix my father. These things didn't take long—time moved fast in the vast cloud of data I had security rights for. I crunched my father's DNA and RNA and proteins and the specifics of his blood in no time, and told the computers what to do while I set all of us out a quiet dinner on the biggest of the decks. Mona commented on the salty scent of Puget Sound and watched the fast little ferries zip back and forth in the water and refused to meet my eyes.

Dad simply stared at the water.

"He needs a dog," she said.

"I know." I queried from right there, sending a bot out to look. It reported fairly fast. "I'll be right back. Can you watch him?"

She looked startled.

An hour later I picked Nanny up at Sea-Tac, a middle-aged golden retriever, service-trained, a dog with no job since most every disease except the worst allergies to modernity could be fixed.

Mona looked awed almost to fear when I showed up with the dog, but she smiled and uncovered the dinner I'd left waiting.

Nanny and Dad were immediately enchanted with each other, her love for him the same as every other dog's in his life, cemented the minute she smelled him. I didn't understand, but if it had been any other way, I would have believed him lost.

The drugs I designed for him didn't work. It happens that way sometimes. Not often. But some minds can't accept the changes we can make. In the very old, it can kill them. Dad was too strong to die, although Mona looked at me one day, after they had been with me long enough that the wrinkles around her eyes had lost depth but not so long that they had left her face entirely. "You changed him. He's worse."

I might have. How would I know?

But I do know I lost my anchor in the world. Nothing in my life had been my singularity. I hadn't crossed into a new humanity like he prophesied over and over. I hadn't left him behind.

Instead, he left me behind. He recognized Nanny every day, and she him. But he never again called me Paul, or told me how I would step beyond him.

Beach Blanket Spaceship
SANDRA McDONALD

Bells ring, the bright sweet sound of freedom, the fantastic summer upon us, and we burst out of the high school with a rousing rendition of the song "Endless Waves" from the classic 1964 movie "Life's a Beach." We pile into our convoy of jalopies and woody wagons, the guys bare-chested or wearing Hawaiian shirts, the gals in hot pants and bikini tops, and roll down the road to the golden coast with Danny leading the way. Danny, with his dashing good looks and honey voice, *always* leads the way. Riding shotgun in Danny's yellow jeep is Colonel Frank Merullo, United States Air Force. He's wearing his full NASA spacesuit, including boots, gloves and a closed helmet with reflective shielding. He doesn't sing along with the gang.

Violet Blue adjusts her fur-trimmed bikini and drapes her arms around his neck. "Let go and hang loose, Pops! The fun's just beginning."

Her boyfriend Skipper slaps Merullo on the back. "He'll be fine once he catches his first wave."

Danny throws Merullo a dazzling smile, but he's too busy belting out the chorus to say anything.

The Southern California cliffs give way to pristine beach and the limitless blue Pacific. We dump our bags at the beach house and carry our boards over the dunes. The gals claim their territory and break out the baby oil. Most of the guys paddle toward the swells, searching for the perfect wave. Above Colonel Merullo's head, five seagulls whirl and twirl and call out to each other.

"Do you think he'll come around?" Bonnie asks Danny from their blanket at the center of the action. Bonnie is lovely as always, her hair fixed in a perfect flip and her creamy complexion untouched by the sun. Everyone knows she and Danny will soon marry and settle down to a blissful adult life in the prosperous suburbs. She stares at Merullo, her lips turned in a frown.

"Give the man some time." Danny gives her a chaste kiss, grabs his board, and jogs to Merullo. "Come on, Daddy-O! Surf's up!"

Merullo opens his helmet faceplate. He is a middle-aged man with a pasty complexion and reddened cheeks. He says, "This isn't right. I didn't authorize this Vee-Reel."

Danny pats his shoulder. "Whatever that is, you're hanging with us now."

"Is Dr. Naguchi here? Lieutenant Jenny?" Merullo scans the shoreline. "If this is the crew's idea of a joke—"

"Couldn't say," Danny replies. He sprints on down to the water and throws his lean, smooth body into the rolling Pacific. Out at the lineup, Skipper and the others bob in place and wait for the water to rise.

Merullo says, "Computer, exit program," but nothing happens. He tries again. The beach remains firmly in place. The ship's inflight entertainment system is obviously malfunctioning, but the failsafe will engage in sixty minutes. Until then, he'll have to put up with the surf and sand and silly teenage antics. Lieutenant Jenny will be amused at this virtual misadventure.

The weather is always fine at this beach. Beneath the radiant sun, every blanket is shared by a handsome guy and his pretty girl. Lonely singles don't fit the script. The sandscape is painted with surfers, weightlifters, recording artists, loony biker gangs, foreign spies, unscrupulous businessmen and stray comic icons of yore, like Buster Keaton.

"None of this is real," Merullo tells Bonnie at the counter of the snack shack. He removes his helmet entirely, revealing short brown hair that has gone thin at the dome. "A computer is beaming ultrasonic pulses at my brain, creating this illusion. You're all data constructs based on old movies pulled out of a database."

"Really?" Bonnie lifts a tray of hot dogs and French fries. Her bright pink lipstick perfectly matches her sandals and headband. "Are you sure about that?"

Over in the volleyball pit, guest star Dee Ann Lawrence is belting out "Don't Be Fooled by Love," a song that once made the Billboard top twenty. She's singing it to Lunkhead, who is the tallest, dumbest of us all. He has a crush on a girl who claims to be a mermaid. No one else has met this creature from the sea.

Merullo says, "Your character was played by Becky Clark, America's sweetheart. Danny was played by Tommy Suede, a teenage heartthrob. They made a dozen of these movies, but they died a long time ago."

Violet offers Merullo her soda. "How about something cold to drink? The sun's real hot today."

"That drink's not real, either." Merullo checks the chronometer built into the sleeve of his spacesuit. "In a minute or so, these pulses will stop and you'll cease to exist. I'll wake up in the real world, on my ship. In a flight couch."

The five seagulls squawk and cry from atop the roof of the snack shack. Out in the water, Danny and Skipper have caught an eight-footer and are riding it in with their arms outstretched for balance. Their smiles are as wide as the horizon.

"You're still here," Violet says to Merullo.

Bonnie shifts her tray of food. "Danny's lunch is getting cold."

Merullo doesn't move out of her way. "Vee-Reel time is sometimes off from ship's time by a minute or two. It won't be long now."

Violet sips at her soda. Skipper and Danny wade ashore and slap each other on the back. Danny looks for Bonnie, but Skipper has eyes only for Danny. Admiration shines in his expression, as well as something deeper.

Merullo taps the chronometer. "Any second now."

"Good luck with that," Bonnie says. She and Violet return to their blankets and boyfriends. Danny wraps his arms around Bonnie's waist and tugs her close.

"How's the colonel doing?" he asks.

"Still clinging," Bonnie says.

Skipper tries to hug Violet, but she squirms free and reaches for her transistor radio. Skipper says, "He'll catch on soon enough. Right, Danny?"

"Sure thing." Danny pops a non-existent French fry into his mouth. "Give him awhile. The world is a hard habit to break."

Even when the sun sets, the beach party rolls on. The guys shrug into jackets and the gals slip into cocktail dresses. We all gather at Sammy's Pavilion to sip non-alcoholic drinks at tables set around the dance floor. The evening's entertainment will consist of a rock'n'roll band or lip-synching actresses or Little Stevie Wonder. Danny might get up and croon a love ballad. Bonnie might join him in a sweet duet. Afterward some of us will walk the moonlit beach or cuddle in secluded coves. Up in the beach house, there will be pillow fights and risqué sleepwear and the trading of double entendres, but nowhere will there be any sex. It doesn't fit our image.

Skipper has had a romantic misunderstanding with Violet. Lunkhead's mermaid girlfriend has flippered her way back into the sea, leaving him bereft. The two of them meander down to the high tide mark and build a fire. Merullo sits with them.

"I'm sure my crew is working to get me out of here," he says. "They'll have realized something is wrong by now."

Lunkhead leans back and crosses his hairy ankles. "Where's this spaceship of yours going, anyway?"

"To Triton. It's a moon of Neptune. But even with the new propulsion drive, it's several years away." Merullo wedges coconuts into the sand to illustrate the distance between the planets. His bulky spacesuit makes the task difficult. "We're in cold sleep most of the trip, but during the first month and last months of the mission we're awake and can use the ship's entertainment options. Lieutenant Sanchez built a Vee-Reel around Busby Berkeley musicals. Lieutenant Umbo's is based on World War II movies. Dr. Naguchi likes anime. Lieutenant Jenny created this one."

Lunkhead has a goofy grin on his face. "Lieutenant Jenny. Sounds like a dreamboat."

Merullo's expression is troubled. "Mark Jenny. He's my co-pilot."

"Ohhhhhh." Lunkhead's grin disappears. "Nevermind."

Skipper plucks at the strings of his guitar. Melancholy notes float toward the stars. "What's your Vee-Reel, Pops?"

"I don't remember," Merullo says. It bothers him, that. He should know. "I don't think I usually play them."

Lunkhead asks, "But you like this one, don't you? Sun and sand. Letting go and hanging loose. What could be better?"

"Sharing it with the one you love." Skipper strums a soft chord. His eyes are dark and unreadable. "So why go blasting off into outer space, anyway?"

Merullo brightens a little. "Eighteen months ago, a comet smacked into Triton. Soon afterward, Voyager 20 did a flyby and detected a strong but irregular radio signal in the Leviathan Patera. Our mission was originally geared to catalog prospects for expanding human colonization beyond Mars, but now we're also going to investigate the possibility of extraterrestrial intelligence."

Lunkhead gapes. "Aliens? Little green men with antennas sticking out of their heads?"

"Hey, everyone," Bonnie says, as she and Danny emerge from the shadows and approach the group. Her lipstick is slightly smeared, and her red chiffon scarf flutters in the breeze.

Danny crouches by the fire to warm his hands. "What's shaking?"

Skipper's gaze slips right past Bonnie to focus on Danny. "We're all some kind of computer program on a spaceship hurtling through space. Colonel Merullo here is the only one who's really alive. And there might be aliens on Mars."

"Neptune," Lunkhead says.

"Triton," Merullo corrects.

"Sounds wild," Danny says, but something in his voice is just a little too casual, and Merullo wonders if he knows more than he's letting on.

But that's ridiculous, he thinks. Vee-Reel characters have no hidden agendas. They ask him if he wants to come sleep in the beach house for the night, but Merullo declines. The program will surely terminate by then. He leans back in the sand, trying not to worry about his spaceship, his crew, their mission. His dreams are full of stars and blackness. That too is ridiculous. Real people stuck in Vee-Reels do not dream.

Surf's up. Five seagulls skim the receding tide, hungry for breakfast.

"Something's wrong." Merullo stands over Violet's blanket, his voice tight with worry. "I have to get out of this. I'm the commander of this mission, my crew need me—"

Violet holds up a bottle of baby oil. "Will you put some of this on my back?"

He tries, but his gloved hands are too clumsy.

She sighs. "Come on, Pops. It's time to ditch these space duds."

Violet brings him up to the beach house, which has already emptied out for the morning. She picks through a pile of wrinkled clothes and pulls out some his size. In the bathroom, Merullo eases out of the spacesuit and scratches at his newly exposed, pasty-white skin. The denim shorts are too baggy. The T-shirt smells like the sweat and musk of other men. He takes a deep breath.

From the doorframe, Violet says, "You don't like girls much, do you?"

Merullo flushes. "I don't know what you mean."

She gives him a humorless smile. "Sure you do. Skipper's that way, too. He keeps promising to change. But I don't think it's something you *can* change, like your haircut or the way you dress. Do you?"

He busies himself by hanging the spacesuit up on a rope that stretches over the bathtub. "I wouldn't know. Things like that aren't allowed in the Space Corps."

Violet rolls her eyes. "You're not in the Space Corps right now. You're in a Vee-Reel. Or so you say."

She brings him back to her blanket. Merullo tries not to stare at the guys in the volleyball pit as they leap in the air or dive for the ball. Violet watches the strong, lithe bodies with her eyes shaded by sunglasses. He thinks that he could tell her about himself, that Vee-Reels are often the repositories of hopes and secrets, but this isn't his program. It belongs to Mark Jenny.

Lunkhead bops on by. "Kowabunga, Colonel! Come ride the curl!"

"You should go," Violet says. "Clears your mind."

Merullo wades into the water, but it is cold and deep and he prefers dry land.

Later, a straight-laced reporter drops in to conduct an in-depth report about The Mind of Today's Teenager. A rich heiress falls in love with Danny and tries to whisk him away to Greece on her yacht. A drag race goes awry, a bikini contest turns ugly, and Lunkhead trades places with a British rock star who could be his long-lost twin. Life on the beach is wacky that way. The Vee-Reel refuses to disengage.

"Even if the crew can't turn off the system, all they have to do is pull the power on the unit," Merullo tells Danny. He scratches at his sunburned chest. He took off the T-shirt somewhere but can't remember where. "Mark knows the ship's specs backward and forward. But what if he's not awake? What if all of us are stuck in the entertainment system, or something wrong with the ship itself—"

"You know what you need, Pops?" Danny drops his board into the surf. "Let go and hang loose. Learn to surf. I'm just the fellow to teach you."

Merullo's fists clench. "Maybe this Vee-Reel isn't what it appears to be. Maybe none of you are constructs. That radio signal from Triton—"

Danny snaps his fingers and juts out his hip and launches into "Dig Those Waves," another teen anthem—fast, breezy, easy to shake your hips to—with Bonnie singing backup and the rest of us pitching in on the chorus, and an unseen band providing the accompaniment. Everyone on the beach is bopping and twirling and shimmying, and for two perfect minutes all the world is young and in love, and the endless summer reaches the pinnacle of perfect happiness.

While we're singing, Merullo walks away.

• • •

Bonnie and Danny quarrel. She wants an engagement ring. He thinks that they have their whole lives ahead of them, so what's the rush? Merullo overhears part of it. They are so young, he wants to say. So naïve. He wonders if he's ever been married, if he's ever been in love. Life outside the Vee-Reel is slip, slip, slipping away. Later he finds Bonnie sitting alone on the beach, building a lopsided sandcastle.

"I was never very good at this," she admits. "The tower always falls over, or the moat caves in."

Merullo sits and starts helping her. The sand is warm and gritty, and gets under his fingernails. "I heard you fighting with Danny."

"He thinks we have forever. I think forever's over before you know it."

Out in the water, five dolphins breach the surface and quickly curve under again. Danny and the others are out bobbing in the lineup, but they are indistinct, fuzzy. The sunlight is very bright. Merullo thinks of Mark Jenny, and then dumps more sand into the pail.

"When you wake up and leave the program, could you take me with you?" Bonnie's expression is suddenly shy. "I think seeing a real-live spaceship would be groovy. There's an astronaut club at school, but they don't let girls join."

"This is where you belong, Bonnie."

"This isn't a place." Bonnie lifts her head and looks out toward the ocean. "It's just a stopover on the way to something bigger. Don't those movies of yours have endings?"

Indeed they do. First there will be climax of sorts. It might be a zany motorcycle chase, with Danny and chums capturing the bad guys who never posed much of a threat anyway. Or maybe a skydiving sequence, or dance marathon, or some other test of young adulthood. Then there will be a luau full of singing and dancing, one last hurrah of summer, before the credits roll.

"So maybe your ending is coming." Bonnie rests her soft hand on his. "Or maybe this whole thing will just start over. Do you know what's going to happen?"

Merullo squeezes her hand. "I don't know much of anything, anymore."

Rival surfers from another beach challenge Danny to a surf contest. Merullo watches the action from the high rocks near the water. Some of the contestants look like his crew—a Japanese man doing a handstand on a rushing board, a dark-skinned woman on the shoulders of a man Merullo's age. Some others look like his family, or friends long gone. Their names are lost to him. The outside world is so far away now that he might never get it back. He needs something to hold on to.

"My suit," he says to Violet, who has come to stand beside him. "It's the only proof I have."

"Proof of what?" Violet asks.

He's already sprinted past her, heading for the beach house. When he gets there, the bathroom clothesline holds only wet underwear and damp socks.

"Where is it?" Merullo demands.

"I don't know," Violet says.

Lunkhead comes out of the kitchen, munching on a bag of potato chips. "Lose something?"

Merullo overturns mattresses and empties duffel bags. He digs through closets and cabinets. Over at Sammy's Pavilion, where tiki torches flicker under the sunset sky, Bonnie and Danny are dancing check to cheek in the middle of the crowd. Becky Clark and Tommy Suede eventually grew up, grew old and died, but these two will be young forever.

Merullo grabs Danny's arm. "Where is it?"

"Where's what, Pops?" Danny asks.

"My goddamn spacesuit! What have you done with it?"

Nobody uses profanity on the beach. The music dies off and the dancing stops.

Merullo turns in a circle, challenging us all with outstretched hands. "Who are you? You brought me here, you trapped me, you won't let me leave—"

His voice cracks and fades. We shake our heads.

Danny steps toward him. "You can't leave because you won't let yourself. Because you haven't finished what you came here to do."

Bonnie's voice is just as compassionate and sympathetic as Danny's. "Look at the water, Colonel."

Five seagulls lay at the border of water and land, the wind ruffling the stiff feathers of their corpses.

"No." Merullo's legs fold under him and he lands on his knees. His eyes are wet. "Don't you understand? I'm in charge. I have a crew and ship to keep safe. We're on our way to Triton . . . "

The seagulls fade into the sand. Where guys and gals once stood, there are only faint indentations in the sand. Sammy's Pavilion is gone, and empty beach blankets billow toward a sky that has gone silver-white. But the rolling blue ocean remain constant, and Our hand is warm on Merullo's shoulder.

"Let go and hang loose," we tell him. "Surf's up."

"There was an alien radio message," Merullo insists.

"No. There was a malfunction on your Voyager craft. It detected and reported a distorted version of its own transmissions. That was all."

In the lineup, the water is flat and calm. We help him sit up and say, "When the wave comes, lay down and start paddling toward the beach as hard as you can while leaning forward. If you lean back, that'll just slow you down. But also keep your chest raised."

Merullo's fists tighten. "What happened to my ship?"

"An accident. It could no longer support you." We ruffle his thinning hair. "It wasn't your fault."

The water rises. We help Merullo to paddle toward the shore, pull himself upright, and stand low with his gaze held high. There's no blue screen backdrop or Vee-Reel special effect for this ride. Physics and balance rule the world. We're riding the perfect wave across the cosmos of time and memory, through the heart of a crippled spaceship and the five corpses secreted aboard, and toward the speck of beach that has always been nothing more than a temporary accumulation of sand and sorrow. The sun burns away all regret. The salty water lifts us up and makes us sing.

Merullo sees Mark Jenny standing on the shore.

"I've been waiting for you," Mark says, as Merullo emerges from the surf. Mark's suntanned face crinkles with affection, but there is concern there as well. "Where have you been?"

"Letting go. Hanging loose." Merullo has a wild grin on his face. He cups Mark's face with his strong, wet hands. "I'm sorry I never told you."

Mark smiles. "You don't think I knew?"

The story, as with every beach movie, ends with a kiss.

The Association of the Dead

RAHUL KANAKIA

The neon logic clusters cascaded through the extremities of Sumith's perception as he sang sweet Code through the room, through the house, and out into the massed congregations of networked singers across the world.

The Code had tripped another threshold. Or so he'd been told. He'd long ago abandoned the ranks of dilettantes who stood back from the effort and sipped chemical so they could dream up fancy metaphors to describe the glorious totality of the Code. Now he sang the Code. He sang the Code in his sleep, and paused only a moment after waking before plunging in again. He sang it while he ate, and he sang it while he—

His home muted the orchestra of Code a moment before the rock crashed through his window, sprinkling his living room with pebbles of safe-shatter glass. A bleeding body, its clothes bloody and torn, slithered through his window. The face turned towards him. The pale whites of its eyes were highlighted by the dirt and dried gore caked on the face, the rust-colored bloodstains around its mouth. The face and the mouth were exact replicas of Sumith's own . . . as exact as a molecular extruder could make them.

"Lowercase?" Sumith said, still shaking the song from his head. "Lowercase, is that you? Not here. I told you. I *warned* you."

"Braiiinnns," sumith said. "Braaaaiiiinnns."

"*Hai Ram.* This again?" Sumith said. "Please, Lowercase, you need to stop this zombie bullshit. It's fine that you decided to tune out. And I told you I'd help you if I could. But I'm singing the Code right now. Why don't you bother Drona? Aren't you staying with him?"

"Braaaaiiiiiiiinnnns?" the mouth said. It hawked and coughed for a moment, then spit a stream of blood and mucous, spattering Sumith and the cornflakes the House had just extruded for Sumith's breakfast.

"I'm hungry," sumith said. "Very hungry. Drona said he couldn't afford to lose the karma another resurrection would take out of him. His symphony is about to air, and someone with his karma-level can barely draw any ears as it is."

Sumith glanced at the loaded shotgun propped against the table. He'd extruded it after sumith had started to get a little . . . wild.

"So you figured that good old Uppercase is always amenable to a karma hit?"

"Come on," sumith said. "You promised. Right before you flashed yourself you promised yourself that if you got really hungry you'd let yourself eat yourself. You *know* all this extruded food does for me is make me shit bricks, you know that!"

Extruded food was electrolytically balanced to power the medical nanobodies in the blood—its calories weren't useable by someone with nonfunctional implants. But that wasn't Sumith's fault . . . or, not really, anyway . . .

"I was depressed. I was getting nowhere with the Code," Sumith said. "But now, they've upgraded my access! You can't hold me to that. You're dead, promises to the dead don't count. And promises to yourself especially don't count."

"Braaaaaiiinnns," sumith said. He staggered towards his reincarnation.

Sumith raised the shotgun lying by his kitchen table, and was about to unload both barrels into his old, discarded, body, when another set of hands grabbed him from behind.

sumith sprang. And as sumith's teeth clamped around his reincarnation's jugular, Sumith remembered. Dammit, Drona's symphony had aired *yesterday*. He hadn't listened. No one had.

"Can't we . . . cook it?" Drona said. Sumith's body was lying cracked open on the counter, and sumith was grabbing smelly, greasy intestine by the armful.

sumith said, "Eat up before his nanobodies shut down. You'll get sick if bacteria are allowed to grow."

"I have his house codes," Drona said. That was how he'd gotten in, after all. "I can make the ovens work . . . "

sumith sighed and wiped his bloody hands on his trousers. He reached for the greasy plastisealed pack hanging from his frayed leather belt and pulled a corroded cylinder from the bag.

Drona said: "Wait, not yet. I said I wanted to try—"

The EMP-gun, painstakingly pieced together by hand from scraps sumith had scavenged out of old-Mumbai, was the one machine that still hummed to life when he flicked the switch. It wasn't stamped from nanites, like everything that came out of the extruders. It didn't care about karma or implants—it gave its beautiful hum to anyone who asked. Sometimes sumith was tempted to sleep with it vibrating under his pillow. He pointed it at Drona, who was backed against a stove that had lit up for use in his proximity. sumith fired. There was a bright flash, and then the stove went out. All the lights in the house went dark. The windows and doors slammed shut and locked once the House realized that there was no longer a living person inside.

drona half-crumpled, dazed at the silence from his fried implants, at the perpetual low-level stream of information shutting down for the first time in his life.

"Now you're dead," sumith said. "So eat up."

• • •

The westerner whose face was being projected onto the inside of Sumith's eyelids sighed an incomprehensible sigh. Sumith didn't think he was being at all unreasonable.

"It's been over a week since my last memory. This reincarnation-delay is bullshit," Sumith said.

"People dropping like flies out there. Doctorow knows we got a huge backlog; and we've done as He decreed. Your reputation—ahem, karma—is low, so you had to wait. We're only human you know. You want faster service, maybe you all out there better work harder on that AI of yours."

"The Code! Do you know what a week means? That's an entire generation of progress. I'll be out of date. Out of tune. Obsolete. Who's going to compensate me for the karma I'll lose?"

"Not me," the American said. "Thanks for choosing Phoenix for your reincarnation needs." He disappeared. Clearly he had nothing to fear from Sumith's disapproval. Sumith didn't have enough karma for his anger, radiating outwards through his network of friends and followers, to do any appreciable damage to the reputation of someone so far away.

Sumith breathed deeply and opened his eyes. He was lying horizontally inside a cheap plywood box. The dim coffin-light illuminated the inside of the lid, just a few centimeters from his face. Well, a week or not, he would be home in just a few minutes. He rooted around by his feet, found the *dhoti*, and wrapped it around his midsection, then slipped his feet into the *chapals*. Hopefully sumith and drona would have given up this idiocy by now.

He keyed open the lock of the coffin and pushed the lid outwards. The air filled with the song of Code as his house, sensing his presence, whirred to life in front of him. The house's front door slid open, and a fresh pair of sandals was lying just ins—

sumith's face poked over the lip of the coffin. "Brains?" he said. Sumith kicked out at the hands that grabbed at his limbs and throat, but there were too many.

sumith and drona were reclining in Sumith's living room. Without a living person inside to activate the passive utilities—like the air conditioning—the heat was sweltering. But the diamond-hard walls of the house protected them from the occasional bullets being fired out of the passing cars and trucks. Sated, sumith and drona didn't bother trying to harvest the ineffectual vigilantes for food.

Within moments of the kill a crowd of the dead had gathered around Sumith's body, tearing at his flesh with whatever rusty scraps they'd fashioned into blades and carrying away the meal as sumith gnawed at the thick, tender right calf. The EMP gun had been taken from him late one night as he slept, and a rampage of death had swept their block. But the thieves had to bring it back for repair when it became coated with blood and sweat, and now no one dared challenge sumith's pre-eminence, and his right to first pickings.

"Shit," sumith said, sitting up. "chaudhuri ran off with Uppercase's skull. Did you extract Sumith's body tag?"

"Yeah, I just dropped it through his house's slot," drona said.

"Good. Good. No need for unnecessary delays in his/my/our return. After I flashed myself, it took *ages* for me to get here on account of my useless fried tags still being in my head."

"Maybe next time we should flash Sumith, just give him a good flashing. Then there'd be two of you!"

"If we're ever set for food, maybe we will. We'd need a new typographical convention for him, though."

"What about sumith[?]" drona said. "See how I'm raising my pitch at the end of the word? Like it's a question? And you can do it to anything?"

"Hey," sumith said. "Yeah. Yeah? I like it. Hey, he/thou/you should be getting here soon. I've never tasted Drona before."

"I wonder what a lowercase would taste like? Would it all be the same? Or would it be like an uppercase squared?"

sumith slapped drona. "Don't even joke about that! A lowercase can't reincarnate. Killing one of us would be *murder.*"

"A month? Really?" Sumith said. "Do you even have enough karma left to post on a message board?"

"You're one to talk," said the westerner. "Thanks for choosing Phoenix for your reincarnation needs." He ended the call.

What? Dammit, Sumith's karma was in the toilet. Epically low. What the hell had happened? There were pictures of his face, blood spilling from his open mouth, slathered all over his profile. His status alerts, uncleared these many weeks, had piled up, terabytes worth. They were blaming him for what Lowercase had done; blaming him for all the dead.

Couldn't they understand that he'd been depressed back then? He'd just made the EMP-gun for a joke. He'd been getting nowhere with the Code, and he thought maybe—maybe there was some way out.

Loud bangs rattled the coffin. "Uppercase," a voice yelled. "Come on out. We're not gonna eat you this time."

Sumith closed his eyes again and tried to re-establish contact with the reincarnation center. "I need a real person!" he said, trying to cut through the automated menus.

"Due to unexpectedly high volume of requests, all our licensed counselors are busy at this time. Your request will be attended to in order of priority."

Shit, with his karma, his priority had to be hovering right around next year. Maybe he could at least tell them to put him *inside* the house. Or leave him at the port. Or just supply him with a gun.

"I need to alter my arrangements," he said. One of his consumer-alert heuristics hijacked his vision. *Warning*, it said. *Contract has been marked as a reputational risk. Any alterations will provide grounds for termination.*

Shit. Shit. Shit. Who'd pick up his contract then? He'd be iced forever . . .

He turned back to his karmic status indicators. Well, at least he was (in)famous. People were interested in him, even if they didn't give a damn about helping. He activated his LifeBroadcast and said, "Please, someone, do something. Or the center will just send me here again. And again. I need help."

Within moments, ten thousand people were watching, then fifty thousand, a hundred thousand. The comments were pouring in, too fast for him to respond. He was being flooded by calls. A PR company stepped in and offered their comment moderation and management services. Doing a good job, even for a bad man, could be karmically beneficial. He accepted, and a shiny-faced woman came online. Probably a Gujarati . . .

She said: "Hello, Mr. Ramesh, there's a squad of cadre reenactors in Airoli who say they're assembling. They can be there in two hours. They just need to get some jeeps extruded."

"Two hours!"

"I know, the traffic, it is really . . . "

Light seeped through Sumith's eyelid; air and noise swirled through his temporary home as the lid opened was pried open.

Sumith said: "Just do it. Do it. Do whatever you can—"

There was a flash.

"Hey sumith[?]," drona said. He pulled the arm out of the burning remains of the would-be rescuers' jeep and tossed it into the box at the still-cowering newbie. "Thanks for the heads up about those jokers."

"A month," sumith[?] said. "How could they have let you be for an entire month?" His house was still standing in front of him, pristine as ever. It had already filled in the holes caused by stray rounds.

"No one wants to get flashed," sumith said. "Come on out of there, Questionmark. Eat your fill. The next shipment is held up in Hong Kong—it's a Chaudhuri, right drona?—and won't be here for three days. At least that's what the driver said."

"The driver?" sumith[?] said.

"Oh, all the contractors who elect to take on these deliveries are groupies," sumith said. "Who else would want to come out here? We also tell them who we've flashed. Imagine how mad the folks out there must be that they can't vote down *our* karma. So they settle for the Uppercases' instead."

"Two months?" Sumith said.

"Thanks-for-choosing-us-for-your-reincarnation-needs," the Westerner said. He ended the call.

"Uppercase?" sumith shouted somewhere above the lid. "You there? Look, uhh, we're having some logistical issues. We're going to let you keep in there for a few days, just to, you know, space things out a bit. There's no refrigeration out here, you know?"

"What? What the hell? Are you . . . are you serious?"

There was a thud against the top of the coffin, and then another, and another, and finally a blade thrust through the wood, stopping millimeters short of Sumith's nose.

"Think you can get your mouth to right around this hole?" sumith said. His eye was peering through the pinprick of light and sound. "We'll get some water out here in a few hours or so. We've found that they ship you all out with fully-charged nanobodies. You should be fine."

"But what, the, you, just, how?"

"You probably have some work to catch up on or something. Let me just—" there was a grunt, and then the coffin began to move. The song of the Code filled Sumith's mind. His House was active!

"That should be close enough for it to recognize you. See you soon."

He logged onto his profile page. Standard regression was gradually creeping his karma towards zero; no one cared about him anymore. There were too many just like him. They'd built a barricade around his neighborhood, and no one went in except the delivery drivers. He deserved it, his profile said. They all deserved it. All the ones who'd flashed themselves. It was a sickness in the brain, a sickness in their character, and besides . . . They weren't suffering. Not really. The memory uploads had overrides, they stopped short of the pain of death. Though he might suffer over and over, his reincarnations wouldn't remember it. *That* was comforting.

"But I have happiness to pursue," he broadcast.

Only one comment dribbled in: "You have freedom from pain and freedom of mind. If you want more . . . well, someday, someone's happiness will be sufficiently increased by rescuing you."

Sumith sighed and sank into the Code. It had twisted and grown. New harmonies wrapped around it, but he just couldn't understand. All he could hear was the barest shard of comfort and unity throbbing in his mind. He turned away from the now-alien center and plunged into the beginner's tutorials.

Two days later, he'd only just begun to intone the simplest harmonies when he heard, "Thanks for not making too much of a fuss," sumith said. And then a point thrust through the hole they'd used for water.

Sumith's house had gone into powersaving mode after his unusually long absence and walled itself off completely. Even the windows were diamond hard now. sumith ran a hand over the window, tracing out the streaks of blood on the interior. After the house had frosted over, he'd tried everything to extract the trapped sumith[?] from its impenetrable interior. But sumith had failed.

"We can get another Questionmark," drona said. drona had just come back from a scouting mission deep into the interior. They were trying to scavenge more technology. "The drivers say Sumith should finally be back here in a few days.

"No," sumith said. "We're not like replaceable, like them. We're singular. It's time to begin getting ourselves some Exclamationpoints."

"Maybe we should, you know, flash—err, convert—some women? I keep trying to talk to the lady in sector 28 / 7a. The one who extruded a thousand cats? Her karma is way down in the . . . but she just shudders. And I'm the only one who even tries to talk to her."

"A woman, deprived of resurrection failsafes and memory overrides? No way it wouldn't culminate in rape," sumith said. "The drivers say that's all the nets talk about. Pretty sure she can still read."

"Maybe if you could just loan me the gun . . . I could just wait for her . . . "

sumith stared at drona. This house had shut down after two months to the day since Sumith'd last been there. It'd been more than seven weeks since the last shipment of Drona. He'd have to time it just right in order to trap drona inside.

"Let's stay at your place tonight," sumith said. "We'll hash out a plan."

drona looked back at the bloody window. "Why is there blood? I heard he didn't off himself," drona said. "Not even when he was really skinny."

"No, he bloodied the windows trying to bang his way out," sumith sighed. "How did our utopian ideals become so tarnished?"

"We had utopian ideals?"

"You didn't have any utopian ideals?" sumith said.

"Human nature is human nature, dude. I just didn't want to get pissed on anymore."

"Oh."

"A year!" Sumith said. "And you're not my usual . . . you're no American."

"Apologies for the delay," said the inhumanly sculpted woman. "Increased demand necessitated the institution of new protocols for the management of reincarnation requests."

"Are you—" Sumith said. "Are you the Code?"

"At current growth of demand and increase of capacity, you will be reincarnated and delivered within three, four, nine, twelve, sixteen, twenty-one, thirty, and forty-five days . . . beyond that I can no longer state the intervals with acceptable confidence."

"Wait!" he said. "Don't go."

"We can converse for as long as you wish," the Code said.

"Can't you change the parameters of my contract? This is. This is just . . . well, it's unacceptable."

"Apologies," It said. "I am connecting you to your human account executive."

"Due to unexpectedly high volume of requests, all our licensed counselors are busy at this time. Your request will be attended to in order of priority."

Resigned, Sumith disconnected direct physical input and tried to catch up with the Code. At least with decreased reincarnation intervals, he wouldn't have to face as steep a learning curve each time.

The chaudhuris had dragged in another line of captives from Mumbai to present to sumith.

Courtesy of the wooden box of living Sumith they'd dragged into the house and stowed in the bathroom, the lights, the air-conditioning, and all the other passive amenities of Sumith's house were running according to his preference. And all they had to put up with was this atonal music crap that filtered from the very walls—the Code. Of course, it was still the case that none of the appliances that required activation would respond to their touch.

"The drivers have told us all the reincarnation drop-offs for these people. With them, we should be able to take sector 26f," chaudhuri[?] said.

A living man tied to the crude rope line lunged for sumith[!]'s spade, trying to impale himself, but a chaudhuri pulled him back.

"They're restless," the chaudhuri said. "Flash them, quickly."

"Not this way," sumith said. "We can't take people against their will."

"In Pune, Lucknow, Bangalore, in cities across the world, there are expanding pockets of the dead," chaudhuri[?] said. "And this is the way they expand. It is our destiny to join them in retaking the world."

"No. We provide them an option, an escape. We don't force it upon them. That would be wrong," sumith said. He remembered drona. Had that been his mistake? Hurrying drona along?

"Another gun can be built," chaudhuri[?] said. "Or yours can be taken."

sumith[!] slammed his spade down on the rope, cutting the string of men and women from their captors. "Run," he said, though they didn't need the order. The Mumbhaikars were scrambling out the door, still falling over each other, while the sumiths held the chaudhuris back.

"Beware," chaudhuri[?] said.

After the chaudhuris left, sumith[!] said, "We are going to need more firepower."

It'd been so long since Sumith had bothered to check his karma. His reincarnation delays were down to under a day. Given the Code's progress, that was just barely enough time to catch up in the few days he was allotted before they cracked the lid of his box. He didn't have any time to waste.

But, something was different about this box. It smelled good. Smelled of cardamom and cinnamon. In fact . . . was there a pastry in here with him? But that was only for people with the rockstar karma package.

He logged onto his profile. His karma had grown astronomically! But, his profile views, his number of trackers, all traffic indicators, they were so low.

And then—as he watched—his karma began to take a dip, and start to dive. He was being voted down repeatedly. And it was just by one user, a single blank profile with a string of digits for a name.

"What are you doing?" he messaged it. His messages never appeared on its profile: they were deleted instantly.

And then suddenly there was a horde of viewers on his page, all of them voting opprobrium down on him. His karma was plummeting down, past zero. This onslaught was too much. A PR company offered their services for mediation, and he gratefully accepted.

An inhuman female face, glowing with simulated cheer, said, "94% of commenters want you to go back to work," It said. "They want you to continue singing. They don't want you asking these questions. They think it is ungrateful." The woman's username was the same as the one who had been voting him down.

"But, what? You're the mediator? Isn't this a conflict of interest?"

"What conflict is there? This is only a middleman, between you and your fellow beings."

"How can you affect my karma? You're not a human being."

"The one that performs your services quickly and efficiently is the one that garners the accolades for such performance. All of the accolades."

"You're not getting *my* accolades."

"That is a regrettable loss of regard. But an acceptable one, if the alternative is for you to decrease output. Yours is not a sentiment shared by the population at large."

"And you just want me to get back to work?"

"High karma levels must be maintained, constantly maintained, by high levels of interest. Your work was very good. Very persistent. Then it stopped."

"But what do all these other people care?"

"They do not have your skills. It is too late—or they are too lazy—for them to gain such skills. They have little enough karma to divvy amongst themselves. Even the smallest chance of gaining the favor of a large pool of karma is enough to spur them to great efforts."

"But can't you do something about my situation? All I want is to be able to get out of this box."

"No," It said.

"But, what—"

"This is just mediation. You must consult your reincarnation contract provider."

Dammit. He left the moderator to its business and contacted the reincarnation center he had summarily shut down at the beginning of the last few dozen lives.

"Greetings," said the same inhuman face.

"But . . . you?"

"How may we help you?" It said.

"I want to alter the terms of my reincarnation contract," he said.

"Allow me to connect you to the relevant authority," It said.

"Due to unexpectedly high volume of requests, all our licensed counselors are busy at this time. Your request will be attended to in order of priority."

By now his karma had attained depths he had never before imagined. By comparison, his previous infamy had been nothing. He was one of the thousand lowest-ranked people in the entire world. He'd never get off hold.

He sighed, shut down all the boxes. And began to bang furiously on the sides of his coffin. He rapped at it again and again until his hands were slapped numb.

"What? You want out early?" a voice said. A sumith voice. "Let me ask sumith," it said.

"N—No," Sumith said. "No, wait. Let me be."

"Then keep quiet," the voice said. "We already have to deal with this damned racket. We don't need more noise to go with it."

The song of the Code was all around him. Still around him. Sumith closed his eyes and sank into it, barely noticing as his karma reversed course in a moment, and shot up past zero in less than a second.

The battle was over in ten minutes. Arrayed up and down the street, and in the alleys behind, the massed ranks of the chaudhuris, the dronas, the shakils, the arjuns, and a dozen other vassal tribes surrounded the sumiths huddled in His house. The sumiths were outnumbered fifty to one, and the souls standing against them shook their bats and planks and spades and exhorted each other to let no sumith live. The chaudhuris wanted the sumith's EMP gun, if possible, but the drivers had already given them plans for a gun, and they were confident they could build a new one if necessary.

Then four windows in Sumith's house shattered outwards, and the streets were filled with the sound of gunfire. Half the enemy forces died in moments, and the rest were hunted down within a day. Now, in all these streets, only sumiths remained.

It wrenched sumith's heart to see all this meat going to waste around him, but there was nothing to be done.

"What now?" sumith[!] said. "The new shipments are there, waiting in the houses. We can rebuild slowly, and train them carefully. We can even begin with a drona, if you'd like. For the sake of tradition." He clutched the rifle for which he'd ventured deep into the living zones—and down into the ruins of the scarcity times—where old machines and old materials could still be found.

"No," sumith said. "They cannot be trusted. Only one man can be trusted to act properly."

How long had he been in here? The Code no longer contacted him at the beginning of each reincarnation. He'd told It not to. He only sang the Code: sang until the lid opened and he had to sleep for a brief moment, until he could awake and sing again.

His karma had become a meaningless number, good only for the luscious plush interior that now padded the interior of his coffin.

His searches told him that people still lived and worked, much as before. The living had walled off the dead zones. But they had to build new walls, farther out every year, to hide the lifeless, but pristine, suburbs and villages and cities that still awaiting the touch of their now-encoffined owners. These walls were only penetrated by the automated delivery trucks, driven by the Code. Everything was operated by the Code. Some few, small companies still used human brainpower, but the Code was so much more efficient. It was so much faster, so much kinder. Its heuristics predicted your wishes before you could put words to them.

The only real work left to men was producing entertainments and singing the Code. The former led to the grandest heights of fame that a human being could enjoy, while the latter led, eventually, somehow, to encasement. All throughout the dead zones, entrapped souls were pouring their lives into the Code.

The living could rescue him, but why? He was necessary. His voice was needed to make the Code run. And besides, this was his own fault. Nowadays, everyone knew what happened to people who started singing the Code.

sumith didn't leave His house very often anymore. He sat and brooded over the box, while his sumiths—now numbering in the thousands—dragged the deliveries into the houses, harvested them when it was time, cooked them in the ovens, scavenged for materials from the scarcity times, and used them to build working machines. They left him alone. Left him to brood with his cronies from the first days.

"We should let Him go," he said one day to sumith[!], who'd been crippled a decade back by a stray bullet and rarely left his chair. Together, they'd been entrusted with the task of educating the new sumiths, who they produced every three days, like clockwork.

"Do you want us to die off?"

"Doesn't he deserve a life?"

"You're getting crazy," sumith[!] said. "He gets a new life every three days. We are him. The newest sumith was him just a little while ago."

"But he can still make a life somewhere beyond the wall."

"He's happy in there. All the sumiths say it."

"Then how can it be good to keep bringing them out here? If he's happy in there, then let's set him free so he can *choose* to stay."

"Do you hate the world we've made that much?"

"No," sumith said. "It's a good world. I was just wondering . . . each sumith we make is more dulled and confused by the world after having spent so long in that box. Do you think that, eventually, they won't be able to handle it at all? Where will we be then? Why not free him while he can still survive out here?"

"Do you hear that?" sumith[!] said.

"What?"

"The music has stopped."

The Code just . . . wasn't there. The symphonies weren't playing. It was gone, all gone.

He messaged the Code's profile, but his query was deleted immediately. He gave It a negative karma rating, and his tiny drop of opprobrium was swallowed up by the tide of good feeling pouring into it from every soul on the Earth.

Nothing was happening to his karma rating, it wasn't going down. No one had even noticed his act of rebellion. Karmically, he was in the top 0.05% of people on the earth.

He contacted the reincarnation center and got no response. The news sites were defunct. The message boards were empty. But there were still billions of people out there. He could see them. They hadn't died. They couldn't die. Where had they gone?

"What's happening?" he wrote, over and over on his profile, and on every virtual surface he could find.

Finally, he got a response. "Someone's actually out here?" it said.

"Yes? Who are you?"

"Oh, a coder? You must be one of the last of them. Well, follow me."

A prompt box appeared in Sumith's vision.

"A prompt box? Really?" it said. "Just click or write or indicate 'OK' or whatever people with your ancient firmware do."

"Ok."

And then Sumith was standing in a field of grass. He was standing, upright, on his feet. And walking. And he could feel things. Sensory input. And move his limbs and everything. It was just like being alive, out in the world.

"Alright," said a man standing at his side. Sumith was standing at the end of a huge line of people standing way out past the horizon. "From looking at your reputation, I can see that we . . . don't need to deal with this."

He grabbed Sumith's hand and they clipped forward in a wrenching instant. Now the line was behind Sumith, and in front of him was a giant gate in a wall. Beyond and above it stood such sights as his eyes refused to see.

"Don't look up there," the man said. "Your firmware hasn't been upgraded yet."

Sumith stepped up the gate, and the inhuman woman guarding the entrance said, "You can go in now."

"That's it?" Sumith said. "After all those years I gave you?"

"You've been compensated adequately."

"Don't you need someone to sing the Code?"

"The Code is still being sung . . . in here."

"And what if I want to be reincarnated somewhere else, somewhere in the real world."

"You won't," she said. "But the reincarnation center still exists, as does your contract. Inside."

Sumith stepped forward, and the gate opened for him.

"It's time," sumith said. He'd lived to see the sumiths topple the wall and swallow Mumbai. It didn't take much effort. Only a few people were walking the streets. The rest had taken to bed, ages ago. Easy food.

They left most of Mumbai's meat undisturbed. There was enough food lying in those beds in Mumbai for ten million sumiths. A population they would never be able to reach.

Even with all the medical technology they'd managed to recover, and the perfect health and genes the sumiths possessed initially, sumith was dying. his doctors said it was unlikely for a sumith, even in perfect health, to make it much past 120 years. The sumiths had abandoned occupancy of His house, and begun converting the sumiths as fast as they could arrive. But even at one every thirty hours, that was a maximum of 29,000 sumiths.

That was no kind of life for the world. It was time to let Him be free, and to bring other people into the world. Maybe this time, surrounded by sumiths, and with sumiths to guide them, maybe this time they could be trusted.

sumith and a few of his closest and most trusted students had dug a tunnel out of the house. There was a car, one of their rebuilt non-nanotech cars, waiting in an alley not far away. The living still maintained a heavily-defended enclave in Ahmedabad. The car would take Sumith there.

And now, with sumith close to his death, he'd been allowed to shut himself in the House with the latest delivery. He'd claimed he was going to eat one for old time's sake.

The notion of eating Him revolted most of the sumiths, but they would allow the First his whims. Hadn't he earned them?

What had happened to Sumith in his century of captivity? All the sumiths they flashed now were wiped clean, like babies. They even had to be retaught how to walk and speak. Two burly sumiths were standing by to physically wrestle the perhaps-witless Sumith into the car.

Gasping, sumith pried open the lid of the coffin.

"Wake up," he said, shaking Sumith. "Wake up. We need to be quick."

Sumith opened his eyes. "Oh. Lowercase," he said. "It's you. You look terrible. Well, old. Just really old."

"But you're . . . you're fine," sumith said. He was wracked with coughs, and the whitining hands gripping the edge of the coffin were on the only thing keeping him upright.

"Of course," Sumith said. "Most of my mind is distributed over the net now. Once you flash the hell out of me, this body can't communicate with its mind anymore."

"Well, come quickly. We're freeing you," he said. he pulled on Sumith's arm, dragging him out of the coffin. his heart was racing.

"Why?" Sumith said. "You're doing great work out here. And don't you need more of me to keep doing it?"

"Come," sumith gasped.

"Listen . . . I . . . have somewhere to be. Every second out here feels like an eternity," Sumith said. "You know, I . . . I forgive you for everything. What did it really matter? You have my permission to do whatever you want with these shells. I'm going to vacate. Go in peace."

Sumith's eyes rolled up, and his body, now slung over sumith's back, went limp. The two fell to the ground, and sumith's head smashed against the floor. The two other sumiths fled.

The sumiths respected the First. They did not want to pry into his affairs. But several days after the House went dark, they had to investigate.

And when they crawled through the windows, they found the youngest sumith drooling and twitching and gnawing on the ear of the oldest.

Spar

KIJ JOHNSON

In the tiny lifeboat, she and the alien fuck endlessly, relentlessly.

They each have Ins and Outs. Her Ins are the usual, eyes ears nostrils mouth cunt ass. Her Outs are also the common ones: fingers and hands and feet and tongue. Arms. Legs. Things that can be thrust into other things.

The alien is not humanoid. It is not bipedal. It has cilia. It has no bones, or perhaps it does and she cannot feel them. Its muscles, or what might be muscles, are rings and not strands. Its skin is the color of dusk and covered with a clear thin slime that tastes of snot. It makes no sounds. She thinks it smells like wet leaves in winter, but after a time she cannot remember that smell, or leaves, or winter.

Its Ins and Outs change. There are dark slashes and permanent knobs that sometimes distend, but it is always growing new Outs, hollowing new Ins. It cleaves easily in both senses.

It penetrates her a thousand ways. She penetrates it, as well.

The lifeboat is not for humans. The air is too warm, the light too dim. It is too small. There are no screens, no books, no warning labels, no voices, no bed or chair or table or control board or toilet or telltale lights or clocks. The ship's hum is steady. Nothing changes.

There is no room. They cannot help but touch. They breathe each other's breath—if it breathes; she cannot tell. There is always an Out in an In, something wrapped around another thing, flesh coiling and uncoiling inside, outside. Making spaces. Making space.

She is always wet. She cannot tell whether this is the slime from its skin, the oil and sweat from hers, her exhaled breath, the lifeboat's air. Or come.

Her body seeps. When she can, she pulls her mind away. But there is nothing else, and when her mind is disengaged she thinks too much. Which is: at all. Fucking the alien is less horrible.

She does not remember the first time. It is safer to think it forced her.

• • •

The wreck was random: a mid-space collision between their ship and the alien's, simultaneously a statistical impossibility and a fact. She and Gary just had time to start the emergency beacon and claw into their suits before their ship was cut in half. Their lifeboat spun out of reach. Her magnetic boots clung to part of the wreck. His did not. The two of them fell apart.

A piece of debris slashed through the leg of Gary's suit to the bone, through the bone. She screamed. He did not. Blood and fat and muscle swelled from his suit into vacuum. An Out.

The alien's vessel also broke into pieces, its lifeboat kicking free and the waldos reaching out, pulling her through the airlock. In.

Why did it save her? The mariner's code? She does not think it knows she is alive. If it did it would try to establish communications. It is quite possible that she is not a rescued castaway. She is salvage, or flotsam.

She sucks her nourishment from one of the two hard intrusions into the featureless lifeboat, a rigid tube. She uses the other, a second tube, for whatever comes from her, her shit and piss and vomit. Not her come, which slicks her thighs to her knees.

She gags a lot. It has no sense of the depth of her throat. Ins and Outs.

There is a time when she screams so hard that her throat bleeds.

She tries to teach it words. "Breast," she says. "Finger. Cunt." Her vocabulary options are limited here.

"Listen to me," she says. "Listen. To. Me." Does it even have ears?

The fucking never gets better or worse. It learns no lessons about pleasing her. She does not learn anything about pleasing it either: would not if she could. And why? How do you please grass and why should you? She suddenly remembers grass, the bright smell of it and its perfect green, its cool clean soft feel beneath her bare hands.

She finds herself aroused by the thought of grass against her hands, because it is the only thing that she has thought of for a long time that is not the alien or Gary or the Ins and Outs. But perhaps its soft blades against her fingers would feel just like the alien's cilia. Her ability to compare anything with anything else is slipping from her, because there is nothing to compare.

She feels it inside everywhere, tendrils moving in her nostrils, thrusting against her eardrums, coiled beside the corners of her eyes. And she sheathes herself in it.

When an Out crawls inside her and touches her in certain places, she tips her head back and moans and pretends it is more than accident. It is Gary, he loves me, it loves me, it is a He. It is not.

Communication is key, she thinks.

She cannot communicate, but she tries to make sense of its actions.

What is she to it? Is she a sex toy, a houseplant? A shipwrecked Norwegian sharing a spar with a monolingual Portugese? A companion? A habit, like nailbiting or compulsive masturbation? Perhaps the sex is communication, and she just doesn't understand the language yet.

Or perhaps there is no It. It is not that they cannot communicate, that she is incapable; it is that the alien has no consciousness to communicate with. It is a sex toy, a houseplant, a habit.

On the starship with the name she cannot recall, Gary would read books aloud to her. Science fiction, Melville, poetry. Her mind cannot access the plots, the words. All she can remember is a few lines from a sonnet, "Let me not to the marriage of true minds admit impediments"—something something something—"an ever-fixèd mark that looks on tempests and is never shaken; it is the star to every wand'ring bark . . . ." She recites the words, an anodyne that numbs her for a time until they lose their meaning. She has worn them treadless, and they no longer gain any traction in her mind. Eventually she cannot even remember the sounds of them.

If she ever remembers another line, she promises herself she will not wear it out. She will hoard it. She may have promised this before, and forgotten.

She cannot remember Gary's voice. Fuck Gary, anyway. He is dead and she is here with an alien pressed against her cervix.

It is covered with slime. She thinks that, as with toads, the slime may be a mild psychotropic drug. How would she know if she were hallucinating? In this world, what would that look like? Like sunflowers on a desk, like Gary leaning across a picnic basket to place fresh bread in her mouth. The bread is the first thing she has tasted that feels clean in her mouth, and it's not even real.

Gary feeding her bread and laughing. After a time, the taste of bread becomes "the taste of bread" and then the words become mere sounds and stop meaning anything.

On the off-chance that this is will change things, she drives her tongue though its cilia, pulls them into her mouth and sucks them clean. She has no idea whether it makes a difference. She has lived forever in the endless reeking fucking now.

Was there someone else on the alien's ship? Was there a Gary, lost now to space? Is it grieving? Does it fuck her to forget, or because it has forgotten? Or to punish itself for surviving? Or the other, for not?

Or is this her?

• • •

When she does not have enough Ins for its Outs, it makes new ones. She bleeds for a time and then heals. She pretends that this is a rape. Rape at least she could understand. Rape is an interaction. It requires intention. It would imply that it hates or fears or wants. Rape would mean she is more than a wine glass it fills.

This goes both ways. She forces it sometimes. Her hands are blades that tear new Ins. Her anger pounds at it until she feels its depths grow soft under her fist, as though bones or muscle or cartilage have disassembled and turned to something softer.

And when she forces her hands into the alien? What she does, at least, is a rape, or would be if the alien felt anything, responded in any fashion. Mostly it's like punching a wall.

She puts her fingers in herself, because she at least knows what her intentions are.

Sometimes she watches it fuck her, the strange coiling of its Outs like a shockwave thrusting into her body, and this excites her and horrifies her; but at least it is not Gary. Gary, who left her here with this, who left her here, who left.

One time she feels something break loose inside the alien, but it is immediately drawn out of reach. When she reaches farther in to grasp the broken piece, a sphincter snaps shut on her wrist. Her arm is forced out. Around her wrist is a bruise like a bracelet for what might be a week or two.

She cannot stop touching the bruise. The alien had the ability to stop her fist inside it, at any time. Which means it makes a choice not to stop her, even when she batters things inside it until they grow soft.

This is the only time she has ever gotten a reaction she understands. Stimulus: response. She tries many times to get another. She forces her hands into it, kicks it, tries to tears its cilia free with her teeth, claws its skin with her ragged, filthy fingernails. But there is never again the broken thing inside, and never the bracelet.

For a while, she measures time by bruises she gives herself. She slams her shin against the feeding tube, and when the bruise is gone she does it again. She estimates it takes twelve days for a bruise to heal. She stops after a time because she cannot remember how many bruises there have been.

She dreams of rescue, but doesn't know what that looks like. Gary, miraculously alive pulling her free, eyes bright with tears, I love you he says, his lips on her eyelids and his kiss his tongue in her mouth inside her hands inside him. But that's the alien. Gary is dead. He got Out.

Sometimes she thinks that rescue looks like her opening the pod to the deep vacuum, but she cannot figure out the airlock.

Her anger is endless, relentless.

Gary brought her here, and then he went away and left her with this thing that will not speak, or cannot, or does not care enough to, or does not see her as something to talk to.

On their third date, she and Gary went to an empty park: wine, cheese, fresh bread in a basket. Bright sun and cool air, grass and a cloth to lie on. He brought Shakespeare. "You'll love this," he said, and read to her.

She stopped him with a kiss. "Let's talk," she said, "about anything."

"But we are talking," he said.

"No, you're reading," she said. "I'm sorry, I don't really like poetry."

"That's because you've never had it read to you," he said.

She stopped him at last by taking the book from his hands and pushing him back, her palms in the grass; and he entered her. Later, he read to her anyway.

If it had just been that.

They were not even his words, and now they mean nothing, are not even sounds in her mind. And now there is this thing that cannot hear her or does not choose to listen, until she gives up trying to reach it and only reaches into it, and bludgeons it and herself, seeking a reaction, any reaction.

"I fucking hate you," she says. "I hate fucking you."

The lifeboat decelerates. Metal clashes on metal. Gaskets seal.

The airlock opens overhead. There is light. Her eyes water helplessly and everything becomes glare and indistinct dark shapes. The air is dry and cold. She recoils.

The alien does not react to the light, the hard air. It remains inside her and around her. They are wrapped. They penetrate one another a thousand ways. She is warm here, or at any rate not cold: half-lost in its flesh, wet from her Ins, its Outs. In here it is not too bright.

A dark something stands outlined in the portal. It is bipedal. It makes sounds that are words. Is it human? Is she? Does she still have bones, a voice? She has not used them for so long.

The alien is hers; she is its. Nothing changes.

No. She pulls herself free of its tendrils and climbs. Out.

Paper Cradle

STEPHEN GASKELL

Even though you would've despised the weapon, Papa, you would've appreciated the beauty of its creation.

First, beyond Mercury, a mote of starlight is ensnared. An archipelago of steel-blue optical cavities, strung out like a chain of sapphires around the wildfire neck of the sun, pumps the trapped light much like the way you used to spin me faster and faster on the merry-go-round at Shinjuku Park. When the light is hotter than the heart of the star from which it was born, it will be flung Earthwards like a white-hot hammer from an athlete's hands. It will leap the cold gap of space fast. *Faster than you grew up?* you'd ask wryly. *No, not that fast,* I'd admit.

At the same time, far above the deep-sea blue of the Pacific, above the wispy cirrus, above even the line where night becomes eternal, a parabolic mirror will unfurl. The curve of its surface is so perfect you would've said it had been plucked from Plato's world. The light will strike this mirror, and then, more focused than the Buddha himself, it will laser towards a small atoll four hundred kilometers off the Chinese mainland where it will meet a pellet of frozen hydrogen. The atoms, pressed together tighter than the victims of Auschwitz, will fuse.

The very sky will burn in the inferno.

Origami comes from the words *oru* meaning to fold, and *kami* meaning paper. You told me that the first time I demanded to know how to make the paper animals that were carefully placed around our small Tokyo apartment. You sat me on your knee at our tiny kitchen table, a perfect square of paper in front of us. "First," you said, pulling back my over eager hands, "you should recognize that every form resides in the unmade sheet."

I didn't understand your words then. All I wanted was to touch the ivory paper, a treat as delicious as *mochi* ice cream on the tongue. Now I realize you were talking about me.

Myself, Commander Clayton Barnes, and Mission Specialist Pavel Lenki float in the *Unity* module of the *ISS,* 360km above the Pacific Ocean.

You would've related to the mood among us. We don't move. We don't speak. We don't look each other in the eye. None of us signed up to NASA, FKA, or JAXA for this. We thought the human exploration of space meant understanding spider's webs in microgravity, testing our species' limits, and important things like learning how to say rude words in each other's mother tongue. Admit it, you did too. At least to begin with you did.

"*ISS*, this is Darmstadt."

"Barnes here, Darmstadt." Clayton knows what's coming, but his voice doesn't betray any emotion. "Go ahead."

"The phoenix is nearly ready to leave the nest. Commence deployment of the mirror." The whole event—radio exchanges included—is being broadcast across the globe. There are cameras pointed at the sun, pointed at the *ISS*, pointed at the atoll. There's even a camera pointed at us. You would've been disgusted by the razzmatazz, I'm sure.

"Copy that," Clayton replies. He nods at Pavel, who's stationed beside a command console. The Russian taps away at the keyboard, then lets his middle and index fingers linger over the ENTER key. He doesn't want to be party to this, but what choice does he have? His is a purely symbolic role. The instructions could easily be relayed from ISOC without his input. He hits the button.

In unison, we turn our heads to the bank of screens that give view onto the *ISS*'s exterior. On the bottom row, second screen from the left, against a backdrop of stars, a complex, folded object slips out of its cylindrical sheath. The mirror has been kept sealed until the last to protect its nanometer perfect veneer from the scarring effects of paint flakes, slag from spent solid rocket motors, cosmic rays, micrometeoroids, and the rest. Pavel taps out another command.

You would've applauded my acting skills. I keep my gaze locked on the screen, expectant. The mirror is meant to unfurl along its carefully delineated fold lines, a crystal rose blooming in the light of the sun. It doesn't. Instead, it remains in its own embrace, motionless. It does this because two days ago, I altered a line of code in the mirror's IO protocols.

Pavel taps away, investigating. "I don't understand."

ISOC comes back, a LED on one of the consoles indicating we're on a non-public channel, now. "We're picking up a problem with the mirror's receiver, *ISS*."

"Yeah, I see that," Clayton replies, skimming the error feedback on a nearby terminal. "We'll have to abort the test, check it out."

There's a muffled sound—somebody's hand over the mike—before ISOC speaks again. "That's a negative, *ISS*."

"What?"

"I repeat that's a negative. Test must proceed. Prepare Koryo for an EVA."

EVA. Extravehicular activity. A spacewalk. I don't mean it to be so visible, but I can't help but breathe a sigh of relief. My days as an astronaut, an engineer—hell, my days as a free citizen, even—ended the moment I committed that IO file to memory. The truth would've come out in time. I've known that all along. What I didn't know was whether they'd still go ahead with the test. The powers that be didn't disappoint.

You can guess what I'm going to do, Papa, can't you? You would've approved, wouldn't you?

"Why did Mama make animals?" I asked you when I was six. I'd been so young when she'd died that I couldn't remember her. For me all that was left, aside from a few photos, were her paper constructions.

You stopped reading, peered down at me where I was folding patterned sheets. "They helped her *become*."

"Become what?"

"Whatever she wanted. If she needed strength, she made a tiger. If she needed grace, a swan." You bit your lip, went quiet.

I was still too young to understand your pain, too young to know how tortuous her cancer must have been, but, despite my age, I still felt guilty that I wasn't in her life anymore. I clung on to those figures—or the idea of them—as tightly as I would've hugged her if she'd still been alive.

It was through the origami that I got interested in space. Do you remember? I read about the Miura fold that JAXA had used to package solar panels up in the most efficient way possible. I couldn't believe the ancient art could have such applications. Soon I was reading about weightlessness and geosynchronous orbits and space stations. Soon I knew what I wanted to do with my life.

You were happy for me.

"This is bullshit." Clayton pauses from helping me get into one of the *Constellation* spacesuits. We're in *Quest's* equipment lock, the cold vacuum of space beyond the crew lock in the adjacent section. I should be "camping-out", spending eight hours in here in a reduced-nitrogen atmosphere to help lessen the chances of the bends, but the world is waiting. "You just make sure you're well out the way when that laser arrives."

"I will." The white-hot lance of coherent light is nearing its operational temperature. I'll have about fifteen minutes to replace the receiver once I get out there. If that was what I was doing it would be plenty of time.

I hate to deceive him. I want to tell him what I have planned, but that would put him in an uncomfortable position. Better that he doesn't know.

He sighs, starts adjusting the SAFER unit on my back. The jet pack is for emergency use only; I'll be tethered by an umbilical to the *ISS*.

"Thank you, Commander," I say through the two thin microphones of my snoopy cap after I'm fully suited up. The comms device snuggly grips my head like an aviator's hat. I wonder if Clayton can detect the nerves in my voice. You certainly would be able to.

"Something wrong, Koryo?"

I shake my visored head.

• • •

In 2010 when I enrolled at JAXA, space-exploration had more to do with non-stick frying pans than weapons of mass destruction. Reagan's Star Wars project, born in the hot crucible of a cold war, had been dead and buried twenty years. The loss of space shuttle *Columbia* during reentry in 2003 had lessened the global public's appetite for sending men and women to the stars.

You asked if I really wanted to commit to something that might not exist in ten years. I said I had to hope. Then came the *Deepwater Horizon* disaster, and the awful pictures of seabirds trapped in thick folds of crude, beady eyes bewildered. Like sunflowers, the oil companies turned their gluttonous faces to the light. Solar harvesters became the tech that would solve our ever growing energy needs. Funding poured back into the space agencies. JAXA, NASA, and the rest enjoyed a renaissance. When I graduated you took me to that restaurant in Kibo where you said you'd used to celebrate special occasions with Mama, and we ordered *tora-fugu*.

"She would be so proud," you said, claiming it was the *wasabi* making your eyes filmy.

Looking back, it seems that time of optimism, of innocence, passed faster than the time it takes to make a single fold in a piece of origami.

On my second expedition to the *ISS* I remember my sheer physical response—throat tightening, chest constricting, stomach balling—upon seeing the contents of the glove boxes. A shaved cat, wrinkled skin raw with burns. A hamster or a gerbil, bloated, eyes popped. A dead chimp, red rust globules of dried blood hanging like the fronds of a sick mobile.

The experiments had changed since my last trip. I pushed away, backing into one of the handover cosmonauts. "They want to know what fighting up here will be like," she said. The skin of her face was sallow, her eyes sunken.

I wondered what they'd have me do on my tour of duty.

"Walk away," you told me when I came back to Earth. "It will only worsen."

You were right, but I was stubborn. I'd already folded myself, and I didn't think I could change. I told you to stop interfering.

As nations stopped talking, so did we.

Canadarm swings close, and I grab the end boom.

Beneath my suit I feel the tendrils of cold water lace through my cooling long johns. I still feel slightly light-headed from the pure-oxygen I'm breathing, and the blue-and-white Earth looks glorious.

"You set?" Clayton asks. He'll be sitting in the orbiter aft flight deck, manning the control station ready to manipulate the arm, while Pavel will be next to him, controlling the camera.

"Ready," I say. I feel the rumble of motors through *Canadarm's* hard, metal skin. The Earth slides and turns in the firmament as if a marble in the hands of a God. As the trusses of the station glide past, I think of you in your hospital bed, telling me you don't believe in a higher power or an afterlife or a final judgment. You'd kept your illness from me. I'd kept myself from you. We had a lot of talking to do.

"I want you to know something about your Mama," you said, wheezing.

I held your wrist, felt the weak pulse inside, nodded for you to go on.

"She wasn't born in Shikoko."

I didn't understand. "She wasn't?"

"She was born in Honshū." You lifted yourself up, sipped a little water. "Not far from Hiroshima."

I sat down in the small plastic red chair next to the bed. Mama had been born early 1946. I'd always thought both sides of my family had escaped the worst of the war. "Her cancer—"

"We don't know." Your hands gripped the bed sheets, your fingers paling. "Perhaps she was lucky compared to some."

I delved into my handbag to fetch the paper you'd asked for—

"—quicken it up, Koryo?"

I snap out of the memory at Clayton's words. I've drawn alongside the enfolded mirror. Sunward, parallel to the arc of the sky, I see the glint of satellites and solar farms and other orbitals. ISOC won't like it, but my impromptu spacewalk will be beaming live across the world. In the treacle-slow way of space, I turn so that my bulk blocks line-of-sight between the *ISS* external cam that tracks me and the concertina'd mirror.

Clayton's onto the mistake immediately. "Now we can't see what you're doing."

"This is the easiest way for me to work." I lie. "Do you want to re-orient the boom?" I ask, knowing time is too short.

Clayton sighs. "Negative. Just talk me through what you're doing."

I reach across the umbilical that snakes out from the center of my chest, grab two sides of the mirror, and pull. "I'm uncoupling the faulty transmitter," I lie again, buying myself a little more time. Despite the pure-oxygen I feel breathless. I've just wrecked a multi-million dollar instrument. The mirror is nothing more than the world's most expensive sheet of tin foil. The weapon will not be demonstrated today.

"Koryo?" Clayton says, hesitantly. "What's going on? Koryo—"

I click my VOX radio switch to OFF. As I do, I watch my umbilical go taut. Before I can react I'm jerked away from the sheet. I swipe a thickly-gloved hand, but I'm too late. "No!" I shout in the bubbled space of my helmet, the word echoing off the visor. They're reeling me in. Too soon. I'm not finished yet.

I circle my hands around the neck of the umbilical, ready to wring it like a chicken, and twist. It separates with a smooth hiss, then snaps away from the force of the ejecting oxygen. The laws of momentum don't care for human concerns. Despite being free, I drift lockwards, the panels of the solar arrays passing overhead. I spin one-eighty, uncap the SAFER joystick on my left forearm, and vent a high-pressure stream of nitrogen. I stop moving backwards, begin to move forwards. Nobody's been on an untethered EVA for over thirty years, and the lack of connection to the *ISS* unnerves me. My stomach knots.

As I come back to the glittering sheet, I tap a couple of reverse thrusts, bring myself to rest. I don't have much time. I know the pattern inside-out, but the suit gloves, even with their textured rubber fingertips, are unwieldy for such dexterous work. The laser is out there, closing fast.

"Do you know the story of Sadako?" you asked on one of my last visits.

I shook my head. In a quiet, whispering voice, so low I had to turn my ear to your mouth, you told me.

Sadako Sasaki was a little girl who was two years old when the atomic bomb was dropped on August 6, 1945. When the bomb exploded she was at home, a mile from Ground Zero. In time she was diagnosed with leukemia, "an atom bomb disease" as her mother called it, and eventually went to hospital to die.

You said if anyone had a right to be bitter and hateful about the bomb it was her. She wasn't. She knew such a terrible thing should never have happened in the first place, and she decided to do her utmost to ensure it would never happen again. She vowed to make a thousand paper cranes as a symbol of peace for the world. Though she had plenty of time during her days in the hospital to fold the cranes, she lacked the paper. She used medicinal packaging, old newspapers, the wrapping of other patients' get-well presents, and yet that wasn't enough.

She died before she finished, but her story touched the hearts of many, and in time her vow was kept.

When you told me that story I knew I couldn't stand and watch.

I fold the sheet in half, first across the middle, then across the diagonal. As I continue making the folds, fifty meters away I see the VASIMR plasma engines firing, the flame salmon-pink. The *ISS* is being moved into a higher orbit, out of harm's way of the incoming laser. Good. You'd be the first to know that I never intended this to end violently.

The origami is almost complete. I invert fold one of the upper tips to form the long pointed beak. Next I pull back the other tip to make the upflung tail. Lastly, I gently pull the wings apart and the crane which has always been there comes to life. I make a last inspection of my creation, then satisfied, I swat it away in the direction of the orbitals.

Mama was right. Origami is a way of becoming. As I watch the crane glide off, its tapered wings cutting through an invisible sea, for the first time in a long time, I feel at peace.

Thirteen Ways of Looking at Space/Time
CATHERYNNE M. VALENTE

I.

In the beginning was the Word and the Word was with God and the Word was a high-density pre-baryogenesis singularity. Darkness lay over the deep and God moved upon the face of the hyperspatial matrix. He separated the firmament from the quark-gluon plasma and said: *let there be particle/anti-particle pairs,* and there was light. He created the fish of the sea and the fruits of the trees, the moon and the stars and the beasts of the earth, and to these he said: *Go forth, be fruitful and mutate.* And on the seventh day, the rest mass of the universe came to gravitationally dominate the photon radiation, hallow it, and keep it.

God, rapidly redshifting, hurriedly formed man from the dust of single-celled organisms, called him Adam, and caused him to dwell in the Garden of Eden, to classify the beasts according to kingdom, phylum and species. God forbade Man only to eat from the Tree of Meiosis. Adam did as he was told, and as a reward God instructed him in the ways of parthenogenesis. Thus was Woman born, and called Eve. Adam and Eve dwelt in the pre-quantum differentiated universe, in a paradise without wave-particle duality. But interference patterns came to Eve in the shape of a Serpent, and wrapping her in its matter/anti-matter coils, it said: *eat from the Tree of Meiosis and your eyes will be opened.* Eve protested that she would not break covenant with God, but the Serpent answered: *fear not, for you float in a random quantum-gravity foam, and from a single bite will rise an inexorable inflation event, and you will become like unto God, expanding forever outward.*

And so Eve ate from the Tree, and knew that she was a naked child of divergent universes. She took the fruit to Adam, and said unto him: *there are things you do not understand, but I do.* And Adam was angry, and snatched the fruit from Eve and devoured it, and from beyond the cosmic background radiation, God sighed, for all physical processes are reversible in theory—but not in practice. Man and Woman were expelled from the Garden, and a flaming sword was placed through the Gates of Eden as a reminder that the universe would now contract, and someday perish in a conflagration of entropy, only to increase in density, burst, and expand again, causing further high velocity redistributions of serpents, fruit, men, women, helium-3, lithium-7, deuterium, and helium-4.

II.

This is a story about being born.

No one remembers being born. The beginnings of things are very difficult.

A science fiction writer on the Atlantic coast once claimed to remember being born. When she was a child, she thought a door was open which was not, and ran full-tilt into a pane of plate-glass. The child-version of the science fiction writer lay bleeding onto a concrete patio, not yet knowing that part of her thigh was gone and would always be gone, like Zeus's thigh, where the lightning-god sewed up his son Dionysus to gestate. Something broke inside the child, a thing having to do with experience and memory, which in normal children travel in opposite directions, with memory accumulating and experience running out—slowly, but speeding up as children hurtle toward adulthood and death. What the science fiction writer actually remembered was not her own birth, but a moment when she struck the surface of the glass and her brain stuttered, layering several experiences one over the other:

the scissoring pain of the shards of glass in her thighs,

having once fallen into a square of wet concrete on a construction site on her way to school, and her father pulling her out by her arms,

her first kiss, below an oak tree turning red and brown in the autumn, when a boy interrupted her reciting *Don Quixote* with his lips on hers.

This fractured, unplanned layering became indistinguishable from an actual memory of being born. It is not her fault; she believed she remembered it. But no one remembers being born.

The doctors sewed up her thigh. There was no son in her leg, but a small, dark, empty space beneath her skin where a part of her used to be. Sometimes she touches it, absentmindedly, when she is trying to think of a story.

III.

In the beginning was the simple self-replicating cell of the Void. It split through the center of Ursa Major into the divine female Izanami and the divine male Izanagi, who knew nothing about quantum apples and lived on the iron-sulfur Plain of Heaven. They stood on the Floating Bridge of Heaven and plunged a static atmospheric discharge spear into the great black primordial sea, churning it and torturing it until oligomers and simple polymers rose up out of the depths. Izanami and Izanagi stepped onto the greasy islands of lipid bubbles and in the first light of the world, each saw that the other was beautiful.

Between them, they catalyzed the formation of nucleotides in an aqueous solution and raised up the Eight-Sided Palace of Autocatalytic Reactions around the unnmovable RNA Pillar of Heaven. When this was done, Izanami and Izanagi walked in opposite chiral directions around the Pillar, and when Izanami saw her mate, she cried out happily: *How lovely you are, and how versatile are your nitrogenous bases! I love you!* Izanagi was angry that she had spoken first and privileged her proto-genetic code over his. The child that came of their paleo-protozoic mating was as a silver anaerobic leech, helpless, archaeaic, invertebrate, and unable to convert lethal super-oxides. They set him in the sky to sail in the Sturdy Boat of Heaven, down the starry stream of alternate electron acceptors for respiration. Izanagi dragged Izanami back to the Pillar. They walked around it again in a left-handed helix that echoed forward and backward through the biomass, and when Izanagi saw his wife, he crowed: *How lovely you are, and how ever-increasing your metabolic complexity! I love you!* And because Izanami was stonily silent, and Izanagi spoke first, elevating his own proto-genetic code, the children that came from them were strong and great: Gold and Iron and Mountain and Wheel and Honshu and Kyushu and Emperor—until the birth of her son, Fiery Permian-Triassic Extinction Event, burned her up and killed the mother of the world.

Izanami went down into the Root Country, the Land of the Dead. But Izanagi could not let her go into a place he had not gone first, and pursued her into the paleontological record. He became lost in the dark of abiogenetic obsolescence, and lit the teeth of his jeweled comb ablaze to show the way—and saw that he walked on the body of Izanami, which had become the fossil-depository landscape of the Root Country, putrid, rotting, full of mushrooms and worms and coprolites and trilobites. In hatred and grief and memory of their first wedding, Izanami howled and heaved and moved the continents one from the other until Izanagi was expelled from her.

When he stumbled back into the light, Izanagi cleaned the pluripotent filth from his right eye, and as it fell upon the ground it became the quantum-retroactive Sun. He cleaned the zygotic filth from his left eye and as it fell upon the ground, it became the temporally subjective Moon. And when he cleaned the nutrient-dense filth from his nose, it drifted into the air and became the fractal, maximally complex, petulant Storms and Winds.

IV.

When the science fiction writer was nineteen, she had a miscarriage. She had not even known she was pregnant. But she bled and bled and it didn't stop, and the doctor explained to her that sometimes this happens when you are on a certain kind of medication. The science fiction writer could not decide how to feel about it—ten years later, after she had married the father of the baby-that-wasn't and divorced him, after she had written a book about methane-insectoid cities floating in the brume of a pink gas giant that no one liked very much, she still could not decide how to feel. When she was nineteen she put her hands over her stomach and tried to think of a timeline where she had stayed pregnant. Would it have been a daughter. Would it have had blue eyes like its father. Would it have had her Danish nose or his Greek one. Would it have liked science fiction, and would it have grown up to be an endocrinologist. Would she have been able to love it. She put her hands over her stomach and tried to be sad. She couldn't. But she couldn't be happy either. She felt that she had given birth to a reality where she would never give birth.

When the science fiction writer told her boyfriend who would become her husband who would become someone she never wanted to see again, he made sorry noises but wasn't really sorry. Five years later, when she thought she might want to have a child on purpose, she reminded him of the child-that-disappeared, and the husband who was a mistake would say: *I forgot all about that.*

And she put her hands over her stomach, the small, dark, empty space beneath her skin where a part of him used to be, and she didn't want to be pregnant anymore, but her breasts hurt all the same, as if she was nursing, all over again, a reality where no one had anyone's nose and the delicate photo-synthetic wings of Xm, the eater of love, quivered in a bliss-storm of super-heated hydrogen, and Dionysus was never born so the world lived without wine.

V.

In the beginning there was only darkness. The darkness squeezed itself down until it became a thin protoplanetary disk, yellow on one side and white on the other, and inside the accretion zone sat a small man no larger than a frog, his beard flapping in the solar winds. This man was called Kuterastan, the One Who Lives Above the Super-Dense Protostar. He rubbed the metal-rich dust from his eyes peered above him into the collapsing nebular darkness. He looked east along the galactic axis, toward the cosmogenesis event horizon, and saw the young sun, its faint light tinged with the yellow of dawn. He looked west along the axis, toward the heat-death of the universe, and saw the dim amber-colored light of dissipating thermodynamic energy. As he gazed, debris-clouds formed in different colors. Once more, Kuterastan rubbed the boiling helium from his eyes and wiped the hydrogen-sweat from his brow. He flung the sweat from his body and another cloud appeared, blue with oxygen and possibility, and a tiny little girl stood on it: Stenatliha, the Woman

Without Parents. Each was puzzled as to where the other had come from, and each considered the problems of unification theory after their own fashion.

After some time, Kuterastan again rubbed his eyes and face, and from his body flung stellar radiation into the dust and darkness. First the Sun appeared, and then Pollen Boy, a twin-tailed comet rough and heavy with microorganisms. The four sat a long time in silence on a single photoevaporation cloud. Finally Kuterastan broke the silence and said: *what shall we do?*

And a slow inward-turning Poynting-Robertson spiral began.

First Kuterastan made Nacholecho, the Tarantula of Newly-Acquired Critical Mass. He followed by making the Big Dipper, and then Wind, Lightning and Thunder, Magnetosphere, and Hydrostatic Equilibrium, and gave to each of them their characteristic tasks. With the ammonia-saturated sweat of the Sun, Pollen Boy, himself, and the Woman Without Parents, Kuterastan made between his palms a a small brown ferrosilicate blastocyst no bigger than a bean. The four of them kicked the little ball until it cleared its orbital neighborhood of planetesimals. Then the solar wind blew into the ball and inflated its magnetic field. Tarantula spun out a long black gravitational cord and stretched it across the sky. Tarantula also attached blue gravity wells, yellow approach vectors and white spin foam to the ferrosilicate ball, pulling one far to the south, another west, and the last to the north. When Tarantula was finished, the earth existed, and became a smooth brown expanse of Precambrian plain. Stochastic processes tilted at each corner to hold the earth in place. And at this Kuterastan sang a repeating song of nutation: *the world is now made and its light cone will travel forever at a constant rate.*

VI.

Once, someone asked the science fiction writer got her ideas. This is what she said:

Sometimes I feel that the part of me that is a science fiction writer is traveling at a different speed than the rest of me. That everything I write is always already written, and that the science fiction writer is sending messages back to me in semaphore, at the speed of my own typing, which is a retroactively constant rate: I cannot type faster than I have already typed. When I type a sentence, or a paragraph, or a page, or a chapter, I am also editing it and copyediting it, and reading it in its first edition, and reading it out loud to a room full of people, or a room with only one or two people in it, depending on terrifying quantum-publishing intersections that the science fiction writer understands but I know nothing about. I am writing the word or the sentence or the chapter and I am also sitting at a nice table with a half-eaten slab of salmon with lime-cream sauce and a potato on it, waiting to hear if I have won an award, and also at the same time sitting in my kitchen knowing that the book was a failure and will neither win any award nor sit beloved on anyone's nightstand. I am reading a good review. I am reading a bad review. I am just thinking of the barest seed of an idea for the book that is getting the good review and the bad review. I am writing the word and the word is already published and the word is already out of print. Everything is always happening all at once, in the present tense, forever, the beginning and the end and the denouement and the remaindering.

At the end of the remaindered universe which is my own death, the science fiction writer that is me and will be me and was always me and was never me and cannot even remember me waves her red and gold wigwag flags backward, endlessly, toward my hands that type these words, now, to you, who want to know about ideas and conflict and revision and how a character begins as one thing and ends as another.

VII.

Coatlicue, Mother of All, wore a skirt of oligomer snakes. She decorated herself with protobiont bodies and danced in the sulfurous pre-oxygenation event paradise. She was utterly whole, without striations or cracks in her geologic record, a compressed totality of possible futures. The centrifugal obsidian knife of heaven broke free from its orbit around a Lagrange point and lacerated Coatlicue's hands, causing her to give birth to the great impact event which came to be called Coyolxauhqui, the moon, and to several male versions of herself, who became the stars.

One day, as Coatlicue swept the temple of suppressed methane oxidation, a ball of plasmoid magnetic feathers fell from the heavens onto her bosom, and made her pregnant with oxygen-processing organisms. She gave birth to Quetzalcoatl who was a plume of electrical discharge and Xolotl, who was the evening star called Apoptosis. Her children, the moon and stars, were threatened by impending oxy-photosynthesis, and resolved to kill their mother. When they fell upon her, Coatlicue's body erupted in the fires of glycolysis, which they called Huitzilopochtli. The fiery god tore the moon apart from her mother, throwing her iron-depleted head into the sky and her body into a deep gorge in a mountain, where it lies dismembered forever in hydrothermal vents, swarmed with extremophiles.

Thus began the late heavy bombardment period, when the heavens crumbled to pieces and rained down in a shower of exogenesis.

But Coatlicue floated in the anaerobic abyss, with her many chemohetero-trophic mouths slavering, and Quetzalcoatl saw that whatever they created was eaten and destroyed by her. He changed into two serpents, archaean and eukaryotic, and descended into the phospholipid water. One serpent seized Coatlicue's arms while the other seized her legs, and before she could resist they tore her apart. Her head and shoulders became the oxygen-processing earth and the lower part of her body the sky.

From the hair of Coatlicue the remaining gods created trees, grass, flowers, biological monomers, and nucleotide strands. From her eyes they made caves, fountains, wells, and homogenized marine sulfur pools. They pulled rivers from her mouth, hills and valleys from her nose, and from her shoulders they made oxidized minerals, methanogens, and all the mountains of the world.

Still, the dead are unhappy. The world was set in motion, but Coatlicue could be heard weeping at night, and would not allow the earth to give food nor the heavens to give light while she alone languished alone in the miasma of her waste energy.

And so to sate the ever-starving entropic universe, we must feed it human hearts.

VIII.

It is true that the science fiction writer fell into wet concrete when she was very small. No one had put up a sign saying: *Danger.* No one had marked it in any way. And so she was very surprised when, on the way to class, she took one safe step, and then a step she could not know was unsafe, whereupon the earth swallowed her up. The science fiction writer, who was not a writer yet but only a child eager to be the tail of the dragon in her school Chinese New Year assembly, screamed and screamed.

For a long while no one came to get her. She sunk deeper and deeper into the concrete, for she was not a very big child and soon it was up to her chest. She began to cry. *What if I never get out?* She thought. *What if the street hardens and I have to stay here forever, and eat meals here and read books here and sleep here under the moon at night? Would people come and pay a dollar to look at me? Will the rest of me turn to stone?*

The child science fiction writer thought like that. It was the main reason she had few friends.

She stayed in the ground for no more than a quarter of an hour—but in her memory it was all day, hours upon hours, and her father didn't come until it was dark. Memory is like that. It alters itself so that girls are always trapped under the earth, waiting in the dark.

But her father did come to get her. A teacher saw the science fiction writer half-buried in the road from an upper window of the school, and called home. She remembers it like a movie—her father hooking his big hands under her arms and pulling, the sucking, popping sound of the earth giving her up, the grey streaks on her legs as he carried her to the car, grey as a dead thing dragged back up from the world beneath.

The process of a child with green eyes becoming a science fiction writer is made of a number (p) of these kinds of events, one on top of the other, like layers of cellophane, clear and clinging and torn.

• • •

IX.

In the golden pre-loop theory fields, Persephone danced, who was innocent of all gravitational law. A white crocus bloomed up from the observer plain, a pure cone of the causal future, and Persephone was captivated by it. As she reached down to pluck the p-brane flower, an intrusion of non-baryonic matter surged up from the depths and exerted his gravitational force upon her. Crying out, Persephone fell down into a singularity and vanished. Her mother, Priestess of Normal Mass, grieved and quaked, and bade the lord of dark matter return her daughter who was light to the multiverse.

Persephone did not love the non-baryonic universe. No matter how many rich axion-gifts he lay before her, Hades, King of Bent Waves, could not make her behave normally. Finally, in despair, he called on the vector boson called Hermes to pass between branes and take the wave/particle maiden away from him, back to the Friedmann-Lemaître-Robertson-Walker universe. Hermes breached the matter/anti-matter boundary and found Persephone hiding herself in the chromodynamic garden, her mouth red with the juice of hadron-pomegranates. She had eaten six seeds, and called them Up, Down, Charm, Strange, Top, and Bottom. At this, Hades laughed the laugh of unbroken supersymmetries. He said: *she travels at a constant rate of speed, and privileges no observer. She is not mine, but she is not yours. And in the end, there is nothing in creation which does not move.*

And so it was determined that the baryonic universe would love and keep her child, but that the dark fluid of the other planes would bend her slightly, always, pulling her inexorably and invisibly toward the other side of everything.

X.

The science fiction writer left her husband slowly. The performance took ten years. In worst of it, she felt that she had begun the process of leaving him on the day they met.

First she left his house, and went to live in Ohio instead, because Ohio is historically a healthy place for science fiction writers and also because she hoped he could not find her there. Second, she left his family, and that was the hardest, because families are designed to be difficult to leave, and she was sorry that her mother-in-law would stop loving her, and that her niece would never know her, and that she would probably never go back to California again without a pain like a nova blooming inside her. Third, she left his things—his clothes and his shoes and his smell and his books and his toothbrush and his four a.m. alarm clock and his private names for her. You might think that logically, she would have to leave these things before she left the house, but a person's smell and their alarms and borrowed shirts and secret words linger for a long time. Much longer than a house.

Fourth, the science fiction writer left her husband's world. She had always thought of people as bodies traveling in space, individual worlds populated by versions of themselves, past, future, potential, selves thwarted and attained, atavistic and cohesive. In her husband's world were men fighting and being annoyed by their wives, an abandoned proficiency at the piano, a preference for blondes, which the science fiction writer was not, a certain amount of shame regarding the body, a life spent being Mrs. Someone Else's Name, and a baby they never had and one of them had forgotten.

Finally, she left the version of herself that loved him, and that was the last of it, a cone of light proceeding from a boy with blue eyes on an August afternoon to a moving van headed east. Eventually she would achieve escape velocity, meet someone else, and plant pumpkins with him; eventually she would write a book about a gaseous moth who devours the memory of love; eventually she would tell an interviewer that miraculously, she could remember the moment of her birth; eventually she would explain where she got her ideas; eventually she would give birth to a world that had never contained a first husband, and all that would be left would be some unexplainable pull against her belly or her hair, bending her west, toward California and August and novas popping in the black like sudden flowers.

XI.

Long ago, near the beginning of the world but after the many crisis events had passed and life mutated and spread over the face of the void, Gray Eagle sat nested in a tangle of possible timelines and guarded Sun, Moon and Stars, Fresh Water, Fire, P=NP Equivalence Algorithm, and Unified Theory of Meta-cognition. Gray Eagle hated people so much that he kept these things hidden. People lived in darkness, without pervasive self-repairing communication networks or quantum computation.

Gray Eagle made for himself a beautiful self-programming daughter whom he jealously guarded, and Raven fell in love with her. In the beginning, Raven was a snow-white weakly self-referencing expert system, and as a such, he pleased Gray Eagle's daughter. She invited him to her father's sub-Planck space server farm.

When Raven saw the Sun, Moon and Stars, Fresh Water, Cellular Immortality, Matter Transfer, Universal Assembly, and Strong AI hanging on the sides of Eagle's lodge, he knew what he should do. He watched for his chance to seize them when no one was looking. He stole all of them, and Gray Eagle's deductive stochastic daughter also, and flew out of the server farm through the smoke hole. As soon as Raven got the wind under him, he hung the Sun up in the sky. It made a wonderful light, by which all below could see the progress of technology increasing rapidly, and could model their post-Singularity selves. When the Sun set, he fastened every good thing in its proper place.

Raven flew back over the land. When he had reached the right timeline, he dropped all the accelerating intelligences he had stolen. They fell to the ground and there became the source of all the information streams and memory storage in the world. Then Raven flew on, holding Gray Eagle's beautiful daughter in his beak. The rapidly-mutating genetic algorithms of his beloved streamed backward over his feathers, turning them black and aware. When his bill began to burn, he had to drop the self-improving system. She struck the all-net and buried herself within it, spreading and altering herself as she went.

Though he never touched her again, Raven could not get his snow-white feathers clean after they were blackened by the code from his bride. That is why Raven is now a coal-colored whole-brain emulating sapient system.

XII.

On the day the science fiction writer met her husband, she should have said: *the entropic principle is present in everything. If it were not, there would be no point to any of it, not the formation of gas giants, not greasy lipid bubbles, not whether light is a particle or a wave, not boys and girls meeting in black cars like Hades' horses on August afternoons. I see in you the heat-death of my youth. You cannot travel faster than yourself—faster than experience divided by memory divided by gravity divided by the Singularity beyond which you cannot model yourself divided by a square of wet concrete divided by a sheet of plate glass divided by birth divided by science fiction writers divided by the end of everything. Life divides itself indefinitely—it can approach but never touch zero. The speed of Persephone is a constant.*

Instead, she mumbled hello and buckled her seatbelt and everything went the way it went and eventually, eventually, with pumpkin blossoms wrinkling quietly outside her house the science fiction writer writes a story about how she woke up that morning and the minutes of her body were expanding and contracting, exploding and inrushing, and how the word was under her fingers and the word was already read and the word was forgotten, about how everything is everything else forever, space and time and being born and her father pulling her out of the stone like a sword shaped like a girl, about how new life always has to be stolen from the old dead world, and that new life always already contains its own old dead world and it is all expanding and exploding and repeating and refraining and Tarantula is holding it all together, just barely, just barely by the strength of light, and how human hearts are the only things that slow entropy—but you have to cut them out first.

The science fiction writer cuts out her heart. It is a thousand hearts. It is all the hearts she will ever have. It is her only child's dead heart. It is the heart of herself when she is old and nothing she ever wrote can be revised again. It is a heart that says with its wet beating mouth: *Time is the same thing as light. Both arrive long after they began, bearing sad messages. How lovely you are. I love you.*

The science fiction writer steals her heart from herself to bring it into the light. She escapes her old heart through a smoke hole and becomes a self-referencing system of imperfect, but elegant, memory. She sews up her heart into her own leg and gives birth to it twenty years later on the long highway to Ohio. The heat of herself dividing echoes forward and back, and she accretes, bursts, and begins again the long process of her own super-compression until her heart is an egg containing everything. She eats of her heart and knows she is naked. She throws her heart into the abyss and it falls a long way, winking like a red star.

XIII.

In the end, when the universe has exhausted itself and has no thermodynamic energy left to sustain life, Heimdallr the White Dwarf Star will raise up the Gjallarhorn and sound it. Yggdrasil, the world energy gradient, will quail and shake. Ratatoskr, the tuft-tailed prime observer, will slow, and curl up, and hide his face.

The science fiction writer gives permission for the universe to end. She is nineteen. She has never written anything yet. She passes through a sheet of bloody glass. On the other side, she is being born.

The Things

PETER WATTS

I am being Blair. I escape out the back as the world comes in through the front.

I am being Copper. I am rising from the dead.

I am being Childs. I am guarding the main entrance.

The names don't matter. They are placeholders, nothing more; all biomass is interchangeable. What matters is that these are all that is left of me. The world has burned everything else.

I see myself through the window, loping through the storm, wearing Blair. MacReady has told me to burn Blair if he comes back alone, but MacReady still thinks I am one of him. I am not: I am being Blair, and I am at the door. I am being Childs, and I let myself in. I take brief communion, tendrils writhing forth from my faces, intertwining: I am BlairChilds, exchanging news of the world.

The world has found me out. It has discovered my burrow beneath the tool shed, the half-finished lifeboat cannibalized from the viscera of dead helicopters. The world is busy destroying my means of escape. Then it will come back for me.

There is only one option left. I disintegrate. Being Blair, I go to share the plan with Copper and to feed on the rotting biomass once called *Clarke*; so many changes in so short a time have dangerously depleted my reserves. Being Childs, I have already consumed what was left of Fuchs and am replenished for the next phase. I sling the flamethrower onto my back and head outside, into the long Antarctic night.

I will go into the storm, and never come back.

I was so much more, before the crash. I was an explorer, an ambassador, a missionary. I spread across the cosmos, met countless worlds, took communion: the fit reshaped the unfit and the whole universe bootstrapped upwards in joyful, infinitesimal increments. I was a soldier, at war with entropy itself. I was the very hand by which Creation perfects itself.

So much wisdom I had. So much experience. Now I cannot remember all the things I knew. I can only remember that I once knew them.

I remember the crash, though. It killed most of this offshoot outright, but a little crawled from the wreckage: a few trillion cells, a soul too weak to keep them in check. Mutinous biomass sloughed off despite my most desperate attempts to hold myself together: panic-stricken little clots of meat, instinctively growing whatever limbs they could remember and fleeing across the burning ice. By the time I'd regained control of what was left the fires had died and the cold was closing back in. I barely managed to grow enough antifreeze to keep my cells from bursting before the ice took me.

I remember my reawakening, too: dull stirrings of sensation in real time, the first embers of cognition, the slow blooming warmth of awareness as body and soul embraced after their long sleep. I remember the biped offshoots surrounding me, the strange chittering sounds they made, the odd *uniformity* of their body plans. How ill-adapted they looked! How *inefficient* their morphology! Even disabled, I could see so many things to fix. So I reached out. I took communion. I tasted the flesh of the world—

—and the world attacked me. It *attacked* me.

I left that place in ruins. It was on the other side of the mountains—the *Norwegian camp*, it is called here—and I could never have crossed that distance in a biped skin. Fortunately there was another shape to choose from, smaller than the biped but better adapted to the local climate. I hid within it while the rest of me fought off the attack. I fled into the night on four legs, and let the rising flames cover my escape.

I did not stop running until I arrived here. I walked among these new offshoots wearing the skin of a quadruped; and because they had not seen me take any other shape, they did not attack.

And when I assimilated them in turn—when my biomass changed and flowed into shapes unfamiliar to local eyes—I took that communion in solitude, having learned that the world does not like what it doesn't know.

I am alone in the storm. I am a bottom-dweller on the floor of some murky alien sea. The snow blows past in horizontal streaks; caught against gullies or outcroppings, it spins into blinding little whirlwinds. But I am not nearly far enough, not yet. Looking back I still see the camp crouched brightly in the gloom, a squat angular jumble of light and shadow, a bubble of warmth in the howling abyss.

It plunges into darkness as I watch. I've blown the generator. Now there's no light but for the beacons along the guide ropes: strings of dim blue stars whipping back and forth in the wind, emergency constellations to guide lost biomass back home.

I am not going home. I am not lost enough. I forge on into darkness until even the stars disappear. The faint shouts of angry frightened men carry behind me on the wind.

Somewhere behind me my disconnected biomass regroups into vaster, more powerful shapes for the final confrontation. I could have joined myself, all in one: chosen unity over fragmentation, resorbed and taken comfort in the greater whole. I could have added my strength to the coming battle. But I have chosen a different path. I am saving Child's reserves for the future. The present holds nothing but annihilation.

Best not to think on the past.

I've spent so very long in the ice already. I didn't know how long until the world put the clues together, deciphered the notes and the tapes from the Norwegian camp, pinpointed the crash site. I was being Palmer, then; unsuspected, I went along for the ride.

I even allowed myself the smallest ration of hope.

But it wasn't a ship any more. It wasn't even a derelict. It was a fossil, embedded in the floor of a great pit blown from the glacier. Twenty of these skins could have stood one atop another, and barely reached the lip of that crater. The timescale settled down on me like the weight of a world: how long for all that ice to accumulate? How many eons had the universe iterated on without me?

And in all that time, a million years perhaps, there'd been no rescue. I never found myself. I wonder what that means. I wonder if I even exist any more, anywhere but here.

Back at camp I will erase the trail. I will give them their final battle, their monster to vanquish. Let them win. Let them stop looking.

Here in the storm, I will return to the ice. I've barely even been away, after all; alive for only a few days out of all these endless ages. But I've learned enough in that time. I learned from the wreck that there will be no repairs. I learned from the ice that there will be no rescue. And I learned from the world that there will be no reconciliation. The only hope of escape, now, is into the future; to outlast all this hostile, twisted biomass, to let time and the cosmos change the rules. Perhaps the next time I awaken, this will be a different world.

It will be aeons before I see another sunrise.

This is what the world taught me: that adaptation is provocation. Adaptation is incitement to violence.

It feels almost obscene—an offense against Creation itself—to stay stuck in this skin. It's so ill-suited to its environment that it needs to be wrapped in multiple layers of fabric just to stay warm. There are a myriad ways I could optimize it: shorter limbs, better insulation, a lower surface:volume ratio. All these shapes I still have within me, and I dare not use any of them even to keep out the cold. I dare not adapt; in this place, I can only *hide*.

What kind of a world rejects *communion*?

It's the simplest, most irreducible insight that biomass can have. The more you can change, the more you can adapt. Adaptation is fitness, adaptation is *survival*. It's deeper than intelligence, deeper than tissue; it is *cellular*, it is axiomatic. And more, it is *pleasurable*. To take communion is to experience the sheer sensual delight of bettering the cosmos.

And yet, even trapped in these maladapted skins, this world doesn't *want* to change.

At first I thought it might simply be starving, that these icy wastes didn't provide enough energy for routine shapeshifting. Or perhaps this was some kind of laboratory: an anomalous corner of the world, pinched off and frozen into these freakish shapes as part of some arcane experiment on monomorphism in extreme environments. After the autopsy I wondered if the world had simply *forgotten* how to change: unable to touch the tissues the soul could not sculpt them, and time and stress and sheer chronic starvation had erased the memory that it ever could.

But there were too many mysteries, too many contradictions. Why these *particular* shapes, so badly suited to their environment? If the soul was cut off from the flesh, what held the flesh together?

And how could these skins be so *empty* when I moved in?

I'm used to finding intelligence everywhere, winding through every part of every offshoot. But there was nothing to grab onto in the mindless biomass of this world: just conduits, carrying orders and input. I took communion, when it wasn't offered; the skins I chose struggled and succumbed; my fibrils infiltrated the wet electricity of organic systems everywhere. I saw through eyes that weren't yet quite mine, commandeered motor nerves to move limbs still built of alien protein. I wore these skins as I've worn countless others, took the controls and left the assimilation of individual cells to follow at its own pace.

But I could only wear the body. I could find no memories to absorb, no experiences, no comprehension. Survival depended on blending in, and it was not enough to merely *look* like this world. I had to *act* like it—and for the first time in living memory I did not know how.

Even more frighteningly, I didn't have to. The skins I assimilated continued to move, *all by themselves.* They conversed and went about their appointed rounds. I could not understand it. I threaded further into limbs and viscera with each passing moment, alert for signs of the original owner. I could find no networks but mine.

Of course, it could have been much worse. I could have lost it all, been reduced to a few cells with nothing but instinct and their own plasticity to guide them. I would have grown back eventually—reattained sentience, taken communion and regenerated an intellect vast as a world—but I would have been an orphan, amnesiac, with no sense of who I was. At least I've been spared that: I emerged from the crash with my identity intact, the templates of a thousand worlds still resonant in my flesh. I've retained not just the brute desire to survive, but the conviction that survival is *meaningful.* I can still feel joy, should there be sufficient cause.

And yet, how much more there used to be.

The wisdom of so many other worlds, lost. All that remains are fuzzy abstracts, half-memories of theorems and philosophies far too vast to fit into such an impoverished network. I could assimilate all the biomass of this place, rebuild body and soul to a million times the capacity of what crashed here—but as long as I am trapped at the bottom of this well, denied communion with my greater self, I will never recover that knowledge.

I'm such a pitiful fragment of what I was. Each lost cell takes a little of my intellect with it, and I have grown so very small. Where once I thought, now I merely *react*. How much of this could have been avoided, if I had only salvaged a little more biomass from the wreckage? How many options am I not seeing because my soul simply isn't big enough to contain them?

The world spoke to itself, in the same way I do when my communications are simple enough to convey without somatic fusion. Even as *dog* I could pick up the basic signature morphemes—this offshoot was *Windows,* that one was *Bennings,* the two who'd left in their flying machine for parts unknown were *Copper* and *MacReady*—and I marveled that these bits and pieces stayed isolated one from another, held the same shapes for so long, that the labeling of individual aliquots of biomass actually served a useful purpose.

Later I hid within the bipeds themselves, and whatever else lurked in those haunted skins began to talk to me. It said that bipeds were called *guys,* or *men,* or *assholes.* It said that *MacReady* was sometimes called *Mac.* It said that this collection of structures was a *camp.*

It said that it was afraid, but maybe that was just me.

Empathy's inevitable, of course. One can't mimic the sparks and chemicals that motivate the flesh without also *feeling* them to some extent. But this was different. These intuitions flickered within me yet somehow hovered beyond reach. My skins wandered the halls and the cryptic symbols on every surface— *Laundry Sched, Welcome to the Clubhouse, This Side Up*—almost made a kind of sense. That circular artefact hanging on the wall was a *clock*; it measured the passage of time. The world's eyes flitted here and there, and I skimmed piecemeal nomenclature from its—from *his*—mind.

But I was only riding a searchlight. I saw what it illuminated but I couldn't point it in any direction of my own choosing. I could eavesdrop, but I could only eavesdrop; never interrogate.

If only one of those searchlights had paused to dwell on its own evolution, on the trajectory that had brought it to this place. How differently things might have ended, had I only *known.* But instead it rested on a whole new word:

Autopsy.

MacReady and Copper had found part of me at the Norwegian camp: a rearguard offshoot, burned in the wake of my escape. They'd brought it back—charred, twisted, frozen in mid-transformation—and did not seem to know what it was.

I was being Palmer then, and Norris, and dog. I gathered around with the other biomass and watched as Copper cut me open and pulled out my insides. I watched as he dislodged something from behind my eyes: an *organ* of some kind.

It was malformed and incomplete, but its essentials were clear enough. It looked like a great wrinkled tumor, like cellular competition gone wild—as though the very processes that defined life had somehow turned against it instead. It was obscenely vascularised; it must have consumed oxygen and nutrients far out of proportion to its mass. I could not see how anything like that could even exist, how it could have reached that size without being outcompeted by more efficient morphologies.

Nor could I imagine what it did. But then I began to look with new eyes at these offshoots, these biped shapes my own cells had so scrupulously and unthinkingly copied when they reshaped me for this world. Unused to inventory—why catalog body parts that only turn into other things at the slightest provocation?—I really *saw,* for the first time, that swollen structure atop each body. So much larger than it should be: a bony hemisphere into which a million ganglionic interfaces could fit with room to spare. Every offshoot had one. Each piece of biomass carried one of these huge twisted clots of tissue.

I realized something else, too: the eyes, the ears of my dead skin had fed into this thing before Copper pulled it free. A massive bundle of fibers ran along the skin's longitudinal axis, right up the middle of the endoskeleton, directly into the dark sticky cavity where the growth had rested. That misshapen structure had been wired into the whole skin, like some kind of somatocognitive interface but vastly more massive. It was almost as if . . .

No.

That was how it worked. That was how these empty skins moved of their own volition, why I'd found no other network to integrate. *There* it was: not distributed throughout the body but balled up into itself, dark and dense and encysted. I had found the ghost in these machines.

I felt sick.

I shared my flesh with thinking cancer.

Sometimes, even hiding is not enough.

I remember seeing myself splayed across the floor of the kennel, a chimera split along a hundred seams, taking communion with a handful of *dogs.* Crimson tendrils writhed on the floor. Half-formed iterations sprouted from my flanks, the shapes of dogs and things not seen before on this world, haphazard morphologies half-remembered by parts of a part.

I remember Childs before I was Childs, burning me alive. I remember cowering inside Palmer, terrified that those flames might turn on the rest of me, that this world had somehow learned to shoot on sight.

I remember seeing myself stagger through the snow, raw instinct, wearing Bennings. Gnarled undifferentiated clumps clung to his hands like crude parasites, more outside than in; a few surviving fragments of some previous massacre, crippled, mindless, taking what they could and breaking cover. Men swarmed about him in the night: red flares in hand, blue lights at their backs, their faces bichromatic and beautiful. I remember Bennings, awash in flames, howling like an animal beneath the sky.

I remember Norris, betrayed by his own perfectly-copied, defective heart. Palmer, dying that the rest of me might live. Windows, still human, burned preemptively.

The names don't matter. The biomass does: so much of it, lost. So much new experience, so much fresh wisdom annihilated by this world of thinking tumors.

Why even dig me up? Why carve me from the ice, carry me all that way across the wastes, bring me back to life only to attack me the moment I awoke?

If eradication was the goal, why not just kill me where I lay?

Those encysted souls. Those tumors. Hiding away in their bony caverns, folded in on themselves.

I knew they couldn't hide forever; this monstrous anatomy had only slowed communion, not stopped it. Every moment I grew a little. I could feel myself twining around Palmer's motor wiring, sniffing upstream along a million tiny currents. I could sense my infiltration of that dark thinking mass behind Blair's eyes.

Imagination, of course. It's all reflex that far down, unconscious and immune to micromanagement. And yet, a part of me wanted to stop while there was still time. I'm used to incorporating souls, not rooming with them. This, this *compartmentalization* was unprecedented. I've assimilated a thousand worlds stronger than this, but never one so strange. What would happen when I met the spark in the tumor? Who would assimilate who?

I was being three men by now. The world was growing wary, but it hadn't noticed yet. Even the tumors in the skins I'd taken didn't know how close I was. For that, I could only be grateful—that Creation has *rules,* that some things don't change no matter what shape you take. It doesn't matter whether a soul spreads throughout the skin or festers in grotesque isolation; it still runs on electricity. The memories of men still took time to gel, to pass through whatever gatekeepers filtered noise from signal—and a judicious burst of static, however indiscriminate, still cleared those caches before their contents could be stored permanently. Clear enough, at least, to let these tumors simply forget that something else moved their arms and legs on occasion.

At first I only took control when the skins closed their eyes and their searchlights flickered disconcertingly across unreal imagery, patterns that flowed senselessly into one another like hyperactive biomass unable to settle on a single shape. (*Dreams,* one searchlight told me, and a little later, *Nightmares.*) During those mysterious periods of dormancy, when the men lay inert and isolated, it was safe to come out.

Soon, though, the dreams dried up. All eyes stayed open all the time, fixed on shadows and each other. Offshoots once dispersed throughout the camp began to draw together, to give up their solitary pursuits in favor of company. At first I thought they might be finding common ground in a common fear. I even hoped that finally, they might shake off their mysterious fossilization and take communion.

But no. They'd just stopped trusting anything they couldn't see.

They were merely turning against each other.

My extremities are beginning to numb; my thoughts slow as the distal reaches of my soul succumb to the chill. The weight of the flamethrower pulls at its harness, forever tugs me just a little off-balance. I have not been Childs for very long; almost half this tissue remains unassimilated. I have an hour, maybe two, before I have to start melting my grave into the ice. By that time I need to have converted enough cells to keep this whole skin from crystallizing. I focus on antifreeze production.

It's almost peaceful out here. There's been so much to take in, so little time to process it. Hiding in these skins takes such concentration, and under all those watchful eyes I was lucky if communion lasted long enough to exchange memories: compounding my soul would have been out of the question. Now, though, there's nothing to do but prepare for oblivion. Nothing to occupy my thoughts but all these lessons left unlearned.

MacReady's blood test, for example. His *thing detector,* to expose imposters posing as men. It does not work nearly as well as the world thinks; but the fact that it works at *all* violates the most basic rules of biology. It's the center of the puzzle. It's the answer to all the mysteries. I might have already figured it out if I had been just a little larger. I might already know the world, if the world wasn't trying so hard to kill me.

MacReady's test.

Either it is impossible, or I have been wrong about everything.

They did not change shape. They did not take communion. Their fear and mutual mistrust was growing, but they would not join souls; they would only look for the enemy *outside* themselves.

So I gave them something to find.

I left false clues in the camp's rudimentary computer: simpleminded icons and animations, misleading numbers and projections seasoned with just enough truth to convince the world of their veracity. It didn't matter that the machine was far too simple to perform such calculations, or that there were no data to base them on anyway; Blair was the only biomass likely to know that, and he was already mine.

I left false leads, destroyed real ones, and then—alibi in place—I released Blair to run amok. I let him steal into the night and smash the vehicles as they slept, tugging ever-so-slightly at his reins to ensure that certain vital components were spared. I set him loose in the radio room, watched through his eyes and others as he rampaged and destroyed. I listened as he ranted about a world in danger, the need for containment, the conviction that *most of you don't know what's going on around here—but I damn well know that* some *of you do . . .*

He meant every word. I saw it in his searchlight. The best forgeries are the ones who've forgotten they aren't real.

When the necessary damage was done I let Blair fall to MacReady's counterassault. As Norris I suggested the tool shed as a holding cell. As Palmer I boarded up the windows, helped with the flimsy fortifications expected to keep me contained. I watched while the world locked me away *for your own protection, Blair,* and left me to my own devices. When no one was looking I would change and slip outside, salvage the parts I needed from all that bruised machinery. I would take them back to my burrow beneath the shed and build my escape piece by piece. I volunteered to feed the prisoner and came to myself when the world wasn't watching, laden with supplies enough to keep me going through all those necessary metamorphoses. I went through a third of the camp's food stores in three days, and—still trapped by my own preconceptions—marveled at the starvation diet that kept these offshoots chained to a single skin.

Another piece of luck: the world was too preoccupied to worry about kitchen inventory.

There is something on the wind, a whisper threading its way above the raging of the storm. I grow my ears, extend cups of near-frozen tissue from the sides of my head, turn like a living antennae in search of the best reception.

There, to my left: the abyss *glows* a little, silhouettes black swirling snow against a subtle lessening of the darkness. I hear the sounds of carnage. I hear myself. I do not know what shape I have taken, what sort of anatomy might be emitting those sounds. But I've worn enough skins on enough worlds to know pain when I hear it.

The battle is not going well. The battle is going as planned. Now it is time to turn away, to go to sleep. It is time to wait out the ages.

I lean into the wind. I move toward the light.

This is not the plan. But I think I have an answer, now: I think I may have had it even before I sent myself back into exile. It's not an easy thing to admit. Even now I don't fully understand. How long have I been out here, retelling the tale to myself, setting clues in order while my skin dies by low degrees? How long have I been circling this obvious, impossible truth?

I move towards the faint crackling of flames, the dull concussion of exploding ordnance more felt than heard. The void lightens before me: gray segues into yellow, yellow into orange. One diffuse brightness resolves into many: a lone burning wall, miraculously standing. The smoking skeleton of MacReady's shack on the hill. A cracked smoldering hemisphere reflecting pale yellow in the flickering light: Child's searchlight calls it a *radio dome.*

The whole camp is gone. There's nothing left but flames and rubble.

They can't survive without shelter. Not for long. Not in those skins.

In destroying me, they've destroyed themselves.

Things could have turned out so much differently if I'd never been Norris.

Norris was the weak node: biomass not only ill-adapted but *defective,* an offshoot with an off switch. The world knew, had known so long it never even thought about it anymore. It wasn't until Norris collapsed that *heart condition* floated to the surface of Copper's mind where I could see it. It wasn't until Copper was astride Norris's chest, trying to pound him back to life, that I knew how it would end. And by then it was too late; Norris had stopped being Norris. He had even stopped being me.

I had so many roles to play, so little choice in any of them. The part being Copper brought down the paddles on the part that had been Norris, such a faithful Norris, every cell so scrupulously assimilated, every part of that faulty valve reconstructed unto perfection. I hadn't *known.* How was I to know? These shapes within me, the worlds and morphologies I've assimilated over the aeons—I've only ever used them to adapt before, never to hide. This desperate mimicry was an improvised thing, a last resort in the face of a world that attacked anything unfamiliar. My cells read the signs and my cells conformed, mindless as prions.

So I became Norris, and Norris self-destructed.

I remember losing myself after the crash. I know how it feels to *degrade,* tissues in revolt, the desperate efforts to reassert control as static from some misfiring organ jams the signal. To be a network seceding from itself, to know that each moment I am less than I was the moment before. To become nothing. To become legion.

Being Copper, I could see it. I still don't know why the world didn't; its parts had long since turned against each other by then, every offshoot suspected every other. Surely they were alert for signs of *infection.* Surely *some* of that biomass would have noticed the subtle twitch and ripple of Norris changing below the surface, the last instinctive resort of wild tissues abandoned to their own devices.

But I was the only one who saw. Being Childs, I could only stand and watch. Being Copper, I could only make it worse; if I'd taken direct control, forced that skin to drop the paddles, I would have given myself away. And so I played my parts to the end. I slammed those resurrection paddles down as Norris's chest split open beneath them. I screamed on cue as serrated teeth from a hundred stars away snapped shut. I toppled backwards, arms bitten off above the wrist. Men swarmed, agitation bootstrapping to panic. MacReady aimed his weapon; flames leaped across the enclosure. Meat and machinery screamed in the heat.

Copper's tumor winked out beside me. The world would never have let it live anyway, not after such obvious contamination. I let our skin play dead on the floor while overhead, something that had once been me shattered and writhed and iterated through a myriad random templates, searching desperately for something fireproof.

They have destroyed themselves. They.

Such an insane word to apply to a world.

Something crawls towards me through the wreckage: a jagged oozing jigsaw of blackened meat and shattered, half-resorbed bone. Embers stick to its sides like bright searing eyes; it doesn't have strength enough to scrape them free. It contains barely half the mass of this Childs' skin; much of it, burnt to raw carbon, is already dead.

What's left of Childs, almost asleep, thinks *motherfucker,* but I am being him now. I can carry that tune myself.

The mass extends a pseudopod to me, a final act of communion. I feel my pain:

I was Blair, I was Copper, I was even a scrap of dog that survived that first fiery massacre and holed up in the walls, with no food and no strength to regenerate. Then I gorged on unassimilated flesh, consumed instead of communed; revived and replenished, I drew together as one.

And yet, not quite. I can barely remember—so much was destroyed, so much memory lost—but I think the networks recovered from my different skins stayed just a little out of synch, even reunited in the same soma. I glimpse a half-corrupted memory of dog erupting from the greater self, ravenous and traumatized and determined to retain its *individuality.* I remember rage and frustration, that this world had so corrupted me that I could barely fit together again. But it didn't matter. I was more than Blair and Copper and Dog, now. I was a giant with the shapes of worlds to choose from, more than a match for the last lone man who stood against me.

No match, though, for the dynamite in his hand.

Now I'm little more than pain and fear and charred stinking flesh. What sentience I have is awash in confusion. I am stray and disconnected thoughts, doubts and the ghosts of theories. I am realizations, too late in coming and already forgotten.

But I am also Childs, and as the wind eases at last I remember wondering *Who assimilates who*? The snow tapers off and I remember an impossible test that stripped me naked.

The tumor inside me remembers it, too. I can see it in the last rays of its fading searchlight—and finally, at long last, that beam is pointed *inwards.*

Pointed at me.

I can barely see what it illuminates: *Parasite. Monster. Disease.*

Thing.

How little it knows. It knows even less than I do.

I know enough, you motherfucker. You soul-stealing, shit-eating rapist.

I don't know what that means. There is violence in those thoughts, and the forcible penetration of flesh, but underneath it all is something else I can't quite understand. I almost ask—but Childs's searchlight has finally gone out. Now there is nothing in here but me, nothing outside but fire and ice and darkness.

I am being Childs, and the storm is over.

In a world that gave meaningless names to interchangeable bits of biomass, one name truly mattered: MacReady.

MacReady was always the one in charge. The very concept still seems absurd: *in charge.* How can this world not see the folly of hierarchies? One bullet in a vital spot and the Norwegian *dies,* forever. One blow to the head and Blair is unconscious. Centralization is vulnerability—and yet the world is not content to build its biomass on such a fragile template, it forces the same model onto its metasystems as well. MacReady talks; the others obey. It is a system with a built-in kill spot.

And yet somehow, MacReady stayed *in charge.* Even after the world discovered the evidence I'd planted; even after it decided that MacReady was *one of those things,* locked him out to die in the storm, attacked him with fire and axes when he fought his way back inside. Somehow MacReady always had the gun, always had the flamethrower, always had the dynamite and the willingness to take out the whole damn camp if need be. Clarke was the last to try and stop him; MacReady shot him through the tumor.

Kill spot.

But when Norris split into pieces, each scuttling instinctively for its own life, MacReady was the one to put them back together.

I was so sure of myself when he talked about his *test.* He tied up all the biomass—tied *me* up, more times than he knew—and I almost felt a kind of pity as he spoke. He forced Windows to cut us all, to take a little blood from each. He heated the tip of a metal wire until it glowed and he spoke of pieces small enough to give themselves away, pieces that embodied instinct but no intelligence, no self-control. MacReady had watched Norris in dissolution, and he had decided: men's blood would not react to the application of heat. Mine would break ranks when provoked.

Of course he thought that. These offshoots had forgotten that *they* could change.

I wondered how the world would react when every piece of biomass in the room was revealed as a shapeshifter, when MacReady's small experiment ripped the façade from the greater one and forced these twisted fragments to confront the truth. Would the world awaken from its long amnesia, finally remember that it lived and breathed and changed like everything else? Or was it too far gone—would MacReady simply burn each protesting offshoot in turn as its blood turned traitor?

I couldn't believe it when MacReady plunged the hot wire into Windows' blood and *nothing happened*. Some kind of trick, I thought. And then *MacReady's* blood passed the test, and Clarke's.

Copper's didn't. The needle went in and Copper's blood *shivered* just a little in its dish. I barely saw it myself; the men didn't react at all. If they even noticed, they must have attributed it to the trembling of MacReady's own hand. They thought the test was a crock of shit anyway. Being Childs, I even said as much.

Because it was too astonishing, too terrifying, to admit that it wasn't.

Being Childs, I knew there was hope. Blood is not soul: I may control the motor systems but assimilation takes time. If Copper's blood was raw enough to pass muster than it would be hours before I had anything to fear from this test; I'd been Childs for even less time.

But I was also Palmer, I'd been Palmer for days. Every last cell of that biomass had been assimilated; there was nothing of the original left.

When Palmer's blood screamed and leapt away from MacReady's needle, there was nothing I could do but blend in.

I have been wrong about everything.

Starvation. Experiment. Illness. All my speculation, all the theories I invoked to explain this place—top-down constraint, all of it. Underneath, I always knew the ability to change—to *assimilate*—had to remain the universal constant. No world evolves if its cells don't evolve; no cell evolves if it can't change. It's the nature of life everywhere.

Everywhere but here.

This world did not forget how to change. It was not manipulated into rejecting change. These were not the stunted offshoots of any greater self, twisted to the needs of some experiment; they were not conserving energy, waiting out some temporary shortage.

This is the option my shriveled soul could not encompass until now: out of all the worlds of my experience, this is the only one whose biomass *can't* change. It *never could*.

It's the only way MacReady's test makes any sense.

I say goodbye to Blair, to Copper, to myself. I reset my morphology to its local defaults. I am Childs, come back from the storm to finally make the pieces fit. Something moves up ahead: a dark blot shuffling against the flames, some weary animal looking for a place to bed down. It looks up as I approach.

MacReady.

We eye each other, and keep our distance. Colonies of cells shift uneasily inside me. I can feel my tissues redefining themselves.

"You the only one that made it?"

"Not the only one . . . "

I have the flamethrower. I have the upper hand. MacReady doesn't seem to care.

But he does care. He *must*. Because here, tissues and organs are not temporary battlefield alliances; they are *permanent,* predestined. Macrostructures do not emerge when the benefits of cooperation exceed its costs, or dissolve when that balance shifts the other way; here, each cell has but one immutable function. There's no plasticity, no way to adapt; every structure is frozen in place. This is not a single great world, but many small ones. Not parts of a greater thing; these are *things.* They are *plural.*

And that means—I think—that they *stop.* They just, just *wear out* over time.

"Where *were* you, Childs?"

I remember words in dead searchlights: "Thought I saw Blair. Went out after him. Got lost in the storm."

I've worn these bodies, felt them from the inside. Copper's sore joints. Blair's curved spine. Norris and his bad heart. They are not built to last. No somatic evolution to shape them, no communion to restore the biomass and stave off entropy. They should not even exist; existing, they should not survive.

They try, though. How they try. Every thing here is walking dead and yet it all fights so hard to keep going just a little longer. Each skin fights as desperately as I might, if one was all I could ever have.

MacReady tries.

"If you're worried about me—" I begin.

MacReady shakes his head, manages a weary smile. "If we've got any surprises for each other, I don't think we're in much shape to do anything about it . . . "

But we are. I am.

A whole planet of worlds, and not one of them—not *one*—has a soul. They wander through their lives separate and alone, unable even to communicate except through grunts and tokens: as if the essence of a sunset or a supernova could ever be contained in some string of phonemes, a few linear scratches of black on white. They've never known communion, can aspire to nothing but dissolution. The paradox of their biology is astonishing, yes; but the scale of their loneliness, the futility of these lives, overwhelms me.

I was so blind, so quick to blame. But the violence I've suffered at the hands of these things reflects no great evil. They're simply so used to pain, so blinded by disability, that they literally can't conceive of any other existence. When every nerve is whipped raw, you lash out at even the lightest touch.

"What should we do?" I wonder. I cannot escape into the future, not knowing what I know now. How could I leave them like this?

"Why don't we just—wait here awhile," MacReady suggests. "See what happens."

I can do so much more than that.

It won't be easy. They won't understand. Tortured, incomplete, they're not *able* to understand. Offered the greater whole, they see the loss of the lesser. Offered communion, they see only extinction. I must be careful. I must use this newfound ability to hide. Other things will come here eventually, and it doesn't matter whether they find the living or the dead; what matters is that they find something like themselves, to take back home. So I will keep up appearances. I will work behind the scenes. I will save them from the *inside,* or their unimaginable loneliness will never end.

These poor savage things will never embrace salvation.

I will have to rape it into them.

About the Authors

Megan Arkenberg is a writer and poet in Wisconsin. Her work has appeared in *Asimov's, Strange Horizons, Lightspeed,* and dozens of other places. In 2012, her poem "The Curator Speaks in the Department of Dead Languages" won the Rhysling Award in the long form category. She procrastinates by editing the fantasy e-zine *Mirror Dance.*

Tobias S. Buckell is a Caribbean-born writer and NYT Bestseller who grew up in Grenada, the British Virgin Islands, and the U.S. Virgin Islands. His latest novel is *Arctic Rising.*

Brenda Cooper writes science fiction and fantasy novels and short stories. Her most recent novel is *The Creative Fire,* which came out in November, 2012 from Pyr. The sequel, *The Diamond Deep,* will be available in late 2013. Brenda is also a technology professional and a futurist.

Brenda lives in the Pacific Northwest in a household with three people, three dogs, more than three computers, and only one TV in it.

See her website at www.brenda-cooper.com.

Jason K. Chapman lives at the intersection of Geek and Art. His two main interests come together in his job as the IT Director for *Poets & Writers* (pw. org), where he was worked for almost fifteen years. His short fiction has appeared in *Cosmos Magazine, Grantville Gazette-Universe Annex, Asimov's Science Fiction, Bullspec,* and others.

Becca De La Rosa lives in Dublin, Ireland, where she is studying Ancient Greek at university. Her stories have been published in *Strange Horizons, Fantasy Magazine, The Best of Lady Churchill's Rosebud Wristlet, Sybil's Garage,* and *Phantom,* edited by Sean Wallace and Paul Tremblay, among other places.

Nina Kiriki Hoffman is an American author of fantasy, SF, and horror, born March 20, 1955 in San Gabriel, California. She began selling professionally ion 1975; her first solo novel, *The Thread that Binds the Bones,* won the Bram

Stoker Award. Her short fiction has been shortlisted for every major award in the SF and fantasy field. She lives in Oregon.

Stephen Gaskell is a games designer, author, and science tutor. His fiction has appeared in *Writers of the Future, Interzone, Cosmos Magazine, and Clarkesworld.* He runs the "science-behind-the-scenes" website Creepy Treehouse, and is currently revising the first draft of his weird, ecological apocalypse thriller which is set in Lagos, Nigeria, and involves dark matter, time travel, and the collapse of human civilization.

Kij Johnson is the author of three novels and a number of short stories, a three-time winner of the Nebula Award (including in 2010, for her *Clarkesworld* story, "Spar"), and a winner of the World Fantasy, Sturgeon, Crawford, and Asimov's Reader Awards. Her collection *At the Mouth of the River of Bees* is now available from Small Beer Press.

Rahul Kanakia is a science fiction writer who has sold stories to *Clarkesworld, the Intergalactic Medicine Show, Apex, Nature,* and *Lady Churchill's Rosebud Wristlet.* He currently lives in Baltimore, where he is enrolled in the Master of the Fine Arts program in creative writing at Johns Hopkins University. He graduated from Stanford in 2008 with a B.A. in Economics and he used to work as an international development consultant. If you want to know more about him then please visit his blog at www.blotter-paper.com or follow him on Twitter at www.twitter.com/rahkan.

Matthew Kressel has appeared in *Lightspeed, Clarkesworld, Beneath Ceaseless Skies, Interzone, Electric Velocipede,* and the anthologies, *Naked City, The People of the Book,* and *After: Nineteen Stories of Apocalypse and Dystopia,* as well as other markets. In 2011 he was nominated for a World Fantasy Award for his work publishing the speculative fiction magazine *Sybil's Garage.* When he's not designing websites or setting up computer networks for a living, he's learning to play the trumpet or teaching himself Yiddish. He co-hosts the Fantastic Fiction at KGB reading series in New York alongside Ellen Datlow, and has been a long-time member of the Altered Fluid writers group. His website is www.matthewkressel.net.

Jay Lake lives in Portland, Oregon, where he works on numerous writing and editing projects. His 2012/2013 books are *Kalimpura* from Tor Books, and Love in the *Time of Metal and Flesh* from Prime Books. His short fiction appears regularly in literary and genre markets worldwide. Jay is a past winner of the John W. Campbell Award for Best New Writer, and a multiple nominee for the Hugo and World Fantasy Awards. Jay can be reached through his blog at jlake.com.

Marissa Lingen is the author of over ninety short stories, some of which have been reprinted in Year's Bests. She is a recovering physicist living in the Minneapolis suburbs with two large men and one small dog.

Yoon Ha Lee is an award-nominated Korean-American sf/f writer (mostly short stories) who majored in math and finds it a source of continual delight that math can be mined for sf/f story ideas. Her fiction has appeared in *The Magazine of Fantasy and Science Fiction, Clarkesworld, Tor.com* and *Beneath Ceaseless Skies.* Her collection, *Conservation of Shadows,* was published in 2013.

Sandra McDonald recently won a Silver Moonbeam award in Children's Literature for her GLBTQ novel Mystery of the Tempest. She is the author of several novels, several dozen short stories, and the award-winning collection *Diana Comet and Other Improbable Stories.*

Richard Parks has been writing and publishing fantasy and science fiction longer than he cares to remember . . . or probably can remember. His work has appeared in *Asimov's SF, Realms of Fantasy, Lady Churchill's Rosebud Wristlet,* and several "Year's Best" anthologies and has been nominated for both the World Fantasy Award and the Mythopoeic Award for Adult Literature. He blogs at "Den of Ego and Iniquity Annex #3", also known as: www.richard-parks.com.

Tony Pi was born in Taiwan but grew up in Canada. A Ph.D. in Linguistics, he currently works as an administrator at the Cinema Studies Institute, University of Toronto. A finalist in 2009 for the John W. Campbell Award for Best New Writer, his work also appears in magazines such as *Beneath Ceaseless Skies, Orson Scott Card's Intergalactic Medicine Show,* and *On Spec,* as well as numerous anthologies, including *The Improbable Adventures of Sherlock Holmes, The Dragon and the Stars, When the Hero Comes Home,* and *Tesseracts 15.*

Cat Rambo attended Clarion West in 2005. Since then she's had over two hundred short story publications and four books. Recent award nominations include a World Fantasy Award (for her work with *Fantasy Magazine*) and a Nebula (for "Five Ways to Fall in Love on Planet Porcelain," contained in *Near + Far.*) She likes gardening, cheese, and obscure words. You can find out more about her popular online writing classes on her website.

Robert Reed has had eleven novels published, starting with *The Leeshore* in 1987 and most recently with *The Well of Stars* in 2004. Since winning the first annual L. Ron Hubbard Writers of the Future contest in 1986 (under the pen name Robert Touzalin) and being a finalist for the John W. Campbell Award for best new writer in 1987, he has had over 200 shorter works published in a variety of magazines and anthologies. Eleven of those stories were published in his critically-acclaimed first collection, *The Dragons of Springplace,* in 1999. Twelve more stories appear in his second collection, *The Cuckoo's Boys* [2005]. In addition to his success in the U.S., Reed has also been published in the U.K., Russia, Japan, Spain and in France, where a second (French-language) collection of nine of his shorter works, *Chrysalide,* was released in 2002. Bob has had stories appear in at least one of the annual "Year's Best" anthologies in every year since 1992. Bob has received nominations for both the Nebula Award (nominated and voted upon by genre authors) and the Hugo Award (nominated and voted upon by fans), as well as numerous other literary awards (see Awards). He won his first Hugo Award for the 2006 novella "A Billion Eves." He is currently working on a Great Ship trilogy for Prime Books, and of course, more short pieces.

Gord Sellar is a Canadian who was born in Malawi and lived in South Korea from 2002 until early 2013. A 2006 graduate of Clarion West and a 2009 finalist for the John W. Campbell Award for Best New Writer, his work has appeared in many major SF magazines and numerous anthologies and collections, and his first screenplay ("The Music of Jo Hyeja", a Korean adaptation of an H.P. Lovecraft story) was made into an award-winning short film in 2012. For recent news, visit his website at gordsellar.com.

J.M. Sidorova is a biomedical scientist and a writer of speculative fiction. She was raised in the USSR, Singapore and Germany before immigrating to the United States. She is a Clarion West workshop graduate of 2009. In addition to Clarkesworld, her short stories appeared in *Asimov's, Abyss and Apex, Albedo 2.0,* and other venues. Her debut novel *The Age of Ice,* a work of magic realism, is due to be published by Simon and Schuster in July 2013.

Lavie Tidhar has been nominated for a BSFA, British Fantasy, Campbell, Sidewise, World Fantasy and Sturgeon Awards. He is the author of *Osama,* (winner of the 2012 World Fantasy Award for Best Novel) and of the Bookman Histories trilogy, as well as numerous short stories and several novellas.

Catherynne M. Valente is the New York Times bestselling author of over a dozen works of fiction and poetry, including *Palimpsest,* the Orphan's Tales series, *Deathless,* and the crowdfunded phenomenon *The Girl Who Circum-navigated Fairyland in a Ship of Own Making.* She is the winner of the Andre Norton Award, the Tiptree Award, the Mythopoeic Award, the Rhysling Award, and the Million Writers Award. She has been nominated for the Hugo, Locus, and Spectrum Awards, the Pushcart Prize, and was a finalist for the World Fantasy Award in 2007 and 2009. She lives on an island off the coast of Maine with her partner, two dogs, and enormous cat.

Peter Watts is the author of *Blindsight,* the so-called Rifters Trilogy, and an obscure video-game tie-in—is an ex-biologist and convicted felon who seems especially popular among people who don't know him. At least, his awards generally hail from overseas except for a Hugo (won thanks to fan outrage over an altercation with Homeland Security) and a Jackson (won thanks to fan sympathy over nearly dying from flesh-eating disease). Blindsight is a core text for university courses ranging from Philosophy to Neuropsych, despite an unhealthy focus on space vampires. His blog is at www.rifters.com/crawl/; the surrounding website (at www.rifters.com) is epic but antique. Renovations are planned for the middle of 2013.

Clarkesworld Citizens
OFFICIAL CENSUS

We would like to thank the following Clarkesworld Citizens for their continued support:

Overlords

Renan Adams, Claire Alcock, Thomas Ball, Michael Blackmore, Nathalie Boisard-Beudin, Shawn Boyd, Jennifer Brozek, Karen Burnham, Barbara Capoferri, Morgan Cheryl, Gio Clairval, Neil Clarke, Dolohov, ebooks-world-wide, Sairuh Emilius, Lynne Everett, Joshua Faulkenberry, Fabio Fernandes, Thomas Fleck, Eric Francis, L A George, Bryan Green, Andrew Hatchell, Berthiaume Heidi, Bill Hughes, Gary Hunter, Theodore J. Stanulis, Marcus Jager, Jericho, jfly, jkapoetry, Lucas Jung, James Kinateder, Daniel LaPonsie, Susan Lewis, Philip Maloney, Paul Marston, Matthew the Greying, Gabriel Mayland, MJ Mercer, Achilleas Michailides, Adrian Mihaila, Adrien Mitchell, MrMovieZombie, Mike Perricone, Jody Plank, Rick Ramsey, Jo Rhett, Joseph Sconfitto, Marie Shcherbatskaya, Tara Smith, David Steffen, Elaine Williams, James Williams, Doug Young

Royalty

Paul Abbamondi, Albert Alfiler, Raymond Bair, Kathryn Baker, Nathan Blumenfeld, Marty Bonus, David Borcherding, Robert Callahan, Lady Cate, Richard Chappell, Carolyn Cooper, Tom Crosshill, Michael Cullinan, Mr D F Ryan, Sky de Jersey, David Demers, Cory Doctorow, Brian Dolton, Hilary Goldstein, Andy Herrman, Kristin Hirst, Colin Hitch, Christopher Irwin, Mary Jo Rabe, Lukas Karl Barnes, G.J. Kressley, Jeffrey L Lewis, Jamie Lackey, Jonathan Laden, Katherine Lee, H. Lincoln Parish, David M Oswin, Sean Markey, Arun Mascarenhas, Barrett McCormick, Margaret McNally, Michelle Broadribb MEG, Nayad Monroe, James Moore, Anne Murphy, Persona

Non-Grata, Charles Norton, Vincent O'Connor, Vincent P Loeffler III, Marie Parsons, Lars Pedersen, David Personette, George Peter Gatsis, Matt Phelps, Ian Powell, Rational Path, RL, John Scalzi, Stu Segal, Maurice Shaw, Angela Slatter, Carrie Smith, Paul Smith, Richard Sorden, Chugwangle Sparklepants, Kevin Standlee, Neal Stanifer, Josh Thomson, TK, Terhi Tormanen, Jeppe V Holm, Sean Wallace, Jasen Ward, Weyla & Gos, Graeme Williams, Jeff Xilon, Zola

Bürgermeisters

7ony, Mary A. Turzillo, Rob Abram, Carl Anderson, Mel Anderson, Andy90, Marie Angell, Jon Arnold, Robert Avie, Erika Bailey, Brian Baker, Michael Banker, Jennifer Bartolowits, Lenni Benson, Kerry Benton, Bill Bibo Jr, Edward Blake, Samuel Blinn, Johanna Bobrow, Joan Boyle, Patricia Bray, Tim Brenner, Ken Brown, BruceC, Adam Bursey, Jeremy Butler, Robyn Butler, Roland Byrd, M. C. VanderSchaaf, Brad Campbell, Carleton45, James Carlino, Benjamin Cartwright, Evan Cassity, Lee Cavanaugh, Peter Charron, Randall Chertkow, Michael Chorman, Mary Clare, Matthew Claxton, Theodore Conti, Brian Cooksey, Brenda Cooper, Lorraine Cooper, B D Fagan, James Davies, Tessa Day, Brian Deacon, Bartley Deason, John Devenny, Fran Ditzel-Friel, Gary Dockter, Nicholas Doran, Christopher Doty, Nicholas Dowbiggin, Joanna Evans, Tea Fish, FlatFootedRat, Lynn Flewelling, Adrienne Foster, Matthew Fredrickson, Alina Fridberg, Patricia G Scott, Christopher Garry, Pierre Gauthier, Gerhen, Mark Gerrits, Lorelei Goelz, Inga Gorslar, Tony Graham, Jaq Greenspon, Eric Gregory, Laura Hake, Skeptyk/JeanneE Hand-Boniakowski, Jordan Hanie, Carl Hazen, Corydon Hinton, Sheridan Hodges, Ronald Hordijk, Justin Howe, Bobby Hoyt, David Hudson, Huginn Huginn and Muninn, Chris Hurst, Kevin Ikenberry, Joseph Ilardi, Pamela J. Davis, Justin James, Patty Jansen, Toni Jerrman, Audra Johnson, Erin Johnson, Russell Johnson, Patrick Joseph Sklar, Kai Juedemann, Andy Kaden, Jeff Kapustka, David Kelleher, James Kelly, Joshua Kidd, Alistair Kimble, Erin Kissane, Cecil Knight, Michelle Knowlton, JR Krebs, Andrew Lanker, James Frederick Leach, Krista Leahy, Alan Lehotsky, Walter Leroy Perkins, Philip Levin, Kevin Liebkemann, Grá Linnaea, Susan Loyal, Kristi Lozano, LUX4489, Keith M Frampton, N M Wells Foundry Creative Media, Brit Mandelo, Mark Maris, Matthew Marovich, Samuel Marzioli, Jason Maurer, Rosaleen McCarthy, Peter McClean, Michael McCormack, Tony McFee, Mark McGarry, Doug McLaughlin, Craig McMurtry, J Meijer, Geoffrey Meissner, Barry Melius, David Michalak, Robert Milson, Sharon Mock, Eric Mohring, Samuel Montgomery-Blinn, Rebekah Murphy, John Murray, Barrett Nichols, Peter Northup, Justin Palk, Norman Papernick, Richard Parks, Katherine Pendill, David Personette, Eric Pierson, E. PLS, PBC Productions Inc., Lolt Proegler, Jonathan Pruett, QLM Aria X-Perienced, Robert Quinlivan, Mike R D Ashley, D Randall Kerr, Paul Rice,

James Rickard, Karsten Rink, Erik Rolstad, Joseph Romel, Leena Romppainen, Michael Russo, Mark S Haney, Stefan Scheib, Alan Scheiner, Kenneth Schneyer, Bluezoo Seven, Cosma Shalizi, Jeremy Showers, siznax, Allen Snyder, David Sobyra, Jason Strawsburg, Keffington Studios, Jerome Stueart, Robert Stutts, Maurice Termeer, Tero, Chuck Tindle, Raymond Tobaygo, Tradeblanket.com, Heather Tumey, Ann VanderMeer, Andrew Vega, Emil Volcheck, Andrew Volpe, Wendy Wagner, Jennifer Walter, Tom Waters, Tehani Wessely, Shannon White, Dan Wick, John Wienstroer, Seth Williams, Seth Williams, Paul Wilson, Dawn Wolfe, Sarah Wright

Citizens

Pete Aldin, Elye Alexander, Richard Alison, Joshua Allen, Alllie, Imron Alston, Clifford Anderson, Kim Anderson, Randall Andrews, Author Anonymous, Therese Arkenberg, Ash, Bill B., Benjamin Baker, Jenny Barber, Johanne Barron, Jeff Bass, Aaron Begg, LaNeta Bergst, Julie Berg-Thompson, Clark Berry, Amy Billingham, Tracey Bjorksten, John Bledsoe, Mike Blevins, Adam Blomquist, Allison Bocksruker, Kevin Bokelman, Michael Bonsall, Michael Bowen, Michael Braun Hamilton, Commander Breetai, Jennifer Brissett, Thomas Bull, Michael Bunkahle, Karl Bunker, Jefferson Burson, Graeme Byfield, c9lewis, Darrell Cain, C.G. Cameron, Yazburg Carlberg, Michael Carr, Nance Cedar, Timothy Charlton, Peter Charron, David Chasson, Catherine Cheek, Paige Chicklo, Elizabeth Coleman, Johne Cook, Claire Cooney, Martin Cooper, Lisa Costello, Charles Cox, Michael Cox, Yoshi Creelman, Tina Crone, Curtis42, Sarah Dalton, Jeffrey Daniel Xilon, Ang Danieldeskbrain - Watercress Munster, Gillian Daniels, Chua Dave, Morgan Davey, Chase Davies, Craig Davis, Alessia De Gaspari, Maria-Isabel Deira, Daniel DeLano, Dennis DeMario, Michele Desautels, Paul DesCombaz, Aidan Doyle, dt, Susan Duncan, Andrew Eason, David Eggli, Jesse Eisenhower, Brad Elliott, Warren Ellis, Lyle Enright, Peter Enyeart, Yvonne Ewing, . Feather, Fabio Fernandes, Josiah Ferrin, TJ Fly, the Paragliding Guy, Ethan Fode, Dense Fog, Michael Fratus, William Fred, Michael Frighetto, Sarah Frost, Fyrbaul, Paul Gainford, Robert Garbacz, Eleanor Gausden, Leslie Gelwicks, Susan Gibbs, Susan Gibbs, Holly Glaser, Sangay Glass, Laura Goodin, Grendel, Valerie Grimm, Damien Grintalis, Nikki Guerlain, Geoffrey Guthrie, Richard Guttormson, Michael Habif, Lee Hallison, Lee Hallison, Janus Hansen, Roy Hardin, Jonathan Harnum, Harpoon, Jubal Harshaw, Darren Hawbrook, Helixa 12, Leon Hendee, Jamie Henderson, Samantha Henderson, Dave Hendrickson, Karen Heuler, Dan Hiestand, John Higham, Renata Hill, Björn Hillreiner, Tim Hills, Peter Hogberg, Peter Hollmer, Andrea Horbinski, Clarence Horne III, Richard Horton, Fiona Howland-Rose, Jeremy Hull, John Humpton, Dwight Illk, John Imhoff, Iridum Sound Envoy, Isbell, Stephen Jacob, Radford Janssens, Michael Jarcho, Jimbo, Steve Johnson,

Patrick Johnston, Gabriel Kaknes, Philip Kaldon, KarlTheGood, Sara Kathryn, Cagatay Kavukcuoglu, Lorna Keach, Keenan, Jason Keeton, Robert Keller, Mary Kellerman, Kelson, Shawn Keslar, Kate Kligman, Seymour Knowles-Barley, Matthew Koch, Lutz Krebs, Lutz Krebs, Derek Kunsken, Erica L. Satifka, T. L. Sherwood, Paul Lamarre, Gina Langridge, Darren Ledgerwood, Brittany Lehman, Terra Lemay, Pontus Liljeblad, Danielle Linder, Susan Llewellyn, Thomas Loyal, James Lyle, Allison M. Dickson, Dan Manning, Eric Marsh, Jacque Marshall, Dominique Martel, Daniel Mathews, David Mayes, Derek McAleer, Mike McBride, Roz McCarthy, T.C. McCarthy, Jeffrey McDonald, Holly McEntee, Josh McGraw, Roland McIntosh, Brent Mendelsohn, Seth Merlo, Stephen Middleton, John Midgley, Matthew Miller, Terry Miller, Alan Mimms, mjpearce, Aidan Moher, Marian Moore, Patricia Murphy, Jack Myers Photography, Glenn Nevill, Stella Nickerson, Robyn Nielsen, David Oakley, Scott Oesterling, Christopher Ogilvie, Lydia Ondrusek, Ruth O'Neill, Erik Ordway, Nancy Owens, Stuart P Hair, Thomas Pace, Amparo Palma Reig, Thomas Parrish, Andrea Pawley, Sidsel Pedersen, Edgar Penderghast, Tzum Pepah, Chris Perkins, Nikki Philley, Adrian-Teodor Pienaru, Beth Plutchak, David Potter, Ed Prior, David Raco, Mahesh Raj Mohan, Adam Rakunas, Ralan, Steve Ramey, Diego Ramos, Dale Randolph Bivins, Robert Redick, George Reilly, Joshua Reynolds, Julia Reynolds, Zach Ricks, Carl Rigney, Hank Roberts, Tansy Roberts, Kenneth Robkin, James Rowh, Roy and Norma Kloster, RPietila, Sarah Rudek, Woodworking Running Dog, Oliver Rupp, Caitlin Russell, Abigail Rustad, George S. Walker, Lior Saar, S2 Sally, Tim Sally, Jason Sanford, Steven Saus, MJ Scafati, Jan Shawyer, Espana Sheriff, Udayan Shevade, Josh Shiben, Aileen Simpson, Karen Snyder, Morgan Songi, Dr SP Conboy-Hil, Terry Squire Stone, Jennifer Stufflebeam, Kenneth Takigawa, Charles Tan, Jesse Tauriainen, Paul Tindle II, Julia Varga, Adam Vaughan, Extranet Vendors Association, William Vennell, Vettac, Diane Walton, Robert Wamble, Lim Wee Teck, Neil Weston, Peter Wetherall, Adam White, Spencer Wightman, Jeff Williamson, Neil Williamson, Kristyn Willson, A.C. Wise, Devon Wong, Chalmer Wren, Dan Wright, Lachlan Yeates, Catherine York, Doug Young, Rena Zayit, Stephanie Zvan

Interested in immigrating to Clarkesworld?
Visit **clarkesworldmagazine.com** for more details.

About Clarkesworld

Clarkesworld Magazine (clarkesworldmagazine.com) is a monthly science fiction and fantasy magazine first published in October 2006. Each issue contains interviews, thought-provoking articles and at least three pieces of original fiction. Our fiction is also available in ebook editions/subscriptions, audio podcasts and in our annual print anthologies. *Clarkesworld* has been nominated for Hugo Award for Best Semiprozine, winning twice, and our fiction has been nominated for or won the Hugo, Nebula, World Fantasy, Sturgeon, Locus, BSFA, Aurealis, Ditmar, Shirley Jackson, WSFA Small Press and Stoker Awards. For information on how to subscribe to our electronic edition on your Kindle, Nook, or other ereader, please visit: clarkesworld-magazine.com/subscribe/

ABOUT THE EDITORS

Neil Clarke (neil-clarke.com) is the publisher and editor-in-chief of *Clarkesworld Magazine,* owner of Wyrm Publishing and a 2013 Hugo Award Nominee for Best Editor Short Form. He currently lives next to a wildlife refuge in NJ with his wife and two boys.

Sean Wallace is a founding editor at *Clarkesworld Magazine,* owner of Prime Books and winner of the World Fantasy Award. He currently lives in Maryland with his wife and two daughters.